JAMES BALDWIN
ANOTHER COUNTRY

"To be James Baldwin is to touch on so many hidden places in Europe, America, the Negro, the white man—to be forced to understand so much."

—Alfred Kazin

"This author retains a place in an extremely select group; that composed of the few genuinely indispensable American writers."

—*Saturday Review*

"He has not himself lost access to the sources of his being—which is what makes him read and awaited by perhaps a wider range of people than any other major American writer."

—*The Nation*

"He is thought-provoking, tantalizing, irritating, abusing and amusing. And he uses words as the sea uses waves, to flow and beat, advance and retreat, rise and take a bow in disappearing . . . the thought becomes poetry and the poetry illuminates the thought."

—Langston Hughes

"He has become one of the few writers of our time."

—Norman Mailer

ANOTHER COUNTRY

JAMES BALDWIN

Published by
Dell Publishing
a division of
Bantam Doubleday Dell Publishing Group, Inc.
666 Fifth Avenue
New York, New York 10103

For Mary S. Painter

Reprinted by arrangement with Doubleday & Company, Inc.
Two previous Laurel editions
Printed in the United States of America
Published simultaneously in Canada
May 1988
10 9 8 7

KRI

They strike one, above all, as giving no account of themselves in any terms already consecrated by human use; to this inarticulate state they probably form, collectively, the most unprecedented of monuments; abysmal the mystery of what they think, what they feel, what they want, what they suppose themselves to be saying.   HENRY JAMES

BOOK ONE

EASY RIDER

> *I told him, easy riders*
> *Got to stay away,*
> *So he had to vamp it,*
> *But the hike ain't far.*
>
> W. C. HANDY

CHAPTER 1

He was facing Seventh Avenue, at Times Square. It was past midnight and he had been sitting in the movies, in the top row of the balcony, since two o'clock in the afternoon. Twice he had been awakened by the violent accents of the Italian film, once the usher had awakened him, and twice he had been awakened by caterpillar fingers between his thighs. He was so tired, he had fallen so low, that he scarcely had the energy to be angry; nothing of his belonged to him any more —*you took the best, so why not take the rest?*—but he had growled in his sleep and bared the white teeth in his dark face and crossed his legs. Then the balcony was nearly empty, the Italian film was approaching a climax; he stumbled down the endless stairs into the street. He was hungry, his mouth felt filthy. He realized too late, as he passed through the doors, that he wanted to urinate. And he was broke. And he had nowhere to go.

The policeman passed him, giving him a look. Rufus turned, pulling up the collar of his leather jacket while the wind nibbled delightedly at him through his summer slacks, and started north on Seventh Avenue. He had been thinking of going downtown and waking up Vivaldo—the only friend he had left in the city, or maybe in the world—but now he decided to walk up as far as a certain jazz bar and night club and look in. Maybe somebody would see him and recognize him, maybe one of the guys would lay enough bread on him for a meal or at least subway fare. At the same time, he hoped that he would not be recognized.

The Avenue was quiet, too, most of its bright lights out. Here and there a woman passed, here and there a man; rarely, a couple. At corners, under the lights, near drug-stores, small knots of white, bright, chattering people showed teeth to each other, pawed each other, whistled for taxis, were whirled away in them, vanished through the doors of drugstores or into the blackness of side streets. Newsstands, like small black blocks on a board, held down corners of the pavements and policemen and taxi drivers and others, harder to place, stomped their feet before them and exchanged such words as they both knew with the muffled vendor within. A sign advertised the chewing gum which would help one to relax and keep smiling. A hotel's enormous neon name challenged the starless sky. So did the names of movie stars and people currently appearing or scheduled to appear on Broadway, along with the mile-high names of the vehicles which would carry them into immortality. The great buildings, unlit, blunt like the phallus or sharp like the spear, guarded the city which never slept.

Beneath them Rufus walked, one of the fallen—for the weight of this city was murderous—one of those who had been crushed on the day, which was every day, these towers fell. Entirely alone, and dying of it, he was part of an unprecedented multitude. There were boys and girls drinking coffee at the drugstore counters who were held back from his condition by barriers as perishable as their dwindling cigarettes. They could scarcely bear their knowledge, nor could they have borne the sight of Rufus, but they knew why he was in the streets tonight, why he rode subways all night long, why his stomach growled, why his hair was nappy, his armpits funky, his pants and shoes too thin, and why he did not dare to stop and take a leak.

Now he stood before the misty doors of the jazz joint, peering in, sensing rather than seeing the frantic black people on the stand and the oblivious, mixed crowd at the bar. The music was loud and empty, no one was doing anything at all, and it was being hurled at the crowd like a malediction in which not even those who hated most deeply any longer believed. They knew that no one heard, that bloodless people cannot be made to bleed. So they blew what everyone had heard before, they reassured everyone that nothing terrible was happening, and the people at the tables found it pleasant to shout over this stunning corroboration and the people at the bar, under cover of the noise they could scarcely have lived without, pursued whatever it was they were after. He wanted to go in and use the bathroom but he was ashamed of the way he looked. He had been in hiding, really, for nearly a month. And he saw himself now, in his mind's eye, shambling through this crowd to the bathroom and crawling out again while everyone watched him with pitying or scornful or mocking eyes. Or, someone would be certain to whisper, *Isn't that Rufus Scott?* Someone would look at him with horror, then turn back to his business with a long-drawn-out, pitying, *Man!* He could not do it—and he danced on one foot and then the other and tears came to his eyes.

A white couple, laughing, came through the doors, giving him barely a glance as they passed. The warmth, the smell of people, whiskey, beer, and smoke which came out to hit him as the doors opened almost made him cry for fair and it made his empty stomach growl again.

It made him remember days and nights, day and nights, when he had been inside, on the stand or in the crowd, sharp, beloved, making it with any chick he wanted, making it to parties and getting high and getting drunk and fooling around with the musicians, who were his friends, who respected him. Then, going home to his own pad, locking his door and taking off his shoes, maybe making himself a drink, maybe listening to some records, stretching out on the bed, maybe calling up some girl. And changing his underwear and his socks and his shirt, shaving, and taking a shower, and making it to Harlem to the barber shop, then seeing his mother and his father and teasing his sister, Ida, and eating: spareribs or pork chops or chicken or greens or cornbread or yams or biscuits. For a moment he thought he would faint with hunger and he moved to a wall of the building and leaned there. His forehead was freezing with sweat. He thought: this is got to stop, Rufus. This shit is got to stop. Then, in weariness and recklessness, seeing no one on the streets and hoping that no one would come through the doors, leaning with one hand against the wall he sent his urine splashing against the stone-cold pavement, watching the faint steam rise.

He remembered Leona. Or a sudden, cold, familiar sickness filled him and he knew he was remembering Leona. And he began to walk, very slowly now, away from the music, with his hands in his pockets and his head down. He no longer felt the cold.

For to remember Leona was also—somehow—to remember the eyes of his mother, the rage of his father, the beauty of his sister. It was to remember the streets of Harlem, the boys on the stoops, the girls behind the stairs and on the roofs, the white policeman who had taught him how to hate, the stickball games in the streets, the women leaning out of windows and the numbers they played daily, hoping for the hit his father never made. It was to remember the juke box, the teasing, the dancing, the hard-on, the gang fights and gang bangs, his first set of drums—bought him by his father —his first taste of marijuana, his first snort of horse. Yes: and the boys too far out, jackknifed on the stoops, the boy dead from an overdose on a rooftop in the snow. It was to remember the beat: *A nigger,* said his father, *lives his whole life, lives and dies according to a beat. Shit, he humps to that beat and the baby he throws up in there, well, he jumps to it and comes out nine months later like a goddamn tambourine.* The beat: hands, feet, tambourines, drums, pianos, laughter, curses, razor blades; the man stiffening with a laugh and a growl and a purr and the woman moistening and softening with a whisper and a sigh and a cry. The beat—in Harlem in the summertime one could almost see it, shaking above the pavements and the roof.

And he had fled, so he had thought, from the beat of Harlem, which was simply the beat of his own heart. Into a boot camp in the South, and onto the pounding sea.

While he had still been in the Navy, he had brought back from one of his voyages an Indian shawl for Ida. He had picked it up some place in England. On the day that he gave it to her and she tried it on, something shook in him which had never been touched before. He had never seen the beauty of black people before. But, staring at Ida, who stood before the window of the Harlem kitchen, seeing that she was no longer merely his younger sister but a girl who would soon be a woman, she became associated with the colors of the shawl, the colors of the sun, and with a splendor incalculably older than the gray stone of the island on which they had been born. He thought that perhaps this splendor would come into the world again one day, into the world they knew. Ages and ages ago, Ida had not been merely the descendant of slaves. Watching her dark face in the sunlight, softened and shadowed by the glorious shawl, it could be seen that she had once been a monarch. Then he looked out of the window, at the air shaft, and thought of the whores on Seventh Avenue. He thought of the white policemen and the money they made on black flesh, the money the whole world made.

He looked back at his sister, who was smiling at him. On her long little finger she twisted the ruby-eyed snake ring which he had brought her from another voyage.

"You keep this up," she said, "and you'll make me the best-dressed girl on the block."

He was glad Ida could not see him now. She would have

said, My Lord, Rufus, you got no right to walk around like this. Don't you know we're counting on you?

Seven months ago, a lifetime ago, he had been playing a gig in one of the new Harlem spots owned and operated by a Negro. It was their last night. It had been a good night, everybody was feeling good. Most of them, after the set, were going to make it to the home of a famous Negro singer who had just scored in his first movie. Because the joint was new, it was packed. Lately, he had heard, it hadn't been doing so well. All kinds of people had been there that night, white and black, high and low, people who came for the music and people who spent their lives in joints for other reasons. There were a couple of minks and a few near-minks and a lot of God-knows-what shining at wrists and ears and necks and in the hair. The colored people were having a good time because they sensed that, for whatever reason, this crowd was solidly with them; and the white people were having a good time because nobody was putting them down for being white. The joint, as Fats Waller would have said, was jumping.

There was some pot on the scene and he was a little high. He was feeling great. And, during the last set, he came doubly alive because the saxophone player, who had been way out all night, took off on a terrific solo. He was a kid of about the same age as Rufus, from some insane place like Jersey City or Syracuse, but somewhere along the line he had discovered that he could say it with a saxophone. He had a lot to say. He stood there, wide-legged, humping the air, filling his barrel chest, shivering in the rags of his twenty-odd years, and screaming through the horn *Do you love me? Do you love me? Do you love me?* And, again, *Do you love me? Do you* love *me? Do you love* me? This, anyway, was the question Rufus heard, the same phrase, unbearably, endlessly, and variously repeated, with all of the force the boy had. The silence of the listeners became strict with abruptly focused attention, cigarettes were unlit, and drinks stayed on the tables; and in all of the faces, even the most ruined and most dull, a curious, wary light appeared. They were being assaulted by the saxophonist who perhaps no longer wanted their love and merely hurled his outrage at them with the same contemptuous, pagan pride with which he humped the air. And yet the question was terrible and real; the boy was blowing with his lungs and guts out of his own short past; somewhere in that past, in the gutters or gang fights or gang shags; in the acrid room, on the sperm-stiffened blanket, behind marijuana or the needle, under the smell of piss in the precinct basement, he had received the blow from which he never would recover and this no one wanted to believe. *Do you love me? Do you love me? Do you love* me? The men on the stand stayed with him, cool and at a little distance, adding and questioning and corroborating, holding it down as well as they could with an ironical self-mockery; but each man knew that the boy was blowing for every one of them. When the set ended they were all soaking. Rufus smelled his odor and the odor of the men around him and "Well, that's it," said the bass man. The crowd was yelling for more but they did their theme song and the lights came on. And he had played the last set of his last gig.

He was going to leave his traps there until Monday afternoon. When he stepped down from the stand there was this blond girl, very plainly dressed, standing looking at him.

"What's on your mind, baby?" he asked her. Everybody was busy all around them, preparing to make it to the party. It was spring and the air was charged.

"What's on *your* mind?" she countered, but it was clear that she simply had not known what else to say.

She had said enough. She was from the South. And something leaped in Rufus as he stared at her damp, colorless face, the face of the Southern poor white, and her straight, pale hair. She was considerably older than he, over thirty probably, and her body was too thin. Just the same, it abruptly became the most exciting body he had gazed on in a long time.

"Honeychild," he said and gave her his crooked grin, "ain't you a long ways from home?"

"I sure am," she said, "and I ain't never going back there."

He laughed and she laughed. "Well, Miss Anne," he said, "if we both got the same thing on our mind, let's make it to that party."

And he took her arm, deliberately allowing the back of his hand to touch one of her breasts, and he said, "Your name's not really Anne, is it?"

"No," she said, "it's Leona."

"Leona?" And he smiled again. His smile could be very effective. "That's a pretty name."

"What's yours?"

"Me? I'm Rufus Scott."

He wondered what she was doing in this joint, in Harlem.

She didn't seem at all the type to be interested in jazz, still less did she seem to be in the habit of going to strange bars alone. She carried a light spring coat, her long hair was simply brushed back and held with some pins, she wore very little lipstick and no other make-up at all.

"Come on," he said. "We'll pile into a cab."

"Are you sure it's all right if I come?"

He sucked his teeth. "If it wasn't all right, I wouldn't ask you. If I say it's all right, it's all *right*."

"Well," she said with a short laugh, "all right, then."

They moved with the crowd, which, with many interruptions, much talking and laughing and much erotic confusion, poured into the streets. It was three o'clock in the morning and gala people all around them were glittering and whistling and using up all the taxicabs. Others, considerably less gala —they were on the western edge of 125th Street—stood in knots along the street, switched or swaggered or dawdled by, with glances, sidelong or full face, which were more calculating than curious. The policemen strolled by; carefully, and in fact rather mysteriously conveying their awareness that these particular Negroes, though they were out so late, and mostly drunk, were not to be treated in the usual fashion; and neither were the white people with them. But Rufus suddenly realized that Leona would soon be the only white person left. This made him uneasy and his uneasiness made him angry. Leona spotted an empty cab and hailed it.

The taxi driver, who was white, seemed to have no hesitation in stopping for them, nor, once having stopped, did he seem to have any regrets.

"You going to work tomorrow?" he asked Leona. Now that they were alone together, he felt a little shy.

"No," she said, "tomorrow's Sunday."

"That's right." He felt very pleased and free. He had planned to visit his family but he thought of what a ball it would be to spend the day in bed with Leona. He glanced over at her, noting that, though she was tiny, she seemed very well put together. He wondered what she was thinking. He offered her a cigarette, putting his hand on hers briefly, and she refused it. "You don't smoke?"

"Sometimes. When I drink."

"Is that often?"

She laughed. "No. I don't like to drink alone."

"Well," he said, "you ain't *going* to be drinking alone for a while."

She said nothing but she seemed, in the darkness, to tense

and blush. She looked out of the window on her side. "I'm glad I ain't got to worry none about getting you home early tonight."

"You ain't got to worry about that, nohow. I'm a big girl."

"Honey," he said, "you ain't no bigger than a minute." She sighed. "Sometimes a minute can be a mighty powerful thing."

He decided against asking what she meant by this. He said, giving her a significant look, "That's true," but she did not seem to take his meaning.

They were on Riverside Drive and nearing their destination. To the left of them, pale, unlovely lights emphasized the blackness of the Jersey shore. He leaned back, leaning a little against Leona, watching the blackness and the lights roll by. Then the cab turned; he glimpsed, briefly, the distant bridge which glowed like something written in the sky. The cab slowed down, looking for the house number. A taxi ahead of them had just discharged a crowd of people and was disappearing down the block. "Here we are," said Rufus; "Looks like a real fine party," the taxi driver said, and winked. Rufus said nothing. He paid the man and they got out and walked into the lobby, which was large and hideous, with mirrors and chairs. The elevator had just started upward; they could hear the crowd.

"What were you doing in that club all by yourself, Leona?" he asked.

She looked at him, a little startled. Then, "I don't know. I just wanted to see Harlem and so I went up there tonight to look around. And I just happened to pass that club and I heard the music and I went in and I *stayed*. I liked the music." She gave him a mocking look. "Is that all right?"

He laughed and said nothing.

She turned from him as they heard the sound of the closing elevator door reverberate down the shaft. Then they heard the drone of the cables as the elevator began to descend. She watched the closed doors as though her life depended on it.

"This your first time in New York?"

Yes, it was, she told him, but she had been dreaming about it all her life—half-facing him again, with a little smile. There was something halting in her manner which he found very moving. She was like a wild animal who didn't know whether to come to the outstretched hand or to flee and kept making startled little rushes, first in one direction and then in the other.

"I was born here," he said, watching her.

"I know," she said, "so it can't seem as wonderful to you as it does to me."

He laughed again. He remembered, suddenly, his days in boot camp in the South and felt again the shoe of a white officer against his mouth. He was in his white uniform, on the ground, against the red, dusty clay. Some of his colored buddies were holding him, were shouting in his ear, helping him to rise. The white officer, with a curse, had vanished, had gone forever beyond the reach of vengeance. His face was full of clay and tears and blood; he spat red blood into the red dust.

The elevator came and the doors opened. He took her arm as they entered and held it close against his chest. "I think you're a real sweet girl."

"You're nice, too," she said. In the closed, rising elevator her voice had a strange trembling in it and her body was also trembling—very faintly, as though it were being handled by the soft spring wind outside.

He tightened his pressure on her arm. "Didn't they warn you down home about the darkies you'd find up North?"

She caught her breath. "They didn't never worry me none. People's just people as far as I'm concerned."

And pussy's just pussy as far as I'm concerned, he thought —but was grateful, just the same, for her tone. It gave him an instant to locate himself. For he, too, was trembling slightly.

"What made you come North?" he asked.

He wondered if he should proposition her or wait for her to proposition him. He couldn't beg. But perhaps she could. The hairs of his groin began to itch slightly. The terrible muscle at the base of his belly began to grow hot and hard.

The elevator came to a halt, the doors opened, and they walked a long corridor toward a half-open door.

She said, "I guess I just couldn't take it down there any more. I was married but then I broke up with my husband and they took away my kid—they wouldn't even let me see him—and I got to thinking that rather than sit down there and go crazy, I'd try to make a new life for myself up here."

Something touched his imagination for a moment, suggesting that Leona was a person and had her story and that all stories were trouble. But he shook the suggestion off. He wouldn't be around long enough to be bugged by her story. He just wanted her for tonight.

He knocked on the door and walked in without waiting

for an answer. Straight ahead of them, in the large living room which ended in open French doors and a balcony, more than a hundred people milled about, some in evening dress, some in slacks and sweaters. High above their heads hung an enormous silver ball which reflected unexpected parts of the room and managed its own unloving comment on the people in it. The room was so active with coming and going, so bright with jewelry and glasses and cigarettes, that the heavy ball seemed almost to be alive.

His host—whom he did not really know very well—was nowhere in sight. To the right of them were three rooms, the first of which was piled high with wraps and overcoats.

The horn of Charlie Parker, coming over the hi-fi, dominated all the voices in the room.

"Put your coat down," he told Leona, "and I'll try to find out if I know anybody in this joint."

"Oh," she said, "I'm sure you know them all."

"Go on, now," he said, smiling, and pushing her gently into the room, "do like I tell you."

While she was putting away her coat—and powdering her nose, probably—he remembered that he had promised to call Vivaldo. He wandered through the house, looking for a relatively isolated telephone, and found one in the kitchen.

He dialed Vivaldo's number.

"Hello, baby. How're you?"

"Oh, all right, I guess. What's happening? I thought you were going to call me sooner. I'd just about given you up."

"Well, I only just made it up here." He dropped his voice, for a couple had entered the kitchen, a blond girl with a disarrayed Dutch bob and a tall Negro. The girl leaned against the sink, the boy stood before her, rubbing his hands slowly along the outside of her thighs. They barely glanced at Rufus. "A whole lot of elegant squares around, you dig?"

"Yeah," said Vivaldo. There was a pause. "You think it's worthwhile making it up there?"

"Well, hell, I don't know. If you got something *better* to do—"

"Jane's here," Vivaldo said quickly. Rufus realized that Jane was probably lying on the bed, listening.

"Oh, you got your grandmother with you, you don't need nothing up here then." He did not like Jane, who was somewhat older than Vivaldo, with prematurely gray hair. "Ain't nothing up here old enough for you."

"That's enough, you bastard." He heard Jane's voice and Vivaldo's, murmuring; he could not make out what was being said. Then Vivaldo's voice was at his ear again. "I think I'll skip it."

"I guess you better. I'll see you tomorrow."

"Maybe I'll come by your pad——?"

"Okay. Don't let grandma wear you out now; they tell me women get real ferocious when they get as old as she is."

"They can't get too ferocious for me, dad!"

Rufus laughed. "You better *quit* trying to compete with me. *You* ain't never going to make it. So long."

"So long."

He hung up, smiling, and went to find Leona. She stood helplessly in the foyer, watching the host and hostess saying good night to several people.

"Think I'd deserted you?"

"No. I knew you wouldn't do that."

He smiled at her and touched her on the chin with his fist. The host turned away from the door and came over to them.

"You kids go on inside and get yourselves a drink," he said. "Go on in and get with it." He was a big, handsome, expansive man, older and more ruthless than he looked, who had fought his way to the top in show business via several of the rougher professions, including boxing and pimping. He owed his present eminence more to his vitality and his looks than he did to his voice, and he knew it. He was not the kind of man who fooled himself and Rufus liked him because he was rough and good-natured and generous. But Rufus was also a little afraid of him; there was that about him, in spite of his charm, which did not encourage intimacy. He was a great success with women, whom he treated with a large, affectionate contempt, and he was now on his fourth wife.

He took Leona and Rufus by the arm and walked them to the edge of the party. "We might have us some real doings if these squares ever get out of here," he said. "Stick around."

"How does it feel to be respectable?" Rufus grinned.

"Shit. I been respectable all my life. It's these *respectable* motherfuckers been doing all the dirt. They been stealing the colored folks blind, man. And niggers helping them do it." He laughed. "You know, every time they give me one of them great big checks I think to myself, they just giving me back a *little* bit of what they been stealing all these years, you know what I mean?" He clapped Rufus on the back. "See that Little Eva has a good time."

The crowd was already thinning, most of the squares were beginning to drift away. Once they were gone, the party would change character and become very pleasant and quiet and private. The lights would go down, the music become softer, the talk more sporadic and more sincere. Somebody might sing or play the piano. They might swap stories of the laughs they'd had, gigs they'd played, riffs they remembered, or the trouble they'd seen. Somebody might break out with some pot and pass it slowly around, like the pipe of peace. Somebody, curled on a rug in a far corner of the room, would begin to snore. Whoever danced would dance more languorously, holding tight. The shadows of the room would be alive. Toward the very end, as morning and the brutal sounds of the city began their invasion through the wide French doors, somebody would go into the kitchen and break out with some coffee. Then they would raid the icebox and go home. The host and hostess would finally make it between their sheets and stay in bed all day.

From time to time Rufus found himself glancing upward at the silver ball in the ceiling, always just failing to find himself and Leona reflected there.

"Let's go out to the balcony," he said to her.

She held out her glass. "Freshen my drink first?" Her eyes were now very bright and mischievous and she looked like a little girl.

He walked to the table and poured two very powerful drinks. He went back to her. "Ready?"

She took her glass and they stepped through the French doors.

"Don't let Little Eva catch cold!" the host called.

He called back. "She may burn, baby, but she sure won't freeze!"

Directly before and beneath them stretched the lights of the Jersey shore. He seemed, from where he stood, to hear a faint murmur coming from the water.

When a child he had lived on the eastern edge of Harlem, a block from the Harlem River. He and other children had waded into the water from the garbage-heavy bank or dived from occasional rotting promontories. One summer a boy had drowned there. From the stoop of his house Rufus had watched as a small group of people crossed Park Avenue, beneath the heavy shadow of the railroad tracks, and came into the sun, one man in the middle, the boy's father, carrying the boy's unbelievably heavy, covered weight. He had never forgotten the bend of the man's shoulders or the stunned angle of his head. A great screaming began from the other end of the block and the boy's mother, her head tied up, wearing her bathrobe, stumbling like a drunken woman, began running toward the silent people.

He threw back his shoulders, as though he were casting off a burden, and walked to the edge of the balcony where Leona stood. She was staring up the river, toward the George Washington Bridge.

"It's real beautiful," she said, "it's just so beautiful."

"You seem to like New York," he said.

She turned and looked at him and sipped her drink. "Oh, I do. Can I trouble you for a cigarette now?"

He gave her a cigarette and lit it for her, then lit one for himself. "How're you making it up here?"

"Oh, I'm doing just fine," she said. "I'm waiting tables in a restaurant way downtown, near Wall Street, that's a real pretty part of town, and I'm rooming with two other girls"— they couldn't go to *her* place, anyway!—"and, oh, I'm doing just fine." And she looked up at him with her sad-sweet, poor-white smile.

Again something warned him to stop, to leave this poor little girl alone; and at the same time the fact that he thought of her as a poor little girl caused him to smile with real affection, and he said, "You've got a lot of guts, Leona."

"Got to, the way I look at it," she said. "Sometimes I think I'll just give up. But—*how* do you give up?"

She looked so lost and comical that he laughed out loud and, after a moment, she laughed too.

"If my husband could see me now," and she giggled, "my, my, my!"

"Why, what would your husband say?" he asked her.

"Why—I don't know." But her laugh didn't come this time. She looked at him as though she were slowly coming out of a dream. "Say—do you think I could have another drink?"

"Sure, Leona," and he took her glass and their hands and their bodies touched for a moment. She dropped her eyes. "Be right back," he said, and dropped back into the room, in which the lights now were dim. Someone was playing the piano.

"Say, man, how you coming with Eva?" the host asked.

"Fine, fine, we lushing it up."

"That ain't nowhere. Blast Little Eva with some pot. Let her get her kicks."

"I'll see to it that she gets her kicks," he said.

"Old Rufus left her out there digging the Empire State

building, man," said the young saxophonist, and laughed.

"Give me some of that," Rufus said, and somebody
handed him a stick and he took a few drags.

"Keep it, man. It's choice."

He made a couple of drinks and stood in the room for a
moment, finishing the pot and digging the piano. He felt
fine, clean, on top of everything, and he had a mild buzz on
when he got back to the balcony.

"Is everybody gone home?" she asked, anxiously. "It's so
quiet in there."

"No," he said, "they just sitting around." She seemed
prettier suddenly, and softer, and the river lights fell behind
her like a curtain. This curtain seemed to move as she
moved, heavy and priceless and dazzling. "I didn't know,"
he said, "that you were a princess."

He gave her her drink and their hands touched again. "I
know you must be drunk," she said, happily, and now, over
her drink, her eyes unmistakably called him.

He waited. Everything seemed very simple now. He
played with her fingers. "You seen anything you want since
you been in New York?"

"Oh," she said, "I want it all!"

"You see anything you want right now?"

Her fingers stiffened slightly but he held on. "Go ahead.
Tell me. You ain't got to be afraid." These words then
echoed in his head. He had said this before, years ago, to
someone else. The wind grew cold for an instant, blowing
around his body and ruffling her hair. Then it died down.

"Do *you?*" she asked faintly.

"Do I what?"

"See anything you want?"

He realized that he was high from the way his fingers
seemed hung up in hers and from the way he was staring at
her throat. He wanted to put his mouth there and nibble it
slowly, leaving it black and blue. At the same time he realized how far they were above the city and the lights below
seemed to be calling him. He walked to the balcony's edge
and looked over. Looking straight down, he seemed to be
standing on a cliff in the wilderness, seeing a kingdom and a
river which had not been seen before. He could make it his,
every inch of the territory which stretched beneath and
around him now, and, unconsciously, he began whistling a
tune and his foot moved to find the pedal of his drum. He
put his drink down carefully on the balcony floor and beat a
riff with his fingers on the stone parapet.

"You never answered my question."

"What?"

He turned to face Leona, who held her drink cupped in both her hands and whose brow was quizzically lifted over her despairing eyes and her sweet smile.

"You never answered mine."

"Yes, I did." She sounded more plaintive than ever. "I said I wanted it all."

He took her drink from her and drank half of it, then gave the glass back, moving into the darkest part of the balcony.

"Well, then," he whispered, "come and get it."

She came toward him, holding her glass against her breasts. At the very last moment, standing directly before him, she whispered in bafflement and rage, "What are you trying to do to me?"

"Honey," he answered, "I'm doing it," and he pulled her to him as roughly as he could. He had expected her to resist and she did, holding the glass between them and frantically trying to pull her body away from his body's touch. He knocked the glass out of her hand and it fell dully to the balcony floor, rolling away from them. Go ahead, he thought humorously; if I was to let you go now you'd be so hung up you'd go flying over this balcony, most likely. He whispered, "Go ahead, fight. I like it. Is this the way they do down home?"

"Oh God," she murmured, and began to cry. At the same time, she ceased struggling. Her hands came up and touched his face as though she were blind. Then she put her arms around his neck and clung to him, still shaking. His lips and his teeth touched her ears and her neck and he told her, "Honey, you ain't got nothing to cry about yet."

Yes, he was high; everything he did he watched himself doing, and he began to feel a tenderness for Leona which he had not expected to feel. He tried, with himself, to make amends for what he was doing—for what he was doing to her. Everything seemed to take a very long time. He got hung up on her breasts, standing out like mounds of yellow cream, and the tough, brown, tasty nipples, playing and nuzzling and nibbling while she moaned and whimpered and her knees sagged. He gently lowered them to the floor, pulling her on top of him. He held her tightly at the hip and the shoulder. Part of him was worried about the host and hostess and the other people in the room but another part of him could not stop the crazy thing which had begun. Her fingers opened his shirt to the navel, her tongue burned his neck and his chest; and his hands pushed up her skirt and caressed the inside of her thighs. Then, after a long, high time, while he shook beneath every accelerating tremor of her body, he forced her beneath him and he entered her. For a moment he thought she was going to scream, she was so tight and caught her breath so sharply, and stiffened so. But then she moaned, she moved beneath him. Then, from the center of his rising storm, very slowly and deliberately, he began the slow ride home.

And she carried him, as the sea will carry a boat: with a slow, rocking and rising and falling motion, barely suggestive of the violence of the deep. They murmured and sobbed on this journey, he softly, insistently cursed. Each labored to reach a harbor: there could be no rest until this motion became unbearably accelerated by the power that was rising in them both. Rufus opened his eyes for a moment and watched her face, which was transfigured with agony and gleamed in the darkness like alabaster. Tears hung in the corners of her eyes and the hair at her brow was wet. Her breath came with moaning and short cries, with words he couldn't understand, and in spite of himself he began moving faster and thrusting deeper. He wanted her to remember him the longest day she lived. And, shortly, nothing could have stopped him, not the white God himself nor a lynch mob arriving on wings. Under his breath he cursed the milk-white bitch and groaned and rode his weapon between her thighs. She began to cry. *I told you,* he moaned, *I'd give you something to cry about,* and, at once, he felt himself strangling, about to explode or die. A moan and a curse tore through him while he beat her with all the strength he had and felt the venom shoot out of him, enough for a hundred black-white babies.

He lay on his back, breathing hard. He heard music coming from the room inside, and a whistle on the river. He was frightened and his throat was dry. The air was chilly where he was wet.

She touched him and he jumped. Then he forced himself to turn to her, looking into her eyes. Her eyes were wet still, deep and dark, her trembling lips curved slightly in a shy, triumphant smile. He pulled her to him, wishing he could rest. He hoped she would say nothing; but, "It was so wonderful," she said, and kissed him. And these words, though they caused him to feel no tenderness and did not take away his dull, mysterious dread, began to call desire back again.

He sat up. "You're a funny little cracker," he said. He watched her. "I don't know what you going to say to your husband when you come home with a little black baby."

"I ain't going to be having no more babies," she said, "you ain't got to worry about that." She said nothing more; but she had much more to say. "He beat that out of me, too," she said finally.

He wanted to hear her story. And he wanted to know nothing more about her.

"Let's go inside and wash up," he said.

She put her head against his chest. "I'm afraid to go in there now."

He laughed and stroked her hair. He began to feel affection for her again. "You ain't fixing to stay here all night, are you?"

"What are your friends going to think?"

"Well, one thing, Leona, they ain't going to call the law." He kissed her. "They ain't going to think nothing, honey."

"You coming in with me?"

"Sure, I'm coming in with you." He held her away from him. "All you got to do is sort of straighten your clothes"— he stroked her body, looking into her eyes—"and sort of run your hand through your hair, like this"—and he brushed her hair back from her forehead. She watched him. He heard himself ask, "Do you like me?"

She swallowed. He watched the vein in her neck throb. She seemed very fragile. "Yes," she said. She looked down. "Rufus," she said, "I really do like you. Please don't hurt me."

"Why should I want to hurt you, Leona?" He stroked her neck with one hand, looking at her gravely. "What makes you think I want to hurt you?"

"People *do*," she said, finally, "hurt each other."

"Is somebody been hurting you, Leona?"

She was silent, her face leaning into his palm. "My husband," she said, faintly. "I thought he loved me, but he didn't—oh, I knew he was rough but I didn't think he was *mean*. And he couldn't of loved me because he took away my kid, he's off some place where I can't never see him." She looked up at Rufus with her eyes full of tears. "He said I wasn't a fit mother because—I—drank too much. I *did* drink too much, it was the only way I could stand living with him. But I would of died for my kid, I wouldn't never of let anything happen to him."

He was silent. Her tears fell on his dark fist. "He's still down there," she said, "my husband, I mean. Him and my mother and my brother is as thick as thieves. They think I ain't never been no good. Well, hell, if people keep telling you you ain't no good"—she tried to laugh—"you bound to turn out pretty bad."

He pushed out of his mind all of the questions he wanted to ask her. It was beginning to be chilly on the balcony; he was hungry and he wanted a drink and he wanted to get home to bed. "Well," he said, at last, "I ain't going to hurt you," and he rose, walking to the edge of the balcony. His shorts were like a rope between his legs, he pulled them up, and felt that he was glued inside them. He zipped up his fly, holding his legs wide apart. The sky had faded down to purple. The stars were gone and the lights on the Jersey shore were out. A coal barge traveled slowly down the river.

"How do I look?" she asked him.

"Fine," he said, and she did. She looked like a tired child. "You want to come down to my place?"

"If you want me to," she said.

"Well, yes, that's what I want." But he wondered why he was holding on to her.

Vivaldo came by late the next afternoon to find Rufus still in bed and Leona in the kitchen making breakfast.

It was Leona who opened the door. And Rufus watched with delight the slow shock on Vivaldo's face as he looked from Leona, muffled in Rufus's bathrobe, to Rufus, sitting up in bed, and naked except for the blankets.

Let the liberal white bastard squirm, he thought.

"Hi, baby," he called, "come on in. You just in time for breakfast."

"I've *had* my breakfast," Vivaldo said, "but you people aren't even decent yet. I'll come back later."

"Shit, man, come on in. That's Leona. Leona, this here's a friend of mine, Vivaldo. For short. His real name is Daniel Vivaldo Moore. He's an Irish wop."

"Rufus is just full of prejudice against everybody," said Leona, and smiled. "Come on in."

Vivaldo closed the door behind him awkwardly and sat down on the edge of the bed. Whenever he was uncomfortable—which was often—his arms and legs seemed to stretch to monstrous proportions and he handled them with be-

wildered loathing, as though he had been afflicted with them
only a few moments before.

"I hope you can eat *something*," Leona said. "There's
plenty and it'll be ready in just a second."

"I'll have a cup of coffee with you," Vivaldo said, "unless you happen to have some beer." Then he looked over at
Rufus. "I guess it was quite a party."

Rufus grinned. "Not bad, not bad."

Leona opened some beer and poured it into a tumbler
and brought it to Vivaldo. He took it, looking up at her with
his quick, gypsy smile, and spilled some on one foot.

"You want some, Rufus?"

"No, honey, not yet. I'll eat first."

Leona walked back into the kitchen.

"Ain't she a splendid specimen of Southern woman-
hood?" Rufus asked. "Down yonder, they teach their wom-
enfolks to *serve*."

From the kitchen came Leona's laugh. "They sure don't
teach us nothing else."

"Honey, as long as you know how to make a man as
happy as you making me, you don't *need* to know nothing
else."

Rufus and Vivaldo looked at each other a moment. Then
Vivaldo grinned. "How about it, Rufus. You going to get
your ass up out of that bed?"

Rufus threw back the covers and jumped out of bed. He
raised his arms high and yawned and stretched.

"You're giving quite a show this afternoon," Vivaldo said,
and threw him a pair of shorts.

Rufus put on the shorts and an old pair of gray slacks and
a faded green sport shirt. "You should have made it to that
party," he said, "after all. There was some pot on the scene
that wouldn't wait."

"Well. I had my troubles last night."

"You and Jane? As usual?"

"Oh, she got drunk and pulled some shit. You know.
She's sick, she can't help it."

"I know *she's* sick. But what's wrong with you?"

"I guess I just like to get beaten over the head." They
walked to the table. "This your first time in the Village,
Leona?"

"No, I've walked around here some. But you don't really
know a place unless you know some of the people."

"You know us now," said Vivaldo, "and between us we
must know everybody else. We'll show you around."

Something in the way Vivaldo said this irritated Rufus. His buoyancy evaporated; sour suspicions filled him. He stole a look at Vivaldo, who was sipping his beer and watching Leona with an impenetrable smile—impenetrable exactly because it seemed so open and good-natured. He looked at Leona, who, this afternoon anyway, drowning in his bathrobe, her hair piled on top of her head and her face innocent of make-up, couldn't really be called a pretty girl. Perhaps Vivaldo was contemptuous of her because she was so plain —which meant that Vivaldo was contemptuous of *him*. Or perhaps he was flirting with her because she seemed so simple and available: the proof of her availability being her presence in Rufus' house.

Then Leona looked across the table and smiled at him. His heart and his bowels shook; he remembered their violence and their tenderness together; and he thought, To hell with Vivaldo. He had something Vivaldo would never be able to touch.

He leaned across the table and kissed her.

"Can I have some more beer?" asked Vivaldo, smiling.

"You know where it is," Rufus said.

Leona took his glass and went to the kitchen. Rufus stuck out his tongue at Vivaldo, who was watching him with a faintly quizzical frown.

Leona returned and set a fresh beer before Vivaldo and said, "You boys finish up now, I'm going to get dressed." She gathered her clothes together and vanished into the bathroom.

There was silence at the table for a moment.

"She going to stay here with you?" Vivaldo asked.

"I don't know yet. Nothing's been decided yet. But I think she wants to—"

"Oh, that's obvious. But isn't this place a little small for two?"

"Maybe we'll find a bigger place. Anyway—you know— I'm not home a hell of a lot."

Vivaldo seemed to consider this. Then, "I hope you know what you're doing, baby. I know it's none of my business, but—"

Rufus looked at him. "Don't you like her?"

"Sure, I like her. She's a sweet girl." He took a swallow of his beer. "The question is—how much do *you* like her?"

"Can't you tell?" And Rufus grinned.

"Well, no frankly—I can't. I mean, sure you like her. But—oh, I don't know."

There was silence again. Vivaldo dropped his eyes.

"There's nothing to worry about," said Rufus. "I'm a big boy, you know."

Vivaldo raised his eyes and said, "It's a pretty big world, too, baby. I hope you've thought of that."

"I've thought of that."

"Trouble is, I feel too paternal toward you, you son of a bitch."

"That's the trouble with all you white bastards."

They encountered the big world when they went out into the Sunday streets. It stared unsympathetically out at them from the eyes of the passing people; and Rufus realized that he had not thought at all about this world and its power to hate and destroy. He had not thought at all about his future with Leona, for the reason that he had never considered that they had one. Yet, here she was, clearly intending to stay if he would have her. But the price was high: trouble with the landlord, with the neighbors, with all the adolescents in the Village and all those who descended during the week ends. And his family would have a fit. It didn't matter so very much about his father and mother—their fit, having lasted a lifetime, was now not much more than reflex action. But he knew that Ida would instantly hate Leona. She had always expected a great deal from Rufus, and she was very race-conscious. She would say, You'd never even have looked at that girl, Rufus, if she'd been black. But you'll pick up any white trash just because she's white. What's the matter—you ashamed of being black?

Then, for the first time in his life, he wondered about that —or, rather, the question bumped against his mind for an instant and then speedily, apologetically, withdrew. He looked sideways at Leona. Now she was quite pretty. She had plaited her hair and pinned the braids up, so that she looked very old-fashioned and much younger than her age.

A young couple came toward them, carrying the Sunday papers. Rufus watched the eyes of the man as the man looked at Leona; and then both the man and the woman looked swiftly from Vivaldo to Rufus as though to decide which of the two was her lover. And, since this was the Village—the place of liberation—Rufus guessed, from the swift, nearly sheepish glance the man gave them as they passed, that he had decided that Rufus and Leona formed the couple. The face of his wife, however, simply closed tight, like a gate.

They reached the park. Old, slatternly women from the slums and from the East Side sat on benches, usually alone, sometimes sitting with gray-haired, matchstick men. Ladies from the big apartment buildings on Fifth Avenue, vaguely and desperately elegant, were also in the park, walking their dogs; and Negro nursemaids, turning a stony face on the grown-up world, crooned anxiously into baby carriages. The Italian laborers and small-business men strolled with their families or sat beneath the trees, talking to each other; some played chess or read *L'Espresso*. The other Villagers sat on benches, reading—Kierkegaard was the name shouting from the paper-covered volume held by a short-cropped girl in blue jeans—or talking distractedly of abstract matters, or gossiping or laughing; or sitting still, either with an immense, invisible effort which all but shattered the benches and the trees, or else with a limpness which indicated that they would never move again.

Rufus and Vivaldo—but especially Vivaldo—had known or been intimate with many of these people, so long ago, it now seemed, that it might have occurred in another life. There was something frightening about the aspect of old friends, old lovers, who had, mysteriously, come to nothing. It argued the presence of some cancer which had been operating in them, invisibly, all along and which might, now, be operating in oneself. Many people had vanished, of course, had returned to the havens from which they had fled. But many others were still visible, had turned into lushes or junkies or had embarked on a nerve-rattling pursuit of the perfect psychiatrist; were vindictively married and progenitive and fat; were dreaming the same dreams they had dreamed ten years before, clothed these in the same arguments, quoted the same masters; and dispensed, as they hideously imagined, the same charm they had possessed before their teeth began to fail and their hair began to fall. They were more hostile now than they had been, this was the loud, inescapable change in their tone and the only vitality left in their eyes.

Then Vivaldo was stopped on the path by a large, good-natured girl, who was not sober. Rufus and Leona paused, waiting for him.

"Your friend's real nice," said Leona. "He's real natural. I feel like we known each other for years."

Without Vivaldo, there was a difference in the eyes which watched them. Villagers, both bound and free, looked them over as though where they stood were an auction block or a stud farm. The pale spring sun seemed very hot on the back of his neck and on his forehead. Leona gleamed before him and seemed to be oblivious of everything and everyone but him. And if there had been any doubt concerning their relationship, her eyes were enough to dispel it. Then he thought, If she could take it so calmly, if she noticed nothing, what was the matter with him? Maybe he was making it all up, maybe nobody gave a damn. Then he raised his eyes and met the eyes of an Italian adolescent. The boy was splashed by the sun falling through the trees. The boy looked at him with hatred; his glance flicked over Leona as though she were a whore; he dropped his eyes slowly and swaggered on —having registered his protest, his backside seemed to snarl, having made his point.

"Cock sucker," Rufus muttered.

Then Leona surprised him. "You talking about that boy? He's just bored and lonely, don't know no better. You could probably make friends with him real easy if you tried."

He laughed.

"Well, that's what's the matter with most people," Leona insisted, plaintively, "ain't got nobody to be with. That's what makes them so evil. I'm telling you, boy, I know."

"Don't call me *boy*," he said.

"Well," she said, looking startled, "I didn't mean nothing by it, honey." She took his arm and they turned to look for Vivaldo. The large girl had him by the collar and he was struggling to get away, and laughing.

"That Vivaldo," said Rufus, amused, "he has more trouble with women."

"He's sure enjoying it," Leona said. "Look like she's enjoying it, too."

For now the large girl had let him go and seemed about to collapse on the path with laughter. People, with a tolerant smile, looked up from the benches or the grass or their books, recognizing two Village characters.

Then Rufus resented all of them. He wondered if he and Leona would dare to make such a scene in public, if such a day could ever come for them. No one dared to look at Vivaldo, out with any girl whatever, the way they looked at Rufus now; nor would they ever look at the girl the way they looked at Leona. The lowest whore in Manhattan would be protected as long as she had Vivaldo on her arm. This was because Vivaldo was white.

He remembered a rainy night last winter, when he had just come in from a gig in Boston, and he and Vivaldo had

gone out with Jane. He had never really understood what
Vivaldo saw in Jane, who was too old for him, and comba-
tive and dirty; her gray hair was never combed, her sweaters,
of which she seemed to possess thousands, were all equally
raveled and shapeless; and her blue jeans were baggy and
covered with paint. "She dresses like a goddamn bull dag-
ger," Rufus had told Vivaldo once, and then laughed at
Vivaldo's horrified expression. His face had puckered as
though someone had just cracked a rotten egg. But he had
never really hated Jane until this rainy night.

It had been a terrible night, with rain pouring down like
great tin buckets, filling the air with a roaring, whining clat-
ter, and making lights and streets and buildings as fluid as
itself. It battered and streamed against the windows of the
fetid, poor-man's bar Jane had brought them to, a bar where
they knew no one. It was filled with shapeless, filthy women
with whom Jane drank, apparently, sometimes, during the
day; and pale, untidy, sullen men, who worked on the docks,
and resented seeing him there. He wanted to go, but he was
trying to wait for the rain to let up a little. He was bored
speechless with Jane's chatter about her paintings, and he
was ashamed of Vivaldo for putting up with it. How had
the fight begun? He had always blamed it on Jane. Finally,
in order not to go to sleep, he had begun to tease Jane a little;
but this teasing revealed, of course, how he really felt about
her, and she was not slow to realize it. Vivaldo watched them
with a faint, wary smile. He, too, was bored, and found
Jane's pretensions intolerable.

"Anyway," Jane said, "you aren't an artist and so I don't
see how you can possibly judge the work I do—"

"Oh, stop it," said Vivaldo. "Do you know how silly you
sound? You mean you just paint for this half-assed gang of
painters down here?"

"Oh, let her swing, man," Rufus said, beginning to enjoy
himself. He leaned forward, grinning at Jane in a way at
once lewd and sardonic. "This chick's too deep for us, man,
we can't dig that shit she's putting down."

"You're the snobs," she said, "not I. I bet you I've reached
more people, honest, hard-working, ignorant people, right
here in this bar, than either of you ever reach. Those people
you hang out with are *dead*, man—at least, these people are
alive."

Rufus laughed. "I thought it smelled funny in here. So
that's it. Shit. It's life, huh?" And he laughed again.

But he was also aware that they were beginning to attract

attention, and he glanced at the windows where the rain streamed down, saying to himself, Okay, Rufus, behave yourself. And he leaned back in the booth, where he sat facing Jane and Vivaldo.

He had reached her, and she struck back with the only weapon she had, a shapeless instrument which might once have been fury. "It doesn't smell any worse in here than it does where you come from, baby."

Vivaldo and Rufus looked at each other. Vivaldo's lips turned white. He said, "You say another word, baby, and I'm going to knock your teeth, both of them, right down your throat."

This profoundly delighted her. She became Bette Davis at once, and shouted at the top of her voice, "Are you threatening me?"

Everyone turned to look at them.

"Oh, shit," said Rufus, "let's go."

"Yes," said Vivaldo, "let's get out of here." He looked at Jane. "Move. You filthy bitch."

And now she was contrite. She leaned forward and grabbed Rufus's hand. "I didn't mean it the way it sounded." He tried to pull his hand away; she held on. He relaxed, not wanting to seem to struggle with her. Now she was being Joan Fontaine. "Please, you *must* believe me, Rufus!"

"I believe you," he said, and rose; to find a heavy Irishman standing in his way. They stared at each other for a moment and then the man spat in his face. He heard Jane scream, but he was already far away. He struck, or thought he struck; a fist slammed into his face and something hit him at the back of the head. The world, the air, went red and black, then roared in at him with faces and fists. The small of his back slammed against something cold, hard, and straight; he supposed it was the end of the bar, and he wondered how he had got there. From far away, he saw a barstool poised above Vivaldo's head, and he heard Jane screaming, keening like all of Ireland. He had not known there were so many men in the bar. He struck a face, he felt bone beneath the bone of his fist, and weak green eyes, glaring into his like headlights at the moment of collision, shuttered in distress. Someone had reached him in the belly, someone else in the head. He was being spun about and he could no longer strike, he could only defend. He kept his head down, bobbing and shifting, pushed and pulled, and he crouched, trying to protect his private parts. He heard the crash of glass. For an instant he saw Vivaldo, at the far end of the bar, blood streaming down from his nose and his forehead, surrounded by three or four men, and he saw the back of a hand send Jane spinning half across the room. Her face was white and terrified. *Good*, he thought, and felt himself in the air, going over the bar. Glass crashed again, and wood splintered. There was a foot on his shoulder and a foot on one ankle. He pressed his buttocks against the floor and drew his free leg in as far as he could; and with one arm he tried to hold back the fist which crashed down again and again into his face. Far behind the fist was the face of the Irishman, with the green eyes ablaze. Then he saw nothing, heard nothing, felt nothing. Then he heard running feet. He was on his back behind the bar. There was no one near him. He pulled himself up and half-crawled out. The bartender was at the door, shooing his customers out; an old woman sat at the bar, tranquilly sipping gin; Vivaldo lay on his face in a pool of blood. Jane stood helplessly over him. And the sound of the rain came back.

"I think he's dead," Jane said.

He looked at her, hating her with all his heart. He said, "I wish to God it was you, you cunt." She began to cry.

He leaned down and helped Vivaldo to rise. Half-leaning on, half-supporting each other, they made it to the door. Jane came behind them. "Let me help you."

Vivaldo stopped and tried to straighten. They leaned, half-in, half-out of the door. The bartender watched them. Vivaldo looked at the bartender, then at Jane. He and Rufus stumbled together into the blinding rain.

"Let me *help* you," Jane cried again. But she stopped in the doorway long enough to say to the bartender, whose face held no expression whatever, "You're going to hear about this, believe me. I'm going to close this bar and have your job, if it's the last thing I ever do." Then she ran into the rain, and tried to help Rufus support Vivaldo.

Vivaldo pulled away from her touch, and slipped and almost fell. "Get away from me. Get away from me. You've been enough help for one night."

"You've got to get in somewhere!" Jane cried.

"Don't you *worry* about it. Don't worry about it. Drop dead, get lost, go fuck yourself. We're going to the hospital."

Rufus looked into Vivaldo's face and became frightened. Both his eyes were closing and the blood poured down from some wound in his scalp. And he was crying.

"What a way to talk to my buddy, man," he said, over and over. "Wow! What a way to talk to my *buddy!*"

"Let's go to her place," Rufus whispered. "It's closer."

Vivaldo did not seem to hear him. "Come on, baby, let's go on over to Jane's, it don't matter."

He was afraid that Vivaldo had been badly hurt, and he knew what would happen at the hospital if two fays and a spade came bleeding in. For the doctors and nurses were, first of all, upright, clean-living white citizens. And he was not really afraid for himself, but for Vivaldo, who knew so little about his countrymen.

So, slipping and sliding, with Jane now circling helplessly around them and now leading the way, like a big-assed Joan of Arc, they reached Jane's pad. He carried Vivaldo into the bathroom and sat him down. He looked into the mirror. His face looked like jam, but the scars would probably heal, and only one eye was closed; but when he began washing Vivaldo, he found a great gash in his skull, and this frightened him.

"Man," he whispered, "you got to go to the hospital."

"That's what I said. All right. Let's go."

And he tried to rise.

"No, man. Listen. If I go with you, it's going to be a whole lot of who shot John because I'm black and you're white. You dig? I'm telling it to you like it is."

Vivaldo said, "I really don't want to hear all that shit, Rufus."

"Well, it's true, whether you want to hear it or not. Jane's got to take you to the hospital, I can't come with you." Vivaldo's eyes were closed and his face was white. "Vivaldo?"

He opened his eyes. "Are you mad at me, Rufus?"

"Shit, no, baby, why should I be mad with you?" But he knew what was bothering Vivaldo. He leaned down and whispered, "Don't you worry, baby, everything's cool. I know you're my friend."

"I love you, you shithead, I really do."

"I love you, too. Now, get on to that hospital, I don't want you to drop dead in this phony white chick's bathroom. I'll wait here for you. I'll be all right." Then he walked quickly out of the bathroom. He said to Jane, "Take him to the hospital, he's hurt worse than I am. I'll wait here."

She had the sense, then, to say nothing. Vivaldo remained in the hospital for ten days and had three stitches taken in his scalp. In the morning Rufus went uptown to see a doctor and stayed in bed for a week. He and Vivaldo never spoke of this night, and though he knew that Vivaldo had finally begun seeing her again, they never spoke of Jane. But from that time on, Rufus had depended on and trusted Vivaldo—

depended on him even now, as he bitterly watched him hors-
ing around with the large girl on the path. He did not know
why this was so; he scarcely knew that it was so. Vivaldo was
unlike everyone else that he knew in that they, all the others,
could only astonish him by kindness or fidelity; it was only
Vivaldo who had the power to astonish him by treachery.
Even his affair with Jane was evidence in his favor, for if he
were really likely to betray his friend for a woman, as most
white men seemed to do, especially if the friend were black,
then he would have found himself a smoother chick, with
the manners of a lady and the soul of a whore. But Jane
seemed to be exactly what she was, a monstrous slut, and
she thus, without knowing it, kept Rufus and Vivaldo equal
to one another.

At last Vivaldo was free and hurried toward them on the
path still grinning, and now waving to someone behind them.

"Look," he cried, "there's Cass!"

Rufus turned and there she was, sitting alone on the rim
of the circle, frail and fair. For him, she was thoroughly
mysterious. He could never quite place her in the white
world to which she seemed to belong. She came from New
England, of plain old American stock—so she put it; she
was very fond of remembering that one of her ancestors had
been burned as a witch. She had married Richard, who was
Polish, and they had two children. Richard had been Vivaldo's English instructor in high school, years ago. They
had known him as a brat, they said—not that he had changed
much; they were his oldest friends.

With Leona between them, Rufus and Vivaldo crossed the
road.

Cass looked up at them with that smile which was at once
chilling and warm. It was warm because it was affectionate;
it chilled Rufus because it was amused. "Well, I'm not sure
I'm speaking to either of you. You've been neglecting us
shamefully. Richard has crossed you *off* his list." She looked
at Leona and smiled. "I'm Cass Silenski."

"This is Leona," Rufus said, putting one hand on Leona's
shoulder.

Cass looked more amused than ever, and at the same time
more affectionate. "I'm very happy to meet you."

"I'm glad to meet *you*," said Leona.

They sat down on the stone rim of the fountain, in the
center of which a little water played, enough for small children to wade in.

"Give an account of yourselves," Cass said. *"Why* haven't you come to see us?"

"Oh," said Vivaldo, "I've been busy. I've been working on my novel."

"He's been working on a novel," said Cass to Leona, "ever since we've known him. Then he was seventeen and now he's nearly thirty."

"That's unkind," said Vivaldo, looking amused at the same time that he looked ashamed and annoyed.

"Well, Richard was working on one, too. Then he was twenty-five and now he's close to forty. So—" She considered Vivaldo a moment. "Only, he's had a brand-new inspiration and he's been working on it like a madman. I think that's one of the reasons he's been rather hoping you'd come by—he may have wanted to discuss it with you."

"What is this new inspiration?" Vivaldo asked. "Offhand, it sounds unfair."

"Ah!"—she shrugged merrily, and took a deep drag on her cigarette—"I wasn't consulted, and I'm kept in the dark. You know Richard. He gets up at some predawn hour and goes straight to his study and stays there until it's time to go to work; comes home, goes straight to his study and stays there until it's time to go to bed. I hardly ever see him. The children no longer have a father, I no longer have a husband." She laughed. "He did manage to grunt something the other morning about it's going very well."

"It certainly *sounds* as though it's going well." Vivaldo looked at Cass enviously. "And you say it's new?—it's not the same novel he was working on before?"

"I gather not. But I really know nothing about it." She dragged on her cigarette again, crushed it under her heel, immediately began searching in her bag for another.

"Well, I'll certainly have to come by and check on all this for myself," said Vivaldo. "At this rate, he'll be famous before I am."

"Oh, I've always known that," said Cass, and lit another cigarette.

Rufus watched the pigeons strutting along the walks and the gangs of adolescents roaming up and down. He wanted to get away from this place and this danger. Leona put her hand on his. He grabbed one of her fingers and held it.

Cass turned to Rufus. "Now *you* haven't been working on a novel, why haven't *you* come by?"

"I've been working uptown. *You* promised to come and hear *me*. Remember?"

"We've been terribly broke, Rufus—"

"When I'm working in a joint, you haven't got to worry about being broke, I told you that before."

"He's a great musician," Leona said. "I heard him for the first time last night."

Rufus looked annoyed. "That gig ended last night. I ain't got nothing to do for a while except take care of my old lady." And he laughed.

Cass and Leona looked briefly at each other and smiled.

"How long have you been up here, Leona?" Cass asked.

"Oh, just a little over a month."

"Do you like it?"

"Oh, I love it. It's just as different as night from day, I can't tell you."

Cass looked briefly at Rufus. "That's wonderful," she said, gravely. "I'm very glad for you."

"Yes, I can feel that," said Leona. "You seem to be a very nice woman."

"Thank you," said Cass, and blushed.

"*How*'re you going to take care of your old lady," Vivaldo asked, "if you're not working?"

"Oh, I've got a couple of record dates coming up; don't you worry about old Rufus."

Vivaldo sighed. "I'm worried about *me*. I'm in the wrong profession—or, rather, I'm not. *In* it, I mean. Nobody wants to hear my story."

Rufus looked at him. "Don't let me start talking to you about *my* profession."

"Things are tough all over," said Vivaldo.

Rufus looked out over the sun-filled park.

"Nobody ever has to take up a collection to bury managers or agents," Rufus said. "But they sweeping musicians up off the streets every day."

"Never mind," said Leona, gently, "they ain't never going to sweep you up off the streets."

She put her hand on his head and stroked it. He reached up and took her hand away.

There was a silence. Then Cass rose. "I hate to break this up, but I must go home. One of my neighbors took the kids to the zoo, but they're probably back by now. I'd better rescue Richard."

"How *are* your kids, Cass?" Rufus asked.

"Much *you* care. It would serve you right if they'd forgotten all about you. They're fine. They've got much more energy than their parents."

Vivaldo said, "I'm going to walk Cass home. What do you think you'll be doing later?"

He felt a dull fear and a dull resentment, almost as though Vivaldo were deserting him. "Oh, I don't know. I guess we'll go along home—"

"I got to go uptown later, Rufus," said Leona. "I ain't got nothing to go to work in tomorrow."

Cass held out her hand to Leona. "It was nice meeting you. Make Rufus bring you by to see us one day."

"Well, it was sure nice meeting you. I been meeting some real nice people lately."

"Next time," said Cass, "we'll go off and have a drink by ourselves someplace, without all these *men*."

They laughed together. "I *really* would like that."

"Suppose I pick you up at Benno's," Rufus said to Vivaldo, "around ten-thirty?"

"Good enough. Maybe we'll go across town and pick up on some jazz?"

"Good."

"So long, Leona. Glad to have met you."

"Me, too. Be seeing you real soon."

"Give my regards," said Rufus, "to Richard and the kids, and tell them I'm coming by."

"I'll do that. Make sure you *do* come by, we'd dearly love to see you."

Cass and Vivaldo started slowly in the direction of the arch. The bright-red, setting sun burned their silhouettes against the air and crowned the dark head and the golden one. Rufus and Leona stood and watched them; when they were under the arch, they turned and waved.

"We better be making tracks," said Rufus.

"I guess so." They started back through the park. "You got some real nice friends, Rufus. You're lucky. They're real fond of you. They think you're somebody."

"You think they do?"

"I know they do. I can tell by the way they talk to you, the way they treat you."

"I guess they *are* pretty nice," he said, "at that."

She laughed. "*You're* a funny boy"—she corrected herself—"a funny *person*. You act like you don't know who you are."

"I know who I am, all right," he said, aware of the eyes that watched them pass, the nearly inaudible murmur that came from the benches or the trees. He squeezed her thin

hand between his elbow and his side. "I'm your boy. You
know what that means?"

"What does it mean?"

"It means you've got to be good to me."

"Well, Rufus, I sure am going to try."

Now, bowed down with the memory of all that had happened since that day, he wandered helplessly back to Forty-
second Street and stopped before the large bar and grill on
the corner. Near him, just beyond the plate glass, stood the
sandwich man behind his counter, the meat arrayed on the
steam table beneath him. Bread and rolls, mustard, relish,
salt and pepper, stood at the level of his chest. He was a big
man, wearing white, with a blank, red, brutal face. From
time to time he expertly knifed off a sandwich for one of the
derelicts within. The old seemed reconciled to being there, to
having no teeth, no hair, having no life. Some laughed together, the young, with dead eyes set in yellow faces, the
slackness of their bodies making vivid the history of their
degradation. They were the prey that was no longer hunted,
though they were scarcely aware of this new condition and
could not bear to leave the place where they had first been
spoiled. And the hunters were there, far more assured and
patient than the prey. In any of the world's cities, on a winter
night, a boy can be bought for the price of a beer and the
promise of warm blankets.

Rufus shivered, his hands in his pockets, looking through
the window and wondering what to do. He thought of walking to Harlem but he was afraid of the police he would encounter in his passage through the city; and he did not see
how he could face his parents or his sister. When he had last
seen Ida, he had told her that he and Leona were about to
make it to Mexico, where, he said, people would leave them
alone. But no one had heard from him since then.

Now a big, rough-looking man, well dressed, white, with
black-and-gray hair, came out of the bar. He paused next to
Rufus, looking up and down the street. Rufus did not move,
though he wanted to; his mind began to race, painfully, and
his empty stomach turned over. Once again, sweat broke
out on his forehead. Something in him knew what was about
to happen; something in him died in the freezing second before the man walked over to him and said:

"It's cold out here. Wouldn't you like to come in and have
a drink with me?"

"I'd rather have a sandwich," Rufus muttered, and thought, *You've really hit the bottom now.*

"Well, you can have a sandwich, too. There's no law that says you can't."

Rufus looked up and down the street, then looked into the man's ice-cold, ice-white face. He reminded himself that he knew the score, he'd been around; neither was this the first time during his wanderings that he had consented to the bleakly physical exchange; and yet he felt that he would never be able to endure the touch of this man. They entered the bar and grill.

"What kind of sandwich would you like?"

"Corned beef," Rufus whispered, "on rye."

They watched while the meat was hacked off, slammed on bread, and placed on the counter. The man paid and Rufus took his sandwich over to the bar. He felt that everyone in the place knew what was going on, knew that Rufus was peddling his ass. But nobody seemed to care. Nobody looked at them. The noise at the bar continued, the radio continued to blare. The bartender served up a beer for Rufus and a whiskey for the man and rang up the money on the cash register. Rufus tried to turn his mind away from what was happening to him. He wolfed down his sandwich. But the heavy bread, the tepid meat, made him begin to feel nauseous; everything wavered before his eyes for a moment; he sipped his beer, trying to hold the sandwich down.

"You were hungry."

Rufus, he thought, you can't make this scene. There's no way in the world you can make it. Don't come on with the man. Just get out of here.

"Would you like another sandwich?"

The first sandwich was still threatening to come up. The bar stank of stale beer and piss and stale meat and unwashed bodies.

Suddenly he felt that he was going to cry.

"No, thank you," he said, "I'm all right now."

The man watched him for a moment.

"Then have another beer."

"No, thank you." But he leaned his head on the bar, trembling.

"Hey!"

Lights roared around his head, the whole bar lurched, righted itself, faces weaved around him, the music from the radio pounded in his skull. The man's face was very close to

his: hard eyes and a cruel nose and flabby, brutal lips. He
smelled the man's odor. He pulled away.

"I'm all right."

"You almost blacked out there for a minute."

The bartender watched them.

"You better have a drink. Hey, Mac, give the kid a drink."

"You sure he's all right?"

"Yeah, he's all right, I know him. Give him a drink."

The bartender filled a shot glass and placed it in front of
Rufus. And Rufus stared into the gleaming cup, praying,
Lord, don't let it happen. Don't let me go home with this
man.

I've got so little left, Lord, don't let me lose it all.

"Drink. It'll do you good. Then you can come on over to
my place and get some sleep."

He drank the whiskey, which first made him feel even
sicker, then warmed him. He straightened up.

"You live around here?" he asked the man. If you touch
me, he thought, still with these strange tears threatening to
boil over at any moment, I'll beat the living shit out of you. I
don't want no more hands on me, no more, no more, no
more.

"Not very far. Forty-sixth Street."

They walked out of the bar, into the streets again.

"It's a lonely city," the man said as they walked. "I'm
lonely. Aren't you lonely, too?"

Rufus said nothing.

"Maybe we can comfort each other for a night."

Rufus watched the traffic lights, the black, nearly deserted
streets, the silent black buildings, the deep shadows of doorways.

"Do you know what I mean?"

"I'm not the boy you want, mister," he said at last, and
suddenly remembered having said exactly these words to
Eric—long ago.

"How do you mean, you're not the boy I want?" And the
man tried to laugh. "Shouldn't I be the best judge of that?"

Rufus said, "I don't have a thing to give you. I don't have
nothing to give nobody. Don't make me go through with
this. Please."

They stopped on the silent Avenue, facing each other.
The man's eyes hardened and narrowed.

"Didn't you know what was going on—back there?"

Rufus said, "I was hungry."

"What are you, anyway—just a cock teaser?"

"I was hungry," Rufus repeated; "I was hungry."

"Don't you have any family—any friends?"

Rufus looked down. He did not answer right away. Then, "I don't want to die, mister. I don't want to kill you. Let me go—to my friends."

"Do you know where to find them?"

"I know where to find—one of them."

There was a silence. Rufus stared at the sidewalk and, very slowly, the tears filled his eyes and began trickling down his nose.

The man took his arm. "Come on—come on to my place."

But now the moment, the possibility, had passed; both of them felt it. The man dropped his arm.

"You're a good-looking boy," he said.

Rufus moved away. "So long, mister. Thanks."

The man said nothing. Rufus watched him walk away.

Then he, too, turned and began walking downtown. He thought of Eric for the first time in years, and wondered if he were prowling foreign streets tonight. He glimpsed, for the first time, the extent, the nature, of Eric's loneliness, and the danger in which this placed him; and wished that he had been nicer to him. Eric had always been very nice to Rufus. He had had a pair of cufflinks made for Rufus, for Rufus's birthday, with the money which was to have bought his wedding rings: and this gift, this confession, delivered him into Rufus's hands. Rufus had despised him because he came from Alabama; perhaps he had allowed Eric to make love to him in order to despise him more completely. Eric had finally understood this, and had fled from Rufus, all the way to Paris. But his stormy blue eyes, his bright red hair, his halting drawl, all returned very painfully to Rufus now.

Go ahead and tell me. You ain't got to be afraid.

And, as Eric hesitated, Rufus added—slyly, grinning, watching him:

"You act like a little girl—or something."

And even now there was something heady and almost sweet in the memory of the ease with which he had handled Eric, and elicited his confession. When Eric had finished speaking, he said slowly:

"I'm not the boy for you. I don't go that way."

Eric had placed their hands together, and he stared down at them, the red and the brown.

"I know," he said.

He moved to the center of his room.

"But I can't help wishing you did. I wish you'd try."

Then, with a terrible effort, Rufus heard it in his voice, his breath:

"I'd do anything. I'd try anything. To please you."

Then, with a smile, "I'm almost as young as you are. I don't know—much—about it."

Rufus had watched him, smiling. He felt a flood of affection for Eric. And he felt his own power.

He walked over to Eric and put his hands on Eric's shoulders. He did not know what he was going to say or do. But with his hands on Eric's shoulders, affection, power, and curiosity all knotted together in him—with a hidden, unforeseen violence which frightened him a little; the hands that were meant to hold Eric at arm's length seemed to draw Eric to him; the current that had begun flowing he did not know how to stop.

At last, he said in a low voice, smiling, "I'll try anything once, old buddy."

Those cufflinks were now in Harlem, in Ida's bureau drawer. And when Eric was gone, Rufus forgot their battles and the unspeakable physical awkwardness, and the ways in which he had made Eric pay for such pleasure as Eric gave, or got. He remembered only that Eric had loved him; as he now remembered that Leona had loved him. He had despised Eric's manhood by treating him as a woman, by telling him how inferior he was to a woman, by treating him as nothing more than a hideous sexual deformity. But Leona had not been a deformity. And he had used against her the very epithets he had used against Eric, and in the very same way, with the same roaring in his head and the same intolerable pressure in his chest.

Vivaldo lived alone in a first-floor apartment on Bank Street. He was home, Rufus saw the light in the window. He slowed down a little but the cold air refused to let him hesitate; he hurried through the open street door, thinking, Well, I might as well get it over with. And he knocked quickly on Vivaldo's door.

There had been the sound of a typewriter; now it stopped. Rufus knocked again.

"Who is it?" called Vivaldo, sounding extremely annoyed.

"It's me. It's me. Rufus."

The sudden light, when Vivaldo opened the door, was a great shock, as was Vivaldo's face.

"My God," said Vivaldo.

He grabbed Rufus around the neck, pulling him inside

and holding him. They both leaned for a moment against Vivaldo's door.

"My God," Vivaldo said again, "where've you been? Don't you know you shouldn't do things like that? You've had all of us scared to death, baby. We've been looking for you everywhere."

It was a great shock and it weakened Rufus, exactly as though he had been struck in the belly. He clung to Vivaldo as though he were on the ropes. Then he pulled away.

Vivaldo looked at him, looked hard at him, up and down. And Vivaldo's face told him how he looked. He moved away from the door, away from Vivaldo's scrutiny.

"Ida's been here; she's half-crazy. Do you realize you dropped out of sight almost a month ago?"

"Yes," he said, and sat down heavily in Vivaldo's easy chair—which sagged beneath him almost to the floor. He looked around the room, which had once been so familiar, which now seemed so strange.

He leaned back, his hands over his eyes.

"Take off your jacket," Vivaldo said. "I'll see if I can scare up something for you to eat—are you hungry?"

"No, not now. Tell me, how is Ida?"

"Well, she's *worried*, you know, but there's nothing wrong with her. Rufus, you want me to fix you a drink?"

"When was she here?"

"Yesterday. And she called me tonight. And she's been to the police. Everybody's been worried, Cass, Richard, everybody—"

He sat up. "The police are looking for me?"

"Well, hell, yes, baby, people aren't supposed to just disappear." He walked into his small, cluttered kitchen and opened his refrigerator, which contained a quart of milk and half a grapefruit. He stared at them helplessly. "I'll have to take you out, I haven't got anything to eat in this joint." He closed the refrigerator door. "You can have a drink, though, I've got some bourbon."

Vivaldo made two drinks, gave one to Rufus and sat down on the other, straight-backed, chair.

"Well, let's have it. What've you been doing, where've you been?"

"I've just been wandering the streets."

"My God, Rufus, in this weather? Where've you been sleeping?"

"Oh. Subways, hallways. Movies sometimes."

"And how'd you eat?"

He took a swallow of his drink. Perhaps it was a mistake to have come. "Oh," he said, astonished to hear the truth come out, "sometimes I sort of peddled my ass."

Vivaldo looked at him. "I guess you had pretty rough competition." He lit a cigarette and threw the pack and the matches to Rufus. "You should have got in touch with somebody, you should have let somebody know what was happening."

"I—couldn't. I just couldn't."

"We're supposed to be friends, you and me."

He stood up, holding an unlit cigarette, and walked around the small room, touching things. "I don't know. I don't know what I was thinking." He lit the cigarette. "I know what I did to Leona. I'm not dumb."

"So do I know what you did to Leona. Neither am I dumb."

"I guess I just didn't think—"

"What?"

"That anyone would care."

In the silence that hung in the room then, Vivaldo rose and went to his phonograph. "You didn't think Ida would care? You didn't think I would care?"

He felt as though he were smothering. "I don't know. I don't know what I thought."

Vivaldo said nothing. His face was pale and angry and he concentrated on looking through his records. Finally he put one on the machine; it was James Pete Johnson and Bessie Smith batting out *Backwater Blues*.

"Well," said Vivaldo, helplessly, and sat down again.

Besides Vivaldo's phonograph, there wasn't much else in his apartment. There was a homemade lamp, brick-supported bookshelves, records, a sagging bed, the sprung easy chair, and the straight-backed chair. There was a high stool before Vivaldo's worktable on which Vivaldo teetered now, his coarse, curly black hair hanging forward, his eyes somber, and his mouth turned down. The table held his pencils, papers, his typewriter, and the telephone. In a small alcove was the kitchen in which the overhead light was burning. The sink was full of dirty dishes, topped by a jaggedly empty and open tin can. A paper sack of garbage leaned against one of the kitchen table's uncertain legs.

There's thousands of people, Bessie now sang, *ain't got no place to go*, and for the first time Rufus began to hear, in the severely understated monotony of this blues, something which spoke to his troubled mind. The piano bore the singer witness, stoic and ironic. Now that Rufus himself had no place to go—*'cause my house fell down and I can't live there no mo'*, sang Bessie—he heard the line and the tone of the singer, and he wondered how others had moved beyond the emptiness and horror which faced him now.

Vivaldo was watching him. Now he cleared his throat and said, "Maybe it would be a good idea for you to make a change of scene, Rufus. Everything around here will just keep reminding you—sometimes it's better just to wipe the slate clean and take off. Maybe you should go to the Coast."

"There's nothing happening on the Coast."

"A lot of musicians have gone out there."

"They're on their ass out there, too. It's no different from New York."

"No, they're working. You might feel differently out there, with all the sunshine and oranges and all." He smiled. "Make a new man out of you, baby."

"I guess you think," said Rufus, malevolently, "that it's time I started trying to be a new man."

There was a silence. Then Vivaldo said, "It's not so much what *I* think. It's what *you* think."

Rufus watched the tall, lean, clumsy white boy who was his best friend, and felt himself nearly strangling with the desire to hurt him.

"Rufus," said Vivaldo, suddenly, "believe me, I know, I know—a lot of things hurt you that I can't really understand." He played with the keys of his typewriter. "A lot of things hurt me that *I* can't really understand."

Rufus sat on the edge of the sprung easy chair, watching Vivaldo gravely.

"Do you blame me for what happened to Leona?"

"Rufus, what good would it do if I *did* blame you? You blame yourself enough already, that's what's wrong with you, what's the good of *my* blaming you?"

He could see, though, that Vivaldo had also hoped to be able to avoid this question.

"Do you blame me or don't you? Tell the truth."

"Rufus, if I wasn't your friend, I think I'd blame you, sure. You acted like a bastard. But I understand that, I think I do, I'm trying to. But, anyway, since you *are* my friend, and, after all, let's face it, you mean much more to me than Leona ever did, well, I don't think I should put you down just because you acted like a bastard. We're *all* bastards. That's why we need our friends."

"I wish I could tell you what it was like," Rufus said, after a long silence. "I wish I could unto it."

"Well, you can't. So please start trying to forget it."

Rufus thought, But it's not possible to forget anybody you were that hung up on, who was that hung up on you. You can't forget anything that hurt so badly, went so deep, and changed the world forever. It's not possible to forget anybody you've destroyed.

He took a great swallow of his bourbon, holding it in his mouth, then allowing it to trickle down his throat. He would never be able to forget Leona's pale, startled eyes, her sweet smile, her plaintive drawl, her thin, insatiable body.

He choked slightly, put down his drink, and ground out his cigarette in the spilling ashtray.

"I bet you won't believe this," he said, "but I loved Leona. I did."

"Oh," said Vivaldo, "believe you! Of course I believe you. That's what all the bleeding was *about*."

He got up and turned the record over. Then there was silence, except for the voice of Bessie Smith.

When my bed get empty, make me feel awful mean and blue,

"Oh, sing it, Bessie," Vivaldo muttered.

My springs is getting rusty, sleeping single like I do.

Rufus picked up his drink and finished it.

"Did you ever have the feeling," he asked, "that a woman was eating you up? I mean—no matter what she was like or what else she was doing—that that's what she was *really* doing?"

"Yes," said Vivaldo.

Rufus stood. He walked up and down.

"She can't help it. And you can't help it. And there you are." He paused. "Of course, with Leona and me—there was lots of other things, too—"

Then there was a long silence. They listened to Bessie.

"Have you ever wished you were queer?" Rufus asked, suddenly.

Vivaldo smiled, looking into his glass. "I used to think maybe I was. Hell, I think I even *wished* I was." He laughed. "But I'm not. So I'm stuck."

Rufus walked to Vivaldo's window. "So you been all up and down that street, too," he said.

"We've all been up the same streets. There aren't a hell of a lot of streets. Only, we've been taught to lie so much about so many things, that we hardly ever know *where* we are."

Rufus said nothing. He walked up and down.

Vivaldo said, "Maybe you should stay here, Rufus, for a couple of days, until you decide what you want to do."

"I don't want to bug you, Vivaldo."

Vivaldo picked up Rufus's empty glass and paused in the archway which led into his kitchen. "You can lie here in the mornings and look at my ceiling. It's full of cracks, it makes all kinds of pictures. Maybe it'll tell you things it hasn't told me. I'll fix us another drink."

Again he felt that he was smothering. "Thanks, Vivaldo."

Vivaldo dragged his ice out and poured two drinks. He came back into the room. "Here. To all the things we don't know."

They drank.

"You had me worried," said Vivaldo. "I'm glad you're back."

"I'm glad to see you," said Rufus.

"Your sister left me a phone number to call in case I saw you. It's the lady who lives next door to you. I guess maybe I should call her now."

"No," said Rufus, after a moment, "it's too late. I'll go on up there in the morning." And this thought, the thought of seeing his parents and his sister in the morning, checked and chilled him. He sat down again in the easy chair and leaned back with his hands over his eyes.

"Rufus," Leona said—time and again—"ain't nothing wrong in being colored."

Sometimes, when she said this, he simply looked at her coldly, from a great distance, as though he wondered what on earth she was trying to say. His look seemed to accuse her of ignorance and indifference. And, as she watched his face, her eyes became more despairing than ever but at the same time filled with some immense sexual secret which tormented her.

He had put off going back to work until he began to be afraid to go to work.

Sometimes, when she said that there was nothing wrong in being colored, he answered:

"Not if you a hard-up white lady."

The first time he said this, she winced and said nothing. The second time she slapped him. And he slapped her. They fought all the time. They fought each other with their hands and their voices and then with their bodies: and the one storm was like the other. Many times—and now Rufus sat very still, pressing darkness against his eyes, listening to the music—he had, suddenly, without knowing that he was going to, thrown the whimpering, terrified Leona onto the bed, the floor, pinned her against a table or a wall; she beat at him, weakly, moaning, unutterably abject; he twisted his fingers in her long pale hair and used her in whatever way he felt would humiliate her most. It was not love he felt during these acts of love: drained and shaking, utterly unsatisfied, he fled from the raped white woman into the bars. In these bars no one applauded his triumph or condemned his guilt. He began to pick fights with white men. He was thrown out of bars. The eyes of his friends told him that he was falling. His own heart told him so. But the air through which he rushed was his prison and he could not even summon the breath to call for help.

Perhaps now, though, he had hit bottom. One thing about the bottom, he told himself, you can't fall any farther. He tried to take comfort from this thought. Yet there knocked in his heart the suspicion that the bottom did not really exist.

"I don't want to die," he heard himself say, and he began to cry.

The music went on, far from him, terribly loud. The lights were very bright and hot. He was sweating and he itched, he stank. Vivaldo was close to him, stroking his head; the stuff of Vivaldo's sweater stifled him. He wanted to stop crying, stand up, breathe, but he could only sit there with his face in his hands. Vivaldo murmured, "Go ahead, baby, let it out, let it all out." He wanted to stand up, breathe, and at the same time he wanted to lie flat on the floor and to be swallowed into whatever would stop this pain.

Yet, he was aware, perhaps for the first time in his life, that nothing would stop it, nothing: this was himself. Rufus was aware of every inch of Rufus. He was flesh: flesh, bone, muscle, fluid, orifices, hair, and skin. His body was controlled by laws he did not understand. Nor did he understand what force within this body had driven him into such a desolate place. The most impenetrable of mysteries moved in this darkness for less than a second, hinting of reconciliation.

And still the music continued, Bessie was saying that she wouldn't mind being in jail but she had to stay there so long.

"I'm sorry," he said, and raised his head.

Vivaldo gave him a handkerchief and he dried his eyes and blew his nose.

"Don't be sorry," said Vivaldo. "Be glad." He stood over Rufus for yet another moment, then he said, "I'm going to take you out and buy you a pizza. You hungry, child, that's why you carrying on like that." He went into the kitchen and began to wash his face. Rufus smiled, watching him, bent over the sink, under the hideous light.

It was like the kitchen in St. James Slip. He and Leona had ended their life together there, on the very edge of the island. When Rufus had ceased working and when all his money was gone, and there was nothing left to pawn, they were wholly dependent on the money Leona brought home from the restaurant. Then she lost this job. Their domestic life, which involved a hideous amount of drinking, made it difficult for her to get there on time and also caused her to look more and more disreputable. One evening, half-drunk, Rufus had gone to the restaurant to pick her up. The next day she was fired. She never held a steady job again.

One evening Vivaldo came to visit them in their last apartment. They heard the whistles of tugboats all day and all night long. Vivaldo found Leona sitting on the bathroom floor, her hair in her eyes, her face swollen and dirty with weeping. Rufus had been beating her. He sat silently on the bed.

"Why?" cried Vivaldo.

"I don't know," Leona sobbed, "it can't be for nothing I did. He's always beating me, for nothing, for nothing!" She gasped for breath, opening her mouth like an infant, and in that instant Vivaldo really hated Rufus and Rufus knew it. "He says I'm sleeping with other colored boys behind his back and it's not true, God knows it's not true!"

"Rufus knows it isn't true," Vivaldo said. He looked over at Rufus, who said nothing. He turned back to Leona. "Get up, Leona. Stand up. Wash your face."

He went into the bathroom and helped her to her feet and turned the water on. "Come on, Leona. Pull yourself together, like a good girl."

She tried to stop sobbing, and splashed water on her face. Vivaldo patted her on the shoulder, astonished all over again to realize how frail she was. He walked into the bedroom.

Rufus looked up at him. "This is my house," he said, "and

that's my girl. You ain't got nothing to do with this. Get your ass out of here."

"You could be killed for this," said Vivaldo. "All she has to do is yell. All *I* have to do is walk down to the corner and get a cop."

"You trying to scare me? Go *get* a cop."

"You must be out of your mind. They'd take one look at this situation and put you *under* the jailhouse." He walked to the bathroom door. "Come on, Leona. Get your coat. I'm taking you out of here."

"I'm not out of *my* mind," Rufus said, "but *you* are. Where you think you taking Leona?"

"I got no place to go," Leona muttered.

"Well, you can stay at my place until you *find* some place to go. I'm not leaving you here."

Rufus threw back his head and laughed. Vivaldo and Leona both turned to watch him. Rufus cried to the ceiling, "He's going to come to *my* house and walk out with *my* girl and he thinks this poor nigger's just going to sit and let him do it. Ain't this a bitch?"

He fell over on his side, still laughing.

Vivaldo shouted, "For Christ's sake, Rufus! *Rufus!*"

Rufus stopped laughing and sat straight up. "What? Who the hell do you think you're kidding? I know you only got one bed in your place!"

"Oh, Rufus," Leona wailed, "Vivaldo's only trying to help."

"You shut up," he said instantly, and looked at her.

"Everybody ain't a animal," she muttered.

"You mean, like me?"

She said nothing. Vivaldo watched them both.

"You mean, like me, bitch? Or you mean, like you?"

"If I'm a animal," she flared—perhaps she was emboldened by the presence of Vivaldo—"I'd like you to tell me who made me one. Just tell me that?"

"Why, your husband did, you bitch. You told me yourself he had a thing on him like a horse. You told me yourself how he did you—he kept telling you how he had the biggest thing in Dixie, black *or* white. And you said you couldn't stand it. Ha-*ha*. *That's* one of the funniest things I *ever* heard."

"I guess," she said, wearily, after a silence, "I told you a lot of things I shouldn't have."

Rufus snorted. "I guess you did." He said—to Vivaldo, the room, the river—"It was her husband ruined this bitch.

Your husband and all them funky niggers screwed you in the Georgia bushes. That's why your husband threw you out. Why don't you tell the truth? I wouldn't have to beat you if you'd tell the truth." He grinned at Vivaldo. "Man, this chick can't get enough——" and he broke off, staring at Leona.

"Rufus," said Vivaldo, trying to be calm, "I don't know what you're putting down. I think you must be crazy. You got a great chick, who'd go all the way for you—and you know it—and you keep coming on with this *Gone with the Wind* crap. What's the matter with your head, baby?" He tried to smile. "Baby, please don't do this. Please?"

Rufus said nothing. He sat down on the bed, in the position in which he had been sitting when Vivaldo arrived.

"Come on, Leona," said Vivaldo at last, and Rufus stood up, looking at them both with a little smile, with hatred.

"I'm just going to take her away for a few days, so you can both cool down. There's no point in going on like this."

"Sir Walter Raleigh—with a hard on," Rufus sneered.

"Look," said Vivaldo, "if you don't trust me, man, I'll get a room at the Y. I'll come back here. Goddammit," he shouted, "I'm not trying to steal your girl. You know me better than that."

Rufus said, with an astonishing and a menacing humility, "I guess you don't think she's good enough for you."

"Oh, shit. You don't think she's good enough for *you.*"

"No," said Leona, and both men turned to watch her, "ain't neither one of you got it right. Rufus don't think he's good enough for *me.*"

She and Rufus stared at each other. A tugboat whistled, far away. Rufus smiled.

"You see? *You* bring it up all the time. *You* the one who brings it up. Now, how you expect me to make it with a bitch like you?"

"It's the way you was raised," she said, "and I guess you just can't help it."

Again, there was a silence. Leona pressed her lips together and her eyes filled with tears. She seemed to wish to call the words back, to call time back, and begin everything over again. But she could not think of anything to say and the silence stretched. Rufus pursed his lips.

"Go on, you slut," he said, "go on and make it with your wop lover. He ain't going to be able to do you no good. Not now. You be back. You can't do without me now." And he lay face downward on the bed. "Me, I'll get me a good night's sleep for a change."

Vivaldo pushed Leona to the door, backing out of the room, watching Rufus.

"I'll be back," he said.

"No, you won't," said Rufus. "I'll kill you if you come back."

Leona looked at him quickly, bidding him to be silent and Vivaldo closed the door behind them.

"Leona," he asked, when they were in the streets, "how long have things been like this? Why do you take it?"

"Why," asked Leona, wearily, "do people take anything? Because they can't help it, I guess. Well, that's me. Before God, I don't know what to do." She began to cry again. The streets were very dark and empty. "I know he's sick and I keep hoping he'll get well and I can't make him see a doctor. He knows I'm not doing none of those things he says, he knows it!"

"But you can't go on like this, Leona. He can get both of you killed."

"He says it's me trying to get us killed." She tried to laugh. "He had a fight last week with some guy in the subway, some real ignorant, unhappy man just didn't like the idea of our being together, you know? and, well, you know, he blamed that fight on me. He said I was encouraging the man. Why, Viv, I didn't even *see* the man until he opened his mouth. But, Rufus, he's all the time looking for it, he sees it where it ain't, he don't see nothing else no more. He says I ruined his life. Well, he sure ain't done mine much good."

She tried to dry her eyes. Vivaldo gave her his handkerchief and put one arm around her shoulders.

"You know, the world is hard enough and people is evil enough without all the time looking for it and stirring it up and making it worse. I keep telling him, I know a lot of people don't like what I'm doing. But I don't care, let them go their way, I'll go mine."

A policeman passed them, giving them a look. Vivaldo felt a chill go through Leona's body. Then a chill went through his own. He had never been afraid of policemen before; he had merely despised them. But now he felt the impersonality of the uniform, the emptiness of the streets. He felt what the policeman might say and do if he had been Rufus, walking here with his arm around Leona.

He said, nevertheless, after a moment, "You ought to leave him. You ought to leave town."

"I tell you, Viv, I keep hoping—it'll all come all right somehow. He wasn't like this when I met him, he's not really like this at all. I *know* he's not. Something's got all twisted up in his mind and he can't help it."

They were standing under a street lamp. Her face was hideous, was unutterably beautiful with grief. Tears rolled down her thin cheeks and she made doomed, sporadic efforts to control the trembling of her little-girl's mouth.

"I love him," she said, helplessly, "I love him, I can't help it. No matter what he does to me. He's just lost and he beats me because he can't find nothing else to hit."

He pulled her against him while she wept, a thin, tired girl, unwitting heiress of generations of bitterness. He could think of nothing to say. A light was slowly turning on inside him, a dreadful light. He saw—dimly—dangers, mysteries, chasms which he had never dreamed existed.

"Here comes a taxi," he said.

She straightened and tried to dry her eyes again.

"I'll come with you," he said, "and come right back."

"No," she said, "just give me the keys. I'll be all right. You go on back to Rufus."

"Rufus said he'd kill me," he said, half-smiling.

The taxi stopped beside them. He gave her his keys. She opened the door, keeping her face away from the driver.

"Rufus ain't going to kill nobody but himself," she said, "if he don't find a friend to help him." She paused, half-in, half-out of the cab. "You the only friend he's got in the world, Vivaldo."

He gave her some money for the fare, looking at her with something, after all these months, explicit at last between them. They both loved Rufus. And they were both white. Now that it stared them so hideously in the face, each could see how desperately the other had been trying to avoid this confrontation.

"You'll *go* there now?" he asked. "You'll *go* to my place?"

"Yes. I'll go. You go on back to Rufus. Maybe you can help him. He needs somebody to help him."

Vivaldo gave the driver his address and watched the taxi roll away. He turned and started back the way they had come.

The way seemed longer, now that he was alone, and darker. His awareness of the policeman, prowling somewhere in the darkness near him, made the silence ominous. He felt threatened. He felt totally estranged from the city in which he had been born; this city for which he sometimes felt a kind of stony affection because it was all he knew of home. Yet he had no home here—the hovel on Bank Street was not a home. He had always supposed that he would, one day, make a home here for himself. Now he began to wonder if anyone could ever put down roots in this rock; or, rather, he began to be aware of the shapes acquired by those who had. He began to wonder about his own shape.

He had often thought of his loneliness, for example, as a condition which testified to his superiority. But people who were not superior were, nevertheless, extremely lonely—and unable to break out of their solitude precisely because they had no equipment with which to enter it. His own loneliness, magnified so many million times, made the night air colder. He remembered to what excesses, into what traps and nightmares, his loneliness had driven him; and he wondered where such a violent emptiness might drive an entire city.

At the same time, as he came closer to Rufus's building, he was trying very hard not to think about Rufus.

He was in a section of warehouses. Very few people lived down here. By day, trucks choked the streets, laborers stood on these ghostly platforms, moving great weights, and cursing. As he had once; for a long time, he had been one of them. He had been proud of his skill and his muscles and happy to be accepted as a man among men. Only—it was they who saw something in him which they could not accept, which made them uneasy. Every once in a while, a man, lighting his cigarette, would look at him quizzically, with a little smile. The smile masked an unwilling, defensive hostility. They said he was a "bright kid," that he would "go places"; and they made it clear that they expected him to go, to which places did not matter—he did not belong to them.

But at the bottom of his mind the question of Rufus nagged and stung. There had been a few colored boys in his high school but they had mainly stayed together, as far as he remembered. He had known boys who got a bang out of going out and beating up niggers. It scarcely seemed possible —it scarcely, even, seemed fair—that colored boys who were beaten up in high school could grow up into colored men who wanted to beat up everyone in sight, including, or perhaps especially, people who had never, one way or another, given them a thought.

He watched the light in Rufus's window, the only light on down here.

Then he remembered something that had happened to him a long time ago, two years or three. It was when he had been spending a lot of time in Harlem, running after the

whores up there. One night, as a light rain fell, he was walking uptown on Seventh Avenue. He walked very briskly, for
it was very late and this section of the Avenue was almost
entirely deserted and he was afraid of being stopped by a
prowl car. At 116th Street he stopped in a bar, deliberately
choosing a bar he did not know. Since he did not know the
bar he felt an unaccustomed uneasiness and wondered what
the faces around him hid. Whatever it was, they hid it very
well. They went on drinking and talking to each other and
putting coins in the juke box. It certainly didn't seem that his
presence caused anyone to become wary, or to curb their
tongues. Nevertheless, no one made any effort to talk to him
and an almost imperceptible glaze came over their eyes
whenever they looked in his direction. This glaze remained,
even when they smiled. The barman, for example, smiled at
something Vivaldo said and yet made it clear, as he pushed
his drink across the bar, that the width of the bar was but a
weak representation of the great gulf fixed between them.

This was the night that he saw the eyes unglaze. Later, a
girl came over to him. They went around the corner to her
room. There they were; he had his tie loosened and his
trousers off and they had been just about to begin when the
door opened and in walked her "husband." He was one of
the smooth-faced, laughing men who had been in the bar.
The girl squealed, rather prettily, and then calmly began to
get dressed again. Vivaldo had first been so disappointed
that he wanted to cry, then so angry that he wanted to kill.
Not until he looked into the man's eyes did he begin to be
afraid.

The man looked down at him and smiled.

"Where was you thinking of putting that, white boy?"

Vivaldo said nothing. He slowly began pulling on his
trousers. The man was very dark and very big, nearly as big
as Vivaldo, and, of course, at that moment, in much better
fighting condition.

The girl sat on the edge of the bed, putting on her shoes.
There was silence in the room except for her low, disjointed,
intermittent humming. He couldn't quite make out the tune
she was humming and this, for some insane reason, drove
him wild.

"You might at least have waited a couple of minutes,"
Vivaldo said. "I never even got it in."

He said this as he was buckling his belt, idly, out of some
dim notion that he might thus, in effect, reduce the fine. The
words were hardly out of his mouth before the man had

struck him, twice, palm open, across the face. Vivaldo staggered backward from the bed into the corner which held the sink and a water glass went crashing to the floor.

"Goddammit," said the girl, sharply, "ain't no need to wreck the joint." And she bent down to pick up the bits of glass. But it also seemed to Vivaldo that she was a little frightened and a little ashamed. "Do what you going to do," she said, from her knees, "and get him out of here."

Vivaldo and the man stared at each other and terror began draining Vivaldo's rage out of him. It was not merely the situation which frightened him: it was the man's eyes. They stared at Vivaldo with a calm, steady hatred, as remote and unanswerable as madness.

"You goddamn lucky you *didn't* get it in," he said. "You'd be a mighty sorry white boy if you had. You wouldn't be putting that white prick in no more black pussy, I can guarantee you that."

Well, if that's the way you feel, Vivaldo wanted to say, why the hell don't you keep her off the streets? But it really seemed better—and it seemed, weirdly enough, that the girl was silently trying to convey this to him—to say as little as possible.

So he only said, after a moment, as mildly as he could, "Look. I fell for the oldest gag in the business. Here I am. Okay. What do you want?"

And what the man wanted was more than he knew how to say. He watched Vivaldo, waiting for Vivaldo to speak again. Vivaldo's mind was filled suddenly with the image of a movie he had seen long ago. He saw a bird dog, tense, pointing, absolutely silent, waiting for a covey of quail to surrender to panic and fly upward, where they could be picked off by the guns of the hunters. So it was in the room while the man waited for Vivaldo to speak. Whatever Vivaldo might say would be turned into an opportunity for slaughter. Vivaldo held his breath, hoping that his panic did not show in his eyes, and felt his flesh begin to crawl. Then the man looked over at the girl, who stood near the bed, watching him, and then he slowly moved closer to Vivaldo. When he stood directly before Vivaldo, his eyes still driving, it seemed, into Vivaldo's as though he would pierce the skull and the brain and possess it all, he abruptly held out his hand.

Vivaldo handed him the wallet.

The man lit a cigarette which he held in the corner of his mouth as he deliberately, insolently, began looking through the wallet. "What I don't understand," he said, with a fearful laziness, "is why you white boys always come uptown, sniffing around our black girls. You don't see none of us spooks downtown, sniffing around your white girls." He looked up. "Do you?"

Don't be so sure, Vivaldo thought, but said nothing. But this had struck some nerve in him and he felt himself beginning to be angry again.

"Suppose I told you that that was my sister," the man said, gesturing toward the girl. "What would *you* do if you found me with your sister?"

I wouldn't give a damn if you split her in two, Vivaldo thought, promptly. At the same time this question made him tremble with rage and he realized, with another part of his mind, that this was exactly what the man wanted.

There remained at the bottom of his mind, nevertheless, a numb speculation as to why *this* question should make him angry.

"I mean, what would you do to me?" the man persisted, still holding Vivaldo's wallet and looking at him with a smile. "I want you to name your own punishment." He waited. Then: "Come on. You know what *you* guys do." And then the man seemed, oddly, a little ashamed, and at the same time more dangerous than ever.

Vivaldo said at last, tightly, "*I* haven't got a sister," and straightened his tie, willing his hands to be steady, and began looking around for his jacket.

The man considered him a moment more, looked at the girl, then looked down to the wallet again. He took out all the money. "This all you got?"

In those days Vivaldo had been working steadily and his wallet had contained nearly sixty dollars. "Yes," Vivaldo said.

"Nothing in your pockets?"

Vivaldo emptied his pockets of bills and change, perhaps five dollars in all. The man took it all.

"I need something to get home on, mister," Vivaldo said.

The man gave him his wallet. "Walk," he said. "You lucky that you can. If I catch your ass up here again, I'll show you what happened to a nigger I know when Mr. Charlie caught him with Miss Anne."

He put his wallet in his back pocket and picked up his jacket from the floor. The man watched him, the girl watched the man. He got to the door and opened it and realized that his legs were weak.

"Well," he said, "thanks for the buggy ride," and stumbled

down the stairs. He had reached the first landing when he heard a door above him open and quick, stealthy footsteps descending. Then the girl stood above him, stretching her hand over the banister.

"Here," she whispered, "take this," and leaned dangerously far over the banister and stuffed a dollar into his breast pocket. "Go along home now," she said, "hurry!" and rushed back up the stairs.

The man's eyes remained with him for a long time after the rage and the shame and terror of that evening. And were with him now, as he climbed the stairs to Rufus's apartment. He walked in without knocking. Rufus was standing near the door, holding a knife.

"Is that for me or for you? Or were you planning to cut yourself a hunk of salami?"

He forced himself to stand where he was and to look directly at Rufus.

"I was thinking about putting it into you, motherfucker."

But he had not moved. Vivaldo slowly let out his breath. "Well, put it down. If I ever saw a poor bastard who needed his friends, you're it."

They watched each other for what seemed like a very long time and neither of them moved. They stared into each other's eyes, each, perhaps, searching for the friend each remembered. Vivaldo knew the face before him so well that he had ceased, in a way, to look at it and now his heart turned over to see what time had done to Rufus. He had not seen before the fine lines in the forehead, the deep, crooked line between the brows, the tension which soured the lips. He wondered what the eyes were seeing—they had not been seeing it years before. He had never associated Rufus with violence, for his walk was always deliberate and slow, his tone mocking and gentle: but now he remembered how Rufus played the drums.

He moved one short step closer, watching Rufus, watching the knife.

"Don't kill me, Rufus," he heard himself say. "I'm not trying to hurt you. I'm only trying to help."

The bathroom door was still open and the light still burned. The bald kitchen light burned mercilessly down on the two orange crates and the board which formed the kitchen table, and on the uncovered wash and bathtub. Dirty clothes lay flung in a corner. Beyond them, in the dim bedroom, two suitcases, Rufus's and Leona's, lay open in the middle of the floor. On the bed was a twisted gray sheet and a thin blanket.

Rufus stared at him. He seemed not to believe Vivaldo; he seemed to long to believe him. His face twisted, he dropped the knife, and fell against Vivaldo, throwing his arms around him, trembling.

Vivaldo led him into the bedroom and they sat down on the bed.

"Somebody's got to help me," said Rufus at last, "somebody's got to help me. This shit has got to stop."

"Can't you tell me about it? You're screwing up your life. And I don't know why."

Rufus sighed and fell back, his arms beneath his head, staring at the ceiling. "I don't know, either. I don't know up from down. I don't know what I'm doing no more."

The entire building was silent. The room in which they sat seemed very far from the life breathing all around them, all over the island.

Vivaldo said, gently, "You know, what you're doing to Leona—that's not right. Even if she were doing what you say she's doing—it's not right. If all you can do is beat her, well then, you ought to leave her."

Rufus seemed to smile. "I guess there *is* something the matter with my head."

Then he was silent again; he twisted his body on the bed; he looked over at Vivaldo.

"You put her in a cab?"

"Yes," Vivaldo said.

"She's gone to your place?"

"Yes."

"You going back there?"

"I thought, maybe, I'd stay here with you for a while—if you don't mind."

"What're you trying to do—be a warden or something?"

He said it with a smile, but there was no smile in his voice.

"I just thought maybe you wanted company," said Vivaldo.

Rufus rose from the bed and walked restlessly up and down the two rooms.

"I don't need no company. I done had enough company to last me the rest of my life." He walked to the window and stood there, his back to Vivaldo. "How I hate them—all those white sons of bitches out there. They're trying to kill me, you think I don't know? They got the world on a string, man, the miserable white cock suckers, and they tying that string around my neck, they killing *me*." He turned into the room again; he did not look at Vivaldo. "Sometimes I lie here and I listen—just listen. They out there, scuffling, making that change, they think it's going to last forever. Sometimes I lie here and listen, listen for a bomb, man, to fall on this city and make all that noise stop. I listen to hear them moan, I want them to bleed and choke, I want to hear them *crying*, man, for somebody to come help them. They'll cry a long time before *I* come down there." He paused, his eyes glittering with tears and with hate. "It's going to happen one of these days, it's got to happen. I sure would like to see it." He walked back to the window. "Sometimes I listen to those boats on the river—I listen to those whistles—and I think wouldn't it be nice to get on a boat again and go some place away from all these nowhere people, where a man could be treated like a man." He wiped his eyes with the back of his hand and then suddenly brought his fist down on the window sill. "You got to fight with the landlord because the landlord's *white!* You got to fight with the elevator boy because the motherfucker's *white*. Any bum on the Bowery can shit all over you because maybe he can't hear, can't see, can't walk, can't fuck—but he's *white!*"

"Rufus. Rufus. What about—" He wanted to say, What about me, Rufus? I'm white. He said, "Rufus, not everybody's like that."

"No? That's news to me."

"Leona loves you—"

"She loves the colored folks so *much*," said Rufus, "sometimes I just can't stand it. You know all that chick knows about me? The *only* thing she knows?" He put his hand on his sex, brutally, as though he would tear it out, and seemed pleased to see Vivaldo wince. He sat down on the bed again. "That's all."

"I think you're out of your mind," said Vivaldo. But fear drained his voice of conviction.

"But she's the only chick in the world for me," Rufus added, after a moment, "ain't that a bitch?"

"You're destroying that girl. Is that what you want?"

"She's destroying me, too," said Rufus.

"Well. Is *that* what you want?"

"What *do* two people want from each other," asked Rufus, "when they get together? Do *you* know?"

"Well, they don't want to drive each other crazy, man. I know that."

"You know more than I do," Rufus said, sardonically. "What do *you* want—when you get together with a girl?"

"What do I *want*?"

"Yeah, what do you *want*?"

"Well," said Vivaldo, fighting panic, trying to smile, "I just want to get laid, man." But he stared at Rufus, feeling terrible things stir inside him.

"Yeah?" And Rufus looked at him curiously, as though he were thinking, *So that's the way white boys make it.* "Is that all?"

"Well"—he looked down—"I want the chick to love me. I want to make her love me. I want to be loved."

There was silence. Then Rufus asked, "Has it ever happened?"

"No," said Vivaldo, thinking of Catholic girls, and whores, "I guess not."

"How do you *make* it happen?" Rufus whispered. "What do you *do*?" He looked over at Vivaldo. He half-smiled. "What do *you* do?"

"What do you mean, what do I do?" He tried to smile; but he knew what Rufus meant.

"You just do it like you was told?" He tugged at Vivaldo's sleeve; his voice dropped. "That white chick—Jane—of yours—she ever give you a blow job?"

Oh, Rufus, he wanted to cry, *stop this crap!* and he felt tears well up behind his eyes. At the same time his heart lunged in terror and he felt the blood leave his face. "I haven't had a chick that great," he said briefly, thinking again of the dreadful Catholic girls with whom he had grown up, of his sister and his mother and father. He tried to force his mind back through the beds he had been in—his mind grew as blank as a wall. "Except," he said, suddenly, "with whores," and felt in the silence that then fell that murder was sitting on the bed beside them. He stared at Rufus.

Rufus laughed. He lay back on the bed and laughed until tears began running from the corners of his eyes. It was the worst laugh Vivaldo had ever heard and he wanted to shake Rufus or slap him, anything to make him stop. But he did nothing; he lit a cigarette; the palms of his hands were wet. Rufus choked, sputtered, and sat up. He turned his agonized face to Vivaldo for an instant. Then: "Whores!" he shouted and began to laugh again.

"What's so funny?" Vivaldo asked, quietly.

"If you don't see it, I can't tell you," Rufus said. He had stopped laughing, was very sober and still. "Everybody's on

the A train—you take it uptown, I take it downtown—it's
crazy." Then, again, he looked at Vivaldo with hatred. He
said, "Me and Leona—she's the greatest lay I ever had. Ain't
nothing we don't do."

"Crazy," said Vivaldo. He crushed out his cigarette on
the floor. He was beginning to be angry. At the same time he
wanted to laugh.

"But it ain't going to work," said Rufus. "It ain't going to
work." They heard the whistles on the river; he walked to
the window again. "I ought to get out of here. I better get
out of here."

"Well, then, *go*. Don't hang around, waiting—just *go*."

"I'm *going* to go," said Rufus. "I'm going to go. I just
want to see Leona one more time." He stared at Vivaldo. "I
just want to get laid—get blowed—loved—one more time."

"You know," said Vivaldo, "I'm not really interested in
the details of your sex life."

Rufus smiled. "No? I thought all you white boys had a
big thing about how us spooks was making out."

"Well," said Vivaldo, "I'm different."

"Yeah," said Rufus, "I bet you are."

"I just want to be your friend," said Vivaldo. "That's all.
But you don't want any friends, do you?"

"Yes, I do," said Rufus, quietly. "Yes, I do." He paused;
then, slowly, with difficulty, "Don't mind me. I know you're
the only friend I've got left in the world, Vivaldo."

And that's why you hate me, Vivaldo thought, feeling still
and helpless and sad.

Now Vivaldo and Rufus sat together in silence, near the
window of the pizzeria. There was little left for them to say.
They had said it all—or Rufus had; and Vivaldo had listened. Music from a nearby night club came at them, faintly,
through the windows, along with the grinding, unconquerable hum of the streets. And Rufus watched the streets with
a helpless, sad intensity, as though he were waiting for
Leona. These streets had claimed her. She had been found,
Rufus said, one freezing night, half-naked, looking for her
baby. She knew where it was, where they had hidden her
baby, she knew the house; only she could not remember the
address.

And then, Rufus said, she had been taken to Bellevue,
and he had been unable to get her out. The doctors had felt
that it would be criminal to release her into the custody of
the man who was the principal reason for her breakdown,

and who had, moreover, no legal claim on her. They had notified Leona's family, and her brother had come from the South and carried Leona back with him. Now she sat somewhere in Georgia, staring at the walls of a narrow room; and she would remain there forever.

Vivaldo yawned and felt guilty. He was tired—tired of Rufus's story, tired of the strain of attending, tired of friendship. He wanted to go home and lock his door and sleep. He was tired of the troubles of real people. He wanted to get back to the people he was inventing, whose troubles he could bear.

But he was restless, too, and unwilling, now that he was out, to go home right away.

"Let's have a nightcap at Benno's," he said. And then, because he knew Rufus did not really want to go there, he added, "All right?"

Rufus nodded, feeling a little frightened. Vivaldo watched him, feeling it all come back, his love for Rufus, and his grief for him. He leaned across the table and tapped him on the cheek. "Come on," he said, "you haven't got to be afraid of anybody."

With these words, at which Rufus looked even more frightened, though a small smile played around the corners of his mouth, Vivaldo felt that whatever was coming had already begun, that the master switch had been thrown. He sighed, relieved, also wishing to call the words back. The waiter came. Vivaldo paid the check and they walked out into the streets.

"It's almost Thanksgiving," said Rufus, suddenly. "I didn't realize that." He laughed. "It'll soon be Christmas, the year will soon be over—" He broke off, raising his head to look over the cold streets.

A policeman, standing under the light on the corner, was phoning in. On the opposite pavement a young man walked his dog. The music from the night club dwindled as they walked away from it, toward Benno's. A heavy Negro girl, plain, carrying packages, and a surly, bespectacled white boy ran together toward a taxi. The yellow light on the roof went out, the doors slammed. The cab turned, came toward Rufus and Vivaldo, and the street lights blazed for an instant on the faces of the silent couple within.

Vivaldo put one arm around Rufus and pushed him ahead of him into Benno's Bar.

The bar was terribly crowded. Advertising men were there, drinking double shots of bourbon or vodka, on the rocks; college boys were there, their wet fingers slippery on the beer bottles; lone men stood near the doors or in corners, watching the drifting women. The college boys, gleaming with ignorance and mad with chastity, made terrified efforts to attract the feminine attention, but succeeded only in attracting each other. Some of the men were buying drinks for some of the women—who wandered incessantly from the juke box to the bar—and they faced each other over smiles which were pitched, with an eerie precision, between longing and contempt. Black-and-white couples were together here —closer together now than they would be later, when they got home. These several histories were camouflaged in the jargon which, wave upon wave, rolled through the bar; were locked in a silence like the silence of glaciers. Only the juke box spoke, grinding out each evening, all evening long, syncopated, synthetic laments for love.

Rufus's eyes had trouble adjusting to the yellow light, the smoke, the movement. The place seemed terribly strange to him, as though he remembered it from a dream. He recognized faces, gestures, voices—from this same dream; and, as in a dream, no one looked his way, no one seemed to remember him. Just next to him, at a table, sat a girl he had balled once or twice, whose name was Belle. She was talking to her boy friend, Lorenzo. She brushed her long black hair out of her eyes and looked directly at him for a moment, but she did not seem to recognize him.

A voice spoke at his ear: "Hey! Rufus! When did they let you out, man?"

He turned to face a grinning chocolate face, topped by processed hair casually falling forward. He could not remember the name which went with the face. He could not remember what his connection with the face had been. He said, "Yeah, I'm straight, how you been making it?"

"Oh, I'm scuffling, man, got to keep scuffling, you know" —eyes seeming to press forward like two malevolent insects, hair flying, lips and forehead wet. The voice dropped to a whisper. "I was kind of strung out there for a while, but I'm straight now. I heard you got busted, man."

"Busted? No, I've just been making the uptown scene."

"Yeah? Well, crazy." He jerked his head around to the door in response to a summons Rufus had not heard. "I got to split, my boy's waiting for me. See you around, man."

Cold air swept into the bar for a moment, then steam and smoke settled again over everything.

Then, while they stood there, not yet having been able to

order anything to drink and undecided as to whether or not they would stay, Cass appeared out of the gloom and noise. She was very elegant, in black, her golden hair pulled carefully back and up. She held a drink and a cigarette in one hand and looked at once like the rather weary matron she actually was and the mischievous girl she once had been.

"What are you doing here?" asked Vivaldo. "And all dressed up, too. What's happening?"

"I'm tired of my husband. I'm looking for a new man. But I guess I came to the wrong store."

"You may have to wait for a fire sale," said Vivaldo.

Cass turned to Rufus and put her hand on his arm.

"It's nice to have you back," she said. Her large brown eyes looked directly into his. "Are you all right? We've all missed you."

He shrank involuntarily from her touch and her tone. He wanted to thank her; he said, nodding and trying to smile, "I'm fine, Cass." And then: "It's kind of nice to be back."

She grinned. "Do you know what I realize every time I see you? That we're very much alike." She turned back to Vivaldo. "I don't see your aging mistress anywhere. Are you looking for a new woman? If so, you too have come to the wrong store."

"I haven't seen Jane for a hell of a long time," said Vivaldo, "and it might be a good idea for us never to see each other again." But he looked troubled.

"Poor Vivaldo," Cass said. After a moment they both laughed. "Come on in the back with me. Richard's there. He'll be very glad to see you."

"I didn't know you people ever set foot in this joint. Can't you bear domestic bliss any longer?"

"We're celebrating tonight. Richard just sold his novel."

"*No!*"

"Yes. *Yes.* Isn't that marvelous?"

"Well, I'll be damned," said Vivaldo, looking a little dazed.

"Come on," Cass said. She took Rufus by the hand and, with Vivaldo ahead of them, they began pushing their way to the back. They stumbled down the steps into the back room. Richard sat alone at a table, smoking his pipe. "Richard," Cass cried, "look what I brought back from the dead!"

"You should have let them rot there." Richard grinned. "Come on in, sit down. I'm glad to see you."

"I'm glad to see *you*," said Vivaldo, and sat down. He and Richard grinned at each other. Then Richard looked at

Rufus briefly and sharply, and looked away. Perhaps Richard had never liked Rufus as much as the others had and now, perhaps, he was blaming him for Leona.

The air in the back room was close, he was aware of his odor, he wished he had taken a shower at Vivaldo's house. He sat down.

"So!" said Vivaldo, "you sold it!" He threw back his head and gave a high, whinnying laugh. "You sold it. That's just great, baby. How does it feel?"

"I held off as long as I could," Richard said. "I kept telling them that my good friend, Vivaldo, was going to come by and look it over for me. They said, 'That Vivaldo? He's a poet, man, he's *bohemian!* He wouldn't read a murder novel, not if it was written by God almighty.' So, when you didn't come by, baby, I figured they were right and I just had to let them have it."

"Shit, Richard, I'm sorry about that. I've just been so hung up——"

"Yeah, I know. Let's have a drink. You, Rufus. What're you doing with yourself these days?"

"I'm just pulling myself together," said Rufus, with a smile. Richard was being kind, he told himself, but in his heart he accused him of cowardice.

"Don't be self-conscious," Cass said. "We've been trying to pull ourselves together for years. You can see what progress we've made. You're in very good company." She leaned her head against Richard's shoulder. Richard stroked her hair and picked up his pipe from the ashtray.

"I don't think it's just a murder story," he said, gesturing with the pipe. "I mean, I don't see why you can't do something fairly serious within the limits of the form. I've always been fascinated by it, really."

"You didn't think much of them when you were teaching me English in high school," said Vivaldo, with a smile.

"Well, I was younger then than you are now. We change, boy, we grow——!" The waiter entered the room, looking as though he wondered where on earth he could be, and Richard called him. "Hey! We're dying of thirst over here!" He turned to Cass. "You want another drink?"

"Oh, yes," she said, "now that our friends are here. I might as well make the most of my night out. Except I'm a kind of dreamy drunk. Do you mind my head on your shoulder?"

"Mind?" He laughed. He looked at Vivaldo. *"Mind!* Why do you think I've been knocking myself out, trying to be a success?" He bent down and kissed her and something appeared in his boyish face, a single-mindedness of tenderness and passion, which made him very gallant. "You can put your head on my shoulder anytime. Anytime, baby. That's what my shoulders are for." And he stroked her hair again, proudly, as the waiter vanished with the empty glasses.

Vivaldo turned to Richard. "When can I read your book? I'm jealous. I want to find out if I should be."

"Well, if you take that tone, you bastard, you can buy it at the bookstore when it comes out."

"Or borrow it from the library," Cass suggested.

"No, really, when can I read it? Tonight? Tomorrow? How long is it?"

"It's over three hundred pages," Richard said. "Come by tomorrow, you can look at it then." He said to Cass, "It's one way of getting him to the house." Then: "You really don't come to see us like you used to—is anything the matter? Because we still love *you*."

"No, nothing's the matter," Vivaldo said. He hesitated. "I had this thing with Jane and then we broke up—and—oh, I don't know. Work wasn't going well, and"—he looked at Rufus—"all kinds of things. I was drinking too much and running around whoring when I should have been—being serious, like you, and getting my novel finished."

"How's it coming—your novel?"

"Oh"—he looked down and sipped his drink—"slow. I'm really not a very good writer."

"Bullshit," said Richard, cheerfully.

He almost looked again like the English instructor Vivaldo had idolized, who had been the first person to tell him things he needed to hear, the first person to take Vivaldo seriously.

"I'm very glad," Vivaldo said, "seriously, *very* glad that you got the damn thing done and that it worked so well. And I hope you make a fortune."

Rufus thought of afternoons and evenings on the stand when people had come up to him to bawl their appreciation and to prophesy that he would do great things. They had bugged him then. Yet how he wished now to be back there, to have someone looking at him as Vivaldo now looked at Richard. And he looked at Vivaldo's face, in which affection and something coldly speculative battled. He was happy for Richard's triumph but perhaps he wished it were his own; and at the same time he wondered what order of triumph it was. And the way the people had looked at Rufus was not unlike this look. They wondered where it came from, this force that they admired. Dimly, they wondered how he stood it, wondered if perhaps it would not kill him soon.

Vivaldo looked away, down into his drink, and lit a cigarette. Richard suddenly looked very tired.

A tall girl, very pretty, carefully dressed—she looked like an uptown model—came into the room, looked about her, peered sharply at their table. She paused, then started out.

"I wish you were looking for me," Vivaldo called.

She turned and laughed. "You're lucky I'm *not* looking for you!" She had a very attractive laugh and a slight Southern accent. Rufus turned to watch her move daintily up the steps and disappear into the crowded bar.

"Well, you scored, old buddy," Rufus said, "go get her."

"No," said Vivaldo, smiling, "better leave well enough alone." He stared at the door where the girl had vanished. "She's pretty, isn't she?" he said partly to himself, partly to the table. He looked at the door again, shifting slightly in his seat, then threw down the last of his drink.

Rufus wanted to say, *Don't let me stop you, man,* but he said nothing. He felt black, filthy, foolish. He wished he were miles away, or dead. He kept thinking of Leona; it came in waves, like the pain of a toothache or a festering wound.

Cass left her seat and came over and sat beside him. She stared at him and he was frightened by the sympathy on her face. He wondered why she should look like that, what her memories or experience could be. She could only look at him this way because she knew things he had never imagined a girl like Cass could know.

"How is Leona?" she asked. "Where is she now?" and did not take her eyes from his face.

He did not want to answer. He did not want to talk about Leona—and yet there was nothing else that he could possibly talk about. For a moment he almost hated Cass; and then he said:

"She's in a home—down South somewhere. They come and took her out of Bellevue. I don't even know where she is."

She said nothing. She offered him a cigarette, lit it, and lit one for herself.

"I saw her brother once. I had to see him, I made him see me. He spit in my face, he said he would have killed me had we been down home."

He wiped his face now with the handkerchief Vivaldo had lent him.

"But I felt like I was already dead. They wouldn't let me see her. I wasn't a relative, I didn't have no right to see her."

There was silence. He remembered the walls of the hospital: white; and the uniforms and the faces of the doctors and nurses, white on white. And the face of Leona's brother, white, with the blood beneath it rushing thickly, bitterly, to the skin's surface, summoned by his mortal enemy. Had they been down home, his blood and the blood of his enemy would have rushed out to mingle together over the uncaring earth, under the uncaring sky.

"At least," Cass said, finally, "you didn't have any children. Thank God for that."

"She did," he said, "down South. They took the kid away from her." He added, "That's why she come North." And he thought of the night they had met.

"She was a nice girl," Cass said. "I liked her."

He said nothing. He heard Vivaldo say, "—but I never know what to do when I'm *not* working."

"You know what to do, all right. You just don't have anybody to do it with."

He listened to their laughter, which seemed to shake him as though it were a drill.

"Just the same," said Richard, in a preoccupied tone, "nobody can work all the time."

Out of the corner of his eye, Rufus watched him stabbing the table with his stir-stick.

"I hope," Cass said, "that you won't sit around blaming yourself too much. Or too long. That won't undo anything." She put her hand on his. He stared at her. She smiled. "When you're older you'll see, I think, that we all commit our crimes. The thing is not to lie about them—to try to understand what you have done, why you have done it." She leaned closer to him, her brown eyes popping and her blond hair, in the heat, in the gloom, forming a damp fringe about her brow. "That way, you can begin to forgive yourself. That's very important. If you don't forgive yourself you'll never be able to forgive anybody else and you'll go on committing the same crimes forever."

"I know," Rufus muttered, not looking at her, bent over the table with his fists clenched together. From far away, from the juke box, he heard a melody he had often played. He thought of Leona. Her face would not leave him. "I know," he repeated, though in fact he did not know. He did not know why this woman was talking to him as she was, what she was trying to tell him.

"What," she asked him carefully, "are you going to do now?"

"I'm going to try to pull myself together," he said, "and get back to work."

But he found it unimaginable that he would ever work again, that he would ever play drums again.

"Have you seen your family? I think Vivaldo's seen your sister a couple of times. She's very worried about you."

"I'm going up there," he said. "I haven't wanted to go—looking this way."

"They don't care how you look," she said, shortly. "*I* don't care how you look. I'm just glad to see you're all right—and I'm not even related to you."

He thought, with a great deal of wonder, That's true, and turned to stare at her again, smiling a little and very close to tears.

"I've always thought of you," she said, "as a very nice person." She gave his arm a little tap and pushed a crumpled bill into his hand. "It might help if you thought of yourself that way."

"Hey, old lady," Richard called, "want to make it in?"

"I guess so," she said, and yawned. "I suppose we've celebrated enough for one night, one book."

She rose and returned to her side of the table and began to gather her things together. Rufus was suddenly afraid to see her go.

"Can I come to see you soon?" he asked, with a smile.

She stared at him across the width of the table. "Please do," she said. "Soon."

Richard knocked his pipe out and put it in his pocket, looking around for the waiter. Vivaldo was staring at something, at someone, just behind Rufus and suddenly seemed about to spring out of his seat. "Well," he said, faintly, "here's Jane," and Jane walked over to the table. Her short, graying hair was carefully combed, which was unusual, and she was wearing a dark dress, which was also unusual. Perhaps Vivaldo was the only person there who had ever seen her out of blue jeans and sweaters. "Hi, everybody," she said, and smiled her bright, hostile smile. She sat down. "Haven't seen any of you for months."

"Still painting?" Cass asked. "Or have you given that up?"

"I've been working like a dog," Jane said, continuing to look around and avoiding Vivaldo's eyes.

"Seems to suit you," Cass muttered, and put on her coat.

Jane looked at Rufus, beginning, it seemed, to recover her self-possession. "How've you been, Rufus?"

"Just fine," he said.

"We've all been dissipating," said Richard, "but you look like you've been being a good girl and getting your beauty sleep every night."

"You look great," said Vivaldo, briefly.

For the first time she looked directly at him. "Do I? I guess I've been feeling pretty well. I've cut down on my drinking," and she laughed a little too loudly and looked down. Richard was paying the waiter and had stood up, his trench coat over his arm. "Are you all leaving?"

"We've got to," said Cass, "we're just dull, untalented, old married people."

Cass glanced over at Rufus saying, "Be good now; get some rest." She smiled at him. He longed to do something to prolong that smile, that moment, but he did not smile back, only nodded his head. She turned to Jane and Vivaldo. "So long, kids. See you soon."

"Sure," Jane said.

"I'll be over tomorrow," said Vivaldo.

"I'm expecting you," Richard said, "don't fail me. So long, Jane."

"So long."

"So long."

Everyone was gone except Jane and Rufus and Vivaldo.

I wouldn't mind being in jail but I've got to stay there so long. . . .

The seats the others had occupied were like a chasm now between Rufus and the white boy and the white girl.

"Let's have another drink," Vivaldo said.

So long. . . .

"Let me buy," Jane said. "I sold a painting."

"Did you now? For a lot of money?"

"Quite a lot of money. That's probably why I was in such a stinking mood the last time you saw me—it wasn't going well."

"You were in a stinking mood, all right."

Wouldn't mind being in jail. . . .

"What're you having, Rufus?"

"I'll stick to Scotch, I guess."

But I've got to stay there. . . .

"I'm sorry," she said, "I don't know what makes me such a bitch."

"You drink too much. Let's just have one drink here. Then I'll walk you home."

They both looked quickly at Rufus.

So long. . . .

"I'm going to the head," Rufus said. "Order me a Scotch with water."

He walked out of the back room into the roaring bar. He stood at the door for a moment, watching the boys and girls, men and women, their wet mouths opening and closing, their faces damp and pale, their hands grim on the glass or the bottle or clutching a sleeve, an elbow, clutching the air. Small flames flared incessantly here and there and they moved through shifting layers of smoke. The cash register rang and rang. One enormous bouncer stood at the door, watching everything, and another moved about, clearing tables and rearranging chairs. Two boys, one Spanish-looking in a red shirt, one Danish-looking in brown, stood at the juke box, talking about Frank Sinatra.

Rufus stared at a small blond girl who was wearing a striped open blouse and a wide skirt with a big leather belt and a bright brass buckle. She wore low shoes and black knee socks. Her blouse was low enough for him to see the beginnings of her breasts; his eye followed the line down to the full nipples, which pushed aggressively forward; his hand encircled her waist, caressed the belly button and slowly forced the thighs apart. She was talking to another girl. She felt his eyes on her and looked his way. Their eyes met. He turned and walked into the head.

It smelled of thousands of travelers, oceans of piss, tons of bile and vomit and shit. He added his stream to the ocean, holding that most despised part of himself loosely between two fingers of one hand. *But I've got to stay there so long. . . .* He looked at the horrible history splashed furiously on the walls—telephone numbers, cocks, breasts, balls, cunts, etched into these walls with hatred. *Suck my cock. I like to get whipped. I want a hot stiff prick up my ass. Down with Jews. Kill the niggers. I suck cocks.*

He washed his hands very carefully and dried them on the filthy roller towel and walked out into the bar. The two boys were still at the juke box, the girl with the striped blouse was still talking to her friend. He walked through the bar to the door and into the street. Only then did he reach in his pocket to see what Cass had pushed into his palm.

Five dollars. Well, that would take care of him until morning. He would get a room at the Y.

He crossed Sheridan Square and walked slowly along West Fourth Street. The bars were beginning to close. People stood before bar doors, trying vainly to get in, or simply delaying going home; and in spite of the cold there were loiterers under street lamps. He felt as removed from them, as he walked slowly along, as he might have felt from a fence, a farmhouse, a tree, seen from a train window: coming closer and closer, the details changing every instant as the eye picked them out; then pressing against the window with the urgency of a messenger or a child; then dropping away, diminishing, vanished, gone forever. *That fence is falling down*, he might have thought as the train rushed toward it, or *That house needs paint*, or *The tree is dead*. In an instant, gone in an instant—it was not his fence, his farmhouse, or his tree. As now, passing, he recognized faces, bodies, postures, and thought *That's Ruth*. Or *There's old Lennie. Son of a bitch is stoned again*. It was very silent.

He passed Cornelia Street. Eric had once lived there. He saw again the apartment, the lamplight in the corners, Eric under the light, books falling over everything, and the bed unmade. Eric—and he was on Sixth Avenue, traffic lights and the lights of taxis blazing around him. Two girls and two boys, white, stood on the opposite corner, waiting for the lights to change. Half a dozen men, in a heavy gleaming car, rolled by and shouted at them. Then there was someone at his shoulder, a young white boy in a vaguely military cap and a black leather jacket. He looked at Rufus with the greatest hostility, then started slowly down the Avenue away from him, waving his rump like a flag. He looked back, stopped beneath the marquee of a movie theater. The lights changed. Rufus and the two couples started toward each other, came abreast in the middle of the Avenue, passed— only, one of the girls looked at him with a kind of pitying wonder in her eyes. *All right, bitch*. He started toward Eighth Street, for no reason; he was simply putting off his subway ride.

Then he stood at the subway steps, looking down. For a wonder, especially at this hour, there was no one on the steps, the steps were empty. He wondered if the man in the booth would change his five-dollar bill. He started down. Then, as the man gave him change and he moved toward the turnstile, other people came, rushing and loud, pushing past him as though they were swimmers and he nothing but an upright pole in the water. Then something began to awaken in him, something new; it increased his distance; it increased his pain. They were rushing—to the platform, to the tracks. Something he had not thought of for many years, something he had never ceased to think of, came back to him as he walked behind the crowd. The subway platform was a dangerous place—so he had always thought; it sloped downward toward the waiting tracks; and when he had been a little boy and stood on the platform beside his mother he had not dared let go her hand. He stood on the platform now, alone with all these people, who were each of them alone, and waited in acquired calmness, for the train.

But suppose something, somewhere, failed, and the yellow lights went out and no one could see, any longer, the platform's edge? Suppose these beams fell down? He saw the train in the tunnel, rushing under water, the motorman gone mad, gone blind, unable to decipher the lights, and the tracks gleaming and snarling senselessly upward forever, the train never stopping and the people screaming at windows and doors and turning on each other with all the accumulated fury of their blasphemed lives, everything gone out of them but murder, breaking limb from limb and splashing in blood, with joy—for the first time, joy, joy, after such a long sentence in chains, leaping out to astound the world, to astound the world again. Or, the train in the tunnel, the water outside, the power failing, the walls coming in, and the water not rising like a flood but breaking like a wave over the heads of these people, filling their crying mouths, filling their eyes, their hair, tearing away their clothes and discovering the secrecy which only the water, by now, could use. It could happen. It could happen; and he would have loved to see it happen, even if he perished, too. The train came in, filling the great scar of the tracks. They all got in, sitting in the lighted car which was far from empty, which would be choked with people before they got very far uptown, and stood or sat in the isolation cell into which they transformed every inch of space they held.

The train stopped at Fourteenth Street. He was sitting at the window and he watched a few people get on. There was a colored girl among them who looked a little like his sister, but she looked at him and looked away and sat down as far from him as she could. The train rolled on through the tunnel. The next stop was Thirty-fourth Street, his stop. People got on; he watched the stop roll by. Forty-second Street. This time a crowd got on, some of them carrying papers, and there were no seats left. A white man leaned on a strap near him. Rufus felt his gorge rise.

At Fifty-ninth Street many came on board and many rushed across the platform to the waiting local. Many white people and many black people, chained together in time and in space, and by history, and all of them in a hurry. In a hurry to get away from each other, he thought, but we ain't never going to make it. We been fucked for fair.

Then the doors slammed, a loud sound, and it made him jump. The train, as though protesting its heavier burden, as though protesting the proximity of white buttock to black knee, groaned, lurched, the wheels seemed to scrape the track, making a tearing sound. Then it began to move uptown, where the masses would divide and the load become lighter. Lights flared and teetered by, they passed other platforms where people waited for other trains. Then they had the tunnel to themselves. The train rushed into the blackness with a phallic abandon, into the blackness which opened to receive it, opened, opened, the whole world shook with their coupling. Then, when it seemed that the roar and the movement would never cease, they came into the bright lights of 125th Street. The train gasped and moaned to a halt. He had thought that he would get off here, but he watched the people move toward the doors, watched the doors open, watched them leave. It was mainly black people who left. He had thought that he would get off here and go home; but he watched the girl who reminded him of his sister as she moved sullenly past white people and stood for a moment on the platform before walking toward the steps. Suddenly he knew that he was never going home any more.

The train began to move, half-empty now; and with each stop it became lighter; soon the white people who were left looked at him oddly. He felt their stares but he felt far away from them. *You took the best. So why not take the rest?* He got off at the station named for the bridge built to honor the father of his country.

And walked up the steps, into the streets, which were empty. Tall apartment buildings, lightless, loomed against the dark sky and seemed to be watching him, seemed to be pressing down on him. The bridge was nearly over his head, intolerably high; but he did not yet see the water. He felt it, he smelled it. He thought how he had never before understood how an animal could smell water. But it was over there, past the highway, where he could see the speeding cars.

Then he stood on the bridge, looking over, looking down. Now the lights of the cars on the highway seemed to be writing an endless message, writing with awful speed in a fine, unreadable script. There were muted lights on the Jersey shore and here and there a neon flame advertising something somebody had for sale. He began to walk slowly to the center of the bridge, observing that, from this height, the city which had been so dark as he walked through it seemed to be on fire.

He stood at the center of the bridge and it was freezing cold. He raised his eyes to heaven. He thought, You bastard, you motherfucking bastard. Ain't I your baby, too? He began to cry. Something in Rufus which could not break shook him like a rag doll and splashed salt water all over his face and filled his throat and his nostrils with anguish. He knew the pain would never stop. He could never go down into the city again. He dropped his head as though someone had struck him and looked down at the water. It was cold and the water would be cold.

He was black and the water was black.

He lifted himself by his hands on the rail, lifted himself as high as he could, and leaned far out. The wind tore at him, at his head and shoulders, while something in him screamed, Why? Why? He thought of Eric. His straining arms threatened to break. *I can't make it this way.* He thought of Ida. He whispered, *I'm sorry, Leona,* and then the wind took him, he felt himself going over, head down, the wind, the stars, the lights, the water, all rolled together, *all right.* He felt a shoe fly off behind him, there was nothing around him, only the wind, *all right, you motherfucking Godalmighty bastard, I'm coming to you.*

CHAPTER 2

It was raining. Cass sat on her living-room floor with the Sunday papers and a cup of coffee. She was trying to decide which photograph of Richard would look best on the front page of the book-review section. The telephone rang.

"Hello?"

She heard an intake of breath and a low, vaguely familiar voice:

"Is this Cass Silenski?"

"Yes."

She looked at the clock, wondering who this could be. It was ten-thirty and she was the only person awake in her house.

"Well"—swiftly—"I don't know if you remember me, but we met once, downtown, in a night club where Rufus was working. I'm his sister—Ida? Ida Scott—"

She remembered a very young, striking, dark girl who wore a ruby-eyed snake ring. "Why, yes, I remember you very well. How are you?"

"I'm fine. Well"—with a small, dry laugh—"maybe I'm not so fine. I'm trying to locate my brother. I been calling Vivaldo's house all morning, but he's not home"—the voice was making an effort not to tremble, not to break—"and so I called you because I thought maybe you'd seen him, Vivaldo, I mean, or maybe you could tell me how to reach him." And now the girl was crying. "You haven't seen him, have you? Or my brother?"

She heard sounds coming from the children's bedroom. "Please," she said, "try not to be so upset. I don't know where Vivaldo is this morning but I saw your brother last night. And he was fine."

"You saw him *last night?*"

"Yes."

"Where'd you see him? Where was he?"

"We had a couple of drinks together in Benno's." Then she remembered Rufus's face and felt a dim, unwilling alarm. "We talked for a while. He seemed fine."

"Oh!"—the voice was flooded with relief and made Cass remember the girl's smile—"wait till I get my hands on him!" Then: "Do you know where he went? Where's he staying?"

The sounds from the bedroom suggested that Paul and Michael were having a fight. "I don't know." I should have asked him, she thought. "Vivaldo would know, they were together, I left them together—look—" Michael screamed and then began to cry, they were going to awaken Richard— "Vivaldo is coming by here this afternoon; why don't you come, too?"

"What time?"

"Oh. Three-thirty, four. Do you know where we live?"

"Yes. Yes, I'll be there. Thank you."

"Please don't be so upset. I'm sure everything will be all right."

"Yes. I'm glad I called you."

"Till later, then."

"Yes. Good-by."

"Good-by."

Cass ran into the children's bedroom and found Paul and Michael rolling furiously about on the floor. Michael was on top. She dragged him to his feet. Paul rose slowly, looking defiant and ashamed. He was eleven, after all, and Michael was only eight. "What's all this noise about?"

"He was trying to take my chess set," Michael said.

The box, the board, and broken chessmen were scattered on both beds and all over the room.

"I was not," Paul said, and looked at his mother. "I was only trying to teach him how to play."

"You don't know *how* to play," said Michael; now that his mother was in the room, he sniffled loudly once or twice and began collecting his property.

Paul *did* know how to play—or knew, anyway, that chess was a game with rules that had to be learned. He played with his father from time to time. But he also loved to torment his brother, who preferred to make up stories about his various chessmen as he moved them about. For this, of course, he did not need a partner. Watching Michael manipulate Richard's old, broken chess set always made Paul very indignant.

"Never mind that," Cass said, "you know that's Michael's

chess set and he can do whatever he wants with it. Now, come on, wash up, and get your clothes on."

She went into the bathroom to supervise their washing and get them dressed.

"Is Daddy up yet?" Paul wanted to know.

"No. He's sleeping. He's tired."

"Can't I go in and wake him?"

"No. Not this morning. Stand still."

"What about his breakfast?" Michael asked.

"He'll have his breakfast when he gets up," she said.

"We never have breakfast together any more," said Paul. "Why can't I go and wake him?"

"Because I told you not to," she said. They walked into the kitchen. *"We* can have breakfast together now, but your father needs his sleep."

"He's always sleeping," said Paul.

"You were out real late last night," said Michael, shyly.

She was a fairly impartial mother, or tried to be; but sometimes Michael's shy, grave charm moved her as Paul's more direct, more calculating presence seldom could.

"What do you care?" she said, and ruffled his reddish blond hair. "And, anyway, how do you know?" She looked at Paul. "I bet that woman let you stay up until all hours. What time did you go to bed last night?"

Her tone, however, had immediately allied them against her. She was their common property; but they had more in common with each other than they had with her.

"Not so late," Paul said, judiciously. He winked at his brother and began to eat his breakfast.

She held back a smile. "What time was it, Michael?"

"I don't know," Michael said, "but it was *real* early."

"If that woman let you stay up one minute past ten o'clock—"

"Oh, it wasn't *that* late," said Paul.

She gave up, poured herself another cup of coffee, and watched them eat. Then she remembered Ida's call. She dialed Vivaldo's number. There was no answer. He was probably at Jane's, she thought, but she did not know Jane's address, or her last name.

She heard Richard moving about in the bedroom and eventually watched him stumble into the shower.

When he came out, she watched him eat a while before she said:

"Richard—? Rufus's sister just called."

"His sister? Oh, yes, I remember her, we met once. What did she want?"

"She wanted to know where Rufus was."

"Well, if she doesn't know, how the hell does she expect us to know?"

"She sounded very worried. She hasn't seen him, you know—in a long time."

"She's complaining? Bastard's probably found some other defenseless little girl to beat up."

"Oh—that hasn't got anything to do with it. She's worried about her brother, she wants to know where he is."

"Well, she hasn't got a very nice *brother;* she'll probably run into him some place one of these days." He looked into her worried face. "Hell, Cass, we saw him last night; there's nothing wrong with him."

"Yes," she said. Then: "She's coming here this afternoon."

"Oh, Christ. What time?"

"I told her about three or four. I thought Vivaldo would be here by then."

"Well, good." He stood up. They walked into the living room. Paul stood at the window, looking out at the wet streets. Michael was on the floor, scribbling in his notebook. He had a great many notebooks, all of them filled with trees and houses and monsters and entirely cryptic anecdotes.

Paul moved from the window to come and stand beside his father.

"Are we going to go now?" he asked. "It's getting late."

For Paul never forgot a promise or an appointment.

Richard winked at Paul and reached down to cuff Michael lightly on the head. Michael always reacted to this with a kind of surly, withdrawn delight; seeming to say to himself, each time, that he loved his father enough to overlook an occasional lapse of dignity.

"Come on, now," Richard said. "You want me to walk you to the movies, you got to get a move on."

Then she stood at the window and watched the three of them, under Richard's umbrella, walking away from her.

Twelve years. She had been twenty-one, he had been twenty-five; it was the middle of the war. She eventually ended up in San Francisco and got paid for hanging around a shipyard. She could have done better, but she hadn't cared. She was simply waiting for the war to be over and for Richard to be home. He ended up in a quartermaster depot in

North Africa where he had spent most of his time, as far as she could gather, defending Arab shoeshine boys and beggars against the cynical and malicious French.

She was in the kitchen, mixing batter for a cake, when Richard came back. He put his head in the kitchen door, water running from the end of his nose.

"How're you feeling now?"

She laughed. "Gloomier than ever. I'm baking a cake."

"That's a terrible sign. I can see there's not much hope for you." He grabbed one of the dish towels and mopped his face.

"What happened to the umbrella?"

"I left it with the boys."

"Oh, Richard, it's so big. Can Paul handle that?"

"No, of course not," he said. "The umbrella's going to get caught in a high wind and they'll be carried away over the rooftops and we'll never see them again." He winked. "That's why I gave it to them. I'm not so dumb." He walked into his study and closed the door.

She put the cake in the oven, peeled potatoes and carrots and left them in the water and calculated the time it would take for the roast beef. She had changed her clothes and set the cake out to cool when the bell rang.

It was Vivaldo. He was wearing a black raincoat and his hair was wild and dripping from the rain. His eyes seemed blacker than ever, and his face paler.

"Heathcliff!" she cried, "how nice you could come!"— and pulled him into the apartment, for it did not seem that he was going to move. "Put those wet things in the bathroom and I'll make you a drink."

"What a bright girl you are," he said, barely smiling. "Christ, it's pissing out there!" He took off his coat and disappeared into the bathroom.

She went to the study door and knocked on it. "Richard. Vivaldo's here."

"Okay. I'll be right out."

She made two drinks and brought them into the living room. Vivaldo sat on the sofa, his long legs stretched before him, staring at the carpet.

She handed him his drink. "How are you?"

"All right. Where're the kids?" He put his drink down carefully on the low table near him.

"They're at the movies." She considered him a moment. "You may be all right but I've seen you look better."

"Well"—again that bleak smile—"I haven't really sobered up yet. I got real drunk last night with Jane. She can't screw if she's sober." He picked up his drink and took a swallow of it, dragged a bent cigarette from one of his pockets and lit it. He looked so sad and beaten for a moment, hunched over the flame of the cigarette, that she did not speak. "Where's Richard?"

"He'll be out. He's in his study."

He sipped his drink, obviously trying to think of something to say, and not succeeding.

"Vivaldo?"

"Yeah?"

"Did Rufus stay at your place last night?"

"Rufus?" He looked frightened. "No. Why?"

"His sister called up to find out where he was."

They stared at each other and his face made her frightened all over again.

"Where did he go?" she asked.

"I don't know. I figured he'd gone to Harlem. He just disappeared."

"Vivaldo, she's coming here this afternoon."

"Who is?"

"His sister, Ida. I told her that I left him with you and that you would be here this afternoon."

"But I don't know where he *is*. I was in the back, talking to Jane—and he said he was going to the head or something —and he never came back." He stared at her, then at the window. "I wonder where he went."

"Maybe," she said, "he met a friend."

He did not trouble to respond to this. "He should have known I wasn't just going to dump him. He could have stayed at my place; I ended up at Jane's place, anyway."

Cass watched him as he banged his cigarette out in the ashtray.

"I have never," she said, mildly, "understood what Jane wanted from you. Or for that matter, what you wanted from her."

He examined his fingernails, they were jagged and in mourning. "I don't know. I just wanted a girl, I guess, someone to share those long winter evenings."

"But she's so much older than you are." She picked up his empty glass. "She's older than *I* am."

"That hasn't got anything to do with it," he said, sullenly. "Anyway, I wanted a girl who—sort of knows the score."

She considered him. "Yes," she said, with a sigh, "that girl certainly knows how to keep score."

"I needed a woman," Vivaldo said, "she needed a man. What's wrong with that?"

"Nothing," she said. "If that's really what both of you needed."

"What do *you* think I was doing?"

"Oh, I don't know," she said. "I really don't know. Only, I've told you, you always seem to get involved with impossible women—whores, nymphomaniacs, drunks—and I think you do it in order to protect yourself—from anything serious. Permanent."

He sighed, smiled. "Hell, I just want to be friends."

She laughed. "Oh, Vivaldo."

"You and I are friends," he said.

"Well—yes. But I've always been the wife of a friend of yours. So you never thought of me—"

"Sexually," he said. Then he grinned. "Don't be so sure."

She flushed, at once annoyed and pleased. "I'm not talking about your fantasies."

"I've always admired you," he said soberly, "and envied Richard."

"Well," she said, "you'd better get over that."

He said nothing. She rattled the ice around in his empty glass.

"Well," he said, "what am I going to do with it? I'm not a monk, I'm tired of running uptown and paying for it—"

"For it's uptown that you run," she said, with a smile. "What a good American you are."

This angered him. "I haven't said they were any better than white chicks." Then he laughed. "Maybe I better cut the damn thing off."

"Don't be such a baby. Really. You should hear yourself."

"You're telling me someone's going to come along who needs it? Needs me?"

"I'm not telling you anything," she said, shortly, "that you don't already know." They heard Richard's study door open. "I'll fix you another drink; you might as well get *good* and drunk." She bumped into Richard in the hall. He was carrying the manuscript. "Do you want a drink now?"

"Love one," he said, and walked into the living room. From the kitchen she heard their voices, a little too loud, a little too friendly. When she came back into the living room, Vivaldo was leafing through the manuscript. Richard stood by the window.

"Just read it," he was saying, "don't go thinking about Dostoievski and all that. It's just a book—a pretty good book."

She handed Richard his drink. "It's a *very* good book," she said. She put Vivaldo's drink on the table beside him. She was surprised and yet not surprised to realize that she was worried about the effect on Richard of Vivaldo's opinion.

"The next book, though, will be better," Richard said. "And very different."

Vivaldo put the manuscript down and sipped his drink. "Well," he said, with a grin, "I'll read it just as soon as I sober up. Whenever," he added, grimly, "that may be."

"And tell me the truth, you hear? You bastard."

Vivaldo looked at him. "I'll tell you the truth."

Years ago, Vivaldo had brought his manuscripts to Richard with almost exactly the same words. She moved away from them both and lit a cigarette. Then she heard the elevator door open and close and she looked at the clock. It was four. She looked at Vivaldo. The bell rang.

"There she is," said Cass.

She and Vivaldo stared at each other.

"Take it easy," Richard said. "What're you looking so tragic about?"

"Richard," she said, "that must be Rufus's sister."

"Well, go let her in. Don't leave her waiting in the hall." As he spoke, the bell rang again.

"Oh, my God," said Vivaldo, and he stood up, looking very tall and helpless. She put down her drink and went to the door.

The girl who faced her was fairly tall, sturdy, very carefully dressed, and somewhat darker than Rufus. She wore a raincoat, with a hood, and carried an umbrella; and beneath the hood, in the shadows of the hall, the dark eyes in the dark face considered Cass intently. There was a hint of Rufus in the eyes—large, intelligent, wary—and in her smile.

"Cass Silenski?"

Cass put out her hand. "Come in. I *do* remember you." She closed the door behind them. "I thought you were one of the most beautiful women I'd ever seen."

The girl looked at her and Cass realized, for the first time, that a Negro girl could blush. "Oh, come on, now, Mrs. Silenski—"

"Give me your things. And please call me Cass."

"Then you call me Ida."

She put the things away. "Shall I make you a drink?"

"Yes, I think I need one," Ida said. "I been scouring this city, I don't know how long, looking for that no-good brother of mine—"

"Vivaldo's inside," Cass said, quickly, wishing to say something to prepare the girl but not knowing what to say. "Will you have bourbon or Scotch or rye? and I think we've got a little vodka—"

"I'll have bourbon." She sounded a little breathless; she followed Cass into the kitchen and stood watching her while she made the drink. Cass handed her the glass and looked into Ida's eyes. "Vivaldo hasn't seen him since last night," she said. Ida's eyes widened, and she thrust out her lower lip, which trembled slightly. Cass touched her elbow. "Come on in. Try not to worry." They walked into the living room.

Vivaldo was standing exactly as she had left him, as though he had not moved at all. Richard rose from the hassock; he had been clipping his nails. "This is my husband, Richard," Cass said, "and you know Vivaldo."

They shook hands and murmured salutations in a silence that began to stiffen like the beaten white of an egg. They sat down.

"Well!" Ida said, shakily, "it's been a long time."

"Over two years," Richard said. "Rufus let us see you a couple of times and then he hustled you out of sight somewhere. Very wise of him, too."

Vivaldo said nothing. His eyes, his eyebrows, and his hair looked like so many streaks of charcoal on a dead white surface.

"But none of you," said Ida, "know where my brother is now?" And she looked around the room.

"He was with me last night," Vivaldo said. His voice was too low; Ida strained forward to hear. He cleared his throat.

"We all saw him," Richard said, "he was fine."

"He was supposed to stay at my place," said Vivaldo, "but we—I—got talking to somebody—and then, when I looked up, he was gone." He seemed to feel that this was not the best way to put it. "There were lots of his friends around; I figured he had a drink with some of them and then maybe went off and decided to stay the night."

"Do you know these friends?" Ida asked.

"Well, I know them when I see them. I don't know—all their *names*."

The silence stretched. Vivaldo dropped his eyes.

"Did he have any money?"

"Well"—he looked to Richard and Cass—"I don't *know*."

"How did he look?"

They stared at each other. "All right. Tired, maybe."

"I'll bet." She sipped her drink; her hand shook a little. "I don't want to make a big fuss over nothing. I'm sure he's all right, wherever he is. I'd just like to *know*. Our Mama and Daddy are having a fit, and"—she laughed, catching her breath roughly—"I guess I am, too." She was silent. Then: "He's the only big brother I got." She sipped her drink, then she put it on the floor beside her chair. She played with the ruby-eyed snake ring on her long little finger.

"I'm sure he's all right," Cass said, miserably aware of the empty sound of the words, "it's just that—well, Rufus is like a lot of people I know. When something goes wrong, when he gets hurt, he just wants to go and hide until it's over. He licks his wounds. Then he comes back." She looked to Richard for help.

He did his best. "I think Cass may be right," he murmured.

"I've been everywhere," said Ida, "everywhere he ever played, I been talking to everybody I could find who ever worked with him, anybody I could find he'd even ever said hello to—I even tried relatives in Brooklyn—" She stopped and turned to Vivaldo. "When you saw him—where did he say he'd been?"

"He didn't say."

"Didn't you ask him?"

"Yes. He wouldn't say."

"I gave you a phone number to call the minute you saw him. Why didn't you call me?"

"It was late when he came to my house, he asked me not to call, he said he was coming to see you in the morning!"

He sounded helpless and close to tears. She stared at him, then dropped her eyes. The silence began to crawl with an acrid, banked hostility emanating from the girl who sat alone, in the round chair, in the center of the room. She looked in turn at each of her brother's friends. "It's funny he didn't make it, then," she said.

"Well, Rufus doesn't talk much," said Richard. "You must know how hard it is to get anything out of him."

"Well," she said, shortly, "*I* would have got it out of him."

"You're his sister," Cass said, gently.

"Yes," Ida said, and looked down at her hands.

"Have you been to the police?" Richard asked.

"Yes." She made a gesture of disgust and rose and walked to the window. "They said it happens all the time—colored men running off from their families. They said they'd try to find him. But they don't care. They don't care what happens —to a black man!"

"Oh, well, now," cried Richard, his face red, "is that fair? I mean, hell, I'm sure they'll look for him just like they look for any other citizen of this city."

She looked at him. "How would you know? I *do* know— know what I'm talking about. I say they don't care—and they *don't* care."

"I don't think you should look at it like that."

She was staring out of the window. "Goddammit. He's out there somewhere. I've got to find him." Her back was to the room. Cass watched her shoulders begin to shake. She went to the window and put her hand on Ida's arm. "I'm all right," Ida said, moving slightly away. She fumbled in the pocket of her suit, then crossed to where she had been sitting and pulled Kleenex out of her handbag. She dried her eyes and blew her nose and picked up her drink.

Cass stared at her helplessly. "Let me freshen it for you," she said, and took the glass into the kitchen.

"Ida," Vivaldo was saying as she reentered, "if there's anything I can do to help you find him—anything at all—" He stopped. "Hell," he said, "I love him, too, I want to find him, too. I've been kicking myself all day for letting him get away last night."

When Vivaldo said, "I love him, too," Ida looked over at him, her eyes very big, as though she were, now, really meeting him for the first time. Then she dropped her eyes. "I don't really know anything you *can* do," she said.

"Well—I could come with you while you look. We could look together."

She considered this; she considered him. "Well," she said, finally, "maybe you could come with me to a couple of places in the Village—"

"All right."

"I can't help it. I have the feeling they think I'm just being hysterical."

"I'll come with you. They won't think *I'm* hysterical."

Richard grinned. "Vivaldo's never hysterical, we all know that." Then he said, "I really don't see the point of all this. Rufus is probably just sleeping it off somewhere."

"Nobody's seen him," Ida cried, "for nearly six *weeks!* Until last night! I *know* my brother, he doesn't do things like this. He always come by the house, no matter where he'd been, or what was happening, just so we wouldn't worry. He used to bring money and things—but even when he was broke, he come anyway. Don't tell me he's just sleeping it off somewhere. Six weeks is a long time." She subsided a little, subsided to a venomous murmur. "And you know what happened—between him and that damn crazy little cracker bitch he got hung up with."

"All right," Richard said, helplessly, after a considerable silence, "have it your own way."

Cass said, "But there's no need to go rushing off in the rain right away. Rufus knows Vivaldo is going to be here. He may come by. I was hoping you would all stay for supper." She smiled at Ida. "Won't you, please? I'm sure you'll feel better. It may all be cleared up by this evening."

Ida and Vivaldo stared at each other, having, it seemed, become allies in the course of the afternoon. "Well?" asked Vivaldo.

"I don't know. I'm so tired and evil I don't seem to be able to think straight."

Richard looked as though he thoroughly agreed with this; and he said, "Look. You've been to the police. You've told everyone you could. You've checked the hospitals, and"—he looked at her questioningly—"the morgue"—and she nodded, not dropping her eyes. "Well. I don't see any point in rushing out in this damn Sunday-afternoon rain, when you hardly even know where you're going. And we all saw him last night. So we know he's around. So why not relax for a couple of hours? Hell, in a couple of hours you may find out you haven't got to go anywhere, he'll turn up."

"Really," said Cass, "there's a very good chance he'll turn up here today." Ida looked at Cass. Then Cass realized that something in Ida was enjoying this—the attention, the power she held for this moment. This made Cass angry, but then she thought: Good. It means that whatever's coming, she'll be able to get through it. Without quite knowing it, from the moment Ida stepped through the door, she was preparing herself for the worst.

"Well," said Ida, loking at Vivaldo, "I asked Mama to call me here—just in case."

"Well, then," said Cass, "it seems to me it's settled." She looked at the clock. "The boys should be home in about another hour. I think what I'll do is fix us all a fresh drink."

Ida grinned. "That's a very friendly idea."

She was terribly attractive when she grinned. Her face,

then, made one think of a mischievous street boy. And at the same time there glowed in her eyes a marvelously feminine mockery. Vivaldo kept watching her, a small smile playing around the corners of his mouth.

The snow which had been predicted for the day before Thanksgiving did not begin to fall until late in the evening—slow, halfhearted flakes, spinning and gleaming in the darkness, melting on the ground.

All day long a cold sun glared down on Manhattan, giving no heat.

Cass woke a little earlier than usual, and fed the children and sent them off to school. Richard ate his breakfast and retired into his study—he was not in a good mood. Cass cleaned the house, thinking of tomorrow's dinner, and went out in the early afternoon to shop and to walk for a little while alone.

She was gone longer than she had intended, for she loved to walk around this city. She was chilled when at last she started home.

They lived just below Twenty-third Street, on the West Side, in a neighborhood that had lately acquired many Puerto Ricans. For this reason it was said that the neighborhood was declining; from what previous height it would have been hard to say. It seemed to Cass very much as it always had, run-down, and with a preponderance of very rough-looking people. As for the Puerto Ricans, she rather liked them. They did not impress her as being rough; they seemed, on the contrary, rather too gentle for their brutal environment. She liked the sound of their talk, soft and laughing, or else violently, clearly, brilliantly hostile; she liked the life in their eyes and the way they treated their children, as though all children were naturally the responsibility of all grownups. Even when the adolescents whistled after her, or said lewd things as she passed and laughed among themselves, she did not become resentful or afraid; she did not feel in it the tense New York hostility. They were not cursing something they longed for and feared, they were joking about something they longed for and loved.

Now, as she labored up the outside steps of the building, one of the Puerto Rican boys she had seen everywhere in the neighborhood opened the door for her with a small, half-smile. She smiled at him and thanked him as forthrightly as she could, and stepped into the elevator.

There was something in Richard's face as he closed the door behind her, and in the loud silence of the apartment. She looked at him and started to ask about the children—but then she heard them in the living room. Richard followed her into the kitchen and she put down her packages. She looked into his face.

"What is it?" she asked. Then, after the instant in which she checked off all the things it wasn't, "Rufus," she said, suddenly, "you've got news about Rufus."

"Yes." She watched the way a small vein in his forehead fluttered. "He's dead, Cass. They found his body floating in the river."

She sat down at the kitchen table.

"When?"

"Sometime this morning."

"How long—how long ago—?"

"A few days. They figured he must have jumped off the George Washington Bridge."

"My God," she said. Then: "Who—?"

"Vivaldo. He called. Just after you went out. Ida had called him."

"My God," she said again, "it's going to kill that poor girl."

He paused. "Vivaldo sounded as though he'd just been kicked in the belly by a horse."

"Where is he?"

"I tried to make him come here. But he was going uptown to the girl—Ida—I don't know what good he can do."

"Well. He was much closer to Rufus than we were."

"Would you like a drink?"

"Yes," she said, "I think I'd like a drink." She sat staring at the table. "I wonder if there was anything—we—anyone —could have done."

"No," he said, pouring a little whiskey in a glass and setting it before her, "there was nothing anyone could have done. It was too late. He wanted to die."

She was silent, sipping the whiskey. She watched the way the sunlight fell on the table.

Richard put his hand on her shoulder. "Don't take it too hard, Cass. After all—"

She remembered his face as it had been the last time she talked to him, the look in his eyes, and his smile when he asked, *Can I come to see you soon?* How she wished, now, that she had stayed and talked to him a little longer. Perhaps —she sipped the whiskey, marveling that the children were so quiet. Tears filled her eyes and dropped slowly down her face, onto the table.

"It's a dirty, rotten shame," she said. "It's a terrible, terrible, terrible thing."

"He was heading that way," said Richard, mildly, "nothing, no one, could have stopped him."

"How do we know that?" Cass asked.

"Oh, honey, you know what he's been like these last few months. We hardly ever saw him but everybody knew."

Knew what? she wanted to ask. Just what in hell did everybody know? But she dried her eyes and stood up.

"Vivaldo tried like hell to stop what he was doing to Leona. And if he could have stopped him from doing *that*—well, then, maybe he could have stopped this, too."

That's true, she thought, and looked at Richard, who, under stress, could always surprise her into taking his measure again.

"I was very fond of him," she said, helplessly. "There was something very sweet in him."

He looked at her with a faint smile. "Well, I guess you're just naturally nicer than I am. I didn't think that. I thought he was a pretty self-centered character, if you want the truth."

"Oh, well," she said, "self-centered—! We don't know a soul who isn't."

"You're not," he said. "You think of other people and you try to treat them right. You spend your life trying to take care of the children—and me—"

"Oh, but you *are* my life—you and the children. What would I do, what would I be, without you? I'm just as self-centered as anybody else. Can't you see that?"

He grinned and rubbed his hand roughly over her head. "No. And I'm not going to argue about it any more." But, after a moment, he persisted. "I don't love Rufus, not the way you did, the way all of you did. I couldn't help feeling, anyway, that one of the reasons all of you made such a kind of—*fuss*—over him was partly just because he was colored. Which is a hell of a reason to love anybody. I just had to look on him as another guy. And I couldn't forgive him for what he did to Leona. You once said you couldn't, either."

"I've had to think about it since then. I've thought about it since then."

"And what have you thought? You find a way to justify it?"

"No. I wasn't trying to justify it. It can't be justified. But now I think—oh, I just don't know enough to be able to judge him. He must—he must have been in great pain. He must have loved her." She turned to him, searching his face. "I'm sure he loved her."

"Some love," he said.

"Richard," she said, "you and I have hurt each other— many times. Sometimes we didn't mean to and sometimes we did. And wasn't it because—just *because*—we loved—love —each other?"

He looked at her oddly, head to one side. "Cass," he said, "how can you compare it? We've never tried to destroy each other—have we?"

They watched each other. She said nothing.

"I've never tried to destroy you. Have you ever tried to destroy me?"

She thought of his face as it had been when they met; and watched it now. She thought of all they had discovered together and meant to each other, and of how many small lies had gone into the making of their one, particular truth: this love, which bound them to one another. She had said No, many times, to many things, when she knew she might have said Yes, because of Richard; believed many things, because of Richard, which she was not sure she really believed. He had been absolutely necessary to her—or so she had believed; it came to the same thing—and so she had attached herself to him and her life had taken shape around him. She did not regret this for herself. I want him, something in her had said, years ago. And she had bound him to her; he had been her salvation; and here he was. She did not regret it for herself and yet she began to wonder if there were not something in it to be regretted, something she had done to Richard which Richard did not see.

"No," she said, faintly. And then, irrepressibly, "But I wouldn't have had to try."

"What do you mean by that?"

"I mean"—he was watching her; she sat down again, playing with the glass of whiskey—"a man meets a woman. And he needs her. But she uses this need against him, she uses it to undermine him. And it's easy. Women don't see men the way men want to be seen. They see all the tender places, all the places where blood could flow." She finished the whiskey. "Do you see what I mean?"

"No," he said, frankly, "I don't. I don't believe all this female intuition shit. It's something women have dreamed up."

"You can *say* that—and in such a tone!" She mimicked

him: "Something women have dreamed up. But *I* can't say that—what men have 'dreamed up' is all there is, the world they've dreamed up *is* the world." He laughed. She subsided. "Well. It's true."

"What a funny girl you are," he said. "You've got a bad case of penis envy."

"So do most men," she said, sharply, and he laughed. "All I meant, anyway," she said, soberly, "is that I had to try to fit myself around you and not try to make you fit around me. That's all. And it hasn't been easy."

"No."

"No. Because I love you."

"Ah!" he said, and laughed aloud, "you *are* a funny girl. I love you, too, you know that."

"I hope you do," she said.

"You know me so well and you don't know that? What happened to all that intuition, all that—*specialized*—point of view?"

"Beyond a certain point," she said, with a sullen smile, "it doesn't seem to work so well."

He pulled her up from the table and put both arms around her, bending his cheek to her hair. "What point is that, my darling?"

Everything, his breath in her hair, his arms, his chest, his odor—was familiar, confining, unutterably dear. She turned her head slightly to look out of the kitchen window. "Love," she said, and watched the cold sunlight. She thought of the cold river and of the dead black boy, their friend. She closed her eyes. "Love," she said again, "love."

Richard stayed with the children Saturday, while Cass and Vivaldo went uptown to Rufus's funeral. She did not want to go but she could not refuse Vivaldo, who knew that he had to be there but dreaded being there alone.

It was a morning funeral, and Rufus was to be driven to the graveyard immediately afterward. Early on that cold, dry Saturday, Vivaldo arrived, emphatically in black and white: white shirt, black tie, black suit, black shoes, black coat; and black hair, eyes, and eyebrows, and a dead-white, bone-dry face. She was struck by his panic and sorrow; without a word, she put on her dark coat and put her hand in his; and they rode down in the elevator in silence. She watched him in the elevator mirror. Sorrow became him. He was reduced to his beauty and elegance—as bones, after a long illness, come forward through the flesh.

They got into a taxi and started uptown. Vivaldo sat beside her, his hands on his knees, staring straight ahead. She watched the streets. Traffic was heavy, but rolling; the cab kept swerving and jerking, slowing down and speeding up but managing not to stop. Then, at Thirty-fourth Street, the red light brought it to a halt. They were surrounded by a violence of cars, great trucks, green buses lumbering across town, and boys, dark boys, pushing wooden wagons full of clothes. The people on the sidewalks overflowed into the streets. Women in heavy coats moved heavily, carrying large packages and enormous handbags—for Thanksgiving was over but signs proclaimed the dwindling number of shopping days to Christmas. Men, relatively unburdened, pursuing the money which Christmas cost, hurried around and past the women; boys in ducktail haircuts swung over the cold black asphalt as though it were a dance floor. Outside the window, as close to her as Vivaldo, one of the colored boys stopped his wagon, lit a cigarette, and laughed. The taxi could not move and the driver began cursing. Cass lit a cigarette and handed it to Vivaldo. She lit another for herself. Then, abruptly, the taxi jerked forward.

The driver turned on his radio and the car was filled suddenly with the sound of a guitar, a high, neighing voice, and a chorus, crying, *"love me!"* The other words were swallowed in the guttural moans of the singer, which were nearly as obscene as the driver's curses had been, but these two words kept recurring.

"My whole family thinks I'm a bum," said Vivaldo. "I'd say they've given me up, except I know they're scared to death of what I'll do next."

She said nothing. He looked out of the cab window. They were crossing Columbus Circle.

"Sometimes—like today," he said, "I think they're probably right and I've just been kidding myself. About everything."

The walls of the park now closed on either side of them and beyond these walls, through speed and barren trees, the walls of hotels and apartment buildings.

"My family thinks I married beneath me," she said. "Beneath *them*." And she smiled at him and crushed out her cigarette on the floor.

"I don't think I ever saw my father sober," he said, "not in all these years. He used to say, 'I want you to tell me the truth now, always tell me the truth.' And then, if I told him the truth, he'd slap me up against the wall. So, naturally, I didn't tell him the truth, I'd just tell him any old lie, I didn't give a shit. The last time I went over to the house to see them I was wearing my red shirt, and he said, 'What's the matter, you turned queer?' Jesus."

She lit another cigarette and she listened. There was a horseback rider on the bridle path, a pale girl with a haughty, bewildered face. Cass had time to think, unwillingly, as the rider vanished forever from sight, that it might have been herself, many years ago, in New England.

"That neighborhood was terrific," Vivaldo said, "you had to be tough, they'd kill you if you weren't, people were dying around us all the time, for nothing. I wasn't really much interested in hanging out with most of those kids, they bored me. But they scared me, too. I couldn't stand watching my father. He's such an awful coward. He spent all his time pretending—well, I don't know *what* he was pretending, that everything was great, I guess—while his wife was going crazy in the hardware store we've got. And he knew that neither me nor my brother had any respect for him. And his daughter was turning into the biggest cock teaser going. She finally got married, I hate to think what her husband must have to promise her each time she lets him have a little bit."

He was silent for a moment. Then, "Of course, he's an asshole, too. Lord. I used to like to just get on a bus and go to some strange part of town by myself and just walk around or go to the movies by myself or just read or just goof. But, no. You had to be a man where I come from, and you had to prove it, prove it all the time. But I could tell you things —" He sighed. "Well, my Dad's still there, sort of helping to keep the liquor industry going. Most of the kids I knew are dead or in jail or on junk. I'm just a bum; I'm lucky."

She listened because she knew that he was going back over it, looking at it, trying to put it all together, to understand it, to express it. But he had not expressed it. He had left something of himself back there on the streets of Brooklyn which he was afraid to look at again.

"One time," he said, "we got into a car and drove over to the Village and we picked up this queer, a young guy, and we drove him back to Brooklyn. Poor guy, he was scared green before we got halfway there but he couldn't jump out of the car. We drove into this garage, there were seven of us, and we made him go down on all of us and we beat the piss out of him and took all his money and took his clothes and left him lying on that cement floor, and, you know, it was winter." He looked over at her, looked directly at her for the first time that morning. "Sometimes I still wonder if they found him in time, or if he died, or what." He put his hands together and looked out of the window. "Sometimes I wonder if I'm still the same person who did those things—so long ago."

No. It was not expressed. She wondered why. Perhaps it was because Vivaldo's recollections in no sense freed him from the things recalled. He had not gone back into it—that time, that boy; he regarded it with a fascinated, even romantic horror, and he was looking for a way to deny it.

Perhaps such secrets, the secrets of everyone, were only expressed when the person laboriously dragged them into the light of the world, imposed them on the world, and made them a part of the world's experience. Without this effort, the secret place was merely a dungeon in which the person perished; without this effort, indeed, the entire world would be an uninhabitable darkness; and she saw, with a dreadful reluctance, why this effort was so rare. Reluctantly, because she then realized that Richard had bitterly disappointed her by writing a book in which he did not believe. In that moment she knew, and she knew that Richard would never face it, that the book he had written to make money represented the absolute limit of his talent. It had not really been written to make money—if only it had been! It had been written because he was afraid, afraid of things dark, strange, dangerous, difficult, and deep.

I don't care, she told herself, quickly. And: It's not his fault if he's not Dostoievski, I don't care. But whether or not she cared didn't matter. *He* cared, cared tremendously, and he was dependent on her faith in him.

"Isn't it strange," she said, suddenly, "that you should be remembering all these things now!"

"Maybe," he said, after a moment, "it's because of her. When I went up there, the day she called me to say Rufus was dead—I don't know—I walked through that block and I walked in that house and it all seemed—I don't know—*familiar.*" He turned his pale, troubled face toward her but she felt that he was staring at the high, hard wall which stood between himself and his past. "I don't just mean that I used to spend a lot of time in Harlem," and he looked away, nervously, "I was hardly ever there in the daytime anyway. I mean, there were the same kids on the block that used to be on my block—they were colored but they were the same, really the same—and, hell, the hallways have the same stink, and everybody's, well, trying to make it but they know they haven't got much of a chance. The same old women, the same old men—maybe they're a little bit more *alive*—and I walked into that house and they were just sitting there, Ida and her mother and her father, and there were some other people there, relatives, maybe, and friends. I don't know, no one really spoke to me except Ida and she didn't say much. And they all looked at me as though—well, as though I had *done* it—and, oh, I wanted so bad to take that girl in my arms and kiss that look off her face and make her know that I didn't do it, *I* wouldn't do it, whoever was doing it was doing it to me, too." He was crying, silently, and he bent forward, hiding his face with one long hand. "I know I failed him, but I loved him, too, and nobody there wanted to know that. I kept thinking, They're colored and I'm white but the same things have happened, really the *same* things, and how can I make them know that?"

"But they didn't," she said, "happen to you *because* you were white. They just happened. But what happens up here" —and the cab came out of the park; she stretched her hands, inviting him to look—"happens *because* they are colored. And that makes a difference." And, after a moment, she dared to add, "You'll be kissing a long time, my friend, before you kiss any of this away."

He looked out of the window, drying his eyes. They had come out on Lenox Avenue, though their destination was on Seventh; and nothing they passed was unfamiliar because everything they passed was wretched. It was not hard to imagine that horse carriages had once paraded proudly up this wide Avenue and ladies and gentlemen, ribboned, beflowered, brocaded, plumed, had stepped down from their carriages to enter these houses which time and folly had so blasted and darkened. The cornices had once been new, had once gleamed as brightly as now they sulked in shame, all tarnished and despised. The windows had not always been blind. The doors had not always brought to mind the distrust and secrecy of a city long besieged. At one time people had cared about these houses—that was the difference; they had been proud to walk on this Avenue; it had once been home, whereas now it was prison.

Now, no one cared: this indifference was all that joined this ghetto to the mainland. Now, everything was falling down and the owners didn't care; no one cared. The beautiful children in the street, black-blue, brown, and copper, all with a gray ash on their faces and legs from the cold wind, like the faint coating of frost on a window or a flower, didn't seem to care that no one saw their beauty. Their elders, great, trudging, black women, lean, shuffling men, had taught them, by precept or example, what it meant to care or not to care: whatever precepts were daily being lost, the examples remained, all up and down the street. The trudging women trudged, paused, came in and out of dark doors, talked to each other, to the men, to policemen, stared into shop windows, shouted at the children, laughed, stopped to caress them. All the faces, even those of the children, held a sweet or poisonous disenchantment which made their faces extraordinarily definite, as though they had been struck out of stone. The cab sped uptown, past men in front of barber shops, in front of barbecue joints, in front of bars; sped past side streets, long, dark, noisome, with gray houses leaning forward to cut out the sky; and in the shadow of these houses, children buzzed and boomed, as thick as flies on flypaper. Then they turned off the Avenue, west, crawled up a long, gray street. They had to crawl, for the street was choked with unhurrying people and children kept darting out from between the cars which were parked, for the length of the street, on either side. There were people on the stoops, people shouting out of windows, and young men peered indifferently into the slow-moving cab, their faces set ironically and their eyes unreadable.

"Did Rufus ever have you up here?" she asked. "To visit his family, I mean."

"Yes," said Vivaldo. "A long time ago. I had almost forgotten it. I *had* forgotten it until Ida reminded me. She was in pigtails then, the cutest little colored girl you ever saw. She was about fifteen. Rufus and I took her to Radio City."

She smiled at his description of Ida, and at his tone, which was unconsciously erotic. The cab crossed the Avenue and stopped on the far corner of the block they had come through, where the chapel stood. Two women stood on the steps of the chapel, talking together in low tones. As Cass watched and Vivaldo paid the driver, a young man joined them and they went inside.

Suddenly, with a curse, she put her hand on her uncovered head.

"Vivaldo," she said, "I can't go in there."

He stared at her blankly, while the taxi driver paused in the act of handing him his change.

"What're you talking about?" he asked. "What's the matter with you?"

"Nothing. Nothing. But a woman's head has to be *covered*. I can't go in there without a hat."

"Of course you can!" But at the same moment he remembered that he had never in his life seen a bareheaded woman in a church.

"No, no, I *can't*. They're all wearing hats, all of them. It would be an insult if I didn't, it would be like coming here in slacks." She paused. "It's a *church*, Vivaldo, it's a funeral, it would be an insult."

He had already conceded her point and he stared at her helplessly. The cab driver still held the change and watched Vivaldo with a careful lack of expression.

"Well, haven't you got a scarf, or something?"

"No." She dug in her handbag, the pockets of her coat, close to tears. "No. Nothing."

"Listen, buddy," the driver said.

Vivaldo's face lightened. "What about your belt? Can't you tie that around your head? It's black."

"Oh, no. That'll never work. Besides—they'd *know* it was my belt."

"Try it."

To end the argument and prove her point, she took off her belt and tied it around her head. "You see? It'll never work."

"What're you people going to do?" the driver asked. "I ain't got all day."

"I'll have to buy something," Cass said.

"We'll be late."

"Well, you go on in. I'll just drive to a store somewhere and I'll come right back."

"Ain't no stores around here, lady," the driver said.

"Of course there are stores somewhere near here," Cass said, sharply. "You go on in, Vivaldo; I'll come right back. What's the address here?"

Vivaldo gave her the address and said, "You'll have to go to 125th Street, that's the only place I know where there are any stores." Then he took his change from the driver and tipped him. "The lady wants to go to 125th Street," he said.

The driver turned in his seat resignedly, and turned on his meter. "You go on in, Vivaldo," Cass said again. "I'm sorry. I'll be right back."

"You have enough money on you?"

"Yes. Go on in."

He got out of the cab, looking helpless and annoyed, and turned into the chapel as the cab pulled away. The driver left her at the corner of 125th Street and Eighth Avenue and she realized, as she hurried down the wide, crowded street, that she was in a strange, unnamable state, neither rage nor tears but close to both. One small, lone, white woman hurrying along 125th Street on a Saturday morning was apparently a very common sight, for no one looked at her at all. She did not see any stores with ladies' hats in the window. But she was hurrying too fast, and looking too hard. If she did not pull herself together, she might very well spend the day wandering up and down this street. For a moment she thought to stop one of the women—one of the women whose faces she watched as though they contained something it was necessary for her to learn—to ask directions. Then she realized that she was mysteriously afraid: afraid of these people, these streets, the chapel to which she must return. She forced herself to walk more slowly. She saw a store and entered it.

A Negro girl came toward her, a girl with red, loosely waved hair, who wore a violently green dress and whose skin was a kind of dusty copper.

"Can I help you?"

The girl was smiling, the same smile—as Cass insisted to herself—that all salesgirls, everywhere, have always worn. This smile made Cass feel poor and shabby indeed. But now she felt it more vehemently than she had ever felt it before. And though she was beginning to shake with a thoroughly mysterious anger, she knew that her dry, aristocratic sharpness, however well it had always worked downtown, would fail of its usual effect here.

"I want," she stammered, "to see a hat."

Then she remembered that she hated hats and never wore them. The girl, whose smile had clearly been taught her by masters, looked as though she sold at least one hat every Saturday morning, to a strange, breathless, white woman.

"Will you come with me?" she asked.

"Well—no," Cass said, suddenly—and the girl turned, impeccably made up eyebrows arched—"I mean, I don't really want a hat." Cass tried to smile; she wanted to run. Silence had fallen over the shop. "I think I'd just like to get a scarf. Black"—and how the word seemed to roll through the shop!—"for my head," she added, and felt that in another moment they would call the police. And she had no way of identifying herself.

"Oh," said the girl. Cass had managed to wipe away the smile. "Marie!" she called, sharply, "will you take care of this lady?"

She walked away and another, older and plainer girl, who was also, however, very carefully dressed and made up, came over to Cass, wearing a very different smile: a bawdy, amused smile, full of complicity and contempt. Cass felt herself blushing. The girl pulled out boxes of scarves. They all seemed sleazy and expensive, but she was in no position to complain. She took one, paid for it, tied it around her head, and left. Her knees were shaking. She managed to find a cab at the corner and, after fighting a small duel with herself, gave the driver the address of the chapel: she had really wanted to tell him to take her home.

The chapel was small and there were not many people in it. She entered as silently as she could, but heads turned at her entrance. An elderly man, probably an usher, hurried silently toward her, but she sat down in the first seat she saw, in the very last row, near the door. Vivaldo was sitting further up, near the middle; the only other white person, as far as she could tell, in the place. People sat rather scattered from each other—in the same way, perhaps, that the elements of Rufus's life had been scattered—and this made the chapel seem emptier than it was. There were many young people there, Rufus's friends, she supposed, the boys and girls who had grown up with him. In the front row sat six figures, the family: no amount of mourning could make Ida's proud back less proud. Just before the family, just below the altar, stood the bier, dominating the place, mother-of-pearl, closed.

Someone had been speaking as she came in, who now sat down. He was very young and he was dressed in the black robes of an evangelist. She wondered if he could be an evangelist, he did not seem to be much more than a boy. But he moved with great authority, the authority indeed of someone who has found his place and made his peace with it. As he sat down, a very thin girl walked up the aisle and the boy in black robes moved to the piano at the side of the altar.

"I remember Rufus," the girl said, "from when he was a big boy and I was just a little girl—" And she tried to smile at the front-row mourners. Cass watched her, seeing that the girl was doing her best not to cry. "—Me and his sister used to sit around trying to console each other when Rufus went off with the big boys and wouldn't let us play with him."

There was a murmur of amusement and sorrow and heads in
the front row nodded. "We lived right next door to each
other; he was like a brother to me." Then she dropped her
head and twisted a white handkerchief, the whitest handkerchief Cass had ever seen, between her two dark hands. She
was silent for several seconds and, once again, a kind of
wind seemed to whisper through the chapel as though everyone there shared the girl's memories and her agony, and
were willing her through it. The boy at the piano struck a
chord. "Sometimes Rufus used to like me to sing this song,"
the girl said, abruptly. "I'll sing it for him now."

The boy played the opening chord. The girl sang in a
rough, untrained, astonishingly powerful voice:

> *I'm a stranger, don't drive me away.*
> *I'm a stranger, don't drive me away.*
> *If you drive me away, you may need me some day,*
> *I'm a stranger, don't drive me away.*

When she finished she walked over to the bier and stood
there for a moment, touching it lightly with both hands.
Then she walked back to her seat.

There was weeping in the front row. Cass watched as Ida
rocked an older, heavier woman in her arms. One of the men
blew his nose loudly. The air was heavy. She wished it were
over.

Vivaldo sat very still and alone, looking straight ahead.
Now, a gray-haired man stepped forward from behind
the altar. He stood watching them for a moment and the
black-robed boy strummed a mournful hymn.

"Some of you know me," he said, finally, "and some of
you don't. My name is Reverend Foster." He paused. "And
I know some of your faces and some of you are strangers to
me." He made a brief bow, first toward Cass, then toward
Vivaldo. "But ain't none of us really strangers. We all here
for the same reason. Someone we loved is dead." He paused
again and looked down at the bier. "Someone we loved and
laughed with and talked with—and got mad at—and prayed
over—is gone. He ain't with us no more. He's gone some
place where the wicked cease from troubling." He looked
down at the bier again. "We ain't going to look on his face
again—no more. He had a hard time getting through this
world and he had a rough time getting out of it. When he
stand before his Maker he going to look like a lot of us
looked when we first got here—like he had a rough time get-

ting through the passage. It was *narrow*." He cleared his throat and blew his nose. "I ain't going to stand here and tell you all a whole lot of lies about Rufus. I don't believe in that. I used to know Rufus, I knew him all his life. He was a bright kid and he was full of the devil and weren't no way in the world of keeping up with him. He got into a lot of trouble, all of you know that. A lot of our boys get into a lot of trouble and some of you know why. We used to talk about it sometimes, him and me—we was always pretty good friends, Rufus and me, even after he jumped up and went off from here and even though he didn't never attend church service like I—we—all wanted him to do." He paused again. "He had to go his way. He had his trouble and he's gone. He was young, he was bright, he was beautiful, we expected great things from him—but he's gone away from us now and it's us will have to make the great things happen. I believe I know how terrible some of you feel. I know how terrible I feel—ain't nothing I can say going to take away that ache, not right away. But that boy was one of the best men I ever met, and I been around awhile. I ain't going to try to judge him. That ain't for us to do. You know, a lot of people say that a man who takes his own life oughtn't to be buried in holy ground. I don't know nothing about that. All *I* know, God made every bit of ground I ever walked on and everything God made is *holy*. And don't none of us know what goes on in the heart of someone, don't many of us know what's going on in our own hearts for the matter of that, and so can't none of us say why he did what he did. Ain't none of us been there and so don't none of us know. We got to pray that the Lord will receive him like we pray that the Lord's going to receive us. That's all. That's *all*. And I tell you something else, don't none of you forget it: I know a lot of people done took their own lives and they're walking up and down the streets today and some of them is preaching the gospel and some is sitting in the seats of the mighty. Now, you remember that. If the world wasn't so full of dead folks maybe those of us that's trying to live wouldn't have to suffer so bad."

He walked up and down behind the altar, behind the bier.

"I know there ain't nothing I can say to you that sit before me—his mother and father, his sister, his kinfolks, his friends—to bring him back or to keep you from grieving that he's gone. I know that. Ain't nothing I can say will make his life different, make it the life that maybe some other man might have lived. It's all been done, it's all written down on high. But don't lose heart, dear ones—don't lose heart. Don't let it make you bitter. Try to understand. Try to understand. The world's already bitter enough, we got to try to be better than the world."

He looked down, then over to the front row.

"You got to remember," he said, gently, "he was *trying*. Ain't many trying and all that tries must suffer. Be proud of him. You got a right to be proud. And that's all he ever wanted in this world."

Except for someone—a man—weeping in the front row, there was silence all over the chapel. Cass thought that the man must be Rufus's father and she wondered if he believed what the preacher said. What had Rufus been to him?—a troublesome son, a stranger while living and now a stranger forever in death. And now nothing else would ever be known. Whatever else had been, or might have been, locked in Rufus's heart or in the heart of his father, had gone into oblivion with Rufus. It would never be expressed now. It was over.

"There's some friends of Rufus's here," said Reverend Foster, "and they going to play something for us and then we going to go."

Two young men walked up the aisle, one carrying a guitar, one carrying a bass fiddle. The thin dark girl followed them. The black-robed boy at the piano flexed his fingers. The two boys stood directly in front of the covered corpse, the girl stood a little away from them, near the piano. They began playing something Cass did not recognize, something very slow, and more like the blues than a hymn. Then it began to be more tense and more bitter and more swift. The people in the chapel hummed low in their throats and tapped their feet. Then the girl stepped forward. She threw back her head and closed her eyes and that voice rang out again:

> *Oh, that great getting-up morning,*
> *Fare thee well, fare thee well!*

Reverend Foster, standing on a height behind her, raised both hands and mingled his voice with hers:

> *We'll be coming from every nation,*
> *Fare thee well, fare thee well!*

The chapel joined them, but the girl ended the song alone:

> *Oh, on that great getting-up morning,*
> *Fare thee well, fare thee well!*

Then Reverend Foster prayed a brief prayer for the safe journey of the soul that had left them and the safe journey, throughout their lives and after death, of all the souls under the sound of his voice. It was over.

The pallbearers, two of the men in the front row, and the two musicians, lifted the mother-of-pearl casket to their shoulders and started down the aisle. The mourners followed.

Cass was standing near the door. The four still faces passed her with their burden and did not look at her. Directly behind them came Ida and her mother. Ida paused for a moment and looked at her—looked directly, unreadably at her from beneath her heavy veil. Then she seemed to smile. Then she passed. And the others passed. Vivaldo joined her and they walked out of the chapel.

For the first time she saw the hearse, which stood on the Avenue, facing downtown.

"Vivaldo," she asked, "are we going to the cemetery?"

"No," he said, "they don't have enough cars. I think only the family's going."

He was watching the car behind the hearse. Ida's parents had already entered the car. She stood on the sidewalk. She looked around her, then walked swiftly over to them. She took each of them by one hand.

"I just wanted to thank you," she said, quickly, "for coming." Her voice was rough from weeping and Cass could not see her face behind the veil. "You don't know what it means to me—to us."

Cass pressed Ida's hand, not knowing what to say. Vivaldo said, "Ida, anything we can do—anything *I* can do—*anything*—!"

"You've done wonders. You been wonderful. I'll never forget it."

She pressed their hands again and turned away. She got into the car and the door closed behind her. The hearse slowly moved out from the curb, and the car, then a second car, followed. Others who had been at the funeral service looked briefly at Cass and Vivaldo, stood together a few moments, and then began to disperse. Cass and Vivaldo started down the Avenue.

"Shall we take a subway?" Vivaldo asked.

"I don't," she said, "think I could face that now."

They continued to walk, nevertheless, aimlessly, in silence. Cass walked with her hands deep in her pockets, staring down at the cracks in the sidewalk.

"I hate funerals," she said, finally, "they never seem to have anything to do with the person who died."

"No," he said, "funerals are for the living."

They passed a stoop where a handful of adolescents stood, who looked at them curiously.

"Yes," she said. And they kept walking, neither seeming to have the energy it would have demanded to stop and hail a cab. They could not talk about the funeral now; there was too much to say; perhaps each had too much to hide. They walked down the wide, crowded Avenue, surrounded, it seemed, by an atmosphere which prevented others from jostling them or looking at them too directly or for too long a time. They reached the mouth of the subway at 125th Street. People climbed up from the darkness and a group of people stood on the corner, waiting for the bus.

"Let's get that cab," she said.

Vivaldo hailed a cab and they got in—as, she could not help feeling they had been expected to do—and they began to roll away from the dark, the violent scene, over which, now, a pale sun fell.

"I wonder," he said. "I wonder."

"Yes? What do you wonder?"

Her tone was sharper than she had intended, she could not have said why.

"What she means when she says she'll never forget it."

Something was going on in her mind, something she could not name or stop; but it was almost as though she were her mind's prisoner, as though the jaws of her mind had closed on her.

"Well, at least that proves that you're intelligent," she said. "Much good may it do you." She watched the cab roll down the Avenue which would eventually turn into the avenue she knew.

"I'd like to prove to her—one day," he said; and paused. He looked out of the window. "I'd like to make her know that the world's not as black as she thinks it is."

"Or," she said, dryly, after a moment, "as white."

"Or as white," he said, mildly. She sensed that he was refusing to react to her tone. Then he said, "You don't like her —Ida."

"I like her well enough. I don't know her."

"I guess that proves my point," he said. "You don't know her and you don't want to know her."

"It doesn't matter whether I like Ida or not," she said. "The point is, you like her. Well, that's fine. I don't know why you want me to object. I *don't* object. But what difference would it make if I did?"

"None," he said, promptly. Then. "Well, some. I'd worry about my judgment."

"Judgment," she said, "has nothing to do with love."

He looked at her sharply, but with gratitude, too. "For it's love we're talking about—?"

"For what you seem to be trying to prove," she said, "it had better be." She was silent. Then she said, "Of course, she may also have something to prove."

"I think she has something to forget," he said. "I think I can help her forget it."

She said nothing. She watched the cold trees and the cold park. She wondered how Richard's work had gone that morning; she wondered about the children. It seemed, suddenly, that she had been away a long time, had failed very great obligations. And all she wanted in the world right now was to get home safely and find everything as she had left it —as she had left it so long ago, this morning.

"You're so juvenile," she heard herself saying. She was using her most matronly tone. "You know so little"—she smiled—"about life. About women."

He smiled, too, a pale, weary smile. "All right. But I want something real to happen to me. I do. How do you find out about"—he grinned, mocking her—"life? About women? Do you know a lot about men?"

The great numbers above faraway Columbus Circle glowed in the gray sky and said that it was twelve twenty-seven. She would get home just in time to make lunch.

Then the depression she had been battling came down again, as though the sky had descended and turned into fog.

"Once I thought I did," she said. "Once I thought I knew. Once I was even younger than you are now."

Again he stared at her but this time said nothing. For a moment, as the road swerved, the skyline of New York rose before them like a jagged wall. Then it was gone. She lit a cigarette and wondered why, in that moment, she had so hated the proud towers, the grasping antennae. She had never hated the city before. Why did everything seem so pale and so profitless: and why did she feel so cold, as though nothing and no one could ever warm her again?

Low in his throat Vivaldo hummed the blues they had heard at the funeral. He was thinking of Ida, dreaming of Ida, rushing ahead to what awaited him with Ida. For a moment she hated his youth, his expectations, possibilities, she hated his masculinity. She envied Ida. She listened to Vivaldo hum the blues.

CHAPTER 3

On a Saturday in early March, Vivaldo stood at his window and watched the morning rise. The wind blew through the empty streets with a kind of dispirited moan; had been blowing all night long, while Vivaldo sat at his worktable, struggling with a chapter which was not going well. He was terribly weary—he had worked in the bookstore all day and then come downtown to do a moving job—but this was not the reason for his paralysis. He did not seem to know enough about the people in his novel. They did not seem to trust him. They were all named, more or less, all more or less destined, the pattern he wished them to describe was clear to him. But it did not seem clear to them. He could move them about but they themselves did not move. He put words in their mouths which they uttered sullenly, unconvinced. With the same agony, or greater, with which he attempted to seduce a woman, he was trying to seduce his people: he begged them to surrender up to him their privacy. And they refused— without, for all their ugly intransigence, showing the faintest desire to leave him. They were waiting for him to find the key, press the nerve, tell the truth. *Then,* they seemed to be complaining, they would give him all he wished for and much more than he was now willing to imagine. All night long, in an increasing rage and helplessness, he had walked from his worktable to his window and back again. He made himself coffee, he smoked cigarettes, he looked at the clock —and the night wore on, but his chapter didn't and he kept feeling that he ought to get some sleep because today, for the first time in several weeks, he was seeing Ida. This was her Saturday off, but she was having a cup of coffee with one of her girl friends in the restaurant where she worked. He was to meet her there, and then they were to visit Richard and Cass.

Richard's novel was about to be published, and it prom-

ised to be very successful. Vivaldo, to his confusion and relief, had not found it very remarkable. But he had not had
the courage to say this to Richard or to admit to himself
that he would never have read the novel if Richard had not
written it.

All the street sounds eventually ceased—motors, and the
silky sound of tires, footfalls, curses, pieces of songs, and
loud and prolonged good nights; the last door in his building
slammed, the last murmurs, rustling, and creaking ended.
The night grew still around him and his apartment grew cold.
He lit the oven. They swarmed, then, in the bottom of his
mind, his cloud of witnesses, in an air as heavy as the oven
heat, clustering, really, around the desired and unknown Ida.
Perhaps it was she who caused them to be so silent.

He stared into the streets and thought—bitterly, but also
with a chilling, stunned sobriety—that, though he had been
seeing them so long, perhaps he had never known them at
all. The occurrence of an event is not the same thing as
knowing what it is that one had lived through. Most people
had not lived—nor could it, for that matter, be said that they
had died—through any of their terrible events. They had
simply been stunned by the hammer. They passed their lives
thereafter in a kind of limbo of denied and unexamined
pain. The great question that faced him this morning was
whether or not he had ever, really, been present at his life.
For if he had ever been present, then he was present still, and
his world would open up before him.

Now the girl who lived across the street, whose name, he
knew, was Nancy, but who reminded him of Jane—which
was certainly why he never spoke to her—came in from her
round of the bars and the coffee houses with yet another
boneless young man. They were everywhere, which explained how she met them, but why she brought them home
with her was a somewhat more sinister question. Those who
wore their hair long wore beards; those who wore theirs short
felt free to dispense with this useful but somewhat uneasy
emphasis. They read poetry or they wrote it, furiously, as
though to prove that they had been cut out for more masculine pursuits. This morning's specimen wore white trousers
and a yachting cap, and a paranoiac little beard jutted out
from the bottom half of his face. This beard was his most
aggressive feature, his only suggestion of hardness or tension. The girl, on the other hand, was all angles, bone,
muscle, jaw; even her breasts seemed stony. They walked
down the street, hand in hand, but not together. They paused

before her stoop and the girl staggered. She leaned against him in an agony of loathing, belching alcohol; his rigidity suggested that her weight was onerous; and they climbed the short steps to the door. Here she paused and smiled at him, coquettishly raising those stony breasts as she pulled back her hair with her hands. The boy seemed to find this delay intolerable. He muttered something about the cold, pushing the girl in before him.

Well, now, they would make it—make what? not love, certainly—and should he be standing at this window twenty-four hours hence, he would see the same scene repeated with another boy.

How could they endure it? Well, he had been there. How he endured it? Whiskey and marijuana had helped; he was a pretty good liar and that had helped; and most women inspired great contempt in him and that had helped. But there was more to it than that. After all, the country, the world—this city—was full of people who got up in the morning and went to bed at night and, mainly, throughout their lives, to the same bed. They did whatever it was they were supposed to do, and they raised their children. And perhaps he didn't like these people very much, but, then, he didn't, on the other hand, know them. He supposed that they existed because he had been told that they did; presumably, the faces he saw on subways and in the streets belonged to these people, who were admirable because they were numerous. His mother and father and his married sister and her husband and their friends were part of this multitude, and his younger brother would belong to them soon. And what did he know about them, really, except that they were ashamed of him? They didn't know that he was real. It seemed that they didn't, for that matter, know that *they* were real, but he was insufficiently simple to find this notion comforting.

He watched a lone man come up the street, his tight black overcoat buttoned to the neck, looking back from time to time as though he hoped he were being followed. Then the garbage truck came up the street, like a gray brainless insect. He watched the garbage being loaded. Then there was nothing, no one. The light was growing stronger. Soon, alarm clocks would begin to ring and the houses would expel the morning people. Then he thought of the scene which would now be occurring between the boy and the girl in the room.

The yellow electric light, self-consciously indirect, would by now have been discovered to be useless and would have

been turned off. The girl would have taken off her shoes and
turned on her radio or her hi-fi set and would be lying on
the bed. The gray light, coming in through the monk's-cloth
blinds, would, with the malice of the noncommittal, be examining every surface, corner, angle, of the unloved room.
The music would not be loud. They would have poured
drinks by now and the girl's drink would be on the table. The
boy's would be between his hands. He would be sitting on
the bed, turned a little away from the girl, staring at the floor.
His cap would have been pushed farther back. And the
silence, beneath the music, would be tremendous with their
fear. Presently, one of them would make a move to conquer
this. If it were the girl, the movement would be sighing and
halting—sighing because of need, halting because of hostility. If it were the boy, the movement would be harshly or
softly brutal: he would lunge over the girl as though rape
were in his mind, or he would try to arouse her lust by means
of feathery kisses, meant to be burning, which he had seen
in the movies. Friction and fantasy could not fail to produce
a physiological heat and hardness; and this sheathed pressure between her thighs would be the girl's signal to moan.
She would toss her head a little and hold the boy more tightly
and they would begin their descent into confusion. Off would
come the cap—as the bed sighed and the gray light stared.
Then his jacket would come off. His hands would push up
the sweater and unlock the brassière. Perhaps both might
wish to pause here and begin a discovery of each other, but
neither would dare. She moaned and clung to darkness, he
removed the sweater. He struggled unlovingly with her
breasts; the sound of her gasps foreshadowed his failure.
Then the record on the hi-fi came to an end, or, on the radio,
a commercial replaced the love song. He pulled up her skirt.
Then the half-naked girl, with a small, apologetic murmur,
rose from the bed, switched off the machine. Standing in
the center of the room, she might mock her nakedness with
a small, cruel joke. Then she would vanish into the john. The
boy would finish his drink and take off everything except
his undershorts. When the girl reappeared, both would be
ready.

Yes, he had been there: chafing and pushing and pounding, trying to awaken a frozen girl. The battle was awful because the girl wished to be awakened but was terrified of the
unknown. Every movement that seemed to bring her closer
to him, to bring them closer together, had its violent recoil,

driving them farther apart. Both clung to a fantasy rather than to each other, tried to suck pleasure from the crannies of the mind, rather than surrender the secrets of the body. The tendrils of shame clutched at them, however they turned, all the dirty words they knew commented on all they did. These words sometimes brought on the climax—joylessly, with loathing, and too soon. The best that he had ever managed in bed, so far, had been the maximum of relief with the minimum of hostility.

In Harlem, however, he had merely dropped his load and marked the spot with silver. It had seemed much simpler for a time. But even simple pleasure, bought and paid for, did not take long to fail—pleasure, as it turned out, was not simple. When, wandering about Harlem, he came across a girl he liked, he could not fail to wish that he had met her somewhere else, under different circumstances. He could not fail to disapprove of her situation and to demand of her more than any girl in such a situation could give. If he did not like her, then he despised her and it was very painful for him to despise a colored girl, it increased his self-contempt. So that, by and by, however pressing may have been the load he carried uptown, he returned home with a greater one, not to be so easily discharged.

For several years it had been his fancy that he belonged in those dark streets uptown precisely because the history written in the color of his skin contested his right to be there. He enjoyed this, his right to *be* being everywhere contested; uptown, his alienation had been made visible and, therefore, almost bearable. It had been his fancy that danger, there, was more real, more open, than danger was downtown and that he, having chosen to run these dangers, was snatching his manhood from the lukewarm waters of mediocrity and testing it in the fire. He had felt more alive in Harlem, for he had moved in a blaze of rage and self-congratulation and sexual excitement, with danger, like a promise, waiting for him everywhere. And, nevertheless, in spite of all this daring, this running of risks, the misadventures which had actually befallen him had been banal indeed and might have befallen him anywhere. His dangerous, overwhelming lust for life had failed to involve him in anything deeper than perhaps half a dozen extremely casual acquaintanceships in about as many bars. For memories, he had one or two marijuana parties, one or two community debauches, one or two girls whose names he had forgotten, one or two addresses which

he had lost. He knew that Harlem was a battlefield and that
a war was being waged there day and night—but of the war
aims he knew nothing.

And this was due not only to the silence of the warriors—
their silence being, anyway, spectacular in that it rang so
loud: it was due to the fact that one knew of battles only
what one had accepted of one's own. He was forced, little by
little, against his will, to realize that in running the dangers
of Harlem he had not been testing his manhood or heighten-
ing his sense of life. He had merely been taking refuge in
the outward adventure in order to avoid the clash and tension of the adventure proceeding inexorably within. Perhaps
this was why he sometimes seemed to surprise in the dark
faces which watched him a hint of amused and not entirely
unkind contempt. He must be poor indeed, they seemed to
say, to have been driven here. They knew that he was driven,
in flight: the liberal, even revolutionary sentiments of which
he was so proud meant nothing to them whatever. He was
just a poor white boy in trouble and it was not in the least
original of him to come running to the niggers.

This sentiment had sometimes seemed to stare out at him
from the eyes of Rufus. He had refused to see it, for he had
insisted that he and Rufus were equals. They were friends,
far beyond the reach of anything so banal and corny as color.
They had slept together, got drunk together, balled chicks
together, cursed each other out, and loaned each other
money. And yet how much, as it turned out, had each kept
hidden in his heart from the other! It had all been a game, a
game in which Rufus had lost his life. All of the pressures
that each had denied had gathered together and killed him.
Why had it been necessary to deny anything? What had been
the point of the game? He turned into the room again and lit
a cigarette and walked up and down. Well, perhaps they had
been afraid that if they looked too closely into one another
each would have found— He looked out of the window,
feeling damp and frightened. Each would have found the
abyss. Somewhere in his heart the black boy hated the white
boy because he was white. Somewhere in his heart Vivaldo
had feared and hated Rufus because he was black. They had
balled chicks together, once or twice the same chick—why?
And what had it done to them? And then they never saw the
girl again. And they never really talked about it.

Once, while he was in the service, he and a colored buddy
had been drunk, and on leave, in Munich. They were in a
cellar some place, it was very late at night, there were candles

on the tables. There was one girl sitting near them. Who had dared whom? Laughing, they had opened their trousers and shown themselves to the girl. To the girl, but also to each other. The girl had calmly moved away, saying that she did not understand Americans. But perhaps she had understood them well enough. She had understood that their by-play had had very little to do with her. But neither could it be said that they had been trying to attract each other—they would never, certainly, have dreamed of doing it that way. Perhaps they had merely been trying to set their minds at ease; at ease as to which of them was the better man. And what had the black boy thought then? But the question was, What had *he* thought? He had thought, Hell, I'm doing all right. There might have been the faintest pang caused by the awareness that his colored buddy was doing possibly a little better than that, but, indeed, in the main, he had been relieved. It was out in the open, practically on the goddamn table, and it was just like his, there was nothing frightening about it.

He smiled—*I bet mine's bigger than yours is*—but remembered occasional nightmares in which this same vanished buddy pursued him through impenetrable forests, came at him with a knife on the edge of precipices, threatened to hurl him down steep stairs to the sea. In each of the nightmares he wanted revenge. Revenge for what?

He sat down again at his worktable. The page on the typewriter stared up at him, full of hieroglyphics. He read it over. It meant nothing whatever. Nothing was happening on that page. He walked back to the window. It was daylight now, and there were people on the streets, the expected, daytime people. The tall girl, with the bobbed hair and spectacles, wearing a long, loose coat, walked swiftly down the street. The grocery store was open. The old Rumanian who ran it carried in the case of milk which had been deposited on the sidewalk. He thought again that he had better get some sleep. He was seeing Ida today, they were having lunch with Richard and Cass. It was eight o'clock.

He stretched out on the bed and stared up at the cracks in the ceiling. He thought of Ida. He had seen her for the first time in seven years ago. She had been about fourteen. It was a holiday of some kind and Rufus had promised to take her out. And perhaps the reason he had asked Vivaldo to come with him was because Vivaldo had had to loan him money. *Because I can't disappoint my sister, man.*

It had been a day rather like today, bright, cold, and hard.

Rufus had been unusually silent and he, too, had been uncomfortable. He felt that he was forcing himself in where he did not belong. But Rufus had made the invitation and he had accepted; neither of them could get out of it now.

They had reached the house around one o'clock in the afternoon. Mrs. Scott had opened the door. She was dressed as though she, too, were going out, in a dark gray dress a little too short for her. Her hair was short but had lately been treated with the curling iron. She kissed Rufus lightly on the cheek.

"Hey, there," she said, "how's my bad boy?"

"Hey, yourself," said Rufus, grinning. There was an expression on his face which Vivaldo had never seen before. It was a kind of teasing flush of amusement and pleasure; as though his mother, standing there in her high heels, her gray dress, and with her hair all curled, had just done something extraordinarily winning. And this flush was repeated in his mother's darker face as she smiled—gravely—back at him. She seemed to take him in from top to toe and to know exactly how he had been getting along with the world.

"This here's a friend of mine," Rufus said, "Vivaldo."

"How do you do?" She gave him her hand, briefly. The brevity was not due to discourtesy or coldness, simply to lack of habit. Insofar as she saw him at all, she saw him as Rufus's friend, one of the inhabitants of the world in which her son had chosen to live. "Sit down, do. Ida'll be right out."

"She ready?"

"Lord, she been getting ready for days. Done drove me nearly wild." They sat down. Vivaldo sat near the window which looked out on a dirty back yard and the back fire escape of other buildings. Across the way, a dark man sat in front of his half-open window, staring out. In spite of the cold, he wore nothing but an undershirt. There was nothing in the yard except cans, bottles, papers, filth, and a single tree. "If anything had happened and you hadn't showed up, I hate to think of the weeping and wailing that would have gone on in this house." She paused and looked toward the door which led to the rest of the apartment. "Maybe you boys like a little beer while you waiting?"

"That all you got to offer us?" Rufus asked, with a smile. "Where's Bert?"

"Bert's down to the store and he ain't back yet. You know how your father is. He going to be sorry he missed you." She turned to Vivaldo. "Would you like a glass of beer, son? I'm sorry we ain't got nothing else—"

"Oh, beer's fine," said Vivaldo, looking at Rufus. "I'd love a glass of beer."

She rose and walked into the kitchen. "What your friend do? He a musician?"

"Naw," said Rufus, "he ain't got no talent."

Vivaldo blushed. Mrs. Scott returned with a quart bottle of beer and three glasses. She had a remarkably authoritative and graceful walk. "Don't you mind my boy," she said, "he's just full of the devil, he can't help it. I been trying to knock it out of him, but I ain't had much luck." She smiled at Vivaldo as she poured his beer. "You look kind of shy. Don't you be shy. You just feel as welcome here as if you was in your own house, you hear?" And she handed him his glass.

"Thank you," said Vivaldo. He took a swallow of the beer, thinking she'd probably be surprised to know how unwelcome he felt in his own house. And then, again, perhaps she wouldn't be surprised at all.

"You look as though you dressed up to go out someplace, too, old lady."

"Oh," she said, deprecatingly, "I'm just going down the block to see Mrs. Braithwaite. You remember her girl, Vickie? Well, she done had her baby. We going to the hospital to visit her."

"Vickie got a baby? *Already?*"

"Well, the young folks don't wait these days, you know that." She laughed and sipped her beer.

Rufus looked over at Vivaldo with a frown. "Damn," he said. "How's she doing?"

"Pretty well—under the *circumstances*." Her pause suggested that the circumstances were grim. "She had a right fine boy, weighed seven pounds." She was about to say more; but Ida entered.

She was already quite tall, nearly as tall as she was going to be. She, too, had been dealing in hot combs and curling irons, Vivaldo's later impression that she had been in pigtails was due to the fact that her hair had been curled tightly all over her head. The dress she wore was long and blue and full, of some rustling material which billowed above her long legs.

She came into the room, looking only at her brother, with an enormous, childlike smile. He and Rufus stood up.

"You see, I got here," said Rufus, smiling, and he and his sister kissed each other on the cheek. Their mother stood watching them with a proud, frowning smile.

"I see you did," said Ida, moving a little away from him,

and laughing. Her delight in seeing her brother was so real that Vivaldo felt a kind of anguish, thinking of his own house, his own sister. "I been *wondering* if you'd make it—you keep so *busy* all the time."

She said the last word with a wry, proud, grown-up exasperation, as one submitting to the penalties imposed by her brother's power and glory. She had not looked at Vivaldo, though she was vividly aware of him. But Vivaldo would not exist until Rufus permitted it.

He permitted it now, tentatively, with one hand on his sister's neck. He turned her toward Vivaldo. "I brought a friend of mine along, Vivaldo Moore. This is my sister, Ida."

They shook hands. Her handshake was as brief as her mother's had been, but stronger. And she looked at Vivaldo differently, as though he were a glamorous stranger, glamorous not only in himself and his color but in his scarcely to-be-imagined relation to her brother.

"Well, now, where," asked Rufus, teasingly, "do you think you'd like to go, young lady?"

And he watched her, grinning. But there was a constraint in the room now, too, which had not been there before, which had entered with the girl who would soon be a woman. She stood there like a target and a prize, the natural prey of someone—somewhere—who would soon be on her trail.

"Oh, I don't care," she said. "Anywhere you-all want to go."

"But you so dressed up—you sure you ain't ashamed to be seen with us?"

He was also dressed up, in his best dark suit and a shirt and tie he had borrowed from Vivaldo.

Ida and her mother laughed. "Boy, you stop teasing your sister," said Mrs. Scott.

"Well, go on, get your coat," Rufus said, "and we'll make tracks."

"We going *far?*"

"We going far enough for you to have to wear a *coat.*"

"She don't mean is you going far," said Mrs. Scott. "She trying to find out *where* you going and what time you coming back."

Ida had moved to the door by which she had entered and stood there, hesitating. "Go on," her mother said, "get your coat and mine, too. I'm going to walk down the block with you."

Ida left and Mrs. Scott smiled and said, "If she thought I

was coming with you today, she be *highly* displeased. She want you all to herself today."

She picked up the empty beer glasses and carried them into the kitchen. "When they were younger," she said to Vivaldo, "Rufus just couldn't do no wrong, far as Ida was concerned." She ran water to rinse out the glasses. "She always been real afraid of the dark, you know? but, shucks, honey, many's the time Ida used to crawl out of her bed, middle of the night, and go running through this dark house to get in bed with Rufus. Look like she just felt *safe* with him. I don't know why, Rufus sure didn't pay her much mind."

"That's not true," said Rufus, "I was always real sweet to my little sister."

She put the glasses down to drain and dried her hands. She peered into a hand mirror and patted her hair and then carefully put on her hat. "You used to tease her something awful," she said.

Ida returned, wearing a coat trimmed with fur, and with her mother's coat over her arm.

"Ah!" cried Rufus, "she's glamorous!"

"She's beautiful," said Vivaldo.

"Now, if you-all going to make fun of me," said Ida, "I ain't going to come with you nowhere."

Mrs. Scott put on her coat and looked critically at her bareheaded daughter. "If she don't stop being so glamorous, she going to end up with the flu." She pulled Ida's collar up higher and buttoned it. "Can't get nobody in this family to wear a hat," she said, "and then they wonder why they always full of cold." Ida made an impatient gesture. "She afraid a hat going to mess up her hair. But she ain't afraid of the wind doing nothing to it." They laughed, Ida a little unwillingly, as though she were embarrassed that the joke was being shared with Vivaldo.

They walked down the wintry block. Children were playing stickball in the streets, but it was otherwise nearly empty. A couple of boys were standing on a nearby stoop and they greeted Ida and Rufus and Mrs. Scott and looked with interest at Vivaldo; looked at him as though he were a member of an enemy gang, which, indeed, he had been, not very long before. An elderly woman slowly climbed the brownstone steps of a run-down building. A black sign jutted out from the building, saying, in white letters, MOUNT OLIVE APOS-TOLIC FAITH CHURCH.

"I don't know where your father done got to," said Mrs. Scott.

"He right around the corner, in Jimmy's Bar," said Ida, shortly. "I doubt if he be home by the time I get back."

"Because I know you ain't intending to be home before four in the morning," said Mrs. Scott, smiling.

"Well, he ain't going to be home by *then*," said Ida, "and you know it well as I do."

A girl came toward them now, narrow-hipped, swift, and rough-looking. She, too, was bareheaded, with short, dirty, broken-off hair. She wore a man's suede jacket, too large for her, and she held it at the neck with her hand. Vivaldo watched Ida watching the girl approach.

"Here come Willa Mae," said Mrs. Scott. "Poor little thing."

Then the girl stood before them, and she smiled. When she smiled her face was very different. She was very young.

"How you-all today?" she asked. "Rufus, I ain't seen you for the longest time."

"Just fine," Rufus said. "How you making it?" He held his head very high and his eyes were expressionless. Ida looked down at the ground and held on to her mother.

"Oh"—she laughed—"I can't complain. Wouldn't do no good nohow."

"You still at the same place?"

"Sure. Where you think I'm going to move to?"

There was a pause. The girl looked at Vivaldo, looked away. "Well, I got to be going," she said. "Nice running into you." She was no longer smiling.

"Nice seeing you," said Rufus.

After the girl had gone, Ida said disapprovingly, "She used to be your girl friend, too."

Rufus ignored this. He said to Vivaldo, "She used to be a nice girl. Some cat turned her on, and then he split." He spat on the sidewalk. "Man, what a scene."

Mrs. Scott halted before steps leading up into a tenement. Ida took Rufus by the arm. "I got to leave you children here," said Mrs. Scott. She looked at Rufus. "What time you going to bring this girl home?"

"Oh, I don't know. It won't be late. I know she want to go out night-clubbing but I ain't going to let her get *too drunk*."

Mrs. Scott smiled and held out her hand to Vivaldo.

"Nice meeting you, son," she said. "You make Rufus bring you by again, you hear? Don't you be a stranger."

"No, ma'am. Thank you, I'll come up again real soon."

But he never did see her again, not until Rufus was dead. Rufus had never invited him home again.

"I'll be seeing *you* later, young lady," she said. She started up the steps. "You children have a good time."

She had been fourteen or fifteen that day. She would be twenty-one or twenty-two now. She had told him that she remembered that day; but he wondered *how* she remembered it. He had not seen her again until she had become a woman and at that time he had not remembered their first meeting. But he remembered it now. He remembered delight and discomfort. What did she remember?

He thought, I've got to get some sleep. *I've got to get some sleep.* But the people in his novel massed against him. They seemed to watch him with a kind of despairing, beseeching reproach. His typewriter, a dark shapeless presence, accused him, reminding him of the days and nights, the weeks, the months, the years by now, that he had spent without sleep, pursuing easier and less honorable seductions. Then he turned on his belly and his sex accused him, his sex immediately filled with blood. He turned on his back with a furious sigh. He thought, *I'm twenty-eight years old. I'm too old for this bit.* He closed his eyes and he groaned. He thought, *I've got to finish that damn novel,* and he thought, *Oh, God, make her love me, oh God, let me love.*

"What a wonderful day!" cried Ida.

He watched her face for a moment, looking extremely pleased himself, and then delicately increased his pressure on her elbow, more for the pleasure this gave him than to hurry them across the broad, impatient, startling avenue.

"Yes," he said, "it's a great day."

They had just come up from the subway and it was perhaps this ascent from darkness to day which made the streets so dazzling. They were on Broadway at Seventy-second Street, walking uptown—for Cass and Richard had moved, they were climbing that well-known ladder, Cass said. The light seemed to fall with an increased hardness, examining and inciting the city with an unsparing violence, like the violence of love, and striking from the city's grays and blacks a splendor as of steel on steel. In the windows of tall buildings flame wavered, alive, in ice.

There was a high, driving wind which brightened the eyes and the faces of the people and forced their lips slightly apart, so that they all seemed to be carrying, to some immense encounter, the bright, fragile bubble of a lifetime of expectation. Bright boys in windbreakers, some of them with girls whose hair, whose fingertips, caught the light, looked into polished delicatessen windows, the windows of shops, paused at the entrances of movie theaters to look at the gleaming stills; and their voices, which shared the harsh quality of the light which covered them, seemed breaking on the air like glass splinters.

Children, in great gangs and clouds, erupted out of side streets with the sound of roller skates and came roaring down on their elders like vengeance long prepared, or the arrow released from the bow.

"I've never *seen* such a day," he said to Ida, and it was true. Everything seemed to be swollen, thrusting and shifting and changing, about to burst into music or into flame or revelation.

Ida said nothing. He felt, rather than saw her smile, and he was delighted all over again by her beauty. It was as though she were wearing it especially for him. She was more friendly with him today than she had ever been. He did not feel today, as he had felt for so long, that she was evading him, locking herself away from him, forcing him to remain a stranger in her life. Today she was gayer and more natural, as though she had at last decided to come out of mourning. There was in her aspect the flavor of something won, the atmosphere of hard decisions past. She had come up from the valley.

She moved with a wonderful, long-legged stride and she carried her head high, as though it had borne, but only yesterday, the weight of an African water jar. Her mother's head had borne the weight of white folks' washing, and it was because Ida had never known what to make of this fact —should she be ashamed of it, or proud?—that there mingled in her regal beauty something of the too-quick, diffident, plebeian disdain. She was working now as a waitress in a chain restaurant on the eastern edge of the Village and her confusion revealed itself in her attitude toward her customers, an attitude which was at once haughty and free. He had often watched her as she crossed the floor in her checkered apron, her face a dark mask behind which belligerence battled with humility. This was in her eyes which never for an instant lost their wariness and which were always ready, within a split second, to turn black and lightless with contempt. Even when she was being friendly there was something in her manner, in her voice, which carried a warning;

she was always waiting for the veiled insult or the lewd suggestion. And she had good reason for it, she was not being fantastical or perverse. It was the way the world treated girls with bad reputations and every colored girl had been born with one.

Now, as she walked beside him, trim and oddly elegant in a heavy, dark blue coat, and with her head covered by an old-fashioned and rather theatrical shawl, he saw that both her vanity and her contempt were being swollen by the glances which rested on her as briefly and unforgettably as the touch of a whip. She was very, very dark, she was beautiful; and he was proud to be with her, artlessly proud, in the shining, overt, male way; but the eyes they passed accused him, enviously, of a sniggering, back-alley conquest. White men looked at her, then looked at him. They looked at her as though she were no better, though more lascivious and rare, than a whore. And then the eyes of the men sought his, inviting a wet complicity.

The women, too. They saw Ida first and might have been happy to admire her if she had been walking alone. But she was with Vivaldo, which gave her the status of a thief. The means that she had used to accomplish this abduction were beneath or perhaps beyond them, but their eyes briefly accused Vivaldo of betrayal, then narrowed against a dream or a nightmare, and turned away.

Ida strode past, seeming not to see them. She conveyed with this stride and her bright, noncommittal face how far she felt them to be beneath her. She had the great advantage of being extraordinary—however she might bear this distinction, or however others might wish to deny it; whereas, her smile suggested, these people, the citizens of the world's most bewildered city, were so common that they were all but invisible. Nothing was simpler for her than to ignore, or to seem to ignore, these people: nothing was farther beyond them than the possibility of ignoring her. And the disadvantage at which they thus were placed, for which, after all, they had only themselves to blame, said something which Vivaldo could scarcely believe concerning the poverty of their lives.

So their passage raised small clouds of male and female hostility which blew into their faces like dust. And Ida accepted this spiteful tribute with a spiteful pride.

"What are you humming?" he asked. She had been humming to herself for a block or so.

She continued humming for another second, coming to

the end of a phrase. Then she said, smiling, "You wouldn't know it. It's an old church song. I woke up with it this morning and it's been with me all day."

"What is it?" he asked. "Won't you sing it for me?"

"You not about to get religion, are you?" She looked at him sideways, grinning. "I used to have religion, did you know that? A long time ago, when I was a little girl."

"No," he said, "there's a whole lot about you I don't know. Sing your song."

She bent her head toward him, leaning more heavily on his arm, as though they were two children. The colors of the shawl flashed.

She sang, in her low, slightly rough voice, whispering the words to him:

> *I woke up this morning with my mind*
> *Stayed on Jesus.*
> *I woke up this morning with my mind*
> *Stayed on Jesus.*

"That's a great way to wake up," he said.
And she continued:

> *I stayed all day with my mind*
> *Stayed on Jesus.*
> *Hallelu, Hallelu*
> *Hallelujah!*

"That's a great song," he said. "That's tremendous. You've got a wonderful voice, you know that?"

"I just woke up with it—and it made me feel, I don't know —different than I've felt for months. It was just as though a burden had been taken off me."

"You still *do* have religion," he said.

"You know, I think I do? It's funny, I haven't thought of church or any of that type stuff for years. But it's still there, I guess." She smiled and sighed. "Nothing ever goes away." And then she smiled again, looking into his eyes. This shy, confiding smile made his heart move up until it hung like a Ferris wheel at its zenith, looking down at the fair. "It seems to go away," she said in a wondering tone, "but it doesn't, it all comes back." And his heart plunged; he watched her face, framed by the brilliant shawl. "I guess it's true, what they used to tell me—if you can get through the worst, you'll see the best."

They turned off the Avenue, toward Cass's house.

"What a beautiful girl you are," he said. She turned from him, irrepressibly humming her song. "You are, you know."

"Well," she said, and turned toward him again, "I don't know if I'm beautiful or not. But I know you're crazy."

"I'm crazy about *you*. I hope you know *that*."

He said it lightly and did not know if he should curse himself for his cowardice or congratulate himself on his restraint.

"I don't know what I'd have done without you," she said, "these last few months. I know I didn't see much of you, but I knew you were there, I felt it, and it helped—oh, more than I'll ever be able to tell you."

"I had the feeling sometimes," he said, "that you thought I was just being a pest." And now he did curse himself for not saying more precisely what he felt and for sounding so much like a child.

But this was his day, apparently—he seemed to be coming to the end of the tunnel in which he had been traveling so long. "A pest!" she cried, and laughed. "If you aren't the cutest thing." Then, soberly, "I was the one who was the *pest*—but I just couldn't help it."

They turned into a gray, anonymous building which had two functionless pillars on either side of the door and an immense plain of imitation marble and leather beyond it. And he suddenly remembered—it had gone entirely out of his mind—that this lunch was for the purpose of celebrating the publication of Richard's first novel. He said to Ida, "You know, this lunch is a celebration and I forgot to bring anything."

The elevator man rose from his chair, looking at them dubiously, and Vivaldo gave him the floor number and then, as the man still seemed to hesitate, the number of the apartment. He closed the door and the elevator began to move upward.

"What are we celebrating?" Ida asked.

"You and me. We finally have a real date together. You didn't call to break it at the last minute and you haven't said you've got to rush right home after just *one* drink." He grinned at Ida, but he was aware that he was speaking partly for the benefit of the elevator man, whom he had never noticed before. But he disliked him intensely now.

"No, come on, now, what are we *really* celebrating? Or maybe I should say what are Richard and Cass celebrating?"

"Richard's novel. It's published. It'll be in all the book-stores Monday."

"Oh, Vivaldo," she said, "that's wonderful. He must feel *wonderful*. A real, honest-to-God published writer."

"Yes," he said, "one of our boys made it." He was touched by her enthusiasm. And he was aware, at the same time, that she had also been speaking for the benefit of the elevator man.

"It must be wonderful for Cass, too," she said. "And for *you*, he's your friend." She looked at him. "When are you going to bring out *your* novel?"

This question, and even more her way of asking it, seemed to contain implications he scarcely dared to trust. "One of these days," he muttered; and he blushed. The elevator stopped and they walked into a corridor. Richard's door was to the left of them. "It looks like I've got my hands full right now."

"What do you mean? It's not working the way you want it to?"

"The novel, you mean?"

"Yes." Then, as they faced each other before the door, "What did you think I meant?"

"Oh, that's what I thought you meant, all right." He thought, *Now listen, don't spoil it, don't rush it, you stupid bastard, don't spoil it.* "It's just that it's not exactly what *I* meant."

"What *did* you mean?" She was smiling.

"I meant—I hoped I'm going to have my hands full now, with you." She called part of her smile back, but she still looked amused. She watched him. "You know—dinners and lunches and—walks—and movies and things—with you. With you." He dropped his eyes. "You know what I mean?" Then, in the warm, electrical silence, he raised his eyes to hers, and he said, "You know what I mean."

"Well," she said, "let's talk about it after lunch, okay?" She turned from him and faced the door. He did not move. She looked at him with her eyes very wide. "Aren't you going to ring the bell?"

"Sure." They watched each other. Ida reached out and touched him on the cheek. He grabbed her hand and held it for a moment against his face. Very gently, she pulled her hand away. "You are the cutest thing I've ever seen," she said, "you *are*. Go on and ring that bell, I'm hungry."

He laughed and pressed the button. They heard the sour buzzing inside the apartment, then confusion, a slammed door, and footsteps. He took one of Ida's hands in both of his. "I want to be with you," he said. "I want you to be with me. I want that more than I've ever wanted anything in the world."

Then the door opened and Cass stood before them, dressed in a rusty orange frock, her hair pulled back and falling around her shoulders. She held a cigarette in one hand, with which she made a gesture of exaggerated welcome.

"Come in, children," she said, "I'm delighted to see you, but there's absolute chaos in this house today. Everything's gone wrong." She closed the door behind them. They heard a child screaming somewhere in the apartment, and Richard's voice raised in anger. Cass listened for a moment, her forehead wrinkled with worry. "That's Michael," she said, helplessly. "He's been impossible all day—fighting with his brother, with his father, with me. Richard finally gave him a spanking and I guess he's going to leave him in his room." Michael's screams diminished and they heard the voices of Michael and his father working out, apparently, the terms of a truce. Cass lifted her head. "Well. I'm sorry to keep you standing in the hall. Take off your things, I'll show you into the living room and give you things to drink and to nibble on—you'll need them, lunch is going to be late, of course. Ida, how are you? I haven't seen you in God knows when." She took Ida's coat and shawl. "Do you mind if I don't hang them up? I'll just dump them in the bedroom, other people are coming over after lunch." They followed her into the large bedroom. Ida immediately walked over to the large, full-length mirror and worriedly patted her hair and applied new lipstick.

"I'm just fine, Cass," she said, "but you're the one—! You got a famous husband all of a sudden. How does it feel?"

"He's not even famous *yet*," said Cass, "and, already I can't stand it. Somehow, it just seems to reduce itself to having drinks and dinners with lots of people you certainly wouldn't be talking to if they weren't"—she coughed—"in the *profession*. God, what a profession. I had no idea." Then she laughed. They started toward the living room. "Try to persuade Vivaldo to become a plumber."

"No, dear," said Ida, "I wouldn't trust Vivaldo with no tools whatever. This boy is just as clumsy as they come. I'm always expecting him to fall over those front feet he's got. Never saw anybody with so *many* front feet." The living room was down two steps and the wide windows opened on a view of the river. Ida seemed checked, but only for an instant, by the view of the river. She walked into the center of the room. "This is wonderful. You people have really got some space."

"We were really very lucky," Cass said. "The people who had it had been here for years and years and they finally decided to move to Connecticut—or some place like that. I don't remember. Anyway, since they'd been here so long the rent hadn't gone up much, you know? So it's really a lot cheaper than most things like this in the city." She looked over at Ida. "You know, you look wonderful, you really do. I'm so glad to see you."

"I'm glad to see you," said Ida, "and I feel fine, I feel better than I've felt, oh, in years." She crossed to the bar, and stood facing Cass. "Look like you people done got serious about your drinking, too," she said, in a raucous, whiskey voice. "Let me have a taste of that there Cutty Sark."

Cass laughed. "I thought you were a bourbon woman." She dropped some ice in a glass.

"When it cames to liquor," Ida said, "I's *anybody's* woman." And she laughed, looking exactly like a little girl. "Let me have some water in that, sugar, I don't want to get carried away here this afternoon." She looked toward Vivaldo, who stood on the steps, watching her. She leaned toward Cass. "Honey, who's that funny-looking number standing in the do'way?"

"Oh, he drops by from time to time. He always looks that way. He's harmless."

"I'll have the same thing the lady's drinking," said Vivaldo, and joined them at the bar.

"Well, I'm glad you told me he's harmless," Ida said, and winked at him, and drummed her long fingernails on the bar.

"I'll have a short drink with you," said Cass, "and then I'm simply going to have to vanish. I've got to finish fixing lunch—and we have to *eat* it—and I'm not even dressed yet."

"Well, I'll help you in the kitchen," Ida said. "What time are all these other people coming over?"

"About five, I guess. There's this TV producer coming, he's supposed to be very bright and liberal—Steve Ellis, does that sound right?"

"Oh, yes," said Ida, "he's supposed to be very good, that man. He's *very* well known." She mentioned a show of his she had seen some months ago, which utilized Negroes, and which had won a great many awards. "Wow." She wiggled her shoulders. "Who else is coming?"

"Well. Ellis. And Richard's editor. And some other writer whose name I can't remember. And I guess they're bringing their wives." She sipped her drink, looking rather weary. "I can't imagine why we're doing this. I guess it's mainly on account of the TV man. But Richard's publishers are giving Richard a small party Monday—in their offices—and he could just as well see all those people then."

"Buck up, old girl," said Vivaldo. "You're just going to have to get used to it."

"I expect so." She gave them a quick, mischievous grin, and whispered, "But they seem so silly!—those I've met. And they're so *serious,* they just *shine* with it."

Vivaldo laughed. "That's treason, Cass. Be careful."

"I know. They really are getting behind the book, though; they have great hopes for it. You haven't seen it yet, have you?" She walked over to the sofa, where books and papers were scattered and picked the book up, thoughtfully. She crossed the room again. "Here it is."

She put the book down on the bar between Ida and Vivaldo. "It's had great advance notices. You know, 'literate,' 'adult,' 'thrilling'—that sort of thing. Richard'll show them to you. It's even been compared to *Crime and Punishment*—because they both have such a simple story line, I guess." Vivaldo looked at her sharply. "Well, I'm only quoting."

The sun broke free of a passing cloud and filled the room. They squinted down at the book on the bar. Cass stood quietly behind them.

The book jacket was very simple, jagged red letters on a dark blue ground: *The Strangled Men. A novel of murder, by Richard Silenski.* He looked at the jacket flap which described the story and then turned the book over to find himself looking into Richard's open, good-natured face. The paragraph beneath the picture summed up Richard's life, from his birth to the present: *Mr. Silenski is married and is the father of two sons, Paul (11) and Michael (8). He makes his home in New York City.*

He put the book down. Ida picked it up.

"It's wonderful," he said to Cass. "You must be proud." He took her face between his hands and kissed her on the forehead. He picked up his drink. "There's always something wonderful about a book, you know?—when it's really, all of a sudden, a book, and it's there between covers. And there's your name on it. It must be a great feeling."

"Yes," said Cass.

"You'll know that feeling soon," said Ida. She was examining the book intently. She looked up with a grin. "I bet I just found out something you never knew," she said to Vivaldo.

"Impossible," said Vivaldo. "I'm sure I know everything Richard knows."

"*I* wouldn't be so sure," said Cass.

"I bet you don't know Cass's real name."

Cass laughed. "He does, but he's forgotten it."

He looked at her. "That's true, I have. What *is* your real name? I know you hate it, that's why nobody ever uses it."

"Richard just did," she said. "I think he did it just to tease me."

Ida showed him the book's dedication page, which read *for Clarissa, my wife.* "That's cute, isn't it?" She looked at Cass. "You sure had me fooled, baby; you just don't seem to be the Clarissa *type.*"

"As it turned out," said Cass, with a smile. Then she looked at Vivaldo. "Ah," she said, "did you happen to note a very small note in today's theatrical section?" She went to the sofa and picked up one of the newspapers and returned to Vivaldo. "Look. Eric's coming home."

"Who's Eric?" Ida asked.

"Eric Jones," Cass said. "He's an actor friend of ours who's been living in France for the last couple of years. But he's been signed to do a play on Broadway this fall."

Vivaldo read. *Lee Bronson has signed Eric Jones, who last appeared locally three seasons ago in the short-lived* Kingdom of the Blind, *for the role of the elder son in the Lane Smith drama,* Happy Hunting Ground, *which opens here in November.*

"Son of a bitch," said Vivaldo, looking very pleased. He turned to Cass. "Have you heard from him?"

"Oh, no," said Cass, "not for a very long time."

"It'll be nice to see him again," Vivaldo said. He looked at Ida. "You'll like him. Rufus knew him, we were all very good friends." He folded the paper and dropped it on the bar. "Everybody's famous, goddammit, except me."

Richard came into the room, looking harried and boyish, wearing an old gray sweater over a white T-shirt and carrying his belt in his hands.

"It's easy to see what you've been doing," said Vivaldo, smiling. "We heard it all the way in here."

Richard looked at the belt shamefacedly and threw it on

the sofa. "I didn't really use it on him. I just made believe I was going to. I probably should have whaled the daylights out of him." He said to Cass, "What's the matter with him all of a sudden? He's never acted like this before."

"I've already told you what I think it is. It's the new house and kind of new excitement, and he doesn't see as much of you as he's used to, and he's reacted to all of this very badly. He'll get over it, but it's going to take a little time."

"Paul's not like that. Hell, he's gone out and made friends already. He's having a ball."

"Richard, Paul and Michael are not at all *alike*."

He stared at her and shook his head. "That's true. Sorry." He turned to Ida and Vivaldo. "Excuse us. We're fascinated by our offspring. We sometimes sit around and talk about them for hours. Ida, you look wonderful, it's great to see you." He took her hand in his, looking into her eyes. "Are you all right?"

"I'm fine, Richard. And it's wonderful to see *you*. Especially now that you're such a success."

"Ah, you mustn't listen to my wife," he said. He went behind the bar. "Everybody's got a drink except me, I guess. And *I*"—he looked very boyish, very secure and happy— "am going to have a dry martini on the rocks." He opened the ice bucket. "Only, there aren't any rocks."

"I'll get you some ice," Cass said. She put her drink on the bar and picked up the ice bucket. "You know, I think we're going to have to buy some ice from the delicatessen."

"Well, I'll go down and do that later, chicken." He pinched her cheek. "Don't worry."

Cass left the room. Richard grinned at Vivaldo. "If you hadn't got here today, I swore I was just going to cut you out of my heart forever."

"You knew I'd be here." He raised his glass. "Congratulations." Then, "What's this I hear about all the TV networks just crying for you?"

"Don't exaggerate. There's just *one* producer who's got some project he wants to talk to me about, I don't even know what it is. But my agent thinks I should see him."

Vivaldo laughed. "Don't sound so defensive. I *like* TV."

"You're a liar. You haven't even got a TV set."

"Well, that's just because I'm *poor*. When I get to be a success like you, I'll go out and buy me the biggest screen on the market." He watched Richard's face and laughed again. "I'm just teasing you."

"Yeah. Ida, see what you can do to civilize this character. He's a barbarian."

"I know," Ida said, sadly, "but I hardly know what to do about it. Of course," she added, "if you were to offer me an autographed copy of your book, I might come up with an inspiration."

"It's a deal," Richard said. Cass came back with the ice bucket and Richard took it from her and set it on the bar. He mixed his drink. Then he joined them on the other side of the bar and put his arm around Cass's shoulders. "To the best Saturday we've ever had," he said, and raised his glass. "May there be many more." He took a large swallow of his drink. "I love you all," he said.

"We love you, too," said Vivaldo.

Cass kissed Richard on the cheek. "Before I go and try to salvage lunch—tell me, just what kind of arrangement *did* you make with Michael? Just so I'll know."

"He's taking a nap. I promised to wake him in time for cocktails. We have to buy him some ginger ale."

"And Paul?"

"Oh, Paul. He'll tear himself away from his cronies in time to come upstairs and get washed and meet the people. Wild horses wouldn't keep him away." He turned to Vivaldo. "He's been bragging about me all over the house."

Cass watched him for a moment. "Very well managed. And now I leave you."

Ida picked up her glass. "Wait a minute. I'm coming with you."

"You don't have to, Ida. I can do it."

"These men can get drunk, too, if we keep them waiting too long. I'll help you, we can get it done in no time." She followed Cass to the doorway. With one foot on the step, she turned. "Now, I'm going to hold you to your promise, Richard. About that book, I mean."

"I'm going to hold you to yours. You're the one who got the dirty end of *this* deal."

She looked at Vivaldo. "Oh, I don't know. I might think of something."

"I hope you know what you're getting into," Cass said. "I don't like that look on Vivaldo's face at *all*."

Ida laughed. "He *is* kind of simple-looking, I declare. Come on. I'll tell you about it in the kitchen."

"Don't believe a word Cass says about me," Vivaldo called.

"Oh, you mean she *knows* something about you? Come

on, Cass, honey, we going to get down to the knitty-gritty
this afternoon." And they disappeared.

"You've always had a thing about colored girls, haven't
you?" Richard asked, after a moment. There was something
curiously wistful in his voice.

Vivaldo looked at him. "No. I've never been involved with
a colored girl."

"No. But you used to do a lot of tomcatting up in Harlem.
And it's so logical, somehow, that you should be trying to
make it with a colored girl now—you certainly scraped the
bottom of the white barrel."

Against his will, Vivaldo was forced to laugh. "Well, I
don't think Ida's color has a damn thing to do with it, one
way or the other."

"Are you sure? Isn't she just another in your long line of
waifs and strays and unfortunates?"

"Richard," Vivaldo said, and he put his glass down on the
bar, "are you trying to bug me? What is it?"

"Of course I'm not trying to bug you," Richard said. "I
just think that maybe it's time you straightened out—settled
down—time you figured out what you want to do and started
doing it instead of bouncing around like a kid. You're not a
kid."

"Well, I think it's time you stopped treating me like one.
I know what I want to do and I *am* doing it. All right? And
I've got to do it my own way. So get off my back." He smiled,
but it was too late.

"I didn't think I was on your back," said Richard. "I'm
sorry."

"I didn't mean it the way it sounded, you know that."

"Let's just forget it, okay?"

"Well, hell, I don't want you mad at me."

"I'm *not* mad at you." He walked to the window and stood
there, looking out. With his back to Vivaldo, he said, "You
didn't really like my book much, did you?"

"So that's it."

"What?" Richard turned, the sunlight full on his face, revealing the lines in his forehead, around and under his eyes,
and around his mouth and chin. The face was full of lines;
it was a tough face, a good face, and Vivaldo had loved it for
a long time. Yet, the face lacked something, he could not
have said what the something was, and he knew his helpless
judgment was unjust.

He felt tears spring to his eyes. "Richard, we talked about
the book and I told you what I thought, I told you that it

was a brilliant idea and wonderfully organized and beautifully written and—" He stopped. He had not liked the book.
He could not take it seriously. It was an able, intelligent,
mildly perceptive *tour de force* and it would never mean
anything to anyone. In the place in Vivaldo's mind in which
books lived, whether they were great, mangled, mutilated, or
mad, Richard's book did not exist. There was nothing he
could do about it. "And you yourself said that the next book
would be better."

"What are you crying about?"

"What?" He wiped his eyes with the back of his hand.
"Nothing." He walked over to the bar and leaned on it.
Some deep and curious cunning made him add, "You talk as
though you didn't want us to be friends any more."

"Oh, crap. Is that what you think? Of course we're
friends, we'll be friends till we die." He walked to the bar
and put his hand on Vivaldo's shoulder, leaning down to
look into his face. "Honest. Okay?"

They shook hands. "Okay. Don't bug me any more."

Richard laughed. "I *won't* bug you any more, you stupid
bastard."

Ida came to the doorway. "Lunch is on the table. Come
on, now, hurry, before it gets cold."

They were all a little drunk by the time lunch was over,
having drunk with it two bottles of champagne; and eventually they sat in the living room again as the sun began to
grow fiery, preparing to go down. Paul arrived, dirty, breathless, and cheerful. His mother sent him into the bathroom to
wash and change his clothes. Richard remembered the ice
that had to be bought for the party and the ginger ale that he
had promised Michael, and he went downstairs to buy them.
Cass decided that she had better change her clothes and put
up her hair.

Ida and Vivaldo had the living room to themselves for a
short time. Ida put on an old Billie Holiday record and she
and Vivaldo danced.

There was a hammer knocking in his throat as she stepped
into his arms with a friendly smile, one hand in his hand,
one hand resting lightly on his arm. He held her lightly at
the waist. His fingers, at her waist, seemed to have become
abnormally and dangerously sensitive, and he prayed that
his face did not show the enormous, illicit pleasure which
entered him through his fingertips. He seemed to feel, beneath the heavy fabric of the suit she wore, the texture of
the cloth of her blouse, the delicate obstruction which was

the fastening of her skirt, the slick material of her slip which seemed to purr and crackle under his fingers, against her smooth, warm skin. She seemed to be unaware of the liberties being taken by his stiff, unmoving fingers. She moved with him, both guiding and being guided by him, effortlessly keeping her feet out of the path of his great shoes. Their bodies barely touched but her hair tickled his chin and gave off a sweet, dry odor and suggested, as did everything about this girl, a deep, slow-burning, carnal heat. He wanted to hold her closer to him. Perhaps, now, at this very moment, as she looked up at him, smiling, he would lower his head and wipe that smile from her face, placing his unsmiling mouth on hers.

"Your hands are cold," he said, for the hand which held his was very dry, and the fingertips were cool.

"That's supposed to mean that I've got a warm heart," said Ida, "but what it really means is poor circulation."

"I prefer," he said, "to believe that you've got a warm heart."

"I was counting on that," she said, with a laugh, "but when you get to know me better you'll find out that I'm the one who's right. I'm afraid," she said, with a teasing, frowning smile, "that I'm usually right." She added, "About me."

"I wish I knew you better," he said.

"So," she said, with a short, light laugh, "do I!"

Richard returned. Michael, grave and shy, came out of his exile and he and Paul were given ginger ales on the rocks. Cass appeared in a high-necked, old-fashioned, burgundy-colored dress, and with her hair up. Richard put on a sport shirt and a more respectable-looking sweater, and Ida vanished to put on her face. The people began to arrive.

The first to arrive was Richard's editor, Loring Montgomery, a chunky, spectacled, man, with smooth, graying hair, who was younger than he looked—nearly ten years younger, in fact, than Richard. He had a diffident manner and a nervous giggle. With him was Richard's agent, a dark-haired, dark-eyed young woman, who wore much silver and a little gold, and whose name was Barbara Wales. She, too, had a giggle but it was not nervous, and a great deal of manner but it was not diffident. She apparently felt that her status as Richard's agent created a bond of intimacy between herself and Cass; who, helplessly and miserably mesmerized, and handicapped by the volume of Miss Wales's voice and the razorlike distinctness of her syllables, trotted obediently behind her into the bedroom where coats and hats were to be deposited and where the women could repair their make-up.

"The bar is over here," Richard called, "whatever you're drinking, come and get it."

"I could stand another drink," Vivaldo said. "I've been drinking all day and I can't get drunk."

"Are you trying to?" asked Ida.

He looked at her and smiled. "No," he said, "no, I'm not trying to. But if I were, I couldn't make it, not today." They stood facing the window. "You're going to have supper with me, aren't you?"

"You're not hungry, al*ready?*"

"No. But I'm going to be hungry around suppertime."

"Well," she said, "ask me around suppertime."

"You're not suddenly going to decide you have to go home, or anything? You're not going to run out on me?"

"No," she said, "I'm going to stick with you until the bitter end. You've got to talk to that agent, you know."

"Do I have to?" He looked in the direction of the glittering Miss Wales.

"Of course you do. I'm sure it's one of the reasons Richard wanted you here this afternoon. And you have to talk to the editor, too."

"Why? I haven't got anything to show him."

"Well, you *will*. I'm sure Richard arranged all this partly for you. Now, you've got to cooperate."

"And what are you going to be doing while I'm having all these conferences?"

"I'll talk to Cass. Nobody's really interested in us; we don't write."

He kissed her hair. "You *are* the cutest thing," he said.

The doorbell rang. This time it was Steve Ellis, who had come with his wife. Ellis was a short, square man with curly hair and a boyish face. The face was just beginning, as is the way with boyish faces, not so much to harden as to congeal. He had a reputation as the champion of doomed causes, reaction's intrepid foe; and he walked into the drawing rooms of the world as though he expected to find the enemy ambushed there. His wife wore a mink coat and a flowered hat, seemed somewhat older than he, and was inclined to be talkative.

"Great meeting you, Silenski," he said. Though he was compelled to look up to Richard, he did so with his head at an odd and belligerent angle, as though he were looking up in order more clearly to sight down. The hand he extended to Richard with a bulletlike directness suggested also the arrogant limpness of hands which have the power to make or break: only custom prevented the hand from being kissed. "I've been hearing tremendous things about you. Maybe we can have a chat a little later."

And his smile was good-natured, open, and boyish. When he was introduced to Ida, he stood stock-still, throwing out his arms as though he were a little boy.

"You're an actress," he said. "You've *got* to be an actress."

"No," said Ida, "I'm not."

"But you *must* be. I've been looking for you for years. You're sensational!"

"Thank you, Mr. Ellis," she said, laughing, "but I am not an actress." Her laugh was a little strained but Vivaldo could not know whether this was due to nerves or displeasure. People stood in smiling groups around them. Cass stood behind the bar, watching.

Ellis smiled conspiratorially and pushed his head a little forward. "What do you *do,* then? Come on, tell me."

"Well, at the moment," Ida said, rather pulling herself together, "I work as a waitress."

"A waitress. Well, my wife's here, so I won't ask you where you work." He stepped a little closer to Ida. "But what do you think about while you walk around waiting on tables?" Ida hesitated, and he smiled again, coaxing and tender. "Come *on.* You can't tell me that all you want is to get to be head waitress."

Ida laughed. Her lips curved rather bitterly, and she said, "No." She hesitated and looked toward Vivaldo, and Ellis followed her look. "I've sometimes thought of singing. That's what I'd like to do."

"Aha!" he cried, triumphantly, "I knew I'd get it out of you." He pulled a card out of his breast pocket. "When you get ready to make the break, and let it be soon, you come and see me. Don't you forget."

"You won't remember my name, Mr. Ellis." She said it lightly and the look with which she measured Ellis gave Vivaldo no clue as to what was going on in her mind.

"Your name," he said, "is Ida Scott. Right?"

"Right."

"Well, I never forget names or faces. Try me."

"That's true," said his wife, "he never forgets a name or a face. I don't know how he does it."

"I," said Vivaldo, "am not an actress."

Ellis looked startled, then he laughed. "You could have fooled me," he said. He took Vivaldo by the elbow. "Come and have a drink with me. Please."

"I don't know why I said that. I was half-kidding."

"But only half. What's your name?"

"Vivaldo. Vivaldo Moore."

"And you're not an actress—?"

"I'm a writer. Unpublished."

"Aha! You're working on something?"

"A novel."

"What's it about?"

"My novel's about Brooklyn."

"The tree? Or the kids or the murderers or the junkies?" Vivaldo swallowed. "All of them."

"That's quite an assignment. And if you don't mind my saying so, it sounds just a little bit old-fashioned." He put his hand before his mouth and burped. "Brooklyn's been done. And done."

No it hasn't, Vivaldo thought. "You mean," he said, with a smile, "that it doesn't have any TV possibilities?"

"It might have, who knows?" He looked at Vivaldo with friendly interest. "You really have a sneer in your voice when you say TV, you know that? What are you so afraid of?" He tapped Vivaldo on the chest. "Art doesn't exist in a vacuum; it isn't just for you and your handful of friends. Christ, if you knew how sick I am of this sensitive-young-man horseshit!"

"I'm sick of it, too," said Vivaldo. "I don't think of myself as a sensitive young man."

"No? You sound like one and you act like one. You look down your nose at everybody. Yes," he insisted, for Vivaldo looked at him in some surprise, "you think that most people are shit and you'd rather die than get yourself dirtied up in any of the *popular* arts." Then he gave Vivaldo a deliberate, insolent once-over. "And here you are, in your best suit, and I bet you live in some dingy, ice-water apartment and you can't even take your girl out to a night club." His voice dropped. "The colored girl, Miss Scott, you see I do remember names, she's your girl, isn't she? That's why you got pissed off at me. Man, you're too touchy."

"I thought you were too free."

"I bet you wouldn't have felt that if she were a white girl."

"I'd have felt that about any girl who happened to be with me."

But he wondered if Ellis were right. And he realized that he would never know, there would never be any way for him to know. He felt that Ellis had treated Ida with a subtle lack of respect. But he had spoken to her in the only way he could, and it was the way he spoke to everyone. All of the people in Ellis' world approached each other under cover of a manner designed to hide whatever they might really be feeling, about each other or about themselves. When confronted with Ida, who was so visibly rejected from the only world they knew, this manner was forced to become relatively personal, self-conscious, and tense. It became entangled with an effort to avoid being called into judgment; with a fear that their spiritual and social promissory notes might suddenly be called up. By being pressed into the service of an impulse that was real, the manner revealed itself as totally false and because it was false, it was sinister.

Then, as Ellis poured himself another applejack and he poured himself another Scotch, he realized that the things which Ellis had, and the things which Richard was now going to have, were the things that he wanted very much. Ellis could get anything he wanted by simply lifting up a phone; headwaiters were delighted to see him; his signature on a bill or a check was simply not to be questioned. If he needed a suit, he bought it; he was certainly never behind in his rent; if he decided to fly to Istanbul tomorrow, he had only to call his travel agent. He was famous, he was powerful, and he was not really much older than Vivaldo, and he worked very hard.

Also, he could get the highest-grade stuff going; he had only to give the girl his card. And then Vivaldo realized why he hated him. He wondered what he would have to go through to achieve a comparable eminence. He wondered how much he was willing to give—to be powerful, to be adored, to be able to make it with any girl he wanted, to be sure of holding any girl he had. And he looked around for Ida. At the same time, it occurred to him that the question was not really what he was going to "get" but how he was to discover his possibilities and become reconciled to them.

Richard, now, was talking, or, rather, listening to Mrs. Ellis; Ida was listening to Loring; Cass sat on the sofa, listening to Miss Wales. Paul stood near her, looking about the room; Cass held him absently and yet rather desperately by the elbow.

"Anyway—I'd like to keep in touch with you, maybe you've got something." And Ellis handed him his card. "Why don't you give me a ring sometime? and I meant what I said to Miss Scott, too. I produce pretty good shows, you know." He grinned and punched Vivaldo on the shoulder. "You won't have to lower your *artistic* standards."

Vivaldo looked at the card, then looked at Ellis. "Thanks," he said. "I'll bear it in mind."

Ellis smiled. "I like you," he said. "I'm even willing to suggest an analyst for you. Let's join the party."

He walked over to Richard and Mrs. Ellis. Vivaldo walked over to Ida.

"I've been trying to find out about your novel," Loring said, "but your young lady here is *most* cagey. She won't give me a clue."

"I keep telling him that I don't know anything about it," Ida said, "but he won't believe me."

"She doesn't know much about it," Vivaldo said. "I'm not sure I know an awful lot about it myself." Abruptly, he felt himself beginning to tremble with weariness. He wanted to take Ida and go home. But she seemed pleased enough to stay; it was not really late; the last rays of the setting sun were fading beyond the river.

"Well," said Loring, "as soon as you *do* have something, I hope you'll get in touch with me. Richard thinks you're tremendously talented and I'd certainly trust his judgment."

He knew that Ida was puzzled and irritated by the mediocrity of his response. He tried to pump up enthusiasm, and watching Ida's face helped. He could not imagine what she thought of Ellis, and rage at himself, his jealousy, his fear, and his confusion, contributed a saving intensity to his evasive reply. Loring seemed more certain than ever that he was a diamond in the rough, and Ida more certain than ever that he was in need of hands to push him.

And he himself felt, in a way he had not felt before, that it was time for him to take the plunge. This was the water, the people in this room; it impressed him, certainly, as far from fine, but it was the only water there was.

Miss Wales now looked over toward him, but he avoided her eyes, giving all of his attention to Ida.

"Let's go," he said, in a low voice, "let's get out of here. I've had it."

"You want to go *now?* You haven't talked to Miss Wales." But he watched her eyes flicker toward the bar, where Ellis stood. And there was something in her face which he could not read, something speculative and hard.

"I don't *want* to talk to Miss Wales."

"Why on earth *not?* You're being silly."

"Look," he said, "is there someone here *you* want to talk to?" *Oh, you idiot!* he groaned to himself. But the words were said.

She looked at him. "I don't know what you mean. What are you talking about?"

"Nothing," he said, sullenly. "I'm just crazy. Don't mind me."

"You were thinking something. What were you thinking?"

"Nothing," he said, "really nothing." He smiled. "I don't care. We can stay if you want to."

"I was only staying," she said, "on account of you."

He was about to say, Well then, we can *go,* but decided that it would be smarter not to. The doorbell rang. He said, "I just wanted to avoid getting involved in a supper deal with any of these people, that's all."

"But *who,*" she persisted, "did you think I wanted to talk to?"

"Oh," he said, "I thought if you were really serious about that singing business, you might have wanted to make an appointment with Ellis. I imagine he could be helpful."

She looked at him wearily, with mockery and pity. "Oh, Vivaldo," she said, "what a busy little mind you've got." Then her manner changed, and she said, very coldly, "You don't really have the right, you know, to worry about who I talk to. And what you're suggesting doesn't flatter me at *all.*" She kept her voice low, but it had begun to shake. "Maybe, now, I'll behave like what you think I am!" She walked over to the bar and stepped between Richard and Ellis. She was smiling. Ellis put one hand on her elbow and his face changed as he spoke to her, becoming greedier and more vulnerable. Richard went behind the bar to pour Ida a drink.

Vivaldo could have joined them, but he did not dare. Her outburst had come so mysteriously, and with such speed, that he was afraid to think of what might happen if he walked over to the bar. And she was right; he was wrong. Who she talked to was none of his business.

But her reaction had been so swift and terrible! Now, his advantage was gone. His patiently amassed and hoarded capital—of understanding and gallantry—had vanished in the twinkling of an eye.

"I'd like you to meet Sydney Ingram. This is Vivaldo Moore."

Cass was at his shoulder, presenting the newcomer, of

whose arrival he had been vaguely aware. He had come alone. Vivaldo recognized his name because the boy's first novel had just been published and he wanted to read it. He was tall, nearly as tall as Vivaldo, with a pleasant, heavy-featured face and a great deal of black hair and, like Vivaldo, was dressed in a dark suit, probably his best one.

"I'm delighted to meet you," Vivaldo said—sincerely, for the first time that evening.

"I've read his novel," Cass said, "it's wonderful, you must read it."

"I want to," said Vivaldo. Ingram smiled, looking uncomfortable, and stared into his glass as though he wished he could drown in it.

"I've circulated enough for the time being," Cass said. "Let me stay with you two for a while." She led them slowly toward the big window. It was twilight, the sun was gone, soon the street lamps would be turned on. "Somehow, I don't think I'm cut out to be a literary hostess."

"You looked fine to me," said Vivaldo.

"You weren't trying to keep up a conversation with me. My attention just keeps wandering, I can't help it. I might as well be in a room full of physicists."

"What are they talking about over at the bar?" Vivaldo asked.

"Steve Ellis's responsibility to the televiewers of America," Ingram said. They laughed. "Don't laugh," said Ingram, "he, too, can become President. At least, he can read and write."

"I should think," said Cass, "that that would disqualify him."

She took each of them by one arm and they stood together in the darkening window, staring out at the highway and the shining water. "What a great difference there is," she said, "between dreaming of something and dealing with it!" Neither Vivaldo nor Ingram spoke. Cass turned to Ingram and, in a voice he had never heard her use before, wistful and desirous, she asked, "Are you working on something new, Mr. Ingram? I hope you are."

And his voice seemed, oddly, to respond to hers. They might have been calling each other across that breadth of water, seeking for each other as the darkness relentlessly fell. "Yes," he said, "I am, it's a new novel, it's a love story."

"A love story!" she said. Then, "And where does it take place?"

"Oh, here in the city. Now."

There was a silence. Vivaldo felt her small hand, under his elbow, tighten. "I'm looking forward to reading it," she said, "very much."

"Not more," he said, "than I am looking forward to finishing it and having it read, especially, if I may say so, by you."

She turned her face to Ingram, and he could not see her smile but he could feel it. "Thank you," she said. She turned to the window again and she sighed. "I suppose I must get back to my physicists."

They watched the street lamps click on.

"I'm going to have a drink," Cass said. "Will anyone join me?"

"Sure," said Vivaldo. They walked to the bar. Richard, Ellis, and Loring were sitting on the sofa. Miss Wales and Mrs. Ellis were standing at the bar. Ida was not in the room.

"Excuse me," said Vivaldo.

"I think somebody's in there!" cried Miss Wales.

He walked down the hall, but did not reach the bathroom. She was sitting in the bedroom, among all the coats and hats, perfectly still.

"Ida—?"

Her hands were folded in her lap and she was staring at the floor.

"Ida, why are you mad at me? I didn't mean anything." She looked up at him. Her eyes were full of tears.

"Why did you have to say what you said? Everything was fine and I was so happy until you said that. You think I'm nothing but a whore. That's the only reason you want to see me." The tears dripped down her face. "All you white bastards are the same."

"Ida, I swear that isn't true. I swear that isn't true." He dropped to one knee beside the bed and tried to take her hands in his. She turned her face away. "Honey, I'm in love with you. I got scared and I got jealous, but I swear I didn't mean what you thought I meant, I didn't, I couldn't. I love you. Ida, please believe me. I love you."

Her body kept shaking and he felt her tears on his hands. He raised her hands to his lips and kissed them. He tried to look into her face, but she kept her face turned away. "Ida. Ida, please."

"I don't know any of these people," she said, "I don't care about them. They think I'm just another colored girl, and they trying to be nice, but they don't care. They don't want to talk to me. I only stayed because you asked me, and you've been so nice, and I was so proud of you, and now you've spoiled it all."

"Ida," he said, "if I've spoiled things between you and me, I don't know how I'm going to live. You can't say that. You've got to take it back, you've got to forgive me and give me another chance. Ida." He put one hand to her face and slowly turned it toward him. "Ida, I love you, I do, more than anything in this world. You've got to believe me. I'd rather die than hurt you." She was silent. "I was jealous and I was scared and that was a very dumb thing I said. But I was just afraid you didn't care about me. That's all. I didn't mean anything bad about you."

She sighed and reached for her purse. He gave her a handkerchief. She dried her eyes and blew her nose. She looked very tired and helpless.

He moved and sat beside her on the bed. She avoided looking at him but she did not move.

"Ida—" and he was shocked by the sound of his voice, it contained such misery. It did not seem to be his voice, it did not seem to be under his control. "I told you, I love you. Do you care about me?" She rose and walked to the mirror. He watched her. "Please tell me."

She looked into the mirror, then picked up her handbag from the bed. She opened it, closed it, then looked in the mirror again. Then she looked at him, "Yes," she said, helplessly, "yes, I do."

He took her face between his hands and kissed her. At first she did not answer him, seemed merely to be enduring him, seemed suspended, hanging, waiting. She was trembling and he tried to control her trembling with the force of his arms and hands. Then something seemed to bend in her, to give, and she put her arms around him, clinging to him. Finally, he whispered in her ear, "Let's get out of here. Let's go."

"Yes," she said, after a moment, "I guess it's time to go." But she did not step out of his arms at once. She looked at him and she said, "I'm sorry I was so silly. I know you didn't mean it."

"I'm sorry, too. I'm just a jealous, no-good bastard, I can't help it, I'm crazy about you."

And he kissed her again.

"—leaving so soon!" said Miss Wales. "And we never got a chance to talk!"

"Vivaldo," said Cass, "I'll call you this week. Ida, I can't call you, will you call me? Let's get together."

"I'm waiting for a script from you, you bum," said Ellis, "just as soon as you climb down out of that makeshift ivory tower. Nice meeting you, Miss Scott."

"He means it," said Mrs. Ellis. "He really means it."

"I was happy to meet you both," said Ingram, "very happy. Good luck with your novel."

Richard walked them to the door. "Are we still friends?"

"Are you kidding? Of course, we're still friends."

But he wondered if they were.

The door closed behind them and they stood in the corridor, staring at each other.

"Shall we go home?" he asked.

She watched him, her eyes very large and dark. "You got anything to eat down there?"

"No. But the stores are still open. We can get something."

She took his arm and they walked to the elevator. He rang the bell. He stared at her as though he could not believe his eyes.

"Good," she said. "We'll get something and I'll cook you a decent supper."

"I'm not very hungry," he said.

They heard the elevator door slam beneath them and the elevator began to rise.

The smell of the chicken she had fried the night before still hung in the room, and the dishes were still in the sink. The wishbone lay drying on the table, surrounded by the sticky glasses out of which they had drunk beer, and by their sticky coffee cups. Her clothes were thrown over a chair, his were mainly on the floor. He had awakened, she was asleep. She slept on her side, her dark head turned away from him, making no sound.

He leaned up a little and watched her face. Her face would now be, forever, more mysterious and impenetrable than the face of any stranger. Strangers' faces hold no secrets because the imagination does not invest them with any. But the face of a lover is an unknown precisely because it is invested with so much of oneself. It is a mystery, containing, like all mysteries, the possibility of torment.

She slept. He felt that she was sleeping partly in order to avoid him. He fell back on his pillow, staring up at the cracks in the ceiling. She was in his bed but she was far from him; she was with him and yet she was not with him. In some deep, secret place she watched herself, she held herself in check, she fought him. He felt that she had decided, long ago, precisely where the limits were, how much she could afford to give, and he had not been able to make her give a penny more. She made love to him as though it were a technique of pacification, a means to some other end. However she might wish to delight him, she seemed principally to wish to exhaust him; and to remain, above all, herself on the banks of pleasure the while she labored mightily to drown him in the tide. *His* pleasure was enough for her, she seemed to say, his pleasure was hers. But he wanted her pleasure to be his, for them to drown in the tide together.

He had slept, but badly, aware of Ida's body next to his, and aware of a failure more subtle than any he had known before.

And his mind was troubled with questions which he had not before permitted to enter but whose hour, now, had struck. He wondered who had been with her before him; how many, how often, how long; what he, or they before him, had meant to her; and he wondered if her lover, or lovers, had been white or black. What difference does it make? he asked himself. What difference does any of it make? One or more, white or black—she would tell him one of these days. They would learn everything about each other, they had time, she would tell him. Would she? Or would she merely accept his secrets as she accepted his body, happy to be the vehicle of his relief? While offering in return (for she knew the rules) revelations intended to pacify and also intended to frustrate him; to frustrate, that is, any attempt on his part to strike deeper into that incredible country in which, like the princess of fairy tales, sealed in a high tower and guarded by beasts, bewitched and exiled, she paced her secret round of secret days.

It was early in the morning, around seven, and there was no sound anywhere. The girl beside him stirred silently in her sleep and threw one hand up, as though she had been frightened. The scarlet eye on her little finger flashed. Her heavy hair was wild and tangled and the face she wore in sleep was not the face she wore when awake. She had taken off all her make-up, so that she had scarcely any eyebrows, and her unpainted lips were softer now, and defenseless. Her skin was darker than it was in the daytime and the round, rather high forehead held a dull, mahogany sheen. She looked like a little girl as she slept, but she was not a very trusting little girl; one hand half-covered her face and the other was hidden between her thighs. It made him think, somehow, of all the sleeping children of the poor. He touched her forehead lightly with his lips, then eased himself quietly out of bed and went into the bathroom. When he came out he stood staring for a moment at the kitchen, then lit a cigarette, and brought an ashtray back to the bed with him. He lay on his belly, smoking, his long arms dangling to the floor, where he had placed the ashtray.

"What time is it?"

He leaned up, smiling. "I didn't know you were awake." And, strangely, he suddenly felt terribly shy, as though this was his first time to awaken, naked, next to a naked girl.

"Oh," she said, "I like to watch people when they think I'm asleep."

"That's good to know. How long have you been watching me?"

"Not long. Just when you came out of the bathroom. I saw your face and I wondered what you were thinking about."

"I was thinking about you." Then he kissed her. "Good morning. It's seven-thirty."

"My Lord. Do you always wake up so early?" And she yawned and grinned.

"No. But I guess I couldn't wait to see you again."

"Now, I'm going to remember that," she said, "when you start waking up at noon and even later and act like you don't want to get up out of the bed."

"Well, I may not be so anxious to jump right out of *bed*." She motioned for his cigarette and he held it for her while she took a drag or two. Then he put the cigarette out in the ashtray. He leaned over her. "How about you?"

"You're sweet," she said, and, after a moment, "you're a deep-sea diver." Each of them blushed. He put his hands on her breasts, which were heavy and wide apart, with reddish-brown nipples. Her large shoulders quivered a little, a pulse beat in her neck. She watched him with a face at once troubled and detached, calm, and, at the same time, frightened.

"Love me," he said. "I want you to love me."

She caught one of his hands as it moved along her belly.

"You think I'm one of those just-love-to-love girls."

"Baby," he said, "I sure hope so; we're going to be great, let me tell you. We haven't even started yet." His voice had dropped to a whisper and their two hands knotted together in a teasing tug of war.

She smiled. "How many times have you said *that?*"

He paused, looking over her head at the blinds which held back the morning. "I don't believe I've ever said it. I've never felt this way before." He looked down at her again and kissed her again. "Never."

After a moment she said, "Neither have I." She said it quickly, as though she had just popped a pill into her mouth and were surprised at its taste and apprehensive about its effects.

He looked into her eyes. "Is that true?"

"Yes." Then she dropped her eyes. "I've got to watch my step with you."

"Why? Don't you trust me?"

"It's maybe that I don't trust myself."

"Maybe you've never loved a man before," he said.

"I've never loved a white man, that's the truth."

"Oh, well," he said, smiling, trying to empty his mind of the doubts and fears which filled it, "be my guest." He kissed her again, a little drunk with her heat, her taste, her smell. "Never," he said, gravely, "never anyone like you." Her hand relaxed a little and he guided it down. He kissed her neck and shoulders. "I love your colors. You're so many different, crazy colors."

"Lord," she said, and laughed, sharply, nervously, and tried to move her hand away, but he held it: the tug of war began again. "I'm the same old color all over."

"You can't see yourself all over. But I can. Part of you is honey, part of you is copper, some of you is gold—"

"Lord. What're we going to do with you this morning?"

"I'll show you. Part of you is black, too, like the entrance to a tunnel—"

"Vivaldo." Her head hit the pillow from side to side in a kind of torment which had nothing to do with him, but for which, just the same, he was responsible. He put his hand on her forehead, already beginning to be damp, and was struck by the way she then looked at him; looked at him as though she were, indeed, a virgin, promised at her birth to him, the bridegroom; whose face she now saw for the first time, in the darkened bridal chamber, after all the wedding guests had gone. There was no sound of revelry anywhere, only silence, no help anywhere if not in this bed, violation by the bridegroom's body her only hope. Yet she tried to smile. "I've never met a man like you before." She said this in a low voice, in a tone that mixed hostility with wonder.

"Well, I told you—I've never met a girl like you before,

either." But he wondered what kind of men she *had* known. Gently, he forced her thighs open; she allowed him to place her hand on his sex. He felt that, for the first time, his body presented itself to her as a mystery and that, immediately, therefore, he, Vivaldo, became totally mysterious in her eyes. She touched him for the first time with wonder and terror, realizing that she did not know how to caress him. It was being borne in on her that he wanted *her:* this meant that she no longer knew what he wanted. "You've slept with lots of girls like me before, haven't you? With colored girls."

"I've slept with lots of all kinds of girls." There was no laughter between them now; they whispered, and the heat between them rose. Her odor rose to meet him, it mingled with his own, sharper sweat. He was between her thighs and in her hands, her eyes stared fearfully into his.

"But with colored girls, too?"

"Yes."

There was a long pause, she sighed a long, shuddering sigh. She arched her head upward, away from him. "Were they friends of my brother's?"

"No. No. I paid them."

"Oh." Her head dropped, she closed her eyes, she brought her thighs together, then opened them. The covers were in his way and he threw them off and then for a moment, half-kneeling, he stared at the honey and the copper and the gold and the black of her. Her breath came in short, sharp, trembling gasps. He wanted her to turn her face to him and open her eyes.

"Ida. Look at me."

She made a sound, a kind of moan, and turned her face toward him but kept her eyes closed. He took her hand again.

"Come on. Help me."

Her eyes opened for a second, veiled, but she smiled. He lowered himself down upon her, slowly, allowing her hands to guide him, and kissed her on the mouth. They locked together, shaking, her hands fluttered upward and settled on his back. *I paid them.* She sighed again, a different sigh, long and surrendering, and the struggle began.

It was not like the thrashing of the night before, when she bucked beneath him like an infuriated horse or a beached fish. Now she was attentive to the point of trembling and because he felt that one thoughtless moment would send her slipping and sliding away from him, he was very attentive, too. Her hands moved along his back, up and down, sometimes seeming to wish to bring him closer, sometimes being tempted to push him away, moved in a terrible, a beautiful indecision, and caused him, brokenly, deep in his throat, to moan. She opened up before him, yet fell back before him, too; he felt that he was traveling up a savage, jungle river, looking for the source which remained hidden just beyond the black, dangerous, dripping foliage. Then, for a moment, they seemed to be breaking through. Her hands broke free, her thighs inexorably loosened, their bellies ground cruelly together, and a curious, low whistle forced itself up through her throat, past her bared teeth. Then she was checked, her hands flew up to his neck, the moment passed. He rested. Then he began again. He had never been so patient, so determined, or so cruel before. Last night she had watched him; this morning he watched her; he was determined to bring her over the edge and into his possession, even, if at the moment she finally called his name, the heart within him burst. This, anyway, seemed more imminent than the spilling of his seed. He was aching in a way he had never ached before, was congested in a new way, and wherever her hands had touched him and then fled, he was cold. Her hands clung to his neck as though she were drowning and she was absolutely silent, silent as a child is silent before it finally summons enough breath to scream, before the blow lands, before the long fall begins. And, ruthlessly, viciously, he pushed her to the edge. He did not know whether her body moved with his or not, her body was so nearly his. He felt the bed throbbing beneath them, and heard it sing. Her hands went wild, flying from his neck to his throat to his shoulders, his chest; she began to thrash beneath him, trying to get away and trying to come closer. Her hands, at last, had their own way and grasped his friendly body, caressing and scratching and burning. *Come on. Come on.* He felt a tremor in her belly, just beneath him, as though something had broken there, and it rolled tremendously upward, seeming to divide her breasts, as though he had split her all her length. And she moaned. It was a curiously warning sound, as though she were holding up one hand against the ocean. The sound of her helplessness caused all of his affection, tenderness, desire, to return. They were almost there. *Come on come on come on come on. Come on!* He began to gallop her, whinnying a little with delight, and, for the first time, became a little cold with fright, that so much of himself, so long dammed up, must now come pouring out. Her moans gave way to sobs and cries. *Vivaldo. Vivaldo. Vivaldo.* She was over the edge.

He hung, hung, clinging to her as she clung to him, calling her name, wet, itching, bursting, blind. It began to pour out of him like the small weak trickle that precedes disaster in the mines. He felt his whole face pucker, felt the wind in his throat, and called her name again, while all the love in him rushed down, rushed down, and poured itself into her.

After a long time, he felt her fingers in his hair and he looked into her face. She was smiling—a thoughtful, baffled smile. "Get your big, white self off me. I can't move."

He kissed her, weary as he could be, and peaceful.

"Tell me something first."

She looked sly and amused and mocking; very much like a woman and very much like a shy, little girl. "What do you want to know?"

He shook her, laughing. "Come on. Tell me."

She kissed him on the tip of his nose. "It never happened to me before—not like this, never."

"Never?"

"Never. Almost—but no, never." Then, "Was I good for you?"

"Yes. Yes. Don't ever leave me."

"Let me get up."

He rolled over on his back and she got out of bed and walked into the bathroom. He watched the tall, dusty body, which now belonged to him, disappear. He heard water running in the bathroom, then he heard the shower. He fell asleep.

He woke up in the early afternoon. Ida was standing before the stove, singing.

> *If you can't give me a dollar,*
> *Give me a lousy dime—*

She had washed the dishes, cleaned up the kitchen, and hung up his clothes. Now she was making coffee.

> *Just want to feed*
> *This hungry man of mine.*

BOOK TWO

ANY DAY NOW

*Why don't you take me in your
arms and carry me out of this lonely place?*
—CONRAD, *Victory*

CHAPTER 1

Eric sat naked in his rented garden. Flies buzzed and boomed in the brilliant heat, and a yellow bee circled his head. Eric remained very still, then reached for the cigarettes beside him and lit one, hoping that the smoke would drive the bee away. Yves's tiny black-and-white kitten stalked the garden as though it were Africa, crouching beneath the mimosas like a panther and leaping into the air.

The house and the garden overlooked the sea. Far down the slope, beyond the sand of the beach, in the thunderous blue of the Mediterranean, Yves's head went under, reappeared, went under again. He vanished entirely. Eric stood up, looking out over the sea, almost poised to run. Yves liked to hold his breath under water for as long as possible, a test of endurance which Eric found pointless and, in Yves's case, frightening. Then Yves's head appeared again, and his arm flashed. And, even from this distance, Eric could see that Yves was laughing—he had known that Eric would be watching from the garden. Yves began swimming toward the beach. Eric sat down. The kitten rushed over and rubbed itself against his legs.

It was the end of May. They had been in this house for more than two months. Tomorrow they were leaving. Not for a long time, perhaps never again, would Eric sit in a garden watching Yves in the water. They would take the train for Paris in the morning and, after two days there, Yves would put Eric on the boat for New York. Eric was to get settled there and then Yves was to join him.

Now that it had all been decided and there could be no turning back, Eric felt a sour and savage apprehension. He watched as Yves stepped out of the water. His brown hair was bleaching from the sun and glowed about his head; his long, wiry body was as brown as bread. He bent down to lift off the scarlet bikini. Then he pulled on an old pair of blue

jeans which he had expropriated from Eric. They were somewhat too short for him, but no matter—Yves was not very
fond of Americans, but he liked their clothes. He stalked up
the slope, toward the house, the red cloth of the bikini
dangling from one hand.

Yves had never mentioned going to America and had
never given Eric any reason to suppose that he nourished
such a desire. The desire arrived, or was, in any case, stated,
only when the possibility arose: for Eric had slowly graduated from near-starvation to dubbing French films to bit
roles in some of the American films produced abroad. One
of these bits had led to television work in England; and then
a New York director had offered him one of the principal
supporting parts in a Broadway play.

This offer had presented Eric with the enormous question
he had spent three years avoiding. To accept it was to bring
his European sojourn to an end; not to accept it was to trans-
form his sojourn into exile. He and Yves had been together
for more than two years and, from the time of their meeting,
his home had been with Yves. More precisely and literally, it
was Yves who had come to live with him, but each was, for
the other, the dwelling place that each had despaired of
finding.

Eric did not want to be separated from Yves. But when
he told Yves that, for this reason, he had decided to reject
the offer, Yves looked at him shrewdly, and sighed. "Then
you should have rejected it right away, or you should never
have told me about it at all. You are being sentimental—
you are maybe being, even, a little cowardly, no? You will
never make a *carriére* here in France, you know that as well
as I. You will just grow old and discontented and you will
make me a terrible life and then *I* will leave *you*. But you can
become a great star, I think, if you play this part. Wouldn't
you like that?"

He paused, smiling, and Eric shrugged, then blushed.
Yves laughed.

"How silly you are!" Then, "I, too, have dreams that I
have never spoken of to you," he said. He was still smiling,
but there was an expression in his eyes which Eric had come
to know. It was the look of a seasoned and able adventurer,
trying to decide between pouncing on his prey and luring his
prey into a trap. Such decisions are necessarily swift and so
it was also the look of someone who was already irresistibly
in motion toward whatever it was he wanted; who would

certainly have it. This expression always frightened Eric a little. It seemed not to belong in Yves's twenty-one-year-old face, to have no relation to his open, childlike grin, his puppylike playfulness, the adolescent ardor with which he embraced, then rejected, people, doctrines, theories. This expression made his face extremely bitter, profoundly cruel, ageless; the nature, the ferocity, of his intelligence was then all in his eyes; the extraordinary austerity of his high forehead prefigured his maturity and decay.

He touched Eric lightly on the elbow, as a very young child might do.

"I have no wish to stay here," he said, "in this wretched mausoleum of a country. Let us go to New York. I will make my future there. There is no future here, for a boy like me."

The word *future* caused in Eric a small trembling, a small recoil.

"You'll hate America," he said, with vehemence. Yves looked at him in surprise. "What kind of future are you dreaming of?"

"I am sure that there is something I can do there," Yves said, stubbornly. "I can find my way. Do you really think that I want to be protected by you forever?" And he considered Eric for a moment as though they were enemies or strangers.

"I didn't know you minded being—*protected*—by me."

"Ne te fâche pas. I do not *mind* it; if I minded it, I would be gone." He smiled and said, gently, reasonably, "But it cannot go on forever, I also am a *man.*"

"What cannot go on forever?" But he knew what Yves meant and he knew that what Yves said was true.

"Why," said Yves, "my youth. It cannot last forever." Then he grinned. "I have always been sure that you would be returning to your country one day. It might as well be now, while you are still fond of me, and I can seduce you into taking me along."

"You're a great little old seducer," said Eric, "and that's the truth."

"Ah," said Yves, wickedly, "with you it was easy." Then he looked at Eric gravely. "So it is decided." It was not a question. "I suppose that I must go and visit my whore of a mother and tell her that she will never see me any more."

And his face darkened and his large mouth grew bitter. His mother had been a bistro waitress when the Germans came to Paris. Yves had then been five years old and his

father had vanished so long before that Yves could scarcely
remember him. But he remembered watching his mother
with the Germans.

"She was really a *putain*. I remember many times sitting
in the café, watching her. She did not know I was watching
—anyway, old people think that children never see anything.
The bar was very long, and it curved. I would always be
sitting behind it, at the far end, around the curve. There was
a mirror above me and I could see them in the mirror. And
I could see them in the zinc of the bar. I remember their
uniforms and the shine on their leather boots. They were
always extremely *correct*—not like the Americans who came
later. She would always be laughing, and she moved very
fast. Someone's hand was always on her—in her bosom, up
her leg. There was always another one at our house, the
whole German army, coming all the time. How horrible a
people."

And then, as though to give his mother a possible, reluctant justice:

"Later, she says that she do it for me, that we would not
have eaten otherwise. But I do not believe that. I think she
liked that. I think she was always a whore. She always managed everything that way. When the Americans came, she
found a very pretty officer. He was very nice to me, I must
say—he had a son of his own in the States that he had only
seen one time, and he pretended that *I* was his son, though I
was much older than his son would have been. He made me
wish that *I* had a father, *one* father, especially"—he grinned
—"an American father, who liked to buy you things and
take you on his shoulder everywhere. I was sorry when he
went away. I am sure that it was he who kept her from getting
her head shaved, as she deserved. She told all kinds of lies
about her work in the Resistance. *Quelle horreur!* that
whole time, it was not very pretty. Many women had their
heads shaved, sometimes for nothing, you know? just because they were pretty or someone was jealous or they had
refused to sleep with someone. But not my mother. *Nous,
nous étions tranquille avec nôtre petit officier* and our beef-
steak and our chocolate candy."

Then, with a laugh:

"Now, she owns that bistro where she used to work. You
see what kind of woman she is? I never go there."

This was not entirely true. He had run away from his
mother at fifteen. Or, more accurately, they had established
a peculiar truce, to the effect that he would make no trouble

for her—that is, he would stay out of the hands of the law; and she would make no trouble for him—that is, she would not use his minority status as a means of having him controlled by the law. So Yves had lived by his wits in the streets of Paris, as a semi-*tapette,* and as a *rat d'hôtel,* until he and Eric had met. And during all this time, at great intervals, he visited his mother—when he was drunk or unbearably hungry or unbearably sad; or, rather, perhaps, he visited the bistro, which was different now. The long, curving counter had been replaced by a long, straight one. Neon swirled on the ceiling and above the mirrors. There were small, plastic-topped tables, in bright colors, and bright, plastic chairs instead of the wooden tables and chairs Yves remembered. There was a juke box now where the soldiers had clumsily manipulated the metal football players of the *baby-foot;* there were Coca-Cola signs, and Coca-Cola. The wooden floor had been covered with black plastic. Only the WC remained the same, a hole in the floor with foot-rests next to it, and torn newspaper hanging from a string. Yves went to the bistro blindly, looking for something he had lost, but it was not there any longer.

He sat in the old, vanished corner and watched his mother. The hair which had been brown was now of a chemical and improbably orange vitality. The figure which had been light was beginning to thicken and spread and sag. But her laugh remained, and she still seemed, in a kind of violent and joyless helplessness, to be seeking and fleeing the hands of men.

Eventually, she would come to his end of the bar.

"Je t'offre quelque chose, m'sieu?" With a bright, forced, wistful smile.

"Un cognac, madame." With a wry grin, and the sketch of a sardonic bow. When she was halfway down the bar, he yelled. *"Un double!"*

"Ah! Bien sûr, m'sieu."

She brought him his drink and a small drink for herself, and watched him. They touched glasses.

"A la vôtre, madame."

"A la vôtre, m'sieu."

But sometimes he said:

"A nos amours."

And she repeated dryly:

"A nos amours!"

They drank in silence for a few seconds. Then she smiled.

"You look very well. You have become very handsome. I'm proud of you."

"Why should you be proud of me? I am just a good-for-nothing, it is just as well that I am good-looking, that's how I live." And he watched her. *"Tu comprends, hein?"*

"If you talk that way, I want to know nothing, nothing, of your life!"

"Why not? It is just like yours, when you were young. Or maybe even now, how can I tell?"

She sipped her cognac and raised her chin. "Why don't you come back? You can see for yourself how well the bar does, it would be a good situation for you. *Et puis*—"

"Et puis quois?"

"I am no longer very, very young, it would be *un soulagement* if my son and I could be friends."

And Yves laughed. "You need friends? Go dig up some of those that you buried in order to get this bar. Friends! *Je veut vivre, moi!"*

"Ah, you are ungrateful." Sometimes, when she said this, she dabbed at her eyes with a handkerchief.

"Don't bother me any more, you know what I think of you, go back to your clients." And the last word was thrown at his mother, like a curse; sometimes, if he were drunk enough, there were tears in his eyes.

He would let his mother get halfway down the bar before he shouted.

"Merci, pour le cognac, madame!"

And she turned, with a slight bow, saying:

"De rien, m'sieu."

Eric had been there with him once, and had rather liked Yves's mother, but they had never gone back. And they had scarcely ever spoken of it. There was something hidden in it which Yves did not want to see.

Now, Yves leaped over the low stone wall and entered the garden, grinning.

"You should have come in the water with me, it was wonderful. It would do wonders for your figure; do you know how fat you are getting?"

He flicked at Eric's belly with his bikini and fell on the ground beside him. The kitten approached cautiously, sniffing Yves's foot as though it were investigating some prehistoric monstrosity, and Yves grabbed it, holding it against his shoulder, and stroking it. The kitten closed its eyes and began to purr.

"You see how she loves me? It is a pity to leave her here, let us take her with us to New York."

"Getting *you* into America is going to be hassle enough,

baby, let's not rock the boat. Besides, New York is full of
alley cats. And alleys." He said this with his eyes closed,
drinking in the sun and the odors of the garden and the
dark, salty odors of Yves. The children from the nearby
house were still on the beach; he could hear their voices.

"You have no sympathy for animals. She will suffer terribly when we go away."

"She'll recover. Cats are much stronger than people."

He kept his eyes closed. He felt Yves turn to look down
at him.

"Why are you so troubled about going to New York?"

"New York's a very troubling place."

"I am not afraid of trouble." He touched Eric lightly on
the chest and Eric opened his eyes. He stared up into Yves's
grave, brown, affectionate face. "But *you* are. You are afraid
of trouble in New York. Why?"

"I'm not *afraid*, Yves. But I *have* had a lot of trouble
there."

"We have had much trouble here, too," said Yves, with
his abrupt and always rather shocking gravity, "and we have
always come out of it and now we are better than ever, I
think, no?"

"Yes," said Eric, slowly, and watched Yves's face.

"Well, then, what use is there to worry?" He pushed
Eric's hair back from his forehead. "Your head is hot. You
have been in the sun too long."

Eric grabbed his hand. The kitten leaped away. "Jesus.
I'm going to miss you."

"It is for so short a time. You will be busy, I will be in
New York before you know we have been apart." He grinned
and put his chin on Eric's chest. "Tell me about New York.
You have many friends there? Many *famous* friends?"

Eric laughed. "Not many famous friends, no. I don't know
if I have *any* friends there now, I've been away so long."

"Who were your friends when you left?" He grinned again
and rubbed his cheek against Eric's. "Boys like me?"

"There *are* no boys like you. Thank God."

"You mean not so pretty as I? Or not so warm?"

He put his hands on Yves's salty, sandy shoulders. He
heard the children's voices from the sea and the buzzing and
booming in the garden. "No. Not so impossible."

"Naturally, now that you are about to leave, you find me
impossible. And from what point of view?"

He drew Yves closer. "From every point of view."

"C'est dommage. Moi, je t'aime bien."

These words were whispered against his ear, and they lay still for a few moments. Eric wanted to ask, Is that true? but he knew that it was true. Perhaps he did not know what it meant, but, there, Yves could not help him. Only time might help, time which surrendered all secrets but only on the inexorable condition, as far as he could tell, that the secret could no longer be used.

He put his lips to Yves's shoulder and tasted the Mediterranean salt. He thought of his friends—what friends? He was not sure that he had ever really been friends with Vivaldo or Richard or Cass; and Rufus was dead. He was not certain who, long, long after the event, had sent him the news—he had the feeling that it had to be Cass. It could scarcely have been Vivaldo, who was made too uneasy by what he knew of Eric's relation to Rufus—knew without being willing to admit that he knew; and it would certainly not have been Richard. No one, in any case, had written very often; he had not really wanted to know what was happening among the people he had fled; and he felt that they had always protected themselves against any knowledge of what was happening in him. No, Rufus had been his only friend among them. Rufus had made him suffer, but Rufus had dared to know him. And when Eric's pain had faded, and Rufus was far away, Eric remembered only the joy that they had sometimes shared, and the timbre of Rufus's voice, his half-beat, loping, cocky walk, his smile, the way he held a cigarette, the way he threw back his head when he laughed. And there was something in Yves which reminded him of Rufus—something in his trusting smile and his brave, tough vulnerability.

It was a Thursday when the news came. It was pouring down rain, all of Paris was wavering and gray. He had no money at all that day, was waiting for a check which was mysteriously entangled in one of the bureaucratic webs of the French cinema industry. He and Yves had just divided the last of their cigarettes and Yves had gone off to try and borrow money from an Egyptian banker who had once been fond of him. Eric had then lived on the Rue de la Montagne Ste. Geneviève, and he labored up this hill, in the flood, bareheaded, with water dripping down his nose and eyelashes and behind his ears and down his back and soaking through his trench-coat pocket, where he had unwisely placed the cigarettes. He could practically feel them disintegrating in the moist, unclean darkness of his pocket, not at all protected by his slippery hand. He was in a kind of numb despair and intended simply to get home and take off his clothes and stay in bed until help came; help would probably be Yves, with the money for sandwiches; it would be just enough help to enable them to get through yet another ghastly day.

He traversed the great courtyard and started up the steps of his building; and behind him, near the *porte-cochère,* the bell of the concierge's *loge* sounded, and she called his name.

He went back, hoping that she was not going to ask him about his rent. She stood in her door, with a letter in her hand.

"This just came," she said. "I thought it might be important."

"Thank you," he said.

She, too, hoped that it might be the money he was waiting for, but she closed her door behind her. It was nearly suppertime and she was cooking; in fact, the entire street seemed to be cooking, and his legs threatened to give way beneath him.

He did not look carefully at the outside of the envelope because his mind was entirely occupied by the recalcitrant check, and he was not expecting a check from America, which was where the letter came from; and he crumpled it up, unread, in his trench-coat pocket and crossed the courtyard and went upstairs to his room. There, he put the letter on the table, dried himself, and undressed and got under the covers. Then he lay the cigarettes out to dry, lit the driest one, and looked at the letter again. It seemed a very ordinary letter, until the paragraph beginning *We were all very fond of him, and I know that you were, too*—yes, it must have been Cass who wrote. Rufus was dead, and by his own hand. Rufus was dead.

Boys like me? Yves had teased. How could he tell the boy who lay beside him now anything about Rufus? It had taken him a long while to realize that one of the reasons Yves had so stirred his heart, stirred it in a way he had almost forgotten it could be stirred, was because he reminded him, somehow, somewhere, of Rufus. And it had taken him almost until this very moment, on the eve of his departure, to begin to recognize that part of Rufus's great power over him had to do with the past which Eric had buried in some deep, dark place; was connected with himself, in Alabama, *when I wasn't nothing but a child;* with the cold white people and the warm, black people, warm at least for him, and as necessary as the sun

which bathed the bodies of himself and his lover now. Lying
in this garden now, so warm, covered, and apprehensive,
he saw them on the angular, blazing streets of his childhood,
and in the shuttered houses, and in the fields. They laughed
differently from other people, so it had seemed to him, and
moved with more beauty and violence, and they smelled like
good things in the oven.

But had he ever loved Rufus? Or had it simply been rage
and nostalgia and guilt? and shame? Was it the body of
Rufus to which he had clung, or the bodies of dark men, seen
briefly, somewhere, in a garden or a clearing, long ago, sweat
running down their chocolate chests and shoulders, their
voices ringing out, the white of their jock-straps beautiful
against their skin, one with his head tilted back before a
dipper—and the water splashing, sparkling, singing down!—
one with his arm raised, laying an axe to the base of a tree?
Certainly he had never succeeded in making Rufus believe
he loved him. Perhaps Rufus had looked into his eyes and
seen those dark men Eric saw, and hated him for it.

He lay very still, feeling Yves's unmoving, trusting weight,
feeling the sun.

"Yves—?"

"*Oui, mon chou?*"

"Let's go inside. I think, maybe, I'd like to take a shower
and have a drink. I'm beginning to feel sticky."

"*Ah, les américains avec leur* drinks! I will surely become
an alcoholic in New York." But he raised his head and kissed
Eric swiftly on the tip of his nose and stood up.

He stood between Eric and the sun; his hair very bright,
his face in shadow. He looked down at Eric and grinned.

"*Alors tu es toujours prêt, toi, d'après ce que je vois.*"
Eric laughed. "*Et toi, salaud?*"

"*Mais moi, je suis français, mon cher, je suis pas puritain,
fort heureusement. T'aura du te rendre compte d'ailleurs.*"
He pulled Eric to his feet and slapped him on the buttocks
with the red bikini. "*Viens.* Take your shower. I think we
have almost nothing left to drink, I will bicycle down to the
village. What shall I get?"

"Some whiskey?"

"Naturally, since that is the most expensive. Are we eating
in or out?"

They started into the house, with their arms around each
other.

"Try to get Madame Belet to come and cook something
for us."

"What do you want to eat?"

"I don't care. Whatever you want."

The house was long and low, built of stone, and very cool and dark after the heat and brightness of the kitchen. The kitten had followed them in and now murmured insistently at their feet.

"Perhaps I will feed her before I go. It will only take a minute."

"She can't be hungry yet, she eats all the time," said Eric. But Yves had already begun preparing the kitten's food.

They had entered through the kitchen and Eric walked through it and through the dining salon, into their bedroom, and threw himself down on the bed. The bedroom also had an entrance on the garden. The mimosas pressed against the window, and beyond these were two or three orange trees, holding hard, small oranges, like Christmas balls. There were olive trees in the garden, too, but they had been long untended; it was not worth anyone's while to pick the olives.

The script of the new play was on the plain wooden table which, along with the fireplace in the dining room, had persuaded them to rent the house; on the table, too, were a few books, Yves's copies of Blaise Cendrars and Jean Genet and Marcel Proust, Eric's copies of *An Actor Prepares* and *The Wings of the Dove* and *Native Son*. Yves's sketch pad was on the floor. So were his tennis shoes and his socks and his underwear, all of these embracing Eric's sport shirts and sandals and bathing trunks—less explicit and more somber than Yves's bikini, these last, as Eric himself was less explicit and more somber.

Yves clattered into the bedroom.

"Are you going to take that shower or not?"

"Yes. Right away."

"Well, start. I am leaving now, I will be back in a moment."

"I know your moments. Try not to get too drunk with the natives." He grinned and stood up.

Yves picked up a pair of socks from the floor, put them on, and put on his tennis shoes, and a faded blue pullover. "Ah. *Celui-là, je te jure.*" He took a comb from his pocket and pulled it through his hair, with the result that it stood up more wildly than ever.

"I'll put you on your bicycle."

They walked past the mimosas. "Hurry back," said Eric, smiling, staring at Yves.

Yves picked up his bicycle. "I will be back before you are

dry." He rolled the bicycle through the gate and onto the road. Eric stood in the garden, watching him. The light was still very bright but, in the mysterious way of southern light, was gathering itself together and would soon be gone. Already, the sea looked darker.

Once past the gate, Yves did not look back. Eric turned into the house.

He stepped into the shower, which was off the bedroom. He fumbled with the knobs, and the water came crashing over him, first too cold, but he forced himself to take it, then too hot; he fumbled with the knobs until the water became more bearable. He soaped himself, wondering if he were really getting fat. His belly seemed firm enough, but he had always had a tendency to be chunky and square; it was just as well that he would soon, in New York, be going again to the gym. And the thought of the gym, while the water fell down over him, he was alone with his body and the water, caused many painful and buried things to stir in him. Now that his flight was so rigorously approaching its end, a light appeared, a backward light, throwing his terrors into relief.

And what were these terrors? They were buried beneath the impossible language of the time, lived underground where nearly all of the time's true feeling spitefully and incessantly fermented. Precisely, therefore, to the extent that they were inexpressible, were these terrors mighty; precisely because they lived in the dark were their shapes obscene. And because the taste for obscenity is universal and the appetite for reality rare and hard to cultivate, he had nearly perished in the basement of his private life. Or, more precisely, his fantasies.

These fantasies began as fantasies of love and soured imperceptibly into fantasies of violence and humiliation. When he was little he had been very much alone, for his mother was a civic leader, always busy with clubs and banquets and speeches and proposals and manifestoes, aloft forever on a sea of flowered hats; and his father, rather submerged by this glittering and resounding tide, made his home in the bank and on the golf course, in hunting lodges, and at poker tables. There seemed to be very little between his father and his mother, very little, that is, beyond habit and courtesy and coercion; and perhaps each had loved him, but this was never real to him, since they so clearly did not love each other. He had loved the cook, a black woman named Grace, who fed him and spanked him and scolded and coddled him, and dried the tears which scarcely anyone else in the household ever saw. But, even more than he had loved Grace, he had loved her husband, Henry.

Henry was younger, or seemed younger, than his wife. He was a trial to Grace, and probably to them all, because he drank too much. He was the handyman and one of his duties was the care of the furnace. Eric still remembered the look and the smell of the glaring furnace room, the red shadows from the furnace playing along the walls, and the sticky-sweet smell of Henry's breath. They had spent many hours together there, Eric on a box at Henry's knee, Henry with his hand on Eric's neck or shoulder. His voice fell over Eric like waves of safety. He was full of stories. He told the story of how he had met Grace, and how he had seduced her, and how (as he supposed) he had persuaded her to marry him; told stories of preachers and gamblers in his part of town— they seemed, in his part of town, to have much in common, and, often, to be the same people—how he had outwitted this one and that one, and how, once, he had managed to escape being put on the chain gang. (And he had explained to Eric what a chain gang was.) Once, Eric had walked into the furnace room where Henry sat alone; when he spoke, Henry did not answer; and when he approached him, putting his hand on Henry's knee, the man's tears scalded the back of his hand. Eric no longer remembered the cause of Henry's tears, but he would never forget the wonder with which he then touched Henry's face, or what the shaking of Henry's body had caused him to feel. He had thrown himself into Henry's arms, almost sobbing himself, and yet somehow wise enough to hold his own tears back. He was filled with an unutterably painful rage against whatever it was that had hurt Henry. It was the first time he had felt a man's arms around him, the first time he had felt the chest and belly of a man; he had been ten or eleven years old. He had been terribly frightened, obscurely and profoundly frightened, but he had not, as the years were to prove, been frightened enough. He knew that what he felt was somehow wrong, and must be kept a secret; but he thought that it was wrong because Henry was a grown man, and colored, and he was a little boy, and white.

Henry and Grace were eventually banished, due to some lapse or offense on Henry's part. Since Eric's parents had never approved of those sessions in the furnace room, Eric always suspected this as the reason for Henry's banishment, which made his opposition to his parents more bitter than ever. In any case, he lived his life far from them, at school by day and before his mirror by night, dressed up in his mother's old clothes or in whatever colorful scraps he had been able to collect, posturing and, in a whisper, declaiming. He knew that this was wrong, too, thought he could not have said why. But by this time he knew that everything he did was wrong in the eyes of his parents, and in the eyes of the world, and that, therefore, everything must be lived in secret.

The trouble with a secret life is that it is very frequently a secret from the person who lives it and not at all a secret for the people he encounters. He encounters, because he *must* encounter, those people who see his secrecy before they see anything else, and who drag these secrets out of him; sometimes with the intention of using them against him, sometimes with more benevolent intent; but, whatever the intent, the moment is awful and the accumulating revelation is an unspeakable anguish. The aim of the dreamer, after all, is merely to go on dreaming and not to be molested by the world. His dreams are his protection against the world. But the aims of life are antithetical to those of the dreamer, and the teeth of the world are sharp. How could Eric have known that his fantasies, however unreadable they were for him, were inscribed in every one of his gestures, were betrayed in every inflection of his voice, and lived in his eyes with all the brilliance and beauty and terror of desire? He had always been a heavy, healthy boy, had played like other children, and fought as they did, made friends and enemies and secret pacts and grandiose plans. And yet none of his playmates, after all, had ever sat with Henry in the furnace room, or ever kissed Henry on his salty face. They did not, weighed down with discarded hats, gowns, bags, sashes, earrings, capes, and necklaces, turn themselves into make-believe characters after everyone in their house was asleep. Nor could they possibly, at their most extended, have conceived of the people he, in the privacy of night, became: his mother's friends, or his mother—his mother as he conceived her to have been when she was young, his mother's friends as his mother was now; the heroines and heroes of the novels he read, and the movies he saw; or people he simply put together out of his fantasies and the available rags. No doubt, at school, the boy with whom he was wrestling failed to feel the curious stabs of terror and pleasure that Eric felt, as they grappled with each other, as one boy pinned the other to the ground; and if Eric saw the girls at all, he saw mainly their clothes and their hair; they were not, for him, as were the boys, creatures in a hierarchy, to be adored or feared or despised. None of them looked on each other as he looked on all of them. His dreams were different—subtly and cruelly and criminally different: this was not known yet, but it was felt. He was menaced in a way that they were not, and it was perhaps this sense, and the instinct which compels people to move away from the doomed, which accounted for the invincible distance, increasing with the years, which stretched between himself and his contemporaries.

And, of course, in Eric's case, in Alabama, his increasing isolation and strangeness was held, even by himself, to be due to the extreme unpopularity of his racial attitudes—or, rather, as far as the world in which he moved was concerned, the lack of any responsible attitudes at all. The town in which Eric lived was celebrated and well-to-do, but it was not very big; as far as Eric was concerned, the South was not very big, certainly, as it turned out, not big enough for him; and he was the only son of very prominent people. So it was not long before his appearance anywhere caused heads to shake, lips to purse, tongues to stiffen or else, violently, venomously, to curl around his name. Which was also, however, his father's name, and Eric, therefore, encountered, very often and very soon, the hideous obsequiousness of people who despised him but who did not dare to say so. They had long ago given up saying anything which they really felt, had given it up so long ago that they were now incapable of feeling anything which was not felt by a mob.

Now, Eric stepped out of the shower, rubbing his body with the enormous, rough, white towel Yves had placed in the bathroom for him. Yves did not like showers, he preferred long, scalding baths, with newspapers, cigarettes, and whiskey on a chair next to the bathtub, and with Eric nearby to talk to, to shampoo his hair, and to scrub his back. The thought of the Oriental opulence which overtook Yves each time he bathed caused Eric to smile. He smiled, but he was troubled, too. And as he put on his bathrobe, his body tingled less from the effect of the towel and the toilet water than from his image, abruptly overwhelming, of Yves leaning back in the bathtub, whistling, the washrag in his hand, a peaceful, abstracted look on his face and his sex gleaming and bobbing in the soapy water like a limp, cylindrical fish; and from his memory, to which his image was somehow the gateway, of that moment, nearly fifteen years ago, when the blow had inexorably fallen and his shame and his battle and his exile had begun. He walked into the dining room and poured himself a drink. Then the bottle was empty and he dropped it in the waste basket. He lit a cigarette and sat down in a chair near the window, overlooking the sea. The sun was sinking and the sea was on fire.

The sun had been sinking on that far-off day, a Sunday, a hot day. The church bells had ceased and the silence of the South hung heavy over that town. The trees along the walks gave no shade. The white houses, with their blank front doors, their blackly shadowed porches, seemed to be in battle with the sun, laboring and shuddering beneath the merciless light. Occasionally, passing a porch, one might discern in its depths a still, shadowed, faceless figure. The interminable pickaninnies were playing in the invincible dirt— where Eric was walking that day, on a back road, near the edge of town, with a colored boy. His name was LeRoy, he was seventeen, a year older than Eric, and he worked as a porter in the courthouse. He was tall and very black, and taciturn; Eric always wondered what he was thinking. They had been friends for a long time, from the time of Henry's banishment. But now their friendship, their effort to continue an impossible connection, was beginning to be a burden for them both. It would have been simpler—perhaps— if LeRoy had worked for Eric's family. Then all would have been permitted, would have been covered by the assumption of Eric's responsibility for his colored boy. But, as things were, it was suspect, it was indecent, that a white boy, especially of Eric's class and difficult reputation, should "run," as Eric incontestably did, after one of his inferiors. Eric had no choice but to run, to insist—LeRoy could certainly not come visiting him.

And yet there was something absolutely humiliating in his position; he felt it very sharply and sadly, and he knew that LeRoy felt it, too. Eric did not know, or perhaps he did not want to know, that he made LeRoy's life more difficult and increased the danger in which LeRoy walked—for LeRoy was considered "bad," as lacking, that is, in respect for white people. Eric did not know, though of course LeRoy did, what was already being suggested about him all over town. Eric had not guessed, though LeRoy knew only too well, that the Negroes did not like him, either. They suspected the motives of his friendliness. They looked for the base one and naturally they found it.

So, shortly before, when Eric had appeared in the road, his hands in his pockets, a hoarse, tuneless whistle issuing from his lips, LeRoy had jumped off his porch and come to meet him, striding toward Eric as though he were an enemy.

There was a snicker from LeRoy's porch, quickly muffled; a screen door slammed; every eye on the street was on them.

Eric stammered, "I just dropped by to see what you were doing."

LeRoy spat in the dusty road. "Ain't doing nothing. Ain't you got nothing to do?"

"You want to take a walk?" Eric asked.

For a moment it really seemed that LeRoy was going to refuse, for his scowl deepened. Then a faint smile touched his lips. "Okay. But I can't walk far. I got to get back."

They began to walk. "I want to get out of this town," Eric said, suddenly.

"You and me both," said LeRoy.

"Maybe we can go North together," Eric said, after a moment, "where do you think's best? New York? or Chicago? or maybe San Francisco?" He had wanted to say Hollywood, because he had a dim notion of trying to become a movie star. But he could not really imagine LeRoy as a movie star, and he did not want to seem to want anything LeRoy could not have.

"I can't be thinking about leaving. I got my Ma and all them kids to worry about." He looked at Eric and laughed, but it was not an entirely pleasant laugh. "Ain't everybody's old man runs a bank, you know." He picked up a pebble and threw it at a tree.

"Hell, my old man don't give me no money. He certainly won't give me any money to go North. He wants me to stay right here."

"He going to die one day, Eric, he going to have to leave it to somebody, now who you think it's going to be? Me?" And he laughed again.

"Well, I'm not going to hang around here the rest of my life, waiting for my papa to die. That's certainly not much to look forward to."

And he tried to laugh, to match his tone to LeRoy's. But he did not really understand LeRoy's tone. What was wrong between them today? For it was no longer merely the world —there was something unspoken between them, something unspeakable, undone, and hideously desired. And yet, on that far-off, burning day, though this knowledge clamored in him and fell all around him, like the sun, and everything in him was aching and yearning for the act, he could not, to save his soul, have named it. It had yet to reach the threshold of his imagination; and it had no name, no name for him anyway, though for other people, so he had heard, it had dreadful names. It had only a shape and the shape was LeRoy and LeRoy contained the mystery which had him by the throat.

And he put his arm around LeRoy's shoulder and rubbed the top of his head against LeRoy's chin.

"Well, you got it to look forward to, whether you like it or not," LeRoy said. He put one hand on Eric's neck. "But I guess you know what *I* got to look forward to." And Eric felt that he wished to say more, but did not know how. They walked on a few seconds in silence and LeRoy's opportunity came. A cream-colored roadster, bearing six young people, three white boys and three white girls, came up the road in a violent swirl and wake of dust. Eric and LeRoy did not have time to move apart, and a great laugh came from the car, and the driver beat out a mocking version of the wedding march on his horn—then kept his entire palm on it as the car shot down the road, away. All of the people in the car were people with whom Eric had grown up.

He felt his face flame and he and LeRoy moved away from each other; and LeRoy looked at him with a curiously noncommittal pity.

"Now *that's* what you supposed to be doing," he said—he said it very gently, looking at Eric, licking his lower lip—"and *that's* where you supposed to be. You *ain't* supposed to be walking around this damn country road with no nigger."

"I don't give a damn about those people," Eric said—but he knew that he was lying and he knew that LeRoy knew it, too—"those people don't mean a thing to me."

LeRoy looked more pitying than ever, and also looked exasperated. The road now was empty, not a creature moved on it; it was yellow-red and brown and trees leaned over it, with fire falling through the leaves; and the road now began to drop beneath them, toward the railroad tracks and the warehouse. This was the town's dividing line and they always turned off the road at this point, into a clump of trees and a rise which overlooked a stream. LeRoy now turned Eric into this haven. His touch was different today; insistent, gentle, ferocious, and resigned.

"Besides," said Eric, helplessly, "you're not a nigger, not for me, you're LeRoy, you're my friend, and I love you." The words took his breath away and tears came to his eyes and they paused in the fiery shadow of a tree. LeRoy leaned against the tree, staring at Eric, with a terrible expression on his black face. The expression on LeRoy's face frightened him, but he labored upward against his fear, and brought out, "I don't know why people can't do what they want to do; what *harm* are we doing to anybody?"

LeRoy laughed. He reached out and pulled Eric against him, under the shadow of the leaves. "Poor little rich boy," he said, "tell me what you want to *do*." Eric stared at him. Nothing could have moved him out of LeRoy's arms, away from his smell, and the terrible, new touch of his body; and yet, in the same way that he knew that everything he had ever wanted or done was wrong, he knew that this was wrong, and he felt himself falling. Falling where? He clung to LeRoy, whose arms tightened around him. "Poor boy," LeRoy murmured again, "poor boy." Eric buried his face in LeRoy's neck and LeRoy's body shook a little—*the chest and belly of a man!*—and then he pushed Eric away and guided him toward the stream and they sat down beside it.

"I guess you know, now," LeRoy said, after a long silence, while Eric trailed his hand in the water, "what they saying about us in this town. I don't care but it can get us in a lot of trouble and you got to stop coming to see me, Eric."

He had *not* known what they were saying, or he had been unable to allow himself to know; but he knew now. He said, staring into the water, and with a totally mysterious abandon, "Well, if we've got the name, we might as well have the game is how I see it. I don't give a shit about those people, let them all go to hell; what have they got to do with you and me?"

LeRoy looked briefly over at Eric and smiled. "You a nice boy, Eric, but you don't know the score. Your Daddy *owns* half the folks in this town, ain't but so much they can do to you. But what they can do to *me*—!" And he spread his hands wide.

"I won't let anything happen to you."

LeRoy laughed. "You *better* get out of this town. Declare, they going to lynch you before they get around to me." He laughed again and rubbed his hand in Eric's bright red hair.

Eric grabbed his hand. They looked at each other, and a total, a dreadful silence fell. "Boy," LeRoy said, weakly. And then, after a moment, "You really out for trouble, ain't you?" And then nothing was said. They lay together beside the stream.

That day. That day. Had he known where that day would lead him would he have writhed as he did, in such an anguished joy, beneath the great weight of his first lover? But if he had known, or been capable of caring, where such a day might lead him, it could never have been his necessity to bring about such a day. He was frightened and in pain and the boy who held him so relentlessly was suddenly a stranger; and yet this stranger worked in Eric an eternal, a healing transformation. Many years were to pass before he could begin to accept what he, that day, in those arms, with the stream whispering in his ear, discovered; and yet that day was the beginning of his life as a man. What had always been hidden was to him, that day, revealed and it did not matter that, fifteen years later, he sat in an armchair, overlooking a foreign sea, still struggling to find the grace which would allow him to bear that revelation. For the meaning of revelation is that what is revealed is true, and must be borne.

But how to bear it? He rose from his seat and paced restlessly into the garden. The kitten lay curled on the stone doorstep, in the last of the sun, asleep. Then he heard Yves's bicycle bell and, shortly, Yves's head appeared above the low stone wall. He passed, looking straight ahead, and then Eric heard him in the kitchen, bumping into things and opening and closing the icebox door.

The Yves stood beside him.

"Madame Belet will be here in a few moments. She is cooking for us a chicken. And I have bought some whiskey and some cigarettes." Then he looked at Eric and frowned. "You are mad to be standing here in your bathrobe. The sun is down and it is getting cold. Come in and get dressed, I will make us both a drink."

"What would I do without you?"

"I wonder." Eric followed him into the house. "I also bought some champagne," Yves said, suddenly, and he turned to face Eric with a small, shy smile, "to celebrate our last night here." Then he walked into the kitchen. "Get dressed," he called, "Madame Belet will be here soon."

Eric stepped into the bedroom and began putting on his clothes. "Are we going out after dinner?"

"Perhaps. That depends. If we are not too drunk on champagne."

"I'd just as soon stay in, I think."

"Oh, perhaps we must have just one last look at our little seaside town."

"We have to get packed, you know, and clean up this house a little, and try to get some sleep."

"Madame Belet will clean it for us. Anyway, we would never be able to get it done. We can sleep on the train. And we do not have so very much to pack."

Eric heard him washing the glasses. Then he began to whistle a tune which sounded like a free improvisation on Bach. Eric combed his hair, which was too long. He decided that he would get it cut very short before he went back to the States.

Eventually, they sat, as they had sat so many evenings, before the window which overlooked the sea. Yves sat on the hassock, the back of his head resting on Eric's knee.

"I will be very sad to leave here," Yves said, suddenly. "I have never been happier than I have been in this house."

Eric stroked Yves's hair and said nothing. He watched the lights that played on the still, black sea, from the sky and the shore.

"I have been very happy, too," he said at last. And then: "I wonder if we will ever be so happy again."

"Yes, why not? But that is not so important—anyway, no matter how happy I may become, and I am sure that I shall have great moments yet, this house will always stay with me. I found out something here."

"And what was that?"

Yves turned his head and looked up at Eric. "I was afraid that I would just remain a street boy forever, that I was no better than my mother." He turned away, toward the window again. "But, somehow, down here in this house with you, I finally realized that that is not so. I have not to be a whore just because I come from whores. I am better than that." He stopped. "I learned that from you. That is really strange, for, you know? in the beginning I thought you thought of me like that. I thought that you were just another sordid American, looking for a pretty, degenerate boy."

"But you are not pretty," Eric said, and sipped his whiskey. "*Au fait, tu es plutôt moche.*"

"Oh, *Ça va.*"

"Your nose turns up." He stroked the tip of Yves's nose. "And your mouth's too big"—Yves laughed—"and your forehead's too high and soon you won't have any hair." He stroked Yves's forehead, stroked his hair. "And those ears, baby! you look like an elephant or a flying machine."

"You are the first person who ever say that I am ugly. Perhaps that is why I am intrigued." He laughed.

"Well. Your eyes are not too bad."

"*Tu parle. J'ai du chien, moi.*"

"Well, yes, baby, now that you mention it, I'm afraid you've got a point."

They were silent for a moment.

"I have been with so many horrible people," Yves said, gravely, "so soon, and for so long. Really, it is a wonder that I am not completely *sauvage*." He sipped his whiskey. Eric could not see his face, but he could imagine the expression it held: hard and baffled and terribly young, with the cruelty that comes from pain and fear. "First, my mother and all those soldiers, *ils étaient mes oncles, tous*," and he laughed, "and then all those awful, slimy men, I no longer know how many." He was silent again. "I lay in the bed, sometimes we never got to bed, and let them grunt and slobber. Some of them were really fantastic, no whore has ever told the truth about who comes to her, I am sure of that, they would chop off her head before they would dare to hear it. But it is happening, it is happening all the time." He leaned up, hugging his knees, staring at the sea. "Then I would take their money; if they made difficulties I could scare them because I was *mineur*. Anyway, it was very easy to scare them. Most of those people are cowards." Then he said, in a low voice, "I never thought that I would be happy to have a man touch me and hold me. I never thought that I would be able, truly, to make love with a man. Or with anyone."

"Why," Eric asked at last, "didn't you use women instead of men, as you despised the men so much?"

Yves was silent. Then, "I don't know. *D'abord*, I took what there was—or allowed what there was to take *me*," and he looked at Eric and grinned. He sipped his whiskey and stood up. "It is simpler with men, it is usually shorter, the money is easier. Women are much more cunning than men, especially those women who would go after a boy like me, and even more unattractive, really." He laughed. "It is much harder work, and it is not so sure." His face dropped again into its incongruous, austere melancholy. "You do not meet many women in the places I have been; you do not meet many human persons at all. They are all dead. Dead." He stopped, his lips pursed, his eyes glittering in the light that fell through the window. "There were many whores in my mother's place, but—well, yes, there have been a few women, but I couldn't stand them, either." He moved to the window and stood there with his back to Eric. "I do not like *l'élégance des femmes*. Every time I see a woman wearing her fur coats and her jewels and her gowns, I want to tear all that off her and drag her some place, to a *pissoir*, and make her smell the smell of many men, the *piss* of many men, and make her know that *that* is what she is for, she is no better than that, she does not fool me with all those shining rags, which, anyway, she only got by blackmailing some stupid man."

Eric laughed, but he was frightened. *"Comme tu es féroce!"* He watched Yves turn from the window and slowly pace the room—long and lean, like a stalking cat, and in the heavy shadows. And he saw that Yves's body was changing, was losing the adolescent, poverty-stricken harshness. He was becoming a man.

And he watched that sullen, wiry body. He watched his face. The dome of his forehead seemed more remarkable than ever, and more pure, and his mouth seemed, at once, more cruel and more defenseless. This nakedness was the proof of Yves's love and trust, and it was also the proof of Yves's force. Yves, one day, would no longer need Eric as he needed Eric now.

Now, Yves tilted back his head and finished his drink and turned to Eric with a smile.

"You are drinking very slowly tonight. What is the matter?"

"I'm getting old." But he laughed and finished his drink and handed his glass to Yves.

And, as Yves walked away from him, as he heard him in the kitchen, as he looked out over the yellow, winking lights along the shore, something opened in him, an unspeakable despair swept over him. Madame Belet had arrived and he heard Yves and the old peasant woman in the kitchen. Their voices were muted.

On the day that Yves no longer needed him, Eric would drop back into chaos. He remembered that army of lonely men who had used him, who had wrestled with him, caressed him, and submitted to him, in a darkness deeper than the darkest night. It was not merely his body they had used, but something else; his infirmity had made him the receptacle of an anguish which he could scarcely believe was in the world. This anguish rendered him helpless, though it also lent him his weird, doomed grace and power, and it baffled him and set the dimensions of his trap. Perhaps he had sometimes dreamed of walking out of the drama in which he was entangled and playing some other role. But all the exits were barred—were barred by avid men; the role he played was necessary, and not only to himself.

And he thought of these men, that ignorant army. They were husbands, they were fathers, gangsters, football players, rovers; and they were everywhere. Or they were, in any case, in all of the places he had been assured they could not be found, and the need they brought to him was one they scarcely knew they had, which they spent their lives denying, which overtook and drugged them, making their limbs as heavy as those of sleepers or drowning bathers, and which could only be satisfied in the shameful, the punishing dark, and quickly, with flight and aversion as the issue of the act. They fled, with the infection lanced but with the root of the infection still in them. Days or weeks or months might pass —or even years—before, once again, furtively, in an empty locker room, on an empty stairway or a roof, in the shadow of a wall in the park, in a parked car, or in the furnished room of an absent friend, they surrendered to the hands, to the stroking and fondling and kissing of the despised and anonymous sex. And yet the need did not seem to be predominantly physical. It could not be said that they were attracted to men. They did not make love, they were passive, they were acted on. The need seemed, indeed, to be precisely this passivity, this gift of illicit pleasure, this adoration. They came, this army, not out of joy but out of poverty, and in the most tremendous ignorance. Something had been frozen in them, the root of their affections had been frozen, so that they could no longer accept affection, though it was from this lack that they were perishing. The dark submission was the shadow of love—if only someone, somewhere, loved them enough to caress them this way, in the light, with joy! But then they could no longer be passive.

Chaos. For the great difference between these men and himself was also the terms of their connection. He saw their vulnerability and they saw his. But they did not love him for this. They used him. He did not love them, either, though he dreamed of it. And the encounter took place, at last, between two dreamers, neither of whom could wake the other, except for the bitterest and briefest of seconds. Then sleep descended again, the search continued, chaos came again.

And there was more to it than that. When the liaison so casually begun survived the first encounters, when a kind of shy affection began to force itself up through the frozen ground, and shame abated, chaos more than ever ruled. For shame had not so much abated as found a partner. Affection had appeared, but through a fissure, a crevice, in the person, through which, behind affection, came all the winds of fear. For the act of love is a confession. One lies about the body but the body does not lie about itself; it cannot lie about the force which drives it. And Eric had discovered, inevitably, the truth about many men, who then wished to drive Eric and the truth together out of the world.

And where was honor in all this chaos? He watched the winking lights and listened to Yves and Madame Belet in the kitchen. Honor. He knew that he had no honor which the world could recognize. His life, passions, trials, loves, were, at worst, filth, and, at best, disease in the eyes of the world, and crimes in the eyes of his countrymen. There were no standards for him except those he could make for himself. There were no standards for him because he could not accept the definitions, the hideously mechanical jargon of the age. He saw no one around him worth his envy, did not believe in the vast, gray sleep which was called security, did not believe in the cures, panaceas, and slogans which afflicted the world he knew; and this meant that he had to create his standards and make up his definitions as he went along. It was up to him to find out who he was, and it was his necessity to do this, so far as the witchdoctors of the time were concerned, alone.

"Mais, bien sûr," he heard Yves saying to Madame Belet, *"je suis tout à fait à votre avis."* Madame Belet was very fond of Yves and gave him the benefit, entirely unsolicited, of her seventy-two years' experience each time she was able to corner him. He could see Yves now, in the kitchen, holding the two drinks in his hand, edging toward the door, a pale, polite, and lonely smile on his face—for he had great respect for old people—waiting for the pause in Madame Belet's flow which would allow him to escape.

Madame Belet was fond of Eric, too, but he had the feeling that this was mainly because she recognized him as Yves's somewhat unlikely benefactor. If Eric had been French, she would have despised him. But France did not, *Dieu merci!* produce such conundrums as Eric, and he was not to be judged by the civilized standards which obtained in her own country.

"And what time are you leaving?" she asked.

"Oh, surely not before noon, Madame."

She laughed and Yves laughed. There was something bawdy in their laughter and he could not avoid the feeling, though he suppressed it at once, that they were laughing in league, against him. "I hope you will like America," said Madame Belet.

"I will become very rich there," said Yves, "and when I come back, I will take you on a pilgrimage to Rome."

For Madame Belet was devout and had never been to

Rome, and it was her great hope to see the Holy City before
she died.

"Ah. You will never come back."

"I will come back," Yves said. But his voice was full of
doubt. And Eric realized, for the first time, that Yves was
afraid.

"People who go to America," said Madame Belet, "never
come back."

"*Au contraire*," said Yves, "they are coming back all the
time."

Coming back to what? Eric asked himself. Madame Belet
laughed again. Then their voices dropped. Yves came back
into the room. He handed Eric his drink and sat again on
the hassock, with his head on Eric's knee.

"I thought I would never get away," he murmured.

"I was thinking of going in to rescue you." He leaned
down and kissed Yves on the neck.

Yves put one hand on Eric's cheek and closed his eyes.
They were still. A pulse beat in Yves's neck. He turned and
he and Eric kissed each other on the mouth. They pulled
slightly away. Yves's eyes were very black and bright in the
unlit, leaping room. They stared into each other's eyes for a
long time, and kissed again. Then Eric sighed and leaned
back and Yves rested once more against him.

Eric wondered what Yves was thinking. Yves's eyes had
carried him back to that moment, nearly two years before,
when, in a darkened hotel room, in the town of Chartres, he
and Yves had first become lovers. Yves had visited the
cathedral once, years before, and he had wanted Eric to see
it. And this gesture, this desire to share with Eric something
he had loved, marked the end of a testing period, signaled
Yves's turning out of that dark distrust with which he was
accustomed to regard the world and with which he had held
Eric at bay. They had known each other for more than three
months and had seen each other every day, but they had
never touched.

And Eric had waited, attentive and utterly chaste. The
change in him was like the change in a spendthrift when his
attention is captured by something worth more than all his
gold, worth more than all the baubles he has ever purchased;
then, instead of scattering, he begins to assess and hoard and
gather up; all that he has becomes valuable because all that
he has may prove to be an unacceptable sacrifice. So Eric
waited, praying that this violated urchin would learn to love
and trust him. And he knew that the only way he could hope

to bring this about was to cease violating himself: if *he* did not love himself, then Yves would never be able to love him, either.

So he did what he alone could do, purified, as well as he could, his house, and opened his doors; established a precarious order in the heart of his chaos; and waited for his guest.

Yves shifted and sat up and lit a cigarette, then lit one for Eric. "I am beginning to be quite hungry."

"So am I. But we'll be eating soon." The kitten wandered in and leaped into Eric's lap. He stroked it with one hand. "Do you remember how we met?"

"I will never forget it. I owe a great deal to Beethoven." Eric smiled. "*And* to the wonders of modern science."

He had been walking along the Rue des St. Pères on a spring evening, and his thoughts had not been pretty. Paris seemed, and had seemed for a long time, the loneliest city under heaven. And whoever prolongs his sojourn in that city—who tries, that is, to make a home there—is doomed to discover that there is no one to be blamed for whatever happens to him. Contrary to its legend, Paris does not offer many distractions; or, those distractions that it offers are like French pastry, vivid and insubstantial, sweet on the tongue and sour in the belly. Then the discontented wanderer is thrown back on himself—if his life is to become bearable, only he can make it so. And, on that spring evening, walking up the long, dark, murmuring street toward the Boulevard, Eric was in despair. He knew that he had a life to make, but he did not seem to have the tools.

Then, as he neared the Boulevard, he heard music. At first, he thought it came from the houses, but then he realized that it was coming from the shadows across the street, where there were no houses. He stood still and listened; to Beethoven's "Emperor" Concerto, which was moving away from him. Then, out of the shadows, ahead of him, and on the other side of the street, he saw the long, lean figure of a boy. He stood on the corner, waiting for the lights to change, and Eric saw that he was carrying a small portable radio, holding it with both hands. Eric walked to the corner, the lights changed, the boy crossed the street, and Eric followed. Down the long, dark street, the boy on one side and he on the other, and with the violence of the music, which was like the violence in his heart, filling the soft, spring air.

They reached the corner of the Rue de Rennes. The concerto was approaching its end. To the right, far from them, squatted the bulk of the Gare Montparnasse; to the left, and somewhat nearer, were the cafés and the Boulevard, and the clean, gray spire of St. Germain-des-Près.

The boy hesitated on the corner; looked over, briefly, and his eyes met Eric's. He turned in the direction of St. Germain-des-Près. Eric crossed the street, *Tum-ta-tum, tum-ta-tum, tum-ta-tum, tum-ta-tum!* went the music.

"Hello," Eric said. "I'm afraid I've got to hear the end of that concerto."

Yves turned and Eric was immediately struck by his eyes. In the candor with which they regarded him, they were like the eyes of a child; and yet there was also something in that scrutiny which was not childish at all. Eric felt his heart pound once, hard, against his chest. Then Yves smiled.

"It is almost ended," he said.

"I know." They walked in silence, listening to the end of the concerto. When it ended, Yves clicked the radio off.

"Will you have a drink with me?" Eric asked. He said, quickly, "I'm all by myself, I've got no one to talk to—and—and you don't run into people playing Beethoven every day."

"That is true," said Yves with a smile. "You have a funny accent, where are you from?"

"America."

"I thought it *must* be America. But which section you are from?"

"The South. Alabama."

"Oh," said Yves, and looked at him with interest, "then you are *raciste*."

"Why, no," said Eric, feeling rather stunned, "we are not all like that."

"Oh," said Yves, majestically, "I read your newspapers. And I have many African friends and I have noticed that Americans do not like that."

"Well," said Eric, "that's not *my* problem. I left Alabama as fast as I could and if I ever go back there, they'll probably kill me."

"Have you been here long?"

"About a year."

"And you still know *no one*?"

"It's hard to make friends with the French."

"Well. It is only that we are more *réservé* than you."

"I'll say you are." They stopped before the Royal St. Germain. "Shall we have a drink here?"

"It does not matter." Yves looked over the tables, which were full; looked through the glass walls into the bar, which was crowded, mostly with young males. "But it is terribly crowded."

"Let's go some place else."

They walked to the corner and crossed the street. All of the cafés were full. They crossed the street again, and passed the Brasserie Lipp. Eric had been watching Yves with more intensity than he realized; as they passed the brasserie, it suddenly flashed through him that Yves was hungry. He did not know how he knew it, for Yves said nothing, did not pause or sigh; and yet Eric could not have been more certain that the boy was faint with hunger had he abruptly collapsed on the sidewalk.

"Look," Eric said, "I've got an idea. I'm starving, I haven't eaten any supper. Come on over to Les Halles with me and let's get something to eat. And by the time we get back, it won't be so crowded over here." Yves looked at him, his head tilted in a kind of wary, waiting surprise.

"It is so far," he murmured. And he stared at Eric with a bright, suspicious bafflement; as though he were thinking, I am willing to play all games, my friend, but what are the rules of this one? and what are the penalties?

"I'll bring you back." He grinned and grabbed Yves's arm and started for the taxi stand. "Come on, be my guest, you'll be doing me a favor. What's your name?"

"Je m'appel Yves."

"My name is Eric."

He had often thought since that, had it not been for that sudden apprehension before the brasserie, he and Yves would never have met again. Their first meal together had given them time, so to speak, to circle around one another. Eric did most of the talking; the burden of proof was on him. And Yves became less wary and less tight. Eric chattered on, delighted by Yves's changing face, waiting for his smile, waiting for his laugh. He wanted Yves to know that he was not trying to strike with him the common, brutal bargain; was not buying him a dinner in order to throw him into bed. And by and by this unspoken declaration caused Yves to nod gravely, as though he were turning it over in his mind. There also appeared in his face a certain fear. It was this fear which Eric sometimes despaired of conquering, in Yves, or in himself. It was the fear of making a total commitment, a vow: it was the fear of being loved.

That day in Chartres they had passed through town and watched women kneeling at the edge of the water, pounding clothes against a flat, wooden board. Yves had watched them for a long time. They had wandered up and down the old crooked streets, in the hot sun; Eric remembered a lizard darting across a wall; and everywhere the cathedral pursued them. It is impossible to be in that town and not be in the shadow of those great towers; impossible to find oneself on those plains and not be troubled by that cruel and elegant, dogmatic and pagan presence. The town was full of tourists, with their cameras, their three-quarter coats, bright flowered dresses and shirts, their children, college insignia, Panama hats, sharp, nasal cries, and automobiles crawling like monstrous gleaming bugs over the laming, cobblestoned streets. Tourist buses, from Holland, from Denmark, from Germany, stood in the square before the cathedral. Tow-haired boys and girls, earnest, carrying knapsacks, wearing khaki-colored shorts, with heavy buttocks and thighs, wandered dully through the town. American soldiers, some in uniform, some in civilian clothes, leaned over bridges, entered bistros in strident, uneasy, smiling packs, circled displays of colored post cards, and picked up meretricious mementos, of a sacred character. All of the beauty of the town, all the energy of the plains, and all the power and dignity of the people seemed to have been sucked out of them by the cathedral. It was as though the cathedral demanded, and received, a perpetual, living sacrifice. It towered over the town, more like an affliction than a blessing, and made everything seem, by comparison with itself, wretched and makeshift indeed. The houses in which the people lived did not suggest shelter, or safety. The great shadow which lay over them revealed them as mere doomed bits of wood and mineral, set down in the path of a hurricane which, presently, would blow them into eternity. And this shadow lay heavy on the people, too. They seemed stunted and misshapen; the only color in their faces suggested too much bad wine and too little sun; even the children seemed to have been hatched in a cellar. It was a town like some towns in the American South, frozen in its history as Lot's wife was trapped in salt, and doomed, therefore, as its history, that overwhelming, omnipresent gift of God, could not be questioned, to be the property of the gray, unquestioning mediocre.

Sometime in the course of the afternoon, though they had only come down from Paris for the day, they decided to spend the night. It was Yves's suggestion, made when they returned to the cathedral and stood on the steps, looking at the saints and martyrs trapped in stone. Yves had been unusually silent all day. And Eric knew him well enough by now not to push him, not to prod, even not to worry. He knew that Yves's silences meant that he was fighting some curious war of his own, was coming to some decision of his own; presently, later today, tomorrow, next week, Yves would abruptly retrace, in speech, the steps he was taking in silence now. And, oddly enough, for it seems not to be the way we live now, for Eric, merely hearing Yves's footfalls at his side, feeling Yves beside him, and watching that changing face, was joy enough—or almost joy enough.

They found a hotel which overlooked a stream and took a double room. Their windows overlooked the water; the towers of the cathedral loomed to the right of them, far away. When they took the room, the sun was setting and great streaks of fire and dull gold were splashed across the still, blue sky.

There were trees just outside the window, bending into the water; and there were a few tables and chairs, but they were empty; there did not seem to be many people in the hotel.

Yves seated himself in the large window and lit a cigarette, looking down at the tables and chairs. Eric stood next to him, his hand on Yves's shoulder.

"Shall we have a drink down there, old buddy?"

"My God, no; we shall be eaten up by bugs. Let's go and find a bistro."

"Okay."

He moved away. Yves stood up. They stared at each other.

"I imagine that we must come back early," Yves said, "there is surely nothing to do in this town." Then he grinned, mischievously. *"Ça va?"*

"It was your idea to come here," Eric said.

"Yes." He turned to the window again. "It is peaceful, yes? And we can be gentle with each other, we can have a moment together." He threw his cigarette out of the window. When he turned to Eric again, his eyes were clouded, and his mouth was very vulnerable. After a moment he said, softly, "Let us go."

But it was very nearly a question. And, now, both of them were frightened. For some reason, the towers seemed closer than they had been; and, suddenly, the two large beds, placed close together, seemed the only objects in the room. Eric felt his heart shake and his blood begin to race and then to thicken. He felt that Yves was waiting for him to move, that everything was in his hands; and he could do nothing.

Then it lifted, the red, dangerous shadow, the moment passed, they smiled at each other. Yves walked to the door and opened it. They descended again into the sleepy, the beautiful town.

For it was not quite the same town it had been a few hours before. In that second in the room, something had melted between them, a gap between them had closed; and now the irresistible current was tugging at them, dragging them slowly, and absolutely surely, to the fulfillment of that promise.

And for this reason they hesitated, they dawdled, they deliciously put it off. They chose to eat in an unadorned bistro because it was empty—empty when they walked in, anyway, though it was taken over after they had been there for a while, by half a dozen drunk and musical French soldiers. The noise they made might have been unbearable at any other time, but, now, it operated as a kind of protective wall between themselves and the world. It gave them something to laugh at—and they needed to laugh; the distraction the soldiers afforded the other people who had entered the bistro allowed them, briefly, to clasp hands; and this small preamble to terror steadied their hearts and minds.

And then they walked through the town, in which not even a cat seemed to be moving; and everywhere they walked, the cathedral was watching them. They crossed a bridge and watched the moon in the water. Their footfalls rang on the cobblestones. The walls of the houses were all black, they walked through great patches of blackness between one far-off street light to another. But the cathedral was lighted.

The trees and the tables and chairs and the water were lit by the moon. Yves locked their door behind them and Eric walked to the window and looked at the sky, at the mighty towers. He heard the murmur of the water and then Yves called his name. He turned. Yves stood on the other side of the room, between the two beds, naked.

"Which bed do you think is better?" he asked.

And he sounded genuinely perplexed, as though it were a difficult decision.

"Whichever you prefer," Eric said, gravely.

Yves pulled back the covers of the bed nearest the window and placed himself between the sheets. He pulled the covers up to his chin and lay on his back, watching Eric. His eyes were dark and enormous in the dark room. A faint smile touched his lips.

And this look, this moment, entered into Eric, to remain

with him forever. There was a terrifying innocence in Yves's face, a beautiful yielding: in some marvelous way, for Yves, this moment in this bed obliterated, cast into the sea of forgetfulness, all the sordid beds and squalid grappling which had led him here. He was turning to the lover who would not betray him, to his first lover. Eric crossed the room and sat down on the bed and began to undress. Again, he heard the murmur of the stream.

"Will you give me a cigarette?" Yves asked. He had a new voice, newly troubled, and when Eric looked at him he saw for the first time how the face of a lover becomes a stranger's face.

"Bien sûr." He lit two cigarettes and gave one to Yves. They watched each other in the fantastic, tiny glow—and smiled, almost like conspirators.

Then Eric asked, "Yves, do you love me?"

"Yes," said Yves.

"That's good," said Eric, "because I'm crazy about you. I love you."

Then, in the violent moonlight, naked, he slowly pulled the covers away from Yves. They watched each other and he stared at Yves's body for a long time before Yves lifted up his arms, with that same sad, cryptic smile, and kissed him. Eric felt beneath his fingers Yves's slowly stirring, stiffening sex. This sex dominated the long landscape of his life as the cathedral towers dominated the plains.

Now, Yves, as though he were also remembering that day and night, turned his head and looked at Eric with a wondering, speculative, and triumphant smile. And at that moment, Madame Belet entered, with a sound of knives and forks and plates, and switched on the lights. Yves's face changed, the sea vanished. Yves rose from the hassock, blinking a little. Madame Belet put the utensils on the table, carefully, and marched out again, returning immediately with a bottle of wine, and a corkscrew. She placed these on the table. Yves went to the table and began opening the wine.

"She thinks you are going to abandon me," said Yves. He poured a tiny bit of wine into his own glass, then poured for Eric. He looked at Eric, quickly, and added more wine to the first glass, and set the bottle down.

"Abandon you?" Eric laughed. Yves looked relieved and a little ashamed. "You mean—she thinks I'm running away from you?"

"She thinks that perhaps you do not really intend to bring

me to New York. She says that Americans are very different
—when—in their own country."

"Well, how the hell does *she* know?" He was suddenly
angry. "And it's none of her fucking business, anyway."
Madame Belet entered, and he glared at her. Imperturbably,
she placed on the table a platter containing *les crudités,* and
a basket full of bread. She reentered the kitchen, Eric staring
malevolently at her straight, chauvinistic back. "If there's
one thing I can't stand, it's malicious old ladies."

They sat down. "She does not really mean any harm,"
Yves said. "She thought that she was speaking for my good."

"She thinks it's good for you to distrust me—just when
I'm about to get on a boat? Doesn't she think we have
enough to worry about?"

"Oh, well. People do not take the relations between boys
seriously, you know that. We will never know many people
who believe we love each other. They do not believe there
can be tears between men. They think we are only playing a
game and that we do it to shock them."

Eric was silent, chewing on the raw vegetables which
seemed to have no taste. He took a swallow of wine, but it
did not help. His belly tightened and his forehead began to
be damp. "I know. And it's going to be worse in New York."

"Oh, well," said Yves, with an odd and moving note of
finality in his voice, "as long as you do not abandon me, I
will not be afraid."

Eric smiled—at the tone, at the statement; but he felt his
forehead flush hotter, and a strange fear closed his throat.
"Is that a promise?" he asked. He asked it lightly, but his
voice sounded stifled; and Yves, who had lowered his head to
his plate, looked up. They watched each other. Eric stared
into Yves's dark eyes, terribly aware of Yves's forehead,
which gleamed like a skull; and, at the same time, with the
most immense desire, he watched Yves's curving, parted lips.
His teeth gleamed. Eric had felt those teeth on his tongue
and on his cheek, and those lips had made him moan and
tremble many times. And the short length of the table
seemed to tremble between them.

"Why don't we pay Madame Belet now," Eric asked,
"and let her go home?"

Yves rose and walked into the kitchen. Eric munched
again on the raw, garlic-flavored vegetables, thinking, *This
is our last night here. Our last night.* Again, he heard their
voices in the kitchen, Madame Belet seeming to protest, then

agreeing to come in the morning. He finished the last of his wine. Then the kitchen door closed and Yves returned.

"I think, perhaps, she is a little angry," Yves said, smiling, "but she is gone. She will come again in the morning, especially to say good-bye to you. I think that is because she wants to make certain that you know how much she dislikes you." He did not sit down again, but stood at his end of the table, his hands on his hips. "She says the chicken is ready, we should not let it get cold." He laughed, and Eric laughed. "I told her it does not matter with chicken, if it is cold or hot, I like it either way." They both laughed again. Then, abruptly, silence fell between them.

Eric rose and crossed to Yves, and they stood for a moment like two wrestlers, watching each other with a kind of physical calculation, smiling and pale. Yves always seemed, a moment before the act, tentative and tremulous; not like a girl—like a boy: and this strangely innocent waiting, this virile helplessness, alway engendered in Eric a positive storm of tenderness. Everything in him, from his heights and depths, his mysterious, hidden source, came rushing together, like a great flood barely channeled in a narrow mountain stream. And it chilled him like that—like icy water; and roared in him like that, and with the menace of things scarcely understood, barely to be controlled; and he shook with the violence with which he flowed toward Yves. It was this violence which made him gentle, for it frightened him. And now he touched Yves lightly and wonderingly on the cheek. Yves's smile faded, he watched Eric, they moved into each other's arms.

There were the wine bottle and the glasses on the table, their plates, the platter, the bread; Yves had left a cigarette burning in an ashtray on the table, it was nearly nothing but ash now, long and gray; and the kitchen light was on. "You say you don't care about the chicken?" Eric whispered, laughing. Yves laughed, giving off a whiff of garlic, of peppery sweat. Their arms locked around each other, then they drew apart, and, holding hands, stumbled into the bedroom, into the great haven of their bed. Perhaps it had never before seemed so much like a haven, so much their own, now that the terrible floodwaters of time were about to overtake it. And perhaps they had never before so belonged to each other, had never before given or taken so much from each other, as they did now, burning and sobbing on the crying bed.

They labored together slowly, violently, a long time: both feared the end. Both feared the morning, when the moon and stars would be gone, when this room would be harsh and sorrowful with sunlight, and this bed would be dismantled, waiting for other flesh. *Love is expensive,* Yves had once said, with his curiously dry wonder. *One must put furniture around it, or it goes.* Now, for a while, there would be no furniture—how long would this night have to last them? What would the morning bring? the imminent morning, behind which were hidden so many mornings, so many nights.

And they moaned. *Soon,* Yves whispered, sounding insistent, like a child, and with a terrible regret. *Soon.* Eric's hands and mouth opened and closed on his lover's body, their bodies strained yet closer together, and Yves's body shook and he called Eric's name as no one had ever called this name before. *Eric. Eric. Eric.* The sound of his breath filled Eric, heavier than the far-off pounding of the sea.

Then they were silent, breathing hard. The sound of the sea returned. They were aware of the light in the living room, the light left burning in the kitchen. But they did not move. They remained still in one another's arms, in their slowly chilling bed. Soon, one of them, it would be Yves, would move, would light two cigarettes. They would lie in bed, smoking, talking and giggling. Then they would shower: *what a mess we are!* Yves would cry, laughing a laugh of triumph. Then they would dress, they would probably eat, they would probably go out. And soon the night would end. But, for the moment, they were simply exhausted and at peace with one another and loath to leave the only haven either of them had ever found.

And, in fact, they did not move again that night, smoked no cigarettes, ate no chicken, did no talking, drank no champagne. They fell asleep as they were, cradled, spoon-fashion, against each other, lulled by the pounding of the sea. Eric woke once, when the kitten crawled into bed, trying to place itself around Yves's neck. But he forced it to the foot of the bed. He turned around, leaning on one elbow, watching Yves's sleeping face. He thought of getting up and turning off all the lights; he felt a little hungry. But nothing seemed important enough to take him out of bed, to take him away from Yves, even for a moment. He lay down again, closing his eyes, and listening to Yves's breathing. He fell asleep, thinking, *Life is very different in New York,* and he woke up with this thought, just as the sun was beginning to rise. Yves was awake and was watching him. Eric thought, *Maybe he'll hate New York. And then, maybe he'll hate me, too.* Yves looked frightened and determined. They were silent. Yves suddenly pulled Eric into his arms as though he were angry, or as though he were lost. By and by they were at peace again, and then they lay there in silence, blue cigarette smoke circling around them in the sunny air, the kitten purring in the sunlight at their feet. Then the sound of Madame Belet in the kitchen told Eric it was time to make tracks.

CHAPTER 2

Eight days later, Eric was in New York, with Yves's last words still ringing in his ears, and his touch and his smell all over his body. And Yves's eyes, like the searchlight of the Eiffel Tower or the sweep of a lighthouse light, lit up, at intervals, the grave darkness around him and afforded him, in the black distance, his only frame of reference and his only means of navigation.

On the last day in Paris, at the last moment, they both suffered from terrible hangovers, having both been up all night, drinking, at a friend's house; their faces were gray and damp; they stank with weariness. There was great shouting and confusion all around them, and the train breathed over them like some unimaginably malevolent beetle. They were almost too tired for sorrow, but not too tired for fear. It steamed out of them both, like the miasma rising from the Gare St. Lazare. In the deep black shadow of this shed, while their friends stood at a discreet distance from them; and the station attendant moved up and down the platform, shouting, *"En voiture, s'il vous plaît! En voiture! En voiture!"*; and the great hand of the great clock approached the zero hour; they stared into each other's faces like comrades who have been through a war.

"*T'ne fait pas,*" Eric murmured.

"*En voiture!*"

Eric moved up to stand in the crowded doorway of the train. There was nothing to say; there was too much to say.

"I hate waiting," he said. "I hate good-byes." He suddenly felt that he was going to cry, and panic threatened to overtake him because of all these people watching. "We will see each other," he said, "very soon. I promise you, Yves. I promise you. *Tu me fait toujours confiance, j'espère?*" And he tried to smile.

Yves said nothing, but nodded, his eyes very bright, his

mouth very vulnerable, his forehead very high, and full of trouble. People were screaming out of windows, were passing last minute items to each other through windows. Eric was the last person standing in the door. He had an awful feeling that he had forgotten something very important. He had paid for Yves's hotel room, they had visited the American embassy and the French authorities, he had left Yves some money—what else? what else? The train began to move. Yves looked stunned for a moment, Eric raised his eyes from Yves's face to say good-bye to all the others. Yves trotted along the platform, then suddenly leaped up on the step, holding on with one hand, and kissed Eric hard on the mouth.

"Ne m'oublie pas," he whispered. "You are all I have in this world."

Then he jumped down, just as the train began to pick up speed. He ran along the platform a little longer, then stopped, his hands in his pockets, staring, and with the wind raising his hair. Eric watched him, waving. The platform narrowed, sloped, ended, the train swerved, and Yves vanished from his sight. It did not seem possible and he stared stupidly at the flying poles and wires, at the sign saying PARIS—ST. LAZARE, at the blank, back walls of buildings. Then tears rolled down his face. He lit a cigarette and stood in the vestibule, while the hideous outskirts of Paris rolled by. Why am I going home? he asked himself. But he knew why. It was time. In order not to lose all that he had gained, he had to move forward and risk it all.

New York seemed very strange indeed. It might, almost, for strange barbarity of manner and custom, for the sense of danger and horror barely sleeping beneath the rough, gregarious surface, have been some impenetrably exotic city of the East. So superbly was it in the present that it seemed to have nothing to do with the passage of time: time might have dismissed it as thoroughly as it had dismissed Carthage and Pompeii. It seemed to have no sense whatever of the exigencies of human life; it was so familiar and so public that it became, at last, the most despairingly private of cities. One was continually being jostled, yet longed, at the same time, for the sense of others, for a human touch; and if one was never—it was the general complaint—left alone in New York, one had, still, to fight very hard in order not to perish of loneliness. This fight, carried on in so many different ways, created the strange climate of the city. The girls along

Fifth Avenue wore their bright clothes like semaphores, trying helplessly to bring to the male attention the news of their mysterious trouble. The men could not read this message. They strode purposefully along, wearing little anonymous hats, or bareheaded, with youthfully parted hair, or crew cuts, accoutered with attaché cases, rushing, on the evidence, to the smoking cars of trains. In this haven, they opened up their newspapers and caught up on the day's bad news. Or they were to be found, as five o'clock fell, in discreetly dim, anonymously appointed bars, uneasy, in brittle, uneasy, female company, pouring down joyless martinis.

This note of despair, of buried despair, was insistently, constantly struck. It stalked all the New York avenues, roamed all the New York streets; was as present in Sutton Place, where the director of Eric's play lived and the great often gathered, as it was in Greenwich Village, where he had rented an apartment and been appalled to see what time had done to people he had once known well. He could not escape the feeling that a kind of plague was raging, though it was officially and publicly and privately denied. Even the young seemed blighted—seemed most blighted of all. The boys in their blue jeans ran together, scarcely daring to trust one another, but united, like their elders, in a boyish distrust of the girls. Their very walk, a kind of anti-erotic, knee-action lope, was a parody of locomotion and of manhood. They seemed to be shrinking away from any contact with their flamboyantly and paradoxically outlined private parts. They seemed —but could it be true? and how had it happened?—to be at home with, accustomed to, brutality and indifference, and to be terrified of human affection. In some strange way they did not seem to feel that they were worthy of it.

Now, late on a Sunday afternoon, having been in New York four days, and not yet having written his parents in the South, Eric moved through the tropical streets on his way to visit Cass and Richard. He was having a drink with them to celebrate his return.

"I'm glad you think it's something to celebrate," he had told Cass over the phone.

She laughed. "That's not very nice. You sound as though you haven't missed us at all."

"Oh, I certainly want to see all of *you*. But I don't know if I ever really missed the city very much. Did you ever notice how ugly it is?"

"It's getting uglier all the time," Cass said. "A perfect example of free enterprise gone mad."

"I wanted to thank you," he said, after a moment, "for writing me about Rufus." And he thought, with a rather surprising and painful venom, Nobody else thought to do it.

"Well, I knew," she said, "that you'd want to know." Then there was a silence. "You never knew his sister, did you?"

"Well, I knew he *had* one. I never met her; she was just a kid in those days."

"She's not a kid now," Cass said. "She's going to be singing Sunday, down in the Village, with some friends of Rufus's. For the first time. We promised to bring you along. Vivaldo will be there."

He thought of Rufus. He did not know what to say. "She's something like her brother, huh?"

"I wouldn't say that. Yes and no." Briefly: "You'll see." This brought them to another silence, and, after a few seconds, they hung up.

He entered their building, stepped into the elevator, and told the elevator man where he was going. He had forgotten the style of American elevator men, but now it came back to him. The elevator man, without a surly word, slammed the elevator gates shut and drove the car upward. The nature of his silence conveyed his disapproval of the Silenskis and all their friends and his vivid sense of being as good as they.

He rang the bell. Cass opened the door at once, looking as bright as the bright day.

"Eric!" She looked him over with the affectionate mockery he now remembered. "How nice you look with your hair so short!"

"How nice," he returned, smiling, "you look with yours so long. Or was it always long. It's that kind of thing a long absence makes you forget."

"Let me look at you." She pulled him into the apartment and closed the door. "You really look wonderful. Welcome home." She leaned forward suddenly and kissed him on the cheek. "Is that the way they do it in Paris?"

"You have to kiss me on both cheeks," he said, gravely.

"Oh." She seemed slightly embarrassed but kissed him again. "Is that better?"

"Much," he said. Then, "Where *is* everybody?" For the large living room was empty, and filled with the sound of the blues. It was the voice of a colored woman, the voice of Bessie Smith, and it hurled him, with violence, into the hot center of his past: *It's raining and it's storming on the sea. I feel like somebody has shipwrecked poor me.*

For a moment Cass looked as though she were sardonically echoing his question. She crossed the room and lowered the volume of the music slightly. "The children are over in the park with some friends of theirs. Richard's in his study, working. But they should all be appearing almost any moment now."

"Oh," he said, "then I'm early. I'm sorry."

"You aren't early, you're on time. And *I'm* glad. I was hoping to have a chance to talk to you alone before we go down to this jam session."

"You've got a pretty agreeable jam session going on right now," he said. Cass went over to the bar, and he threw himself down on the sofa. "It's mighty nice and cool in here. It's awful outside. I'd forgotten how hot New York could be."

The large windows were open and the water stretched beyond the windows, very bright and peaceful, but murkier than the Mediterranean. The breeze that filled the room came directly from the water; seemed, almost, to bring with it the spice and stink of Europe and the murmur of Yves's voice. Eric leaned back, held in a kind of peaceful melancholy, comforted by the beat of Bessie's song, and looked over at Cass.

The sun surrounded her golden hair which was piled on top of her head and fell over her brow in girlish, somewhat too artless and incongruous curls. This was meant to soften a face, the principal quality of which had always been a spare, fragile boniness. There was a fine crisscross of wrinkles now around the large eyes; the sun revealed that she was wearing a little too much make-up. This, and something indefinably sorrowful in the line of her mouth and jaw, as she stood silently at the bar, looking down, made Eric feel that Cass was beginning to fade, to become brittle. Something icy had touched her.

"Do you want gin or vodka or bourbon or Scotch or beer? or tequila?" She looked up, smiling. Though the smile was genuine, it was weary. It did not contain the mischievous delight that he remembered. And there were tiny lines now around her neck, which he had never noticed before.

We're getting old, he thought, and it damn sure didn't take long.

"I think I'd better stick to whiskey. I get too drunk too fast on gin—and I don't know what this evening holds."

"Ah," she said, "farsighted Eric! And what *kind* of whiskey?"

"In Paris, when we order whiskey—which, for a very long time, I didn't dare to do—we always mean Scotch."

"You loved Paris, didn't you? You must have, you were gone so long. Tell me about it."

She made two drinks and came and sat beside him. From far away, he heard the muffled *cling!* of a typewriter bell.

It's a long old road, Bessie sang, *but I'm going to find an end.*

"It doesn't seem so long," he said, "now that I'm back." He felt very shy now, for when Cass said *You loved Paris* he at once thought, Yves is there. "It's a great city, Paris, a beautiful city—and—it was very good for me."

"I see that. You seem much happier. There's a kind of light around you."

She said this very directly, with a rueful, conspiratorial smile: as though she knew the cause of his happiness, and rejoiced for him.

He dropped his eyes, but raised them again. "It's just the sun," he said, and they both laughed. Then, irrepressibly, "I *was* very happy there, though."

"Well, you didn't leave because you weren't happy there any more?"

"No." *And when I get there, I'm going to shake hands with a friend.* "A guy I know who thinks he has great psychic powers"—he sipped his whiskey, smiling—"Frenchman, persuaded me that I'd become a great star if I came home and did this play. And I just haven't got the guts to go against the stars, to say nothing of arguing with a Frenchman. So."

She laughed. "I didn't know the French went in for things like that. I thought they were very logical."

"French logic is very simple. Whatever the French do is logical because the French are doing it. That's the really unbeatable advantage French logic has over all others."

"I see," she said, and laughed again. "I hope you read the play before your friend consulted the stars. Is it a good part?"

"It's the best part," he said, after a moment, "that I've ever had."

Again, briefly, he heard the typewriter bell. Cass lit a cigarette, offered one to Eric, and lit it for him. "Are you going to settle here now, or are you planning to go back, or what?"

"I don't," he said quickly, "have any plans for going back, a lot—maybe everything—depends on what happens with this play."

She sensed his retreat, and took her tone from him. "Oh. I'd love to come and watch rehearsals. I'd run out and get coffee for you, and things like that. It would make me feel that I'd contributed to your triumph."

"Because you're sure it's going to be a triumph," he said, smiling. "Wonderful Cass. I guess it's a habit great men's wives get into."

Weeping and crying, tears falling on the ground.

The atmosphere between them stiffened a little, nevertheless, with their knowledge of why he had allowed his career in New York to lapse for so long. Then he allowed himself to think of opening night, and he thought, Yves will be here. This thought exalted him and made him feel safe. He did not feel safe now, sitting here alone with Cass; he had not felt safe since stepping off the boat. His ears ached for the sound of Yves's footfalls beside him: until he heard this rhythm, all other sounds were meaningless. *Weeping and crying, tears falling on the ground.* All other faces were obliterated for him by the blinding glare of Yves's absence. He looked over at Cass, longing to tell her about Yves, but not daring, not knowing how to begin.

"Great men's wives, indeed!" said Cass. "How I'd love to explode *that* literary myth." She looked at him, gravely sipping her whiskey, without seeming to taste it. *When I got to the end, I was so worried down.* "You seem very sure of yourself," she said.

"I do?" He was profoundly astonished and pleased. "I don't *feel* very sure of myself."

"I remember you before you went away. You were miserable then. We all wondered—*I* wondered—what would become of you. But you aren't miserable now."

"No," he said, and, under her scrutiny, blushed. "I'm not miserable any more. But I still don't know what's going to become of me."

"Growth," she said, "is what will become of you. It's what *has* become of you." And she gave him again her oddly intimate, rueful smile. "It's very nice to see, it's very—enviable. I don't envy many people. I haven't found myself envying *anyone* for a long, long time."

"It's mighty funny," he said, "that you should envy *me*." He rose from the sofa, and walked to the window. Behind him, beneath the mighty lament of the music, a heavy silence gathered: Cass, also, had something to talk about, but he did not want to know what it was. *You can't trust nobody, you might as well be alone*. Staring out over the water, he asked, "What was Rufus like—near the end?"

After a moment, he turned and looked at her. "I hadn't meant to ask you that—but I guess I really want to know."

Her face, despite the softening bangs, grew spare and contemplative. Her lips twisted. "I told you a little of it," she said, "in my letter. But I didn't know how you felt by that time and I didn't see any point in burdening you." She put out her cigarette and lit another one. "He was very unhappy, as—as you know." She paused. "Actually, we never got very close to him. Vivaldo knew him better than—than *we* did, anyway." He felt a curious throb of jealousy: *Vivaldo!* "We didn't see much of him. He became very involved with a Southern girl, a girl from Georgia—"

Found my long lost friend, and I might as well stayed at home!

"You didn't tell me *that*," he said.

"No. He wasn't very nice to her. He beat her up a lot—"

He stared at her, feeling himself grow pale, remembering more than he wanted to remember, feeling his hope and his hope of safety threatened by invincible, unnamed forces within himself. He remembered Rufus's face, his hands, his body, and his voice, and the constant humiliation. "Beat her up? What for?"

"Well—who knows? Because she was Southern, because she was white. I don't know. Because he was Rufus. It was very ugly. She was a nice girl, maybe a little pathetic—"

"Did she like to be beaten up? I mean—did something in her like it, did she like to be—debased?"

"No, I don't think so. I really don't think so. Well, maybe there's something in everybody that likes to be debased, but I don't think life's that simple. I don't trust all these formulas." She paused. "To tell the truth, I think she probably loved Rufus, really loved him, and wanted Rufus to love her."

"How abnormal," he said, "can you get!" He finished his drink.

A very faint, wry amusement crossed her face. "Anyway, their affair dragged on from bad to worse and she was finally committed to an institution—"

"You mean, a madhouse?"

"Yes."

"Where?"

"In the South. Her family came and got her."

"My God," he said. "Go on."

"Well, then, Rufus disappeared—for quite a long time, that's when I met his sister, she came to see us, looking for him—and came back once, and—*died*." Helplessly, she opened one bony hand, then closed it into a fist.

Eric turned back to the window. "A Southern girl," he said. He felt a very dull, very distant pain. It all seemed very long ago, that gasping and trembling, freezing and burning time. The pain was distant now because it had scarcely been bearable then. It could not really be recollected because it had become a part of him. Yet, the power of this pain, though diminished, was not dead: Rufus's face again appeared before him, that dark face, with those dark eyes and curving, heavy lips. It was the face of Rufus when he had looked with love on Eric. Then, out of hiding, leaped his other faces, the crafty, cajoling face of desire, the remote face of desire achieved. Then, for a second, he saw Rufus's face as he stared on death, and saw his body hurtling downward through the air: into that water, the water which stretched before him now. The old pain receded into the home it had made in him. But another pain, homeless as yet, began knocking at his heart—not for the first time: it would force an entry one day, and remain with him forever. *Catch them. Don't let them blues in here. They shakes me in my bed, can't sit down in my chair.*

"Let me fix you a fresh drink," Cass said.

"Okay." She took his glass. As she walked to the bar, he said, "You knew about us, I guess? I guess everybody knew —though we thought we were being so smart, and all. And, of course, he always had a lot of girls around."

"Well, so did you," she said. "In fact, I vaguely remember that you were thinking of getting married at one point."

He took his drink from the bar, and paced the room. "Yes. I haven't thought of her in a long time, either." He paused and grimaced sourly. "That's right, I certainly did have a few girls hanging around. I hardly even remember their names." As he said this, the names of two or three old girl friends flashed into his mind. "I haven't thought about them for years." He came back to the sofa, and sat down. Cass watched him from the bar. "I might," he said, painfully, "have had them around just on account of Rufus—trying to prove something, maybe, to him and to myself."

The room was growing darker. Bessie sang, *The blues has got me on the go. They runs around my house, in and out of my front door.* Then the needle scratched aimlessly for a second, and the record player clicked itself off. Eric's attention had painfully snagged itself on the memory of those unloved, but not wholly undesired girls. Their texture and their odor floated back to him: and it was abruptly astonishing that he had not thought of that side of himself for so long. It had been because of Yves. This thought filled him with a hideous, unwilling resentment: he remembered Yves's hostile adventures with the girls of the Latin Quarter and St. Germain-des-Prés. These adventures had not touched Eric because they so clearly had not touched Yves. But now, superbly, like a diver coming to the surface, his terror bobbed, naked, to the surface of his mind: he would lose Yves, here. It would happen here. And he, he would have no woman, and he would have no Yves. His flesh began to itch, he felt himself beginning to sweat.

He turned and smiled at Cass, who had moved to the sofa, and sat very still beside him in the gloom. She was not watching him. She sat with her hands folded in her lap, busy with thoughts of her own.

"This is one hell of a party," he said.

She rose, smiling, and shook herself a little. "It is, isn't it? I was beginning to wonder where the children are—they should be home by now. And maybe I'd better turn on some lights." She switched on a lamp near the bar. Now, the water and the lights along the water glowed more softly, suggesting the imminent night. Everything was pearl gray, shot with gold. "I'd better go and rouse Richard."

"I didn't know," he said, "that it would be so easy to feel at home again."

She looked at him quickly, and grinned. "Is that good?"

"I don't know yet." He was about to say something more, something about Yves, but he heard Richard's study door open and close. He turned to face Richard as he came into the room; he looked very handsome and boyish and big.

"So we finally got you back here! I'm told it took every penny Shubert Alley could scrape together. How are you, you old bastard?"

"I'm fine, Richard, it's good to see you." They clung together, briefly, in the oddly truncated, shrinking, American embrace, and stepped back to look at one another. "I hear that you're selling more books than Frank Yerby."

"Better," said Richard, "but not more." He looked over at Cass. "How are you, chicken? How's the headache?"

"Eric started telling me about Paris, and I forgot all

about it. Why don't *we* go to Paris? I think it would do wonders for us."

"Do wonders for our bank account, too. Don't you let this lousy ex-expatriate come here and turn your head." He walked over to the bar and poured himself a drink. "Did you leave many broken hearts over there?"

"They were very restrained about it. Those centuries of breeding mean something, you know."

"That's what they kept telling me when I was over there. It didn't seem to mean much, though, beyond poverty and corruption and disease. How did you find it?"

"I had a ball. I loved it. Of course, I wasn't in the Army—"

"Did you like the French? I couldn't stand them; I thought they were as ugly and as phony as they come."

"I didn't feel that. They can be pretty damn exasperating —but, hell, I liked them."

"Well. Of course, you're a far more patient sort than I've ever been." He grinned. "How's your French?"

"*Du trottoir*—of the sidewalk. But fluent."

"You learn it in bed?"

He blushed. Richard watched him and laughed.

"Yes. As a matter of fact."

Richard carried his drink to the sofa and sat down. "I can see that traveling hasn't improved your morals any. You going to be around awhile?"

Eric sat down in the armchair across the room from Richard. "Well, I've got to be here at least until the play opens. But after that—who knows?"

"Well," said Richard, and raised his glass, "here's hoping. May it run longer than *Tobacco Road*."

Eric shuddered. "Not with me in it, bud." He drank, he lit a cigarette; a certain familiar fear and anger began to stir in him. "Tell me about yourself, bring me up to date."

But, as he said this, he realized that he did not care what Richard had been doing. He was merely being polite because Richard was married to Cass. He wondered if he had always felt this way. Perhaps he had never been able to admit it to himself. Perhaps Richard had changed—but *did* people change? He wondered what he would think of Richard if he were meeting him for the first time. Then he wondered what Yves would think of these people and what these people would think of Yves.

"There isn't much to tell. You know about the book— I'll get a copy for you, a coming-home present—"

"*That* should make you glad you've returned," said Cass.

Richard looked at her, smiling. "No sabotage, please." He said to Eric, "Cass still likes to make fun of me." Then, "There's a new book coming, Hollywood may buy the first one, I've got a TV thing coming up."

"Anything for me in the TV bit?"

"It's cast. Sorry. We probably couldn't have afforded you, anyway." The doorbell rang. Cass went to answer it.

There was suddenly a tremendous commotion at the door, sobbing and screaming, but Eric did not react until he saw the change in Richard's face, and heard Cass's cry. Then Richard and Eric stood up and the children came pounding into the room. Michael was sobbing and blood dripped from his nose and mouth onto his red-and-white-striped T-shirt. Paul was behind him, pale and silent, with blood on his knuckles and smeared across his face; and his white shirt was torn.

"It's all right, Cass," Richard said, quickly, "it's all right. They're not dead." Michael ran to his father and buried his bloody face in his father's belly. Richard looked at Paul. "What the hell's been going on?"

Cass pulled Michael away and looked into his face. "Come on, baby, let me wash this blood away and see what's happened to you." Michael turned to her, still sobbing, in a state of terror. Cass held him. "Come on, darling, everything's all right, hush now, darling, come on." Michael was led away, his hand in Cass's trembling hand, and Richard looked briefly at Eric, over Paul's head.

"Come on," he said to Paul, "what happened? You get into a fight or did you beat him up, or what?"

Paul sat down, pressing his hands together. "I don't really know what happened." He was on the edge of tears himself; his father waited. "We had been playing ball and then we were getting ready to come home, we weren't doing anything, just fooling around and walking. I wasn't paying much attention to Mike, he was behind me with some friends of his. Then"—he looked at his father—"some colored—colored boys, they came over this hill and they yelled something, I couldn't hear what they yelled. One of them tripped me up as he passed me and they started beating up the little kids and we came running down to stop them." He looked at his father again. "We never saw any of them before, I don't know where they came from. One of them had Mike down on the ground, and was punching him, but I got him off." He looked at his bloody fist. "I think I knocked a couple of teeth down his throat."

"Good for you. You didn't get hurt yourself? How do you feel?"

"I feel all right." But he shuddered.

"Stand up, come over here, let me look at you."

Paul stood up and walked over to his father, who knelt down and stared into his face, prodding him gently in the belly and the chest, stroking his neck and his face. "You got a pretty bad crack in the jaw, didn't you?"

"Mike's hurt worse than I am." But he suddenly began to cry. Richard's lips puckered; he gathered his son into his arms. "Don't cry, Paul, it's all over now."

But Paul could not stop, now that he had begun. "Why would they want to do a thing like that, Daddy? We never even *saw* them before!"

"Sometimes—sometimes the world is like that, Paul. You just have to watch out for people like that."

"Is it because they're colored and we're white? Is that why?"

Again, Richard and Eric looked at each other. Richard swallowed. "The world is full of all kinds of people, and sometimes they do terrible things to each other, but—that's not why."

"Some colored people are very nice," said Eric, "and some are not so nice—like white people. Some are nice and some are terrible." But he did not sound very convincing and he wished he had held his peace.

"This kind of thing's been happening more and more here lately," Richard said, "and, frankly, I'm willing to cry Uncle and surrender the island back to the goddamn Indians. I don't think that they ever intended that we should be happy here." He gave a small, dry laugh, and turned his attention to Paul again. "Would you recognize any of these boys if you saw them again?"

"I think so," Paul said. He caught his breath and dried his eyes. "I know I'd recognize one of them, the one I hit. When the blood came out of his nose and mouth, it looked so—*ugly*—against his skin."

Richard watched him a moment. "Let's go inside and clean up and see what's happening to old Michael."

"Michael can't fight," Paul said, "you know? And kids are always going to be picking on him."

"Well, we're going to have to do something about that. He'll have to *learn* how to fight." He walked to the door, with his arm on Paul's shoulder. He turned to Eric. "Make

yourself at home, will you? We'll be back in a few minutes."
And he and Paul left the room.

Eric listened to the voices of the children and their parents, racing, indistinct, bewildered. "All kids get into fights," said Richard, "let's not make a big thing out of it." "They didn't really get into a fight," Cass said. "They were *attacked*. That's not the same thing at all, it seems to me." "Cass, let's not make it any worse than it is." "I still think we ought to call the doctor; *we* don't know anything about the human body, how do *we* know there isn't something broken or bleeding inside? It happens all the time, people dropping dead two days after an accident." "Okay, okay, stop being so hysterical. You want to scare them to death?" "I am not hysterical and *you* stop being the Rock of Gibraltar. I'm not part of your public, I *know* you!" "Now, what does that mean?" "Nothing. Nothing. Will you please call the *doctor?*" Michael's voice broke in, high and breaking, with a child's terror. "Why, that's the silliest thing I ever heard," Cass said, in another tone and with great authority; "of course no one's going to come in here while you're asleep. Mama and Daddy are here and so is Paul." Michael's voice interrupted her again. "It's all right, we aren't *going* out," Cass said. "We aren't going out *tonight*," Richard said, "and Paul and I are going to teach you some tricks so kids won't be bothering *you* any more. By the time *we* get through, those guys will be afraid of *you*. If they just see you coming, boy, they'll take off in a cloud of dust." He heard Michael's unsteady laugh. Then he heard the sound of the phone being dialed, and Richard's voice, and the small ring of the phone as Richard hung up.

"I guess we won't be going downtown with you, after all," Richard said, coming back into the room. "I'm sorry. I'm sure they're all right but Cass wants the doctor to look at them and we have to wait for him to get here. Anyway, I don't think we should leave them alone tonight." He took Eric's glass from his hand. "Let me spike this for you." He walked over to the bar; he was not as calm as he pretended to be. "Little black bastards," he muttered, "they could have killed the kid. Why the hell can't they take it out on each other, for Christ's sake!"

"They beat Michael pretty badly?"

"Well—they loosened one of his teeth and bloodied his nose—but, mainly, they *scared* the shit out of him. Thank God Paul was with him." Then he was silent. "I don't know.

This whole neighborhood, this whole city's gone to hell. I keep telling Cass we ought to move—but she doesn't want to. Maybe this will help her change her mind."

"Change my mind about what?" Cass asked. She strode to the low table before the sofa, picked up her cigarettes, and lit one.

"Moving out of town," Richard said. He watched her as he spoke and spoke too quietly, as though he were holding himself in.

"I've no objection to moving. We just haven't been able to agree on where to move."

"We haven't agreed on where to move because all you've done is offer objections to every place I suggest. And, since you haven't made any counter-suggestions, I conclude that you don't really want to move."

"Oh, Richard. I simply am not terribly attracted to any of those literary colonies you want us to become a part of—"

Richard's eyes turned as dark as deep water. "Cass doesn't like writers," he said, lightly, to Eric, "not if they make a living at it, anyway. She thinks writers should never cease starving and whoring around, like our good friend, Vivaldo. That's fine, boy, that's really being responsible and artistic. But all the rest of us, trying to love a woman and raise a family and make some loot—we're whores."

She was very pale. "I have never said anything at all like that."

"No? There are lots of ways of saying"—he mimicked her—"things like that. You've said it a thousand times. You must think I'm dumb, chicken." He turned again to Eric, who stood near the window, wishing he could fly out of it. "If she was *stuck* with a guy like Vivaldo—"

"Leave Vivaldo out of this! What has *he* got to do with it?"

Richard gave a surprisingly merry laugh, and repeated, "If she was stuck with a guy like that, maybe you wouldn't hear some pissing and moaning! Oh, what a martyrdom! And how she'd love it!" He took a swallow of his drink and crossed the room toward her. "And you know why? You want to know why?" There was a silence. She lifted her enormous eyes to meet his. "Because you're just like all the other American cunts. You want a guy you can feel sorry for, you love him as long as he's helpless. Then you can *pitch in,* as you love to say, you can be his *helper. Helper!*" He threw back his head and laughed. "Then, one fine day, the guy feels chilly between his legs and feels around for his cock and balls and finds she's helped herself to them and locked them in the linen closet." He finished his drink and, roughly, caught his breath. His voice changed, becoming almost tender with sorrow. "That's the way it is, isn't it sugar? You don't like me now as well as you did once."

She looked terribly weary; her skin seemed to have loosened. She put one hand lightly on his arm. "No," she said, "that's not the way it is." Then a kind of fury shook her and tears came to her eyes. "You haven't any right to say such things to me; you're blaming me for something I haven't anything to do with at all!" He reached out to touch her shoulder; she moved away. "You'd better go, Eric, this can't be much fun for you. Make our excuses, please, to Vivaldo and Ida."

"You can say that the Silenskis, that model couple, were having their Sunday fight," said Richard; his face very white, breathing hard, staring at Cass.

Eric set his drink down, carefully; he wanted to run. "I'll just say you had to stay in on account of the kids."

"Tell Vivaldo to take it as a warning. This is what happens if you have kids, this is what happens if you get what you want." And, for a moment, he looked utterly baffled and juvenile. Then, "Hell, I'm sorry, Eric. We never meant to submit you to such a melodramatic afternoon. Please come and see us again; we don't do this all the time, we really don't. I'll walk you to the door."

"It's all right," Eric said. "I'm a big boy, I understand." He walked over to Cass and they shook hands. "It was nice seeing you."

"It was good seeing you. Don't let all that light fade."

He laughed, but these words chilled him, too. "I'll try to keep burning," he said. He and Richard walked to the hall door. Cass stood still in the center of the living room.

Richard opened the door. "So long, kid. Can we call you —has Cass got your number?"

"Yes. And I have yours."

"Okay. See you soon."

"Sure thing. So long."

"So long."

The door closed behind him. He was again in the anonymous, breathing corridor, surrounded by locked doors. He found his handkerchief and wiped his forehead, thinking of the millions of disputes being waged behind locked doors. He rang for the elevator. It arrived, driven by another, older man who was eating a sandwich; he was dumped into the streets again. The long block on which Cass and Richard lived was quiet and empty now, waiting for the night. He hailed a cab on the avenue and was whirled downtown.

His destination was a bar on the eastern end of the Village, which had, until recently, been merely another neighborhood bar. But now it specialized in jazz, and functioned sometimes as a showcase for younger but not entirely untried or unknown talents or personalities. The current attraction was advertised in the small window by a hand-printed, cardboard poster; he recognized the name of a drummer he and Rufus had known years ago, who would not remember him; in the window, too, were excerpts from newspaper columns and magazines, extolling the unorthodox virtues of the place.

The unorthodox, therefore, filled the room, which was very small, low-ceilinged, with a bar on one side and tables and chairs on the other. At the far end of the bar, the room widened, making space for more tables and chairs, and a very narrow corridor led to the rest rooms and the kitchen; and in this widened space, catty-corner to the room, stood a small, cruelly steep bandstand.

Eric had arrived during a break. The musicians were leaping down from the stand, and mopping their brows with large handkerchiefs, and heading for the street door which would remain open for about ten minutes. The heat in the room was terrifying, and the electric fan in the center of the ceiling could have done nothing to alleviate it. And the room stank: of years of dust, of stale, of regurgitated alcohol, of cooking, of urine, of sweat, of lust. People stood three and four deep at the bar, sticky and shining, far happier than the musicians, who had fled to the sidewalk. Most of the people at the tables had not moved, and they seemed quite young; the boys in sport shirts and seersucker trousers, the girls in limp blouses and wide skirts.

On the sidewalk, the musicians stood idly together, still fanning themselves with their handkerchiefs, their faces blandly watchful, ignoring the occasional panhandlers, and the policeman who walked up and down with his lips pursed and his eyes blind with unnamable suspicions and fears.

He wished he had not come. He was afraid of seeing Vivaldo, he was afraid of meeting Ida; and he began to feel, standing helplessly in the center of this sweltering mob, unbearably odd and visible, unbearably a stranger. It was not a new sensation, but he had not felt it for a long time: he felt marked, as though, presently, someone would notice him and then the entire mob would turn on him, laughing and calling him names. He thought of leaving, but, instead, inched into the bar and ordered a drink. He had no idea how he would go about finding Ida or Vivaldo. He imagined that he would have to wait until she began to sing. But, presumably, they would also be watching for him, for his red hair.

And he sipped his drink, standing uncomfortably close to a burly college boy, unpleasantly jostled by the waiter, who was loading his tray next to him. And he was, indeed, beginning to attract a certain, covert attention; he did not look American, exactly: they were wondering how to place him.

He saw them before they saw him. Something made him turn around and look out through the door, to the sidewalk; and Ida and Vivaldo, loosely swinging hands, walked up and began talking to the musicians. Ida was wearing a tight, white, low-cut dress, and her shoulders were covered with a bright shawl. On the little finger of one hand, she wore a ruby-eyed snake ring; on the opposite wrist, a heavy, barbaric-looking bracelet, of silver. Her hair was swept back from her forehead, piled high, and gleaming, like a crown. She was far more beautiful than Rufus and, except for a beautifully sorrowful, quicksilver tension around the mouth, she might not have reminded him of Rufus. But this detail, which he knew so well, caught him at once, and so did another detail, harder, for a moment, to place. She laughed at something said by one of the musicians, throwing her head back: her heavy silver earrings caught the light. Eric felt a pounding in his chest and between his shoulderblades, as he stared at the gleaming metal and the laughing girl. He felt, suddenly, trapped in a dream from which he could not awaken. The earrings were heavy and archaic, suggesting the shape of a feathered arrow: *Rufus never really liked them.* In that time, eons ago, when they had been cufflinks, given him by Eric as a confession of his love, Rufus had hardly ever worn them. But he had kept them. And here they were, transformed, on the body of his sister. The burly college boy, looking straight ahead, seemed to nudge Eric with his knee. Eric moved a little out from the bar and moved nearer the door, so that they would see him when they looked his way.

He stood sipping his drink in the bar; they stood on the twilit sidewalk. Eric watched Vivaldo and used these moments to remember him. Vivaldo seemed more radiant than he had ever been, and less boyish. He was still very slim, very lean, but he seemed, somehow, to have more weight.

In Eric's memory, Vivaldo always put one foot down lightly, like a distrustful colt, ready, at any moment, to break and run; but now he stood where he stood, the ground bore him, and his startled, sniffing, maverick quality was gone. Or perhaps not entirely gone: his black eyes darted from face to face as he spoke, as he listened, investigating, weighing, watching, his eyes hiding more than they revealed. The conversation took a more somber turn. One of the musicians had brought up the subject of money—of unions, and, with a gesture toward the spot where Eric stood, of working conditions. Vivaldo's eyes darkened, his face became still, and he looked briefly down at Ida. She watched the musician who was speaking with a proud, bitter look on her face. "So maybe you better give it another thought, gal," the musician concluded. "I've thought about it," she said, looking down, touching one of the earrings. Vivaldo took this hand in his, and she looked up at him; he kissed her lightly on the tip of the nose. "Well," said another musician, wearily, "we better be making it on in." He turned and entered the bar, saying, "Excuse me, man," to Eric as he passed. Ida whispered something in Vivaldo's ear; he listened, frowning. His hair fell over his forehead, and he threw his head back, sharply, with a look of annoyance, and saw Eric.

For a moment they simply stared at each other. Another musician, entering the bar, passed between them. Then, Vivaldo said, "So there you are. I didn't really believe you'd make it; I didn't really believe you'd be back."

"But I'm here," said Eric, grinning, "now, what do you think of that?"

Vivaldo suddenly raised his arms and laughed—and the policeman moved directly behind him, glowering, seeming to wait for an occult go-ahead signal—and covered the space between himself and Eric and threw both arms around him. Eric nearly dropped the glass he was holding, for Vivaldo had thrown him off balance; he grinned up into Vivaldo's grinning face; and he was aware, behind Vivaldo, of Ida, inscrutably watching, and the policeman, waiting.

"You fucking red-headed Rebel," Vivaldo shouted, "you haven't changed a bit! Christ, I'm glad to see you, I'd no *idea* I'd be so glad to see you." He released Eric, and stepped back, oblivious, apparently, to the storm he was creating. He dragged Eric out of the bar, into the street, over to Ida. "Here's the sonofabitch we've been talking about so long, Ida; here's Eric. He's the last human being to get out of Alabama."

The policeman seemed to take a dim, even a murderous view of this, and, ceasing to wait on occult inspiration, peered commandingly into the bar. The signal he then received caused him, slowly, to move a little away. But Vivaldo beamed on Eric as though Eric were his pride and joy; and said again, to Ida, staring at Eric, "Ida, this is Eric. Eric, meet Ida." And he took their hands and placed them together.

Ida grasped his hand, laughing, and looked into his eyes. "Eric," she said, "I think I've heard more about you than I've ever heard about any living human being. I'm so glad to meet you, I can't tell you. I'd decided you weren't nothing but a myth."

The touch of her hand shocked him, as did her eyes and her warmth and her beauty. "I'm delighted to meet you, too," he said. "You can't have heard more about me—you can't have heard *better* about me—than I've heard about you."

They held each other's eyes for a second, she still smiling, wearing all her beauty as a great queen wears her robes—and establishing that distance between them, too—and then one of the musicians came to the doorway, and said, "Ida, honey, the man says come on with it if you coming." And he disappeared.

Ida said, "Come on, follow me. They've got a table for us way in back somewhere." She took Eric's arm. "They're doing me a favor, letting me sit in. I've never sung in public before. So I can't afford to bug them."

"You see," said Vivaldo, behind them, "you got off the boat just in time for a great occasion."

"You should have let *him* say that," said Ida.

"I was just about to," said Eric, "believe me." They squeezed through the crowd to the slightly wider area in the back. Here, Ida paused, looking about her.

She looked up at Eric. "What happened to Richard and Cass?"

"They asked me to apologize for them. They couldn't come. One of the kids was sick."

He felt, as he said this, a faint tremor of disloyalty—to Ida: as though she were mixed up in his mind with the colored children who had attacked Paul and Michael in the park.

"*Today* of all days," she sighed—but seemed, really, scarcely to be concerned about their absence. Her eyes continued to search the crowd; she sighed again, a sigh of private resignation. The musicians were ready, attempts were being made to silence the mob. A waiter appeared and seated them at a tiny table in a corner next to the ladies' room, and took their order. The malevolent heat, now that they were trapped in this spot, began rising from the floor and descending from the ceiling.

Eric did not really listen to the music, he could not; it remained entirely outside him, like some minor agitation of the air. He watched Ida and Vivaldo, who sat opposite him, their profiles turned toward the music. Ida watched with a bright, sardonic knowingness, as though the men on the stand were beating out a message she had commanded them to convey; but Vivaldo's head was slightly lowered and he looked up at the bandstand with a wry, uncertain bravado, as though there were an incipient war going on between himself and the musicians, having to do with rank and color and authority. He and Ida sat very still, very straight, not touching—it was as though, before this altar, touch was forbidden them.

The musicians sweated on the stand, like horses, played loudly and badly, with a kind of reckless contempt, and failed, during their first number, to agree on anything. This did not, of course, affect the applause, which was loud, enthusiastic, and prolonged. Only Vivaldo made no sound. The drummer, who, from time to time, had let his eyes travel from Ida to Vivaldo—then bowed his head to the drums again—registered Vivaldo's silence with a broad, mocking grin, and gestured to Ida.

"It's your turn now," he said. "Come on up here and see what *you* can do to civilize these devils." And, with the merest of glances at Eric and Vivaldo, "I think you might have had enough practice by now."

Ida looked into his eyes with an unreadable smile, which yet held some hint of the vindictive. She crushed out her cigarette, adjusted her shawl, and rose, demurely. "I'm glad you think I'm ready," she said. "Keep your fingers crossed for me, sugar," she said to Vivaldo, and stepped up on the stand.

She was not announced; there was merely a brief huddle with the piano player; and then she stepped up to the mike. The piano player began the first few bars, but the crowd did not take the hint.

"Let's try it again," said Ida, in a loud, clear voice.

At this, heads turned to look at her; she looked calmly down on them. The only sign of her agitation was in her

hands, which were tightly, restlessly clasped before her—
she was wringing her hands, but she was not crying.

Somebody said, in a loud whisper, "Dig, man, that's the
Kid's kid sister."

There were beads of sweat on her forehead and on her
nose, and one leg moved out, trembling, moved back. The
piano player began again, she grabbed the mike like a
drowning woman, and abruptly closed her eyes:

> *You*
> *Made me leave my happy home.*
> *You took my love and now you've gone,*
> *Since I fell for you.*

She was not a singer yet. And if she were to be judged
solely on the basis of her voice, low, rough-textured, of no
very great range, she never would be. Yet, she had something which made Eric look up and caused the room to fall
silent; and Vivaldo stared at Ida as though he had never
seen her before. What she lacked in vocal power and, at the
moment, in skill, she compensated for by a quality so mysteriously and implacably egocentric that no one has ever
been able to name it. This quality involves a sense of the
self so profound and so powerful that it does not so much
leap barriers as reduce them to atoms—while still leaving
them standing, mightily, where they were; and this awful
sense is private, unknowable, not to be articulated, having,
literally, to do with something else; it transforms and lays
waste and gives life, and kills.

She finished her first number and the applause was
stunned and sporadic. She looked over at Vivaldo with a
small, childish shrug. And this gesture somehow revealed to
Eric how desperately one could love her, how desperately
Vivaldo was in love with her. The drummer went into a
down-on-the-levee-type song, which turned out to be a
song Eric had never heard before:

> *Betty told Dupree*
> *She wanted a diamond ring.*
> *And Dupree said, Betty,*
> *I'll get you most any old thing.*

"My God," muttered Vivaldo, "she's been working."

His tone unconsciously implied that he had not been, and
held an unconscious resentment. And this threw Eric in on

himself. Neither had he been working—for a long time; he
had merely been keeping his hand in. It had been because of
Yves; so he had told himself; but was this true? He looked at
Vivaldo's white, passionate face and wondered if Vivaldo
were now thinking that he had not been working because of
Ida: who had not, however, allowed *him* to distract *her.*
There she was, up on the stand, and unless all the signs were
false, and no matter how hard or long the road might be, she
was on her way. She had started.

> *Give Mama my clothes,*
> *Give Betty my diamond ring.*
> *Tomorrow's Friday,*
> *The day I got to swing.*

She and the musicians were beginning to enjoy each other
and to egg each other on as they bounced through this ballad
of cupidity, treachery, and death; and Ida had created in
the room a new atmosphere and a new excitement. Even the
heat seemed less intolerable. The musicians played for her
as though she were an old friend come home and their pride
in her restored their pride in themselves.

The number ended and Ida stepped off the stand, wet and
triumphant, the applause crashing about her ears like foam.
She came to the table, looking at Vivaldo with a smile and a
small, questioning frown, and, standing, took a sip of her
drink. They called her back. The drummer reached down
and lifted her, bodily, onto the stand, and the applause continued. Eric became aware of a shift in Vivaldo's attention.
He looked at Vivaldo's face, which was stormier than ever,
and followed his eyes. Vivaldo was looking at a short square
man with curly hair and a boyish face who was standing at
the end of the bar, looking up at Ida. He grinned and waved
and Ida nodded and Vivaldo looked up at the stand again:
with narrowed eyes and pursed lips, with an air of grim
speculation.

"Your girl friend's got something," Eric said.

Vivaldo glanced over at him. "It runs in the family," he
said. His tone was not friendly; it was as though he suspected Eric of taunting him; and so referred, obliquely, to
Rufus, with the intention of humbling Eric. Yet, in a moment he relented. "She's going to be terrific," he said, "and,
Lord, I'm going to have to buy me a baseball bat to keep all
the hungry cats away." He grinned and looked again at the
short man at the bar.

Ida stepped up to the microphone. "This song is for my brother," she said. She hesitated and looked over at Vivaldo. "He died just a little before Thanksgiving, last year." There was a murmur in the room. Somebody said, "What did I tell you?"—triumphantly; there was a brief spatter of applause, presumably for the dead Rufus; and the drummer bowed his head and did an oddly irreverent riff on the rim of his drum: *klook-a-klook, klook-klook, klook-klook!*

Ida sang:

> *Precious Lord, take my hand,*
> *Lead me on, let me stand.*

Her eyes were closed and the dark head on the long dark neck was thrown back. Something appeared in her face which had not been there before, a kind of passionate, triumphant rage and agony. Now, her fine, sensual, free-moving body was utterly still, as though being held in readiness for a communion more total than flesh could bear; and a strange chill came into the room, along with a strange resentment. Ida did not know how great a performer she would have to become before she could dare expose her audience, as she now did, to her private fears and pain. After all, her brother had meant nothing to them, or had never meant to them what he had meant to her. They did not wish to witness her mourning, especially as they dimly suspected that this mourning contained an accusation of themselves—an accusation which their uneasiness justified. They endured her song, therefore, but they held themselves outside it; and yet, at the same time, the very arrogance and innocence of Ida's offering compelled their admiration.

> *Hear my cry, hear my call,*
> *Take my hand, lest I fall,*
> *Precious Lord!*

The applause was odd—not quite unwilling, not quite free; wary, rather, in recognition of a force not quite to be trusted but certainly to be watched. The musicians were now both jubilant and watchful, as though Ida had abruptly become their property. The drummer adjusted her shawl around her shoulders, saying, "You been perspiring, don't you let yourself catch cold"; and, as she started off the stand, the piano player rose and, ceremoniously, kissed her on the brow. The bass player said, "Hell, let's tell the folks her *name."* He grabbed the microphone and said, "Ladies and gentlemen, you've been listening to Miss Ida Scott. This is her first—*exposure,"* and he mopped his brow, ironically. The crowd laughed. He said, "But it won't be her last." The applause came again, more easily this time, since the role of judge and bestower had been returned to the audience. "We have been present," said the bass player, "at an historic event." This time the audience, in a paroxysm of self-congratulation, applauded, stomped, and cheered.

"Well," said Vivaldo, taking both her hands in his, "it looks like you're on your way."

"Were you proud of me?" She made her eyes very big: the curve of her lips was somewhat sardonic.

"Yes," he said, after an instant, gravely, "but, then, I'm always proud of you."

Then she laughed and kissed him quickly on the cheek. "My darling Vivaldo. You ain't seen nothing yet."

"I'd like," said Eric, "to add my voice to the general chorus of joy and gratitude. You were great, you really were."

She looked at him. Her eyes were still very big and something in her regard made him feel that she disliked him. He brushed the thought away as he would have brushed away a fly. "I'm not great yet," she said, "but I will be," and she raised both hands and touched her earrings.

"They're very beautiful," he said, "your earrings."

"Do you like them? My brother had them made for me—just before he died."

He paused. "I knew your brother a little. I was very sorry to hear about his—his death."

"Many, many people were," said Ida. "He was a very beautiful man, a very great artist. But he made"—she regarded him with a curious, cool insolence—"some very bad connections. He was the kind who believed what people said. If you told Rufus you loved him, well, he believed you and he'd stick with you till death. I used to try to tell him the world wasn't like that." She smiled. "He was much nicer than I am. It doesn't pay to be too nice in this world."

"That may be true. But you seem nice—you seem very nice—to me."

"That's because you don't know me. But ask Vivaldo!" And she turned to Vivaldo, putting her arm on his.

"I have to beat her up from time to time," said Vivaldo, "but, otherwise, she's great." He stuck out his hand to the short man, who now stood behind Ida. "Hello there, Mr. Ellis. What brings you all the way down here?"

Ellis raised his eyebrows exaggeratedly and threw out his palms. "What do you think brings me down here? I had an uncontrollable desire to see Sammy's Bowery Follies."

Ida turned, smiling, still leaning on Vivaldo. "My God. I saw you down there at the bar, but I scarcely dared believe it was you."

"None other," he said, "and you know"——he looked at her with tremendous admiration——"you are an extraordinary young woman. I've always thought so, I must say, but now I've seen it. I doubt if even you know how great a career is within your grasp."

"I've got an awfully long way to go, Mr. Ellis, I've got such an awful lot to learn."

"If you ever stop feeling that way, I will personally take a hairbrush to you." He looked up at Vivaldo. "You have not called me and I take that very unkindly."

Vivaldo suppressed whatever rude retort was on his tongue. He said, mildly, "I just don't think I've got much of a future in TV."

"*Oh,* what an abysmal lack of imagination!" He shook Ida playfully by the shoulder. "Can't you do anything with this man of yours? *Why* does he insist on holding his light under a bushel?"

"The truth is," said Ida, "that the last time anybody made up Vivaldo's mind for him was the last time they changed his diapers. And that was *quite* a long time ago. Anyway," and she rubbed her cheek against Vivaldo's shoulder, "I wouldn't dream of trying to change him. I like him the way he is."

There was something very ugly in the air. She clung to Vivaldo, but Eric felt that there was something in it which was meant for Ellis. And Vivaldo seemed to feel this, too. He moved slightly away from Ida and picked up her handbag from the table—to give his hands something to do?—and said, "You haven't met our friend, he just came in from Paris. This is Eric Jones; this is Steve Ellis."

They shook hands. "I know your name," said Ellis. "Why?"

"He's an actor," said Ida, "and he's opening on Broadway in the fall."

Vivaldo, meanwhile, was paying the check. Eric took out his wallet, but Vivaldo waved it away.

"I *have* heard of you. I've heard quite a *lot* about you,"

and he looked Eric appraisingly up and down. "Bronson's
signed you for *Happy Hunting Ground*. Is that right?"

"That's right," said Eric. He could not tell whether he
liked Ellis or not.

"It's kind of an interesting play," Ellis said, cautiously,
"and, from what I've heard of you, it ought to do very good
things for you." He turned back to Ida and Vivaldo. "Could
I persuade you to have *one* drink with me in some secluded,
air-conditioned bar? I really don't think," he said to Ida,
"that you ought to make a habit of working in such infernos.
You'll end up dying of tuberculosis, like Spanish bullfighters,
who are always either too hot or too cold."

"Oh, I guess we have time for *one* drink," said Ida, looking doubtfully at Vivaldo, "what do you think, sweetie?"

"It's your night," said Vivaldo. They started toward the
door.

"I'd like to mix maybe just a *little* bit of business in with
this drink," said Ellis.

"I figured that," said Vivaldo. "What an eager beaver you
are."

"The secret," said Ellis, "of my not inconsiderable success." He turned to Ida. "I thought you told me yesterday
that Dick Silenski and his wife would be here—?"

Something happened, then, in her face and in his—in his,
wry panic and regret, quickly covered; in hers, an outraged
warning, quickly dissembled. They entered the wide, hot
street. "Eric saw them," she said, calmly, "something happened, they couldn't come."

"The kids got into a fight in the park," said Eric. "Some
colored kids beat them up." He heard Ida's breathing
change; he told himself he was a bastard. "I left them waiting
for the doctor."

"You didn't tell me that," cried Vivaldo, "Jesus! I'd better
call them up!"

"That isn't what you told me, either," said Ida.

"They weren't very badly hurt," said Eric, "just bloody
noses. But they thought they'd better have a doctor look at
them and of course they didn't want to leave them alone."

"I'll call them," said Vivaldo, "as soon as we get to a bar."

"Yes, sweetie," said Ida, "you'd better do that. What a terrible thing to have happen."

Vivaldo said nothing; kicked at a beer can on the sidewalk. They were walking west through a dark wilderness of
tenements, of dirty children, of staring adolescents, and
sweating grownups. "When you say colored boys," Ida pur-

sued, after a moment, "do you mean that was the *reason* for the fight?"

"There didn't," said Eric, "seem to be any *other* reason. They'd never seen the boys before."

"I imagine," said Ida, "that it was in some kind of retaliation—for something some other boys had done to them."

"I guess that must be it," said Eric.

They reached the crowded park at the bottom of Fifth Avenue. Eric had not seen the park for many years and the melancholy and distaste which weighed him down increased as they began to walk through it. Lord, here were the trees and the benches and the people and the dark shapes on the grass; the children's playground, deserted now, with the swings and the slides and the sandpile; and the darkness surrounding this place, in which the childless wretched gathered to act out their joyless rituals. His life, his entire life, rose to his throat like bile tonight. The sea of memory washed over him, again and again, and each time it receded another humiliated Eric was left writhing on the sands. How hard it was to be despised! how impossible not to despise oneself! Here were the peaceful men in the lamplight, playing chess. A sound of singing and guitar-playing came from the center of the park; idly, they walked toward it; they each seemed to be waiting and fearing the resolution of their evening. There was a great crowd gathered in the small fountain; this crowd broke down, upon examination, into several small crowds, each surrounding one, two, or three singers. The singers, male and female, wore blue jeans and long hair and had more zest than talent. Yet, there was something very winning, very moving, about their unscrubbed, unlined faces, and their blankly shining, infantile eyes, and their untried, unhypocritical voices. They sang as though, by singing, they could bring about the codification and the immortality of innocence. Their listeners were of another circle, aimless, empty, and corrupt, and stood packed together in the stone fountain merely in order to be comforted or inflamed by the touch and the odor of human flesh. And the policemen, in the lamplight, circled around them all.

Ida and Vivaldo walked together, Eric and Ellis walked together; but all of them were far from one another. Eric felt, dimly, that he ought to make some attempt to talk to the man beside him, but he had no desire to talk to him; he wanted to leave, and he was afraid to leave. Ida and Vivaldo had also been silent. Now, as they walked from group to singing group, intermittently, through romanticized Western ballads and toothless Negro spirituals, he heard their voices. And he knew that Ellis was listening, too. This knowledge forced him, finally, to speak to Ellis.

He heard Ida. "—sweetie, don't *be* like that."

"Will you stop calling me *sweetie?* That's what you call every miserable cock sucker who comes sniffing around your ass."

"*Must* you talk that way?"

"Look, don't you pull any of that *lady* bullshit on me."

"—you talk. I'll never understand white people, never, never, never! How *can* you talk that way? How can you expect anyone else to respect you if you don't respect yourselves?"

"*Oh.* Why the fuck did I ever get tied up with a *house* nigger? And I am not *white people!*"

"—I warn you, I warn you!"

"—*you're* the one who starts it! You *always* start it!"

"—I knew you would be *jealous. That's* why!"

"You picked a fine way to keep me from being—jealous, baby."

"Can't we talk about it *later?* Why do you always have to spoil everything?"

"Oh, sure, sure, I'm the one who spoils everything, all right!"

Eric said, to Ellis, "Do you think any of these singers have a future on TV?"

"On daytime TV maybe," Ellis said, and laughed.

"You're a hard man," said Eric.

"I'm just realistic," Ellis said. "I figure everybody's out for himself, to make a buck, whether he says so or not. And there's nothing wrong with that. I just wish more people would admit it, that's all. Most of the people who think they disapprove of me don't disapprove of me at all. They just wish that they were me."

"I guess that's true," said Eric—mortally bored.

They began walking away from the music. "Did you live abroad a long time?" Ellis asked, politely.

"About three years."

"Where?"

"Paris, mostly."

"What made you go? There's nothing for an actor to do over there, is there? I mean, an American actor."

"Oh, I did a couple of things for American TV." Coming toward them, on the path, were two glittering, loud-talking fairies. He pulled in his belly, looking straight ahead. "And I saw a lot of theater—I don't know—it was very good for me." The birds of paradise passed; their raucous cries faded.

Ida said, "I always feel so *sorry* for people like that."

Ellis grinned. "Why should you feel sorry for them? They've got each other."

The four of them now came abreast, Ida putting her arm through Eric's.

"A couple of the waiters on my job are like that. The way some people treat them—! They tell me about it, they tell me everything. I like them, I really do. They're very sweet. And, of course, they make wonderful escorts. You haven't got to worry about them."

"They don't cost much, either," said Vivaldo. "I'll pick one up for you next week and we can keep him around the house as a pet."

"I simply am not able, today, am I, to say anything that will please you?"

"Stop trying so hard. Ellis, where are you taking us for this business-mixed-with-pleasure drink?"

"Curb your enthusiasm. We're practically there." They turned away from the park, toward Eighth Street, and walked into a downstairs bar. Ellis was known here, naturally; they found a booth and ordered.

"Now, the extent of the *business*," Ellis said, looking from Ida to Vivaldo, "is very simple. I've helped other people and I think I can help Miss Scott." He looked at Ida. "You aren't ready yet. You've got a hell of a lot of work to do and a hell of a lot to learn. And I'd like you to drop by my office one afternoon this week so we can go into all this in detail. You've got to study and work and you've got to keep alive while you're doing all that and maybe I can help you work that out." Then he looked at Vivaldo. "And you can come, too, if you think I'm trying to exploit Miss Scott unfairly. Is it your intention to act as her agent?"

"No."

"You don't have any reason to distrust me; you just don't like me, is that it?"

"Yes," said Vivaldo after a moment, "I guess that's right."

"Oh, Vivaldo," Ida moaned.

"That's all right. It's always good to know where you stand. But you certainly aren't going to allow this—*prejudice*—to stand in Miss Scott's way?"

"I wouldn't dream of it. Anyway, Ida does what she wants."

Ellis considered him. He looked briefly at Ida. "Well. That's reassuring." He signaled for the waiter and turned to Ida. "What day shall we make it? Tuesday, Wednesday?"

"Wednesday might be better," she said, hesitantly.

"Around three o'clock?"

"Yes. That's fine."

"It's settled, then." He made a note in his engagement book, then took out his billfold, picked up the check and gave a ten-dollar bill to the waiter. "Give these people anything they want," he said, "it's on me."

"Oh, are you going now?" asked Ida.

"Yes. My wife will kill me if I don't get home in time to see the kids before I go to the studio. See you Wednesday." He held out his hand to Eric. "Glad to have met you, Red; all the best. Maybe you'll do a show for me, one day." He looked down at Vivaldo. "So long, genius. I'm sorry you don't like me. Maybe one of these days you ought to ask yourself why. It's no good blaming *me*, you know, if you don't know how to get or how to hold on to what you want." Then he turned and left. Vivaldo watched the short legs going up the stairs into the street.

He wiped his forehead with his wet handkerchief and the three of them sat in silence for a moment. Then, "I'm going to call Cass," Vivaldo said, and rose and walked toward the phone booth in the back.

"I understand," said Ida, carefully, "that you were a very good friend of my brother's."

"Yes," he said, "I was. Or at least I tried to be."

"Did you find it so very hard—to be his friend?"

"No. No, I hadn't meant to suggest that." He tried to smile. "He was very wrapped up in his music, he was very much—himself. I was younger then, I may not always have —understood." He felt sweat in his armpits, on his forehead, between his legs.

"Oh." She looked at him from very far away. "You may have wanted more from him than he could give. Many people did, men *and* women." She allowed this to hang between them for an instant. Then, "He was terribly attractive, wasn't he? I always think that that was the reason he died, that he was too attractive and didn't know how—how to keep people away." She sipped her drink. "People don't have any mercy. They tear you limb from limb, in the name of love. Then, when you're dead, when they've killed you by what they made you go through, they say you didn't have any character. They weep big, bitter tears—not for *you*. For themselves, because they've lost their toy."

"That's a terribly grim view," he said, "of love."

"I know what I'm talking about. That's what most people mean, when they say love." She picked up a cigarette and waited for him to light it. "Thank you. You weren't here, you never saw Rufus's last girl friend—a terrible little whore of a nymphomaniac, from Georgia. She *wouldn't* let him go, he tried all kinds of ways of getting away from her. He even thought of running away to Mexico. She got him so he couldn't work—I swear, there's nothing like a Southern white person, especially a Southern *woman*, when she gets her hooks into a Negro man." She blew a great cloud of smoke about his head. "And now she's still living, the filthy white slut, and Rufus is dead."

He said, hoping that she would really hear him but knowing she would not, perhaps *could* not, "I hope you don't think *I* loved your brother in that terrible way that you describe. I think we really *were* very good friends, and—and it was an awful shock for me to hear that he was dead. I was in Paris when I heard."

"Oh! I'm not accusing *you*. You and I are going to be friends. Don't you think so?"

"I certainly hope so."

"Well, that settles it, as far as I'm concerned." Then, smiling, with her eyes very big, "What did you do in Paris all that time?"

"Oh"—he smiled—"I tried to grow up."

"Couldn't you have done that here? Or didn't you want to?"

"I don't know. It was more fun in Paris."

"I'll bet." She crushed out her cigarette. "*Have* you grown up?"

"I don't know," he said, "any longer, if people *do*."

She grinned. "You've got a point there, Buster."

Vivaldo came back to the table. She looked up at him. "Well? How are the kids?"

"They're all right. Cass sounded a little distraught, but she sends her love to both of you and hopes to see you soon. Are we going to hang around here, or what are we going to do?"

"Well, let's have supper," Ida said.

Vivaldo and Eric looked at each other for the briefest of seconds. "You'll have to count me out," said Eric, quickly.

"I'm bushed, I've had it, I'm going to go home and hit the sack."

"It's so *early,*" Ida said.

"Well, I just got off a boat and I'm still vibrating." He stood up. "I'll take a rain check on it."

"Well," she looked at Vivaldo, humorously, "I'm sorry the lord and master isn't in a better mood." She moved herself out of the booth. "I've got to go to the little girl's room. Wait for me upstairs."

"I'm sorry," said Vivaldo, as they climbed the stairs into the street, "I'd really looked forward to sitting around and bullshitting with you tonight and all, but I guess you really better leave us alone. You understand, don't you?"

"Of course I understand," said Eric. "I'll give you a call next week sometime." They stood on the sidewalk, watching the aimless mob.

"It must feel very strange for you," said Vivaldo, "to be back here. But I hope you won't think we're not friends any more, because we are. I care a lot about you, Eric. I just want you to know that, so you won't think I'm putting you down gently, sort of, tonight. It's just one of those things." He stared outward, looking very weary. "Sometimes that girl gets me so I don't know if I'm coming or going."

"I know a little bit about it," Eric said. "No sweat." He held out his hand; Vivaldo held it for a moment. "I'll give you a call in a couple of days, all right? Say good-bye to Ida for me."

"All right, Eric. Be well."

Eric smiled. "Stay well."

He turned and started walking toward Sixth Avenue, but he did not really know where he was going. He felt Vivaldo's eyes on his back; then Vivaldo was swallowed up in the press of people behind him.

On the corner of Sixth Avenue, he watched and waited, the lights banged on and off. A truck came by; he looked up into the face of the truck driver, and felt an awful desire to join that man and ride in that truck wherever the truck was going.

But he crossed the street and started walking toward his apartment. It was the safest place to be, it was the only place to be. Strange people—they seemed strange to him now, but, one day, again, he might be one of them—passed him with that ineffable, sidelong, desperate look; but he kept his eyes on the pavement. *Not yet, not you. Not yet. Not yet.*

CHAPTER 3

On the Wednesday afternoon that Ida went off to see Ellis,
Cass called Vivaldo at the midtown bookshop where he
worked and asked if she could buy him a drink when his day
was over. The sound of her voice, swift, subdued, and unhappy, had the effect of jolting him out of his own bewilderment. He asked her to pick him up at the shop at six.

She arrived at the exact time, wearing a green summer
dress which made her look very young, carrying an absurdly
large straw handbag. Her hair was pulled back and fell over
her shoulders; and, for a moment, watching her push
through the doors, both blurred and defined by the heavy
sunlight, she looked like the Cass of his adolescence, of years
ago. She had then been the most beautiful, the most golden
girl on earth. And Richard had been the greatest, most beautiful man.

She seemed terribly wound up—seemed to blaze, nearly,
with some private, barely contained passion. She smiled at
him, looking both young and weary; and for a moment he
was faintly aware of her personal heat, her odor.

"How are you, Vivaldo? It's been rather a while since
we've seen each other."

"I guess it has. And it's been my fault. How are things
with you?"

She shrugged humorously, raising her hands like a child.
"Oh. Up and down." Then, after a moment, "Rather down
right now." She looked around the store. People were peering into bookshelves rather the way children peered in at the
glass-enclosed fish in the aquarium. "Are you free? Can we
leave now?"

"Yes. I was just waiting for you." He said good night to
his employer and they walked into the scalding streets. They
were in the Fifties, on the East Side. "Where shall we have
this drink?"

"I don't care. Some place with air conditioning. And without a TV set. I couldn't care less about baseball."

They started walking uptown, and east, as though each wished to get as far away as possible from the world they knew and their responsibilities in it. The presence of others, walking past them, walking toward them, erupting rudely out of doorways and taxicabs, and springing up from the curbs, intruded painfully on their stillness and seemed to menace their connection. And each man or woman that passed seemed also to be carrying some intolerable burden; their private lives screamed from their hot and discontented faces.

"On days like this," Cass said, suddenly, "I remember what it was like—I *think* I remember—to be young, *very* young." She looked up at him. "When everything, touching and tasting—everything—was so new, and even suffering was wonderful because it was so complete."

"That's hindsight, Cass. I wouldn't want to be that young again for anything on earth."

But he knew what she meant. Her words had taken his mind away—for a moment—from his cruel visions of Ida and Ellis. ("You told me you hadn't seen him since that party." "Well. I *did* go to see him once, just to tell him about the jam session." "Why did you have to see him, why didn't you just call?" "I wasn't sure he'd *remember* me from just over the phone. And then I didn't tell you because I knew how you'd behave." "I don't care what you say, baby, I know what he's after, he just wants to get inside your drawers." "Oh, Vivaldo. You think I don't know how to handle little snots like that?" And she gave him a look, which he did not know how to answer, which almost stated *Look how I handled you.*)

But now he thought of himself at fifteen or sixteen—swimming in the Coney Island surf, or in the pool in his neighborhood; playing handball in the playground, sometimes with his father; lying in the gutter after a street fight, vomiting, praying that no enemy would take this occasion to kick his brains in. He remembered the fear of those days, fear of everything, covered with a mocking, staccato style, defended with the bullets of dirty words. Everything was for the first time; at fifteen or sixteen; and what was her name? Zelda. Could that possibly be right? On the roof, in the summertime, under the dirty city stars.

All for the first time, in the days when acts had no consequences and nothing was irrecoverable, and love was simple and even pain had the dignity of enduring forever: it was unimaginable that time could do anything to diminish it. Where was Zelda now? She might easily have been transformed into the matron with fleshy, spreading buttocks and metallically unlikely blond hair who teetered on high heels just before them now. She, too, somewhere, some day, had looked on and touched everything for the first time and felt the summer air on her breasts like a blessing and been entered and had the blood run out, for the first time.

And what was Cass thinking?

"Oh, no," she said, slowly, "I certainly don't mean that I want to *be* that miserable girl again. I was just remembering how different it was then—how different from now."

He put one arm around her thin shoulders. "You sound sad, Cass. Tell me what's the matter."

He guided her into a dark, cool cocktail lounge. The waiter led them to a small table for two, took their orders, and disappeared. Cass looked down at the tabletop and played with the salted peanuts in the red plastic dish.

"Well, that's why I called you—to talk to you. But it's not so easy. I'm not sure I *know* what's the matter." The waiter returned and set their drinks down before them. "That's not true. I guess I *do* know what's the matter."

Then she was silent. She sipped her drink nervously and lit a cigarette.

"I guess it's about Richard and me," she said at last. "I don't know what's going to become of us. There doesn't seem to be anything between us any more." She spoke in an odd, breathless way, almost like a schoolgirl, and as though she did not believe what she was saying. "Oh, I guess that's not right. There's a hell of a lot between us, there *must* be. But none of it seems to work. Sometimes—sometimes I think he hates me—for being married, for the children, for the work he does. And other times I know that isn't true, that can't be true." She bit her lower lip and stubbed out her cigarette and tried to laugh. "Poor Vivaldo. I know you've got troubles of your own and don't know *what* to do about the maunderings of a middle-aged, self-centered matron."

"Now that you mention it," he said, "I guess you *are* practically decrepit." He tried to smile; he did not know what to say. Ida and Ellis, thrust hastily to the back of his mind, were, nevertheless, dimly accomplishing their unspeakable violations of his manhood. "It really just sounds like a kind of summer storm—don't *all* married people have them?"

"I really don't know anything *about* all married people.

I'm not sure I know anything about marriage." She sipped her drink again, saying, irrelevantly, "I wish I could get drunk." Then she giggled, her proud face suddenly breaking. "I wish I could get drunk and go out and pick up a truck driver or a taxi driver or anybody who'd touch me and make me feel like a woman again." She hid her face with one bony hand and her tears dripped through her fingers. Keeping her head down, she searched fiercely through the absurd straw handbag and finally came up with a small bit of Kleenex. With this, miraculously, she managed to blow her nose and dry her eyes. "I'm sorry," she said, "I've just been sitting around brooding too long."

"What have you been brooding about, Cass? I thought you and Richard had it made." These words sounded, in his own ears, stiff and uncaring. But he had known Cass and Richard too long and been too young when he met them; he had never really thought of Cass and Richard as lovers. Sometimes, of course, he had watched Cass move, realizing that, small as she was, she was all woman and all there, had good legs and nice breasts and knew how to twist her small behind; and, sometimes, watching Richard's great paw on her wrist, wondered how she bore his weight. But he had the tendency of all wildly disorganized people to suppose that the lives of others were tamer and less sensual and more cerebral than his own. And for the very first time he had the sense of Cass as a passionate woman who had merely been carrying on a legal love affair; who writhed as beautifully and shamelessly in Richard's arms as the women Vivaldo had dreamed about for all these years. "I guess," he added, "I must sound pretty dumb. Forgive me."

She smiled—smiled as though she had read his thoughts. "No, you don't. Perhaps I also thought we had it made. But nobody ever has it made." She lit another cigarette, straightening her shoulders, slowly circling, as she had for many weeks now, around some awful decision. "I keep telling myself it's because of the way our lives have changed, now that Richard's becoming so well known. But it isn't that. It's something that's been there all along." Now she was very grave and dry. She looked at Vivaldo through the smoke of her cigarette, narrowing her eyes. "You know, I used to look at you and all your horrible adventures and compare you to Richard and me and think how lucky we were. He was the first"—she faltered and looked down—"the very first man I ever had, and I was the first for him, too—*really* the first, the first girl, anyway, he ever *loved*."

And she looked down again, as though the burden of confession were too great. Yet they were united in the knowledge that what she had begun she must now finish.

"And you think he doesn't love you any more?"

She did not answer. She covered her forehead with her ringed left hand and stared into the dish of salted peanuts as though the answer to all riddles were hidden there. The tiny arrows on her wrist watch said it was twenty-five minutes to seven. Ida would have left Ellis hours ago and would have visited her singing teacher. She would now be in the restaurant, her station set up, and her uniform on, preparing for the dinner rush. He could see her closed, haughty face as she approached a table, manipulating her pad and pencil as though it were a sword and shield. She would not have stayed long with Ellis—he was a busy man. But how long did it take for those guys to bang off a quick one, in the middle of the afternoon, in their inviolable offices? He tried to concentrate on Cass and her trouble. Perhaps he had taken her out for a drink; perhaps he had persuaded her not to go to work, and had invited her for dinner; perhaps they were together now. (Where?) Perhaps Ellis had persuaded her to meet him at midnight in a theatrical bar, the kind of place where it would do her good to be seen with him. But no, not that; it would certainly not do Ellis any good to be seen with *her*. Ellis was far too smart for that—just as he was far too smart to make any verbal comparisons between his power and Vivaldo's. But he would lose no opportunity to force Ida to make these comparisons for herself.

He was making himself sick with his fears and his fantasies. If Ida loved him, then Ellis and the whole great glittering world did not matter. If she did not love him, there was nothing he could do about it and the sooner everything came to an end between them, the better. But he knew that it was not as simple as that, that he was not being honest. She might very well love him and yet—he shuddered and threw down his drink—be groaning on some leather couch under the weight of Ellis. Her love for him would in no way blunt the force of her determination to become a singer—to pursue the career which now seemed so easily within her grasp. He could even see the truth of her loving and vehement assertion that it was he, his love, which had given her the courage to begin. This did not cheer him, the assertion containing to his ears the suggestion that his role now was finished and he was fouling up everything by failing to deliver his exit lines. He shook his head. In half an hour—no, an hour—he would call the restaurant.

"Oh, Cass," he heard himself saying, "I wish I could do something to help."

She smiled and touched his hand. The tiny arrows on her wrist had not moved. "Thank you," she said—very gravely. Then, "I don't know if Richard loves me any more or not. He doesn't see me any more—he doesn't see me. He hasn't touched me"—she raised her eyes to Vivaldo's and two tears spilled over and rolled down her face; she made no move to check them—"he hasn't touched me in, oh, I don't know how long. I've never been very aggressive; I've never had to be." She struck at her tears with the back of her hand. "I sit in that house like—like a housekeeper. I take care of the kids and make meals and scrub toilet bowls and answer the phone and he just—doesn't see me. He's always *working*. He's always busy with deals with—with Ellis, I guess, and his agent and all those horrible people. Maybe he's mad at me because I don't like them very much and I can't help it." She caught her breath, found another wad of Kleenex, and again accomplished miracles with it. "In the beginning, I sort of teased him about them. I don't any more, but I guess it's too late. I know they're busy and important but I can't help it, I don't think it's serious *work*. Maybe Richard's right, he says I'm a New England snob and a man-killer but God knows I don't mean to be and—I don't think Richard's work is any good any more and he can't forgive me for *that*. What am I to do?" And she put both hands to her forehead, looking down, and began to cry again. He looked cautiously around the dark lounge. No one was noticing them. It was, suddenly a quarter to seven.

Ineptly, he asked, "Have you and Richard talked about this at all?"

She shook her head. "No. We've just had fights. We don't seem to be able to talk to each other any more. I know that people say that there comes a time in marriage when everything goes out of it except companionship, but this *can't* be what they were talking about, not this, not so soon. I won't have it!" And now the extraordinary violence in her voice did cause a few heads to turn in their direction.

He took both her hands, smiling. "Easy, girl, easy. Let me buy you another drink."

"That would be nice." The drink before her was mainly water, but she finished it. Vivaldo signaled the waiter for another round.

"Does Richard know where you are now?"

"No—yes. I told him I was going to have a drink with you."

"What time does he expect you back?"

She hesitated. "I don't know. I left supper in the oven. I told him if I wasn't back in time for supper to feed the children and eat himself. He just grunted and walked into his study." She lit a cigarette, looking both desperate and distant; and he knew that there was more in her mind than she was telling. "I guess I'll go on back, though. Or maybe I'll go to a movie."

"Would you like to have supper with me?"

"No. I don't feel like eating. Besides"—the waiter came with their drinks; she waited until he left—"Richard's a little jealous of you."

"Of *me*? Why is he jealous of *me*?"

"Because you may become a real writer. And now he never will be. And he knows it. And *that's* the whole trouble." She made this pronouncement with the utmost coolness and Vivaldo began to see, for the first time, how deadly it must be for Richard, now, to deal with a woman like Cass. "Goddammit. I wouldn't care if he couldn't *read*." And she grinned and took a swallow of her drink.

"Yes, you would," he said. "You can't help it."

"Well. If he couldn't read, and knew it, he could learn. I could teach him. But *I* don't care if he's a writer or not. He's the one who dreamed all that up." She paused, bony and thoughtful. "He's a carpenter's son," she said, "the fifth son of a carpenter who came from Poland. Maybe that's why it's so important. A hundred years ago he'd have been like his father and opened a carpenter's shop. But now he's got to be a writer and help Steve Ellis sell convictions and soap." Ferociously, she ground out her cigarette. "And neither he, nor anyone else in that gang, can tell the difference between them." She lit another cigarette at once. "Don't misunderstand me; I've got nothing against Ellis, or any of those people. They're just ordinary Americans, trying to get ahead. So is Richard, I guess."

"And so is Ida," he said.

"Ida?"

"I think she's been seeing him. I know she had a date to see Ellis this afternoon. He's promised to help her—with her career." And he smiled, bleakly.

Suddenly, she laughed. "My God. Aren't we a wonderful pair of slobs. Sitting here in this dark place, full of self-pity and alcohol, while our lovers are out there in the real world, seeing real people, doing real things, bringing real bacon into real homes—are they real? are they? Sometimes I wake up at night with that question in my mind and I walk around the house and go and look at the children. I don't want them to be like *that*. I don't want them to be like me, either." She turned her face sideways, looking helplessly at the wall. With her golden hair down, and all the trouble in her face, she looked unbelievably young. "What am I to do?"

"I always thought," he ventured, "that it was easier for women."

She turned and looked at him; she did not look as young any more. "That *what* was easier?"

"Knowing what to do."

She threw back her head and laughed. "Oh, Vivaldo. Why?"

"I don't know. Men have to think about so many things. Women only have to think about men."

She laughed again. "What's so easy about that?"

"It isn't? I guess it isn't."

"Vivaldo. If men don't know what's happening, what they're doing, where they're going—what are women to do? If Richard doesn't know what kind of world he wants, how am I to help him make it? What am I to tell our sons?" The question hung in the air between them; sluggishly (it was ten past seven) it struck echoes in him of Ida's tone and Ida's eyes when they quarreled. *Oh. All you white boys make me* sick. *You want to find out what's happening, baby, all you got to do is pay your* dues!

Was there, in all that rage, a plea?

"I'll buy you one more drink," he said.

"Yes. Let me go home or do whatever I'm going to do with just a tiny hint of drunkenness. Excuse me a moment." Jauntily, she signaled the waiter; then gathered up her great handbag and walked to the ladies' room.

All you got to do is pay your dues. He sat, islanded by the vague hum, the meaningless music, of the cocktail lounge, and recalled lapses and errors from his life with Ida which, at the time, he had blamed on her. Their first quarrel had occurred about a month after she had moved in, in April. His mother had called, one Sunday afternoon, to remind him of a birthday party, the following week, for his younger brother, Stevie. His mother assumed that he would not want to come, that he would try to get out of it, and this made her voice, before he could say anything, querulous and complaining. This he could not bear, which made *his* tone sharp and hostile. And there they were, then, the aging, frightened woman and her grown son, acting out their kindergarten drama. Ida, in the kitchen, watched and listened. Vivaldo, watching her, suddenly laughed and before he realized what he was saying, he asked, "Do you mind if I bring a girl friend?" And, as he said this, he felt Ida stiffen and become absolutely concentrated with rage.

"If she's a nice girl," his mother was saying. "You know we love to meet your friends."

He felt immediate contrition, seeing, in his mind's eye, her bewildered face, knowing how she wondered why her eldest son should cause, and appear to wish to cause her, so much pain. At the same time he was aware of Ida's ominous humming in the kitchen.

"She's a very nice girl," he said, promptly, sincerely. Then he faltered, involuntarily stealing a glance at Ida. He did not know how to say, *Mama, she's a colored girl,* knowing that his mother, and who on earth could blame her? would immediately decide that this was but one more attempt on his part to shock and humiliate his family. "I want you two to meet one day, I really do." And this sounded totally insincere. He was thinking, *I guess I really am going to have to tell them, I'm going to have to make them accept it.* And then, at once. *Oh, fuck it, why?* He glanced again at Ida. She was smoking a cigarette and leafing through a magazine.

"Well," said his mother, doubtfully, more than willing, albeit in her fashion, to come flying down the road to meet him, "try to bring her to the party. Everybody will be here and they all ask about you, we haven't seen you in so long. I know your father misses you though he'll never say a thing and Stevie misses you, too, and we all do, Danny." They called him Danny at home.

Everybody: his sister and his brother-in-law, his brother and father and mother, the uncles and aunts and cousins, and the resulting miasma of piety and malice and suspicion and fear. The invincible chatter of people, concerning people, who had no reality for him, the talk about money, of children's illnesses, of doctor's bills, of pregnancies, of unlikely and unlovely infidelities occurring between ciphers and neuters in a vacuum, the ditchwater-dull, infantile dirty stories, and the insane talk about politics. They should, really, all of them, still be living in stables, with horses and cows, and should not be expected to tax themselves with matters beyond their comprehension. He hated himself for the sincerity of this reflection and was baffled, as always, by the particular and dangerous nature of its injustice.

"Okay," he said, trying to stop his mother's flow. She was telling him that his father's stomach trouble had returned. *Stomach trouble, my ass. He just hasn't got any liver left any more, that's all. One of these days he's just going to spatter all over those walls, and what a stench.*

"Are you going to bring your girl friend?"

"I don't know. I'll see."

He could just see Ida with all of them. He, alone, was bad enough; he, alone, distressed and frightened them enough. Ida would reduce them to a kind of speechless hysteria and God knew what his father would say under the impression that he was putting the dark girl at her ease.

More chatter from his mother: it was as though each of her contacts with Vivaldo was so brief and so menaced that she tried to establish in minutes a communion which had not been accomplished in years.

"I'll *be* there," he said, "good-bye," and hung up.

Yet, he had loved her once, he loved her still, he loved them all.

He looked at the silent telephone, then looked over at Ida.

"Want to come to a birthday party?"

"No, thank you, sweetie. You want to educate your family, you get them some slides, you hear? *Colored* slides," and she raised her eyes, mockingly, from the magazine.

He laughed, but felt so guilty about Ida and about his mother that he was unable to let well enough alone.

"I'd like to take you over with me one of these days. It might do them some good. They're such cornballs."

"What might do them some good?" Her attention was still on her magazine.

"Why—meeting you. They're not bad people. They're just very limited."

"I've told you, I'm not at all interested in the education of your family, Vivaldo."

Obscurely, deeply, he was stung. "Don't you think there's any hope for them?"

"I don't give a damn if there's any hope for them or not. But I know that I am not about to be bugged by any more white jokers who still can't figure out whether I'm human or not. If they don't know, baby, sad on them, and I hope they drop dead slowly, in great pain."

"That's not very Christian," he said, lightly. But he was ready to drop it.

"It's the best I can do. I learned all my Christianity from white folks."

"Oh, shit," he said, "here we go again."

The magazine came flying at him and hit him across the bridge of the nose.

"What do you mean, you white motherfucker!" She mimicked him. *"Here we go again!* I've been living in this house for over a month and you *still* think it would be a big joke to take me home to see your mother! Goddammit, you think she's a better woman than I am, you big, white, liberal asshole?" She caught her breath and started toward him, crouching, her hands on her hips. "Or do you think it would serve your whore of a mother right to bring your nigger whore home for her to see? Answer me, goddammit!"

"Will you shut up? You're going to have the police down here in a minute."

"Yes, and when they come, I'm going to tell them you dragged me in off the streets and refused to pay me, yes, I am. You think I'm a whore, well, you treat me like a whore, goddamn your white prick, *pay!*"

"Ida, it was a dumb thing to say, and I'm sorry, all *right.* I didn't mean what you thought I meant. I wasn't trying to put you down."

"Yes, you did. You meant exactly what I thought you meant. And you know why? Because you can't help it, that's why. Can't none of you white boys help it. Every damn one of your sad-ass white chicks think they got a cunt for peeing through, and they don't piss nothing but the best ginger ale, and if it wasn't for the spooks wouldn't a damn one of you white cock suckers *ever* get laid. That's *right.* You are a fucked-up group of people. You hear me? A *fucked*-up group of people."

"All right," he said, wearily, "so we're a fucked-up group of people. So shut up. We're in enough trouble here, as it is."

And they were, because the landlord and the neighbors and the cop on the corner disapproved of Ida's presence. But it was not the most tactful thing he could have said at that moment.

She said, with a contrition absolutely false and murderous, "That's true. I forgot." She turned from him into the kitchen again, reached up in the cupboard and hurled all of his dishes, of which, thank heaven, there were not many, to the floor. "I just think I'll give them something to complain about," she said. There were only two glasses and she smashed these against the refrigerator. Vivaldo had placed himself against the record player, and, as Ida stalked the kitchen, water standing in her eyes, he began to laugh. She rushed at him, slapping and clawing, and he held her off with one hand, still laughing. His belly hurt. Other people in the building were pounding on their pipes and on the walls and on the ceiling, but he could not stop laughing. He ended up on the floor, on his back, howling, and finally, Ida, unwillingly, began to laugh, too. "Get up off the floor, you fool. Lord, what a fool you are."

"I'm just a fucked-up group of people," he said. "Lord, have mercy on me." Ida laughed, helplessly, and he pulled her down on top of him. "Have mercy on me, baby," he said. "Have mercy." The pounding continued, and he said, "There sure are a fucked-up group of people in this house, they won't even let you make love in peace."

Now, Cass returned, with her hair recombed and new make-up on and with her eyes bright and dry. She seated herself in the booth again and picked up her drink. "I'm ready whenever you are," she said. Then, "Thank you, Vivaldo. If I couldn't have found a friend to talk to, I think I would have died."

"You wouldn't have," he said, "but I know what you mean. Here's to you, Cass." And he raised his glass. It was twenty minutes to eight, but, now, he was afraid to call the restaurant. He would wait until he and Cass had separated.

"What are you going to do?" he asked.

"I don't know. I think I may break—is it the sixth commandment? Adultery."

"I mean, right now."

"That's what I thought you meant."

They both laughed. Yet, it crossed his mind that she meant it. "Anyone I know?"

"Are you kidding? Just *think* of the people you know."

He smiled. "All right. But please don't do anything silly, Cass."

She looked down. "I don't think I will," she murmured. Then, "Let's get the bill."

They signaled the waiter, and paid him, and walked into the streets again. The sun was going down, but the heat had not lessened. The stone and steel and wood and brick and asphalt which had soaked in the heat all day would be giving it back all night. They walked two blocks, to the corner of Fifth Avenue, in silence; and in this silence something lived which made Vivaldo oddly reluctant to leave Cass alone.

The corner on which they stood was absolutely deserted, and there was very little traffic.

"Which way are you going?" he asked her.

She looked up and down the Avenue—up and down. From the direction of the park there came a green and yellow cab.

"I don't know. But I think I'll go to that movie."

The cab stopped, several blocks from them, waiting for a red light. Cass abruptly put up her hand.

Again, he volunteered. "Would you like me to come with you? I could act as your protection."

She laughed. "No, Vivaldo, thank you. I don't want to be protected any more." And the cab swerved toward them. They both watched it approach, it slowed and stopped. He looked at her with his eyebrows very high.

"Well—" he said.

She opened the door and he held it. "Thank you, Vivaldo," she said. "Thank you for everything. I'll be in touch with you in a few days. Or call me, I'll be home."

"Okay, Cass." He made a fist and touched her on the chin. "Be good."

"You, too. Good-bye." She got into the cab and he slammed the door. She leaned forward to the driver, the cab rolled forward, downtown. She turned back to wave at him and the cab turned west.

It was like waving good-bye to land: and she could not guess what might have befallen her when, and if, she ever saw land again.

At Twelfth Street and Seventh Avenue she made the driver carry her one block more, to the box office of the Loew's Sheridan; then she paid him and walked out and actually climbed the stairs to the balcony of this hideous place of worship, and sat down. She lit a cigarette, glad of the darkness but not protected by it; and she watched the screen, but all she saw were the extraordinarily unconvincing wiggles of a girl whose name, incredibly enough, appeared to be Doris Day. She thought, irrelevantly, *I never should come to movies, I can't stand them,* and then she began to cry. She wept looking straight ahead, this latter rain coming between her and James Cagney's great, red face, which seemed, at least, thank heaven, to be beyond the possibilities of make-up. Then she looked at her watch, noting that it was exactly eight o'clock. Is that good or bad? she wondered idiotically—knowing, which was always part of her trouble, that she was being idiotic. *My God, you're thirty-four years old, go on downstairs and call him.* But she forced herself

to wait, wondering all the time if she were waiting too long
or would be calling too early. Finally, during the heaviest of
the wide screen's technicolored stormy weather, she walked
down the stairs and entered the phone booth. She dialed his
number and got the answering service. She crawled back
upstairs and found her seat again.

But she could not bear the movie, which showed no signs
of ever ending. At nine o'clock, she walked downstairs again,
intending to walk and have a drink somewhere and go home.
Home. And she dialed the number again.

It rang once, twice; then the receiver was picked up; there
was a silence. Then, in an aggressive drawl:

"Hello?"

She caught her breath.

"Hello?"

"Hello. Eric?"

"Yes."

"Well, it's me. Cass."

"Oh," and then, quickly, "How are you, Cass, it's good of
you to call me. I've been sitting here trying to read this play
and going out of my mind and feeling suicidal."

"I imagine," she said, "that you may have been expecting
this call." For never let it be said, she thought, now really
in the teeth of irreality and anguish, that I don't lay my cards
on the table.

"What did you say, Cass?" But she knew, from the rhythm
of his question, that he had understood her.

"I said, 'You may have been expecting this call.' "

After a moment, he said, "Yes. In a way." Then, "Where
are you, Cass?"

"I'm around the corner from your house. Can I come up?"

"Please do."

"All right. I'll be there in about five minutes."

"Okay. Oh, Cass—"

"Yes?"

"I haven't got anything in the house to drink. If you'll pick
up a bottle of Scotch, I'll pay you for it when you get here."

"Any special kind?"

"Oh, I don't care. Any kind *you* like."

A stone, miraculously enough, seemed to rise from her
heart for a moment. She laughed. "Black Label?"

"Crazy."

"In a minute, then."

"In a minute. I'll be here."

She hung up, staring for a moment at the shining black

instrument of her—deliverance? She marched into the street, found a liquor store and bought a bottle; and the weight of the bottle in her straw handbag somehow made everything real; as the purchase of a railroad ticket proves the imminence of a journey.

What would she say to him? what would he say to her?

He called, "Is that you, Cass?" She called back, "Yes!" and ran clumsily up the steps, like a schoolgirl. She reached his doorway out of breath, and he stood there, in a T-shirt and a pair of old army pants, smiling and pale. His reality shocked her and so did his beauty—or his vigor, which, in a man, is so nearly the same thing. She might have been seeing him for the first time—his short, disordered red hair, a rather square forehead with lines burned into it, heavier eyebrows than she remembered and darker eyes, set farther back. His chin had a tiny cleft—she had never noticed it before. His mouth was wider than she remembered, his lips were fuller, his teeth were slightly crooked. He had not shaved and his red beard bristled and gleamed in the weak yellow light on the landing. His trousers had no belt and his bare feet were in leather sandals. He said, "Come in," and she brushed quickly past his body. He closed the door behind her.

She walked into the center of the room and stared about her, seeing nothing; then they stared at each other, terribly driven, terribly shy, not daring to imagine what came next. He was frightened, but very self-contained. She felt that he was studying her, preparing himself for whatever this new conundrum might prove to be. He had made no decisions at all as yet, was trying to attune himself to her; which placed her under the necessity of finding out what was in his heart by revealing what was in hers. And she did not yet know what was in her heart—or did not want to know.

He took her bag from her and set it on the bookcase. The way he did this made her realize that he was unaccustomed to having women in his room. The Shostakovich Fifth Symphony was on his record player; the play, *Happy Hunting Ground*, lay open on his bed, under his night light. The only other light in the room came from a small lamp on his desk. His apartment was small and spare, absolutely monastic; it was less a place to live in than it was a place to work; and she felt, suddenly and sharply, how profoundly he might resent the intrusion into his undecorated isolation of the feminine order and softness.

"Let's have a drink," he said, and took the bottle from her bag. "How much do I owe you?"

She told him, and he paid her, shyly, with some crumpled bills which were lying on the mantelpiece, next to his keys. He moved into the kitchen, tearing the wrapper off the bottle. She watched him as he found glasses and ice. His kitchen was a mess and she longed to offer to clean it up for him, but she did not dare, not yet. She moved heavily to the bed and sat down on the edge of it and picked up the play.

"I can't tell if that play's any good or not. I can't tell any more, anyway." Whenever he was unsure, his Southern accent became more noticeable.

"Which character are you playing?"

"Oh, I'm playing one of the bad cats, the one they call Malcolm." She looked at the cast of characters and found that Malcolm was the son of Egan. The script was heavily underlined and there were long notes in the margin. One of these notes read, *On this, maybe remember what you know of Yves,* and she looked at the underlined sentence, *No, I don't want no damn aspirin. Man got a headache, why don't you let him find out what kind of headache it is?* Eric called, "Do you want water, or just ice?"

"A little water, thanks."

He came back into the room and handed her her highball. "I play the last male member of a big, rich American family. They got rich by all kinds of swindles and by shooting down people, and all that jazz. But I can't do that by the time I'm a man because it's all been done and they've changed the laws. So I get to be a big labor leader instead, and my dad tries to get me railroaded to jail as a Communist. It gives us a couple of nice scenes. The point is, there's not a pin to choose beween us." He grinned. "It'll probably be a big, fat flop."

"Well, just make sure we have tickets to opening night." A brief silence fell, and her *we* resounded more insistently than the drums of Shostakovich.

"Oh, I'm going to try to pack the house with my friends," he said, "never fear." Silence fell again. He sat down on the bed beside her, and looked at her. She looked down.

"You make me feel very strange," he said. "You make me feel things I didn't think I'd ever feel again."

"What do I make you feel?" she asked. And then, "You do the same for me." She sensed that he was taking the initiative for her sake.

He leaned forward and put one hand on her hand; then

rose, and walked away from her, leaving her alone on the bed. "What about Richard?"

"I don't know," she said. "I don't know what's going to happen between Richard and me." She forced herself to look into his eyes, and she put her drink down on the night table. "But it isn't *you* that's come between Richard and me —*you* don't have anything to do with that."

"I don't *now*, you mean. Or I don't *yet*." He put his cigarette down in the ashtray on the mantelpiece behind him. "But I guess I know what you mean, in a way." He still seemed very troubled and his trouble now propelled him toward her again, to the bed. He felt her trembling, but still he did not touch her, only stared at her with his troubled and searching eyes, and with his lips parted. "Dear Cass," he said, and smiled, "I know we have *now*, but I don't think we have much of a future." She thought, Perhaps if we take *now*, we can have a future, too. It depends on what we mean by "future." She felt his breath on her face and her neck, then he leaned closer, head down, and she felt his lips there. She raised her hands to stroke his head and his red hair. She felt his violence and his uncertainty, and this made him seem much younger than she. And this excited her in a way that she had never been excited before; she glimpsed, for the first time, the force that drove older women to younger men; and then she was frightened. She was frightened because she had never before found herself playing so anomalous a role and because nothing in her experience had ever suggested that her body could become a trap for boys, and the tomb of her self-esteem. She had embarked on a voyage which might end years from now in some horrible villa, near a blue sea, with some unspeaking, unspeakably phallic, Turk or Spaniard or Jew or Greek or Arabian. Yet, she did not want it to stop. She did not quite know what was happening now, or where it would lead, and she was afraid; but she did not want it to stop. She saw the smoke from Eric's cigarette curling up from the mantelpiece—she hoped it was still in the ashtray; the play script was beneath her head, the symphony was approaching its end. She was aware, as though she stood over them both with a camera, of how sordid the scene must appear: a married woman, no longer young, already beginning to moan with lust, pinned down on this untidy and utterly transient bed by a stranger who did not love her and whom she could not love. Then she wondered about that: love; and wondered if anyone really knew anything about it. Eric put one hand on her breast, and it was a new touch, not Richard's, no; but she knew that it was Eric's; and was it love or not? and what did Eric feel? *Sex,* she thought, but that was not really the answer, or if it was, it was an answer which clarified nothing. For now, Eric leaned up from her with a sigh and walked back to his cigarette. He leaned there for a moment, watching her; and she understood that the weight between them, of things unspoken, made any act impossible. On what basis were they to act? for their blind seeking was not a foundation which could be expected to bear any weight.

He came back to the bed and sat down; and he said, "Well. Listen. I know about Richard. I don't altogether believe you when you say that I don't have anything to do with what's happening between you and Richard, because obviously I do, I do *now,* anyway, if only because I'm here." She started to say something, but he raised his hand to silence her. "But that's all right. I don't want to make an issue out of that, I'm not very well placed to defend—conventional morality." And he smiled. "Something is happening between us which I don't really understand, but I'm willing to trust it. I have the feeling, somehow, that I *must* trust it." He took her hand and raised it to his unshaven cheek. "But I have a lover, too, Cass; a boy, a French boy, and he's supposed to be coming to New York in a few weeks. I really don't know what will happen when he gets here, but"—he dropped her hand and rose and paced his room again—"he *is* coming, and we *have* been together for over two years. And that means something. Probably, if it hadn't been for him, I would never have stayed away so long." And he turned on her now all of his intensity. "No matter *what* happens, I loved him very much, Cass, and I still do. I don't think I've ever loved anyone quite like that before, and"—he shuddered—"I'm not sure I'll ever love anyone quite like that again."

She felt not at all frightened by his lover. She remembered the name written in the margin: *Yves.* But it was better for the name of his lover to fall from his lips. She felt very strangely moved, as though she might be able to help him endure the weight of the boy who had such power over him.

"He sounds very remarkable," she said. "Tell me his name, tell me about him."

He came back to the bed and sat down. His drink was finished, and he sipped from hers.

"There isn't much to tell. His name is Yves." He paused, "I can't imagine what he'll think of the States."

"Or of all of us," she said.

He assented, with a smile. "Or of all of us. I'm not sure I know what *I* think." They laughed; she took a sip of her highball; the atmosphere between them began to be easier, as though they were friends. "But—I'm responsible for him when he gets here. He wouldn't be coming if it weren't for me." He looked at her. "He's the son of somebody he can scarcely remember at all, and his mother runs a bistro in Paris. He hates his mother, or thinks he does."

"That's not the usual pattern, is it?" Then she wished that she had held her tongue, or could call the words back. But it was too late, really, to do more than blandly compound her error: "I mean, from what we're told, most men with a sexual bias toward men love their mothers and hate their fathers."

"We haven't been told much," he observed, mildly sardonic. "I used to know street boys in Paris who hadn't had any opportunity to hate their mother *or* their fathers. Of course, they hated *les flics*—the cops—and I suppose some safe slug of an American would work it out that they hated the cops because they were father-figures—we know a hell of a lot about father-figures here because we don't know anything about fathers, we've made them obsolete—but it seems just as likely to me that they hated the cops because the cops liked to beat the shit out of them."

It was strange how she now felt herself holding back—not from him, but from such a vision of the world. She did not want him to see the world this way because such a vision could not make him happy, and whatever made him unhappy menaced her. She had never had to deal with a policeman in her life, and it had never entered her mind to feel menaced by one. Policemen were neither friends nor enemies; they were part of the landscape, present for the purpose of upholding law and order; and if a policeman—for she had never thought of them as being very bright—seemed to forget his place, it was easy enough to make him remember it. Easy enough if one's own place was more secure than his, and if one represented, or could bring to bear, a power greater than his own. For all policemen were bright enough to know who they were working for, and they were not working, anywhere in the world, for the powerless.

She stroked Eric's hair, remembering how she and Richard, when they had first met, had argued over this very question: for he had been very conscious, in those days, of his poverty and her privilege. He had called her the icebound heiress of all the ages, and she had worked very hard to prove him wrong and to dissociate herself, in his mind, from those who wielded the knout of power.

Eric put his head in her lap. He said, "Well, anyway, that's the story, or all the story I know how to tell you now. I just thought you ought to know." He hesitated; she watched his Adam's apple move as he swallowed; and he said, "I can't promise you anything, Cass."

"I haven't asked you to promise me anything." She bent down and kissed him on the mouth. "You're very beautiful," she said, "and very strong. I'm not afraid."

He looked up at her, looking upside down, so that he was for her at that moment both child and man, and her thighs trembled. He kissed her again and took the two clips out of her hair, so that her golden hair fell over him. He turned and held her beneath him on the bed. Like children, with that very same joy and trembling, they undressed and uncovered and gazed on each other; and she felt herself carried back to an unremembered, unimaginable time and state when she had not been Cass, as she was now, but the plain, mild, arrogant, waiting *Clarissa*, when she had not been weary, when love was on the road but not yet at the gates. He looked on her body as though such a body were a new creation, still damp from the vast firmament; and his wonder infected her. She watched his naked body as he crossed the room to turn off the lamp, and thought of the bodies of her children, Paul and Michael, which had come, so miraculously formed, and so heavy and secret with promise, out of her; and, like the water which sprang in the desert when Moses struck the rock with his rod, tears sprang to her eyes. He glowed in the light which came from the lamp above her head. She could not bear to turn it off. She watched him as he bent to take the long-silent record off the machine, and the green eye of the machine clicked off; then he turned to face her, very grave indeed, and with his eyes darker and set farther back than ever. Now, less than ever, did she know what love was—but she smiled, for joy, and he answered her with a small, triumphant laugh. They were oddly equal: perhaps each could teach the other, concerning love, what neither now knew. And they were equal in that both were afraid of what unanswerable and unimaginable riddles might be uncovered in so merciless a light.

She switched off the lamp at the head of the bed, and watched him come to her in the gloom. He took her like a boy, with that singlemindedness, and with a boy's passion to please: and she had awakened something in him, an animal long caged, which came pounding out of its captivity now with a fury which astounded and transfigured them both. Eventually, he slept on her breast, like a child. She watched him, watched his parted lips and and the crooked teeth dully gleaming, and the thin, silver trickle of saliva, flowing on to her; and watched the tiny pulsations in the vein of one arm, the red hairs gleaming on it, thrown heavily across her hip; one leg was thrust out behind him, one knee pointed toward her; the little finger of the hand farthest from her, on the edge of the bed, palm upward, twitched; his sex and his belly were hidden.

She looked at her watch. It was ten past one. She would have to go home and she was relieved to discover that she was apprehensive, but not guilty. She really felt that a weight had rolled away, and that she was herself again, in her own skin, for the first time in a long time.

She moved slowly out from beneath his weight, kissed his brow and covered him. Then she went into the bathroom and stepped into the shower. She sang to herself in an undertone as the water crashed over her body, and used the towel which smelled of him with joy. She dressed, still humming, and combed her hair. But the pins were on the night table. She came out, to find him sitting up, smoking a cigarette. They smiled at each other.

"How are you, baby?" he asked.

"I feel wonderful. How are you?"

"I feel wonderful, too," and he laughed, sheepishly. Then, "You have to go?"

"Yes. Yes, I do." She came to the night table and put the pins in her hair. He reached up and pulled her down on the bed and kissed her. It was a strange kiss, in its sad insistence. His eyes seemed to be seeking in her something he had despaired of finding, and did not yet trust.

"Will Richard be awake?"

"I don't think so. It doesn't matter. We're very seldom together in the evenings; he works, I read, or got out to the movies, or watch TV." She touched his cheek. "Don't worry."

"When will I see you?"

"Soon. I'll call you."

"Does it matter if I call you? Or would you rather I didn't?"

She hesitated. "It doesn't matter." They both thought, *It doesn't matter yet.* He kissed her again.

"I wish you could spend the night," he said. He laughed

again. "We were just beginning to get started, I hope you know that."

"Oh, yes," she said, "I can tell." He placed his rough cheek next to hers. "But I've got to go now."

"Shall I walk you to a taxi?"

"Oh, Eric, don't be silly. There's just no point to that at all."

"I'd like to. I'll only be a minute." He jumped out of bed and entered the bathroom. She listened to the water splashing and flushing and looked around his apartment, which already seemed terribly familiar. She would try to get down and clean it up sometime in the next few days. It would be difficult to get away in the daytime, except, perhaps, on Saturdays. Then it occurred to her that she needed a smoke screen for this affair and that she would have to use Vivaldo and Ida.

Eric came out of the bathroom and pulled on his shorts and his trousers and his T-shirt. He stuck his feet into his sandals. He looked scrubbed and sleepy and pale. His lips were swollen and very red, like those of heroes and gods of antiquity.

"All ready?" he asked.

"All ready." He picked up her bag and gave it to her. They kissed briefly again, and walked down the stairs into the streets. He put his arm around her waist. They walked in silence, and the street they walked was empty. But there were people in the bars, gesticulating and seeming to howl in the yellow light, behind the smoky glass; and people in the side streets, loitering and skulking; dogs on leashes, sniffing with their masters. They passed the movie theater, and were on the Avenue, facing the hospital. And in the shadow of the great, darkened marquee, they smiled into each other's faces.

"I'm glad you called me," he said. "I'm so glad."

She said, "I'm glad you were home."

They saw a cab coming crosstown and Eric put up his hand.

"I'll call you in a few days," she said, "around Friday or Saturday."

"All right, Cass." The cab stopped and he opened the door and put her in, leaned in and kissed her. "Be good, little gal."

"You, too." He closed the door on her, and waved. The cab began to move, and she watched him move, alone, into the long, dark street.

There were no phone booths on deserted Fifth Avenue
and Vivaldo walked the high, silent block to Sixth Avenue
and entered the first bar he came to, heading straight for the
phone booth. He rang the number of the restaurant and
waited quite a while before an irritated male voice answered.
He asked for Miss Ida Scott.

"She didn't come in tonight. She called in sick. Maybe
you can get her at home."

"Thank you," he said. But the man had already hung
up. He felt nothing at all, certainly not astonishment; yet, he
leaned against the phone for an instant, freezing and faint.
Then he dialed his own number. There was no answer.

He walked out of the phone booth into the bar, which
was a workingman's bar, and there was a wrestling match on
the TV screen. He ordered a double shot and leaned on the
bar. He was surrounded by precisely those men he had
known from his childhood, from his earliest youth. It was
as though, hideously, after a long and fruitless voyage, he
had come home, to find that he had become a stranger. They
did not look at him—or did not seem to look at him; but,
then, that was the style of these men; and if they usually saw
less than was present, they also, often, saw more than one
guessed. Two Negroes near him, in working clothes, seemed
to have a bet on the outcome of the wrestling match, which
they did not, however, appear to be watching very closely.
They kept talking to each other in a rumbling, humorous
monotone—a smile kept playing on both their faces—and
every once in a while they ordered a new round of drinks,
or exploded with laughter, or turned their attention again to
the screen. All up and down the bar, men stood silently,
usually singly, watching the TV screen, or watching nothing.
There were booths beside the bar, near the back. An elderly
Negro couple and a young Negro couple shared one booth,
another booth held three aimless youths, drinking beer, in
the very last booth an odd-looking man, who might have
been a Persian, was feeling up a pasty-faced, string-haired
girl. The Negro couples were in earnest conversation—the
elderly Negro woman leaned forward with great vehemence;
and the three youths were giggling and covertly watching
the dark man and the pasty girl; and if this evening ended
as all the others had, they would presently drive off to some
haven and watch each other masturbate. The bartender was
iron-haired and pablum-faced, with spectacles, and leaned
on a barrel at one end of the bar, watching the screen.

Vivaldo watched the screen, seeing two ancient, flabby men throwing each other around on a piece of canvas; from time to time a sensually grinning blonde advertised soap—but her grin was far less sensual than the wrestling match—and a strong-jawed neuter in a crew cut puffed rapaciously, with unnerving pleasure, on a cigarette. Then, back to the groaning wrestlers, who really should have been home in bed, possibly with each other.

Where was she? *Where* was she? With Ellis, certainly. Where? She had called the restaurant; but she had not called him. And she would say, "But we didn't have any plans for tonight, sweetie, I *knew* you were seeing Cass, and I was sure you'd have supper with *her!*" Where was she? the hell with her. She would say, "Oh, honey, don't be like that, suppose I made a fuss every time you went out and had a drink with someone else? I trust you, now, you've got to trust me. Suppose I really make it as a singer and have to see lots of people, what're you going to do *then?*" She trusted him because she didn't give a damn about him, the hell with her. The hell with her. The hell with her.

Oh, Ida. She would say, "Mama called me after you left and she was real upset; Daddy got into a fight this week end and he was cut kind of bad and I just left the hospital this very minute. Mama wanted me to stay with her but I knew you'd be worried, so I came on home. You know, they don't like the idea of my living down here with you one bit, maybe they'll get used to it, but I'm sure that's what makes my Daddy so evil, he just can't get over Rufus, you know, sugar, please make me a little drink, I'm just about dead."

The hell with her. The hell with her.

She would say, "Oh, Vivaldo, why do you want to be so mean when you know how much I love you?" She would sound exasperated and very close to tears. And then, even though he knew that she was using him against himself, hope rose up hard in him, his throat became tight with pain, he willed away all his doubts. Perhaps she loved him, perhaps she did: but if she did, how was it, then, that they remained so locked away from one another? Perhaps it was he who did not know how to give, did not know how to love. Love was a country he knew nothing about. And he thought, very unwillingly, that perhaps he did not love her. Perhaps it was only because she was not white that he dared to bring her the offering of himself. Perhaps he had felt, somewhere, at the very bottom of himself, that she would not dare despise him.

And if this was what she suspected, well, then, her rage was bottomless and she would never be conquered by him.

He walked out of the bar into the streets again, not knowing what to do but knowing he could not go home. He wished he had a friend, a male friend, with whom he could talk; and this made him realize that, with the dubious exception of Rufus, he had never had a friend in his life. He thought of calling Eric, but Eric had been away too long. He no longer knew anything about Eric's life and tonight he did not want to know.

So he walked. He passed the great livid scar of Forty-second Street, knowing that he could not endure sitting through a movie tonight; and on, down lonely Sixth Avenue, until he came to the Village. Again, he thought of calling Eric and again dismissed it. He walked eastward to the park; there were no singers there tonight, only shadows in the shadows of the trees; and a policeman coming into the park as he walked out of it. He walked along MacDougal Street. Here were the black-and-white couples, defiantly white, flamboyantly black; and the Italians watched them, hating them, hating, in fact, all the Villagers, who gave their streets a bad name. The Italians, after all, merely wished to be accepted as decent Americans and probably could not be blamed for feeling that they might have had an easier time of it if they had not been afflicted with so many Jews and junkies and drunkards and queers and spades. Vivaldo peered into the bars and coffee houses, half-hoping to see a familiar and bearable face. But there were only the rat-faced boys, with beards, and the infantile, shapeless girls, with the long hair.

"How're you and your spade chick making it?"

He turned, and it was Jane. She was drunk and with an uptown, seersucker type, who probably worked in advertising.

He stared at her and she said, quickly, with a laugh, "Oh, now, don't get mad, I was only teasing you. Don't old girl friends have *some* rights?" And to the man beside her, she said, "This is an old friend of mine, Vivaldo Moore. And *this* is Dick Lincoln."

Vivaldo and Dick Lincoln acknowledged each other with brief, constrained nods.

"How are you, Jane?" Vivaldo asked, politely, beginning to move, at the same time, in what he hoped was not their direction.

But they, naturally, began to move with him.

"Oh, I'm fine," she said. "I seem to have made an incredible recovery—"

"Have you been ill?"

She looked at him. "Yes, as a matter of fact. Nerves. Due to a love affair that didn't work out."

"Someone I know?"

She laughed, breathily. "You bastard."

"It's just that I'm terribly accustomed to your dramatics. But I'm glad that everything's working out for you now."

"Oh, everything's fine now," she said, and made a grotesquely girlish little skip, holding heavily onto Lincoln's hand. "Dick doesn't care much about soul-searching, but he's good at what he cares about." The man she thus described moved stiffly beside her, his face a ruddy mask of uncertainty, clearly determined to do the right thing, whatever the right thing might prove to be.

"Come and have a drink with us," Jane said. They were standing on the corner, in the lights spilling outward from a bar. The light illumined and horribly distorted her face, so that her eyes looked like coals of fire and her mouth stretched joylessly back upon the gums. "For old times' sake."

"No, thank you," he said. "I'm going on home. I've had a long, hard day."

"Rushing home to your chick?"

"Good thing to rush home to, if you've got one," Dick Lincoln said, putting his pink, nerveless hand on Jane's shoulder.

Somehow, she bore it; but not without another girlish twitch. She said, "Vivaldo's got a great chick." She turned to Dick Lincoln. "I bet you think you're a liberal," she said, "but this boy, baby, he's miles ahead of you. He's miles ahead of *me;* why, if I was as liberal as my friend, Vivaldo, here"—she laughed; a very tall Negro boy passed them, looking at them briefly—"why, I wouldn't be with *you,* you poor white slob. I'd be with the biggest, blackest buck I could find!" Vivaldo felt his skin prickling. Dick Lincoln blushed. Jane laughed, and Vivaldo realized that others, both black and white, were watching them. "Maybe I should have gone with her brother," Jane said, "would you have liked me better if I had? Or were you going with *him,* too? Can't ever tell about a liberal," and she turned her face, laughing, into Dick Lincoln's shoulder.

Lincoln stared helplessly into Vivaldo's eyes. "She's all yours, mister," Vivaldo said, and at this Jane looked up at him, not laughing at all, her face livid and old with rage. And all his anger left him at once.

"So long," he said, and turned away. He wanted to leave before Jane precipitated a race riot. And he also realized that he had become the focus of two very different kinds of attention. The blacks now suspected him of being an ally—though not a friend, never a friend!—and the whites, particularly the neighborhood Italians, now knew that he could not be trusted. "Hurry home," Jane called behind him, "hurry home! Is it true that they've got hotter blood than ours? Is her blood hotter than mine?" And laughter rang down the street behind this call, the suppressed, bawdy laughter of the Italians—for, after all, Vivaldo was one of them, and a male, and, apparently, a gifted one—and the delighted, vindictive laughter of the Negroes. For a moment, behind him, they were almost united—but then, each, hearing the other's laughter, choked their laughter off. The Italians heard the laughter of black men; the black men remembered that it was a black girl Vivaldo was screwing.

He crossed the avenue. He wanted to go home and he wanted to eat and he wanted to get drunk and, also, perhaps out of simple fury, he wanted to get laid—but he did not feel that anything good would happen to him tonight. And he felt that if he were a real writer, he would simply go home and work and throw everything else out of his mind, as Balzac had done and Proust and Joyce and James and Faulkner. But perhaps they had never held in their minds the nameless things he held in his. He felt a very peculiar, a deadly resignation: he knew that he would not go home until it was too late for him to go anywhere else, or until Ida answered the phone. Ida: and he felt an eerie premonition, as though he were old, walking years from now through familiar streets where no one knew or noticed him, thinking of his lost love, and wondering, *Where is she now? Where is she now?* He passed the movie theater and the tough boys and tough men who always stood outside it. It was ten o'clock. He turned west on Waverly Place and walked to a crowded bar where he could get a hamburger. He forced himself to have a hamburger and a beer before he called his apartment again. There was no answer. He went back to the bar and ordered a whiskey and realized that he was running out of money. If he were going to keep on drinking he would have to go to Benno's, where he had a tab.

He drank his whiskey very slowly, watching and listening

to the crowd around him. They had been college boys, mostly, in his day, but both he and they had grown older and he gathered, from the conversations around him, that the college boys had graduated into the professions. He had his eye, vaguely, on a frail, blond girl, who also seemed, somewhat less vaguely, to have her eye on him: incredibly enough, she seemed to be a lawyer. And he was abruptly very excited, as he had been years ago, at the prospect of making it with a chick above his station, a chick he was not even supposed to be able to look at. He was from the slums of Brooklyn and that stink was on him, and it turned out to be the stink that they were looking for. They were tired of boys who washed too much, who had no odor in their armpits and no sweat on their balls. He looked at the blonde again, wondering what she was like with no clothes on. She was sitting at a table near the door, facing him, toying with a daiquiri glass, and talking to a heavy, gray-haired man, who had a high giggle, who was a little drunk, and whom Vivaldo recognized as a fairly well-known poet. The blonde reminded him of Cass. And this made him realize—for the first time, it is astonishing how well the obvious can be hidden—that when he had met Cass, so many years ago, he had been terribly flattered that so highborn a lady noticed such a stinking boy. He had been overwhelmed. And he had adored Richard without reserve, not, as it turned out, because of Richard's talent, which, in any case, he had then been quite unable to judge, but merely because Richard possessed Cass. He had envied Richard's prowess, and had imagined that this envy was love.

But, surely, there had been love in it, or they could never have been friends for so long. (Had they been friends? what had they ever, really, said to one another?) Perhaps the proof of Vivaldo's love resided in the fact that he had never thought of Cass carnally, as a woman, but only as a lady, and Richard's wife. But, more probably, it was only that they were older and he had needed older people who cared about him, who took him seriously, whom he could trust. For this, he would have paid any price whatever. They were not much older now, he was nearly twenty-nine, Richard was thirty-seven or thirty-eight, Cass was thirty-three or thirty-four: but they had seemed, especially in the blazing haven of their love, much older then.

And now—now it seemed that they were all equal in misery, confusion, and despair. He looked at his face in the mirror behind the bar. He still had all his hair, there was no gray in it yet; his face had not begun to fall at the bottom

and shrivel at the top; and he wasn't yet all ass and belly.
But, still—and soon; and he stole a look at the blonde again.
He wondered about her odor, juices, sounds; for a night,
only for a night; then abruptly, with no warning, he found
himself wondering how Rufus would have looked at this girl,
and an odd thing happened: all desire left him, he turned absolutely cold, and then desire came roaring back, with legions.
Aha, he heard Rufus snicker, *you don't be careful, motherfucker, you going to get a* black *hard on.* He heard again
the laughter which had followed him down the block. And
something in him was breaking; he was, briefly and horribly,
in a region where there were no definitions of any kind,
neither of color, nor of male and female. There was only
the leap and the rending and the terror and the surrender.
And the terror: which all seemed to begin and end and begin
again—forever—in a cavern behind the eye. And whatever
stalked there *saw,* and spread the news of what it saw
throughout the entire kingdom of whomever, though the eye
itself might perish. What order could prevail against so grim
a privacy? And yet, without order, of what value was the
mystery? Order. Order. *Set thine house in order.* He sipped
his whiskey, light-years removed now from the blonde
and the bar and yet, more than ever and most unpleasantly
present. When people no longer knew that a mystery could
only be approached through form, people became—what
the people of this time and place had become, what he had
become. They perished within their despised clay tenements,
in isolation, passively, or actively together, in mobs, thirsting
and seeking for, and eventually reeking of blood. Of rending
and tearing there can never be any end, and God save the
people for whom passion becomes impersonal!

He went into the phone booth again, and, hopelessly, rang
his number. It rang and rang. He hung up and stood in the
booth for a moment. Now he wondered if something had
happened to Ida, if there really had been some family crisis:
but it was too late, now, to call the woman who lived next
door to Ida's family. Again, he thought of calling Eric and
again decided against it. He walked through the bar, slowly,
for he was down to carfare and hot-dog money, and would
have to leave.

He said, to the poet, but looking at the girl, as he came up
to the table, "I just want to say that I know who you are and
I've admired your work for a long time and—thank you."

The poet looked up, astonished, and the girl laughed, and
said, "That's very sweet of you. Are you a poet, too?"

"No," he said. He found himself thinking that it had been a long time since he had been with a white girl. He could not help wondering what it might now be like. "I'm a novelist. Unpublished."

"Well, when you *do* get published, you may make some money," the poet said. "Clever bastard you were, to choose a field which *may* allow you to pay at least a modest rent."

"I don't know if I'm clever," Vivaldo said, "it just turned out like that." He was curious about the girl, curious indeed; but other necessities crowded the center of his mind; perhaps they would meet again. "Well, I just wanted to say thank you, that's all. So long."

"Thank *you*," said the poet.

"Good luck!" cried the girl.

He waved his hand in a kind of parody of a hipster and walked out. He walked over to Benno's. It looked as desolate as a graveyard. There were a couple of people there whom he knew, though he usually avoided them; but he was on a tab tonight, as everyone, instinctively, seemed to know; and, anyway, no one in a bar on a Wednesday night was in a position to be choosy.

Certainly not the three people whose table he joined, who were also running out of money and who were *not* on a tab. One of these was the Canadian-born poet, Lorenzo, moonfaced, with much curly hair; and his girl, a refugee from the Texas backwater, scissor-faced, with much straight hair, and a thumb-chewing giggle; and their sidekick, older, lantern-jawed, with tortured lips, who scowled when he was pleased—which was rare—and smiled a pallid smile when he was frightened—which was almost always—so that he enjoyed the reputation of being extremely good-natured.

"Hi, Vi," cried the poet, "Come on over and join us!"

There was, indeed, nothing else to do, unless he left the bar; so he ordered himself a drink and sat down. They were all drinking beer, and most of their beer was gone. He was introduced, for perhaps the thirtieth time, to Belle and to Harold.

"How *are* you, man?" Lorenzo asked. "Nobody ever sees you any more." He had an open, boyish grin, and it summed him up precisely, even though he was beginning to be rather old for a boy. Still, and especially by contrast with his boy and his girl, he seemed the most vivid person at the table and Vivaldo rather liked him.

"I'm up and I'm down," Vivaldo said—and Belle giggled,

chewing on her thumb—"and I'm turning into a serious
person; that's why you never see me any more."

"Your writing?" asked Lorenzo, still smiling. For he was
one of those poets who escaped the terrors of writing by
writing all the time. He carried a small notebook with him
wherever he went and scribbled in it, and when he got drunk
enough, read the results aloud. It lay before him, closed, on
the table now.

"I'm trying," said Vivaldo. He looked above their heads
at the window, out into the streets. "It's a dead night."

"It sure is," said Harold. He looked over at Vivaldo with
his little smile. "Where's your chick, man? Don't tell me
she's got away."

"No. She's uptown, at some kind of family deal." He
leaned forward. "We have a deal, dig, she won't bug me with
her family and I won't bug her with mine."

Belle giggled again. Lorenzo laughed. "You ought to
bring them together. It'd be the biggest battle since the Civil
War."

"Or since Romeo and Juliet," Belle suggested.

"I've been trying to do that in a long poem," Lorenzo
said, "you know, Romeo and Juliet today, only she's black
and he's white—"

"And Mercutio's passing," grinned Vivaldo.

"Yes. And everybody else is *all* fucked up—"

"Call it," suggested Harold, *"Pickaninnies Everywhere."*

"Or *Everybody's Pickaninnies."*

"Or, *Checkers, Anyone?"*

They all howled. Belle, still clinging to her thumbnail,
laughed until tears rolled down her face.

"You people are *high!"* said Vivaldo.

This sent them off again. "Baby," cried Lorenzo, "one
day, you've got to tell me how you figured *that* out!"

"You want to turn on?" Harold asked.

It had been a long time. He had become bored by the
people with whom one turned on, and really rather bored
with marijuana. Either it did not derange his senses enough,
or he was already more than sufficiently deranged. And he
found the hangover crushing and it interfered with his work
and he had never been able to make love on it.

Still, it had been a long time. It was only ten past eleven,
he did not know what he was going to do with himself. He
wanted to enter into, or to forget, the chaos at his center.

"Maybe," he said. "Let me buy a round first. What're you
drinking?"

"We could make it on back to my pad," said Harold, scowling his little scowl.

"I'm having beer," said Lorenzo. His expression indicated that he would rather have had something else, but did not wish to seem to be taking advantage of Vivaldo.

Vivaldo turned to Belle. "And you?"

She dropped her hand and leaned forward. "Do you think I could have a brandy Alexander?"

"God," he said, "if you can drink it, I guess they can make it." She leaned back again, unsmiling, oddly ladylike, and he looked at Harold.

"Beer, dad," Harold said. "Then we'll split."

So he walked over to the bar, and ordered the round, making a special trip to carry the brimming, viscous Alexander. He knew that Lorenzo liked rye and so he bought him a straight one and a bottle of beer, and a beer for Harold, and a double bourbon for himself. Let's go for broke, he thought, the hell with it. Let's see what happens. And he really could not tell, because he did not want to know, whether he was acting out of panic or recklessness or pain. There was certainly something he did not want to think about: he did not want to think about where Ida was, or what she was doing now. Not now, later for you, baby. He did not want to go home and lie awake, waiting, or walk up and down, staring at his typewriter and staring at the walls. Later for all that, later. And beneath all this was the void where anguish lived and questions crouched, which referred only to Vivaldo and to no one else on earth. Down there, down there, lived the raw, unformed substance for the creation of Vivaldo, and only he, Vivaldo, alone, could master it.

"Here's how," he said, and, unsteadily, they raised their glasses, and drank.

"Thanks, Vivaldo," said Lorenzo, and downed his whiskey in a single swallow. Vivaldo looked at the young face, which was damp and a little gray and would soon be damper and grayer. The veins in the nose were thickening and darkening; and, sometimes, as now, when Lorenzo looked straight before him, the eyes were more baffled and infinitely lonelier than those of a child.

And at such moments Belle watched him, too, sympathy struggling to overcome the relentless vacuity in her face. And Harold seemed hooded then, like a great bird watching from a tree.

"I'd love to go back to Spain," said Lorenzo.

"Do you know Spain?" asked Vivaldo.

"He used to live there," Belle said. "He always talks about
Spain when we get high. We were supposed to go this summer." She bent her head over her cocktail glass, disappearing for a moment, like some unprecedented turtle, behind
the citadel of her hair. "Are we going to go, baby?"

Lorenzo spread his hands, helplessly. "If we can get
enough bread, we'll go."

"It shouldn't cost much to get to Spain," Harold said.
"And you can live there for almost nothing."

"It's a wonderful place," said Lorenzo. "I lived in Barce-
lona, on a fellowship, for over a year. And I traveled all over
Spain. You know, I think they're the grooviest people in the
world, the sweetest cats I ever met, I met in Spain. That's
right. They'll do anything for you, baby, lend you their
shirts, tell you the time, show you the ropes—"

"Lend you their sisters." Harold laughed.

"No, man, they love their sisters—"

"But hate their mothers?"

"No, man, they love them, too. Like they never heard of
Freud." Harold laughed. "They'll take you home and feed
you, they'll share anything they've got with you and they'll
be hurt if you don't take it."

"Mothers, sisters, or brothers," Harold said. "Take them
away. Open up the window and let that foul air out."

Lorenzo ignored this, looking around the table and nodding gravely. "That's the truth, men, they're great people."

"What about Franco?" Belle asked. She seemed rather
proud to know that Franco existed.

"Oh, Franco's an asshole, he doesn't count."

"Bull*shit* he doesn't count," cried Harold, "you think all
those uniforms that *we* help Franco pay for are walking
around Spain just for kicks? You think they don't have real
bullets in those guns? Let me tell you, dad, those cats are for
real, they *shoot* people!"

"Well. That doesn't have anything to do with the people,"
said Lorenzo.

"Yeah. But I bet you wouldn't like to be a Spaniard,"
Harold said.

"I'm sick of all this jazz about the happy Spanish peasant,"
Vivaldo said. He thought of Ida. He leaned over to Lorenzo.
"I bet you wouldn't want to be a nigger here, would you?"

"Oh!" laughed Lorenzo, "your chick sure has you brainwashed!"

"Brainwashed, hell. You wouldn't want to be colored
here and you wouldn't want to be Spanish there." There was

a curious tension in his chest and he took a large swallow of his whiskey. "The question is—what *do* we want to be?"

"I want to be me," said Belle, with an unexpected ferocity, and chewed her thumbnail.

"Well," asked Vivaldo, and looked at her, "what's stopping you?"

She giggled and chewed; she looked down. "I don't know. It's hard to get straight." She looked over at him as though afraid he might reach over and strike her. "You know what I mean?"

"Yes," he said, after a long moment and a long sigh, "I sure do know what you mean."

They all dropped abruptly into silence. Vivaldo thought of his spade chick, his dark girl, his beloved Ida, his mysterious torment and delight and hope, and thought of his own white skin. What did she see when she looked at him? He dilated his nostrils, trying to smell himself: what was that odor like for her? When she tangled her fingers in his hair, his "fine Italian hair," was she playing with water, as she claimed, or was she toying with the notion of uprooting a forest? When he entered that marvelous wound in her, *rending and tearing! rending and tearing!* was she surrendering, in joy, to the Bridegroom, Lord, and Savior? or was he entering a fallen and humiliated city, entering an ambush, watched from secret places by hostile eyes? Oh, Ida, he thought, I'd give up my color for you, I would, only take me, take me, love me as I am! Take me, take me, as I take you. How did he take her, what did he bring to her? Was it his pride and his glory that he brought, or his shame? If he despised his flesh, then he must despise hers—and *did* he despise his flesh? And if she despised her flesh, then she must despise his. Who can blame her, he thought, wearily, if she does? and then he thought, and the thought surprised him, who can blame *me*? They were always threatening to cut the damn thing off, and what were all those fucking confessions about? *I have sinned in thought and deed.* I have sinned, I have sinned, I have sinned —and it was always better, to undercut Hell's competition, to sin, if you had to sin, alone. What a pain in the ass old Jesus Christ had turned out to be, and it probably wasn't even the poor, doomed, loving, hopheaded old Jew's fault.

Harold was watching him. He asked, "You want to turn on now or you want another drink first?" His voice was extremely rough, and he was scowling and smiling at the same time.

"Oh, I don't care," Vivaldo said, "I'm with the crowd." He thought of making another phone call, but realized that he was afraid to. The hell with it. It was one-fifteen. And he was, at last, thank heaven, at least a little drunk.

"Oh, let's split," said Lorenzo. "We've got beer at home."

They rose and left Benno's and walked west to Harold's pad. He lived in a narrow dark street near the river, on the top floor. The climb was discouraging, but the apartment was clean and not too disordered—it was not at all the kind of apartment one would have expected Harold to have—with carpets on the floor and burlap covering the windows. There was a hi-fi set, and records; and science-fiction magazines lay scattered about. Vivaldo flopped down on the narrow couch against the wall, in a kind of alcove formed by two bookcases. Belle sat on the floor near the window. Lorenzo went to the john, then to the kitchen, and returned with a quart bottle of beer.

"You forgot to bring glasses," Belle told him.

"So who needs glasses? We're all friends." But he obediently returned to the kitchen.

Harold, meanwhile, like a meticulous and scientific host, was busily preparing the weed. He seated himself at the coffee table, near Vivaldo, and placed on a sheet of newspaper tweezers, cigarettes, cigarette papers, and a Bull Durham sack full of pot.

"It's great stuff," he told Vivaldo, "chick brought it in from Mexico only yesterday. And, baby, this shit travels *well!*"

Vivaldo laughed. Lorenzo returned with the glasses and looked worriedly over at Vivaldo.

"You feeling all right?"

"I feel fine. Just quiet. You know."

"Groovy." He set a glass of beer carefully on the floor near Vivaldo, and poured a glass for Harold.

"He's going to feel just swinging," said Harold, as happy and busy as bees, "just as soon as he connects with old Mother Harold's special recessed filter-tips. Baby! Are you going to wail!"

Lorenzo poured a glass of beer for Belle, and set the bottle on the floor beside her. "How about some sides?"

"Go, baby."

Vivaldo closed his eyes, feeling an anticipatory languor and lewdness. Lorenzo put on something at once bell-like and doleful, by the Modern Jazz Quartet.

"Here."

He looked up. Harold stood above him with a glowing stick.

He sat up, smiling vaguely, and carefully picked up his beer from the floor before taking the stick from Harold. Harold watched him, smiling intensely, as he took a long, shaky drag. He took a swallow of his beer and gave the stick back. Harold inhaled deeply and expertly, and rubbed his chest.

"Come on over to the window," Belle called.

Her voice sounded high and pleased, like a child's. And, exactly as though he were responding to a child, Vivaldo, though he preferred to remain alone on the sofa, walked over to the window. Harold followed him. Belle and Lorenzo sat on the floor, sharing a stick between them, and staring out at the New York rooftops.

"It's strange," Belle said. "It's so ugly by day and so beautiful at night."

"Let's go up on the roof," said Lorenzo.

"Oh! What a groovy idea!"

They gathered up the makings, and the beer, and Belle picked up a blanket; and, like children, they tiptoed out of the apartment, up the stairs to the roof. And there they seemed bathed in silence, all alone. Belle spread the blanket, which was not big enough for them all. She and Lorenzo shared it. Vivaldo took another large drag and squatted on the edge of the roof, his arms hugging his knees.

"Don't *do* that, man," Lorenzo whispered, "you're too near the edge, I can't bear to watch it."

Vivaldo smiled and moved back, stretching out on his belly beside them.

"I'm sorry. I'm like that, too. I can hang over the edge myself, but I can't watch anybody else do it."

Belle grabbed his hand. He looked up at her pale, thin face, framed by the black hair. She smiled, and she was prettier than she had seemed in the bar. "I like you," she said. "You're a real groovy cat. Lorenzo always said you were, but I never believed him." Her accent, too, was more noticeable now; she sounded like the simplest and most innocent of country girls—if country girls were innocent, and he supposed, at some point in their lives, they had to be.

"Why, thank you," he said. Lorenzo, palely caught in the lights of heaven and earth, grinned over at him. Vivaldo pulled his hand from Belle's hand and reached over and struck Lorenzo lightly on the cheek. "I like you, too, both of you."

"How you feeling, dad?" It was Harold, who seemed to be quite far away.

"I feel wonderful." And he did, in a strange, untrustworthy way. He was terribly aware of his body, the length of his limbs, and the soft wind ruffling his hair, and of Lorenzo and Belle, poised like two cherubim together, and of Harold, the prince of darkness, industrious, indefatigable keeper of the weed. Harold was sitting in the shadow of the chimney, rolling another stick. Vivaldo laughed. "Baby, you really love your work."

"I just love to see people happy," said Harold, and suddenly grinned; he, too, seemed very different from what he had been in the bar, younger and softer; and somewhere beneath it all, much sadder, so that Vivaldo regretted all his harsh, sardonic judgments. What happened to people? why did they suffer so hideously? And at the same time he knew that he and Harold could never be friends and that none of them, really, would ever get any closer to each other than they were right now.

Harold lit his stick and passed it to Vivaldo. "Go, baby," he said—very tenderly, watching Vivaldo with a smile.

Vivaldo took his turn, while the others watched him. It was a kind of community endeavor, as though he were a baby just learning to use the potty or just learning how to walk. They all but applauded when he passed it on to Lorenzo, who took his turn and passed it on to Belle. "Ooh," said Lorenzo, "I'm flying," and leaned back with his head in Belle's lap.

Vivaldo turned over on his back, head resting on his arms, knees pointing to the sky. He felt like singing. "My chick's a singer," he announced.

The sky looked, now, like a vast and friendly ocean, in which drowning was forbidden, and the stars seemed stationed there, like beacons. To what country did this ocean lead? for oceans always led to some great good place: hence, sailors, missionaries, saints, and Americans.

"Where's she singing?" asked Lorenzo. His voice seemed to drop gently from the air: Vivaldo was watching heaven.

"She's not, right now. But she will be soon. And she's going to be great."

"I've seen her," Belle said, "she's beautiful."

He turned his head in the direction of the voice. "You've seen her? Where?"

"In the restaurant where she works. I went there with
somebody—not with Lorenzo," and he heard her giggle,
"and the cat I was with told me she was your girl." There
was a silence. Then, "She's very tough."

"Why do you say that?"

"Oh, I don't know. She just seemed—very tough, that's
all. I don't mean she wasn't nice. But she was very sure of
herself, you could tell she wasn't going to take any shit."

He laughed. "Sounds like my girl, all right."

"I wish I looked like her," Belle said. "My!"

"I like you just the way you are," said Lorenzo. Out of
the corner of his eye, and from far away, Vivaldo watched
his arms go up and saw Belle's dark hair fall.

Just above my head.

That was a song that Ida sometimes sang, puttering in-
efficiently about the kitchen, which always seemed sandy
with coffee grounds and vaguely immoral with dead cigarettes on the burned, blistered paint of the shelves.

Perhaps the answer was in the songs.

> *Just above my head,*
> *I hear music in the air.*
> *And I really do believe*
> *There's a God somewhere.*

But was it *music* in the air, or *trouble* in the air? He began
whistling another song:

> *Trouble in mind, I'm blue,*
> *But I won't be blue always,*
> *'Cause the sun's going to shine*
> *In my back door someday.*

Why *back* door? And the sky now seemed to descend, no
longer phosphorescent with possibilities, but rigid with the
mineral of choices, heavy as the weight of the finite earth,
onto his chest. He was being pressed: *I'm pressing on,* Ida
sometimes sang, *the upward way!*

What in the world did these songs mean to her? For he
knew that she often sang them in order to flaunt before him
privacies which he could never hope to penetrate and to
convey accusations which he could never hope to decipher,
much less deny. And yet, if he could enter this secret place,
he would, by that act, be released forever from the power of
her accusations. His presence in this strangest and grim-

mest of sanctuaries would prove his right to be there; in the same way that the prince, having outwitted all the dangers and slaughtered the lion, is ushered into the presence of his bride, the princess.

> *I loves you, Porgy, don't let him take me.*
> *Don't let him handle me with his hot hands.*

To whom, to whom, did she sing this song?

The blues fell down this morning. The blues my baby gave to me. Water trickled past his ear, onto his wrist. He did not move and the slow tears rolled from the corners of his eyes.

"You're groovy, too," he heard Belle say.

"For real?"

"For real."

"Let's try to make it to Spain. Let's really try."

"I'll get dressed up Monday, uptown style"—she giggled —"and I'll get a job as receptionist somewhere. I hate it, it's such a drag, but, that way, we can get away from here."

"Do that, baby. And I'll get a job, too, I promise."

"You don't have to promise."

"But I do."

He heard their kiss, it seemed light and loving and dry, and he envied them their deadly and unshakable innocence.

"Let's ball."

"Not here. Let's go downstairs."

He heard Lorenzo's laugh. "What's the matter, you shy?"

"No." He heard a giggle and a whisper. "Let's go down."

"They're stoned out of their heads, they don't care."

She giggled again. "Look at them."

He closed his eyes. He felt another weight on his chest, a hand, and he looked into Harold's face. Terribly weary and lined and pale, and his hair was damp and curled on his forehead. And yet, beneath this spectacular fatigue, it was the face of a very young boy which stared at him.

"How're you doing?"

"Great. It was great charge."

"I knew you'd dig it. I like you, man."

He was surprised and yet not surprised by the intensity in Harold's eyes. But he could not bear it; he turned his face away; then he put the weight of Harold's head on his chest.

"Please, man," he told him after a moment, "don't bother. It's not worth it, nothing will happen. It's been too long."

"What's been too long?"

And Vivaldo smiled to himself suddenly, a smile as sad
as his tears, thinking of shooting matches and other con-
tests on rooftops and basements and in locker rooms and
cars half his lifetime ago. And he had dreamed of it since,
though it was only now that he remembered the dreams that
he had dreamed. Feeling very cold now, inwardly cold, with
Harold's hand on his cock and Harold's head on his chest,
and knowing that: yes, something *could* happen, he recalled
his fantasies—of the male mouth, male hands, the male organ, the male ass. Sometimes, a boy—who always rather reminded him of his younger brother, Stevie, and perhaps this
was the prohibition, as, in others, it might be the key—passed
him, and he watched the boy's face and watched his ass, and
he felt something, wanting to touch the boy, to make the boy
laugh, to slap him across his young behind. So he knew that
it was there, and he probably wasn't frightened of it any
more; but it was, possibly, too expensive for him, it did not
matter enough. So he said to Harold, gently, "Understand
me, man, I'm not putting you down. But my time with boys
was a long time ago. I've been busy with girls. I'm sorry."

"And nothing can happen now?"

"I'd rather not. I'm sorry."

Harold smiled. "I'm sorry, too." Then, "Can I lie here
with you, like this, just the same?"

Vivaldo held him and closed his eyes. When he opened
them, the sky was a great brass bowl above him. Harold lay
near him, one hand on Vivaldo's leg, asleep. Belle and
Lorenzo lay wrapped in the blanket, like two dirty children.
He stood up, moving too close to the edge, getting a dreadful
glimpse of the waiting, baking streets. His mouth felt like
Mississippi in the days when cotton was king. He hurried
down the stairs into the streets, hurrying home to Ida. She
would say, "My God, Vivaldo, where've you been? I've been
calling this house all night to let you know I had to go and
sit in with some fellows in Jersey City. I keep telling you we
better get an answering service, but you never hear anything
I say!"

CHAPTER 4

And the summer came, the New York summer, which is like no summer anywhere. The heat and the noise began their destruction of nerves and sanity and private lives and love affairs. The air was full of baseball scores and bad news and treacly songs; and the streets and the bars were full of hostile people, made more hostile by the heat. It was not possible in this city, as it had been for Eric in Paris, to take a long and peaceful walk at any hour of the day or night, dropping in for a drink at a bistro or flopping oneself down at a sidewalk café—the half-dozen grim parodies of sidewalk cafés to be found in New York were not made for flopping. It was a city without oases, run entirely, insofar, at least, as human perception could tell, for money; and its citizens seemed to have lost entirely any sense of their right to renew themselves. Whoever, in New York, attempted to cling to this right, lived in New York in exile—in exile from the life around him; and this, paradoxically, had the effect of placing him in perpetual danger of being forever banished from any real sense of himself.

In the evenings, and on week ends, Vivaldo sat in his undershorts at the typewriter, his buttocks sticking to the chair, sweat rolling down his armpits and behind his ears and dripping into his eyes and the sheets of paper sticking to each other and to his fingers. The typewriter keys moved sluggishly, striking with a dull, wet sound—moved, in fact, rather the way his novel moved, lifelessly, pushed forward, inch by inch by recalcitrant inch, almost entirely by the will. He scarcely knew what his novel was about any longer, or why he had ever wished to write it, but he could not let it go. He could not let it go, nor could he close with it, for the price of that embrace was the loss of Ida's, or so he feared. And this fear kept him suspended in a pestilential, dripping limbo.

Their physical situation, in any case, was appalling. Their

apartment was too small. Even had they both kept regular hours, had worked all day and come home only in the evenings, they would have been cramped; but some weeks Vivaldo worked nights in the bookstore and some weeks he worked days; and Ida, too, was on a kind of universal, unpredictable shift at the restaurant, sometimes working lunch and supper, sometimes either, sometimes both. They each hated their jobs—which did not help their relationship with one another—but Ida was the most popular waitress her boss had, which gave her a certain leeway, and Vivaldo could no longer accept those more demanding and more lucrative jobs which offered him a future he did not want. They were both, as it were, racing before a storm, struggling to "make it" before they were sucked into that quicksand, which they saw all around them, of an aimless, defeated, and defensive bohemia. And this meant that they could not hope to improve their physical situation, being scarcely able to maintain the apartment that they had.

Vivaldo had often suggested that they move out of the Village, into the lower East Side, where cheap lofts were available, lofts which could be made extremely attractive. But Ida had vetoed this. Her most important reason was never stated, but Vivaldo eventually realized that she had a horror of that neighborhood because Rufus's last attempt at domestic life, or at life itself, had been made down there.

She told Vivaldo, "I wouldn't feel safe, honey, coming home at night or coming home in the daytime. You don't know those people the way I do, because they've never treated you the way they've treated me. Some of those cats, baby, if they catch you alone on a subway platform, or coming up the steps to *your* apartment, they don't think nothing of opening up their pants and asking you to give them a blow job. That's *right*. And, look, baby, I was down there, it was on Mott Street, with Rufus, a couple of years ago, to see some people for Sunday brunch. They were white. And we went out on the fire escape to look at a wedding procession down the street. So some of the people on the block saw us. Well, do you know that three white men came up to that apartment, one with a blackjack and one with a gun and one with a knife, and they threw us out of there. They said"—and she laughed—"that we were giving their street a bad name."

She watched his face for a moment. "It's true," she said, gently. Then, "Let's just stay here, Vivaldo, until we can do better. It's rough, but it's not as rough as it might be."

So they tried to keep their door open, but there were risks attached to this, particularly if Ida were home, lounging on the sofa in her brief blue playsuit or practicing arrangements with the help of the record player. The sound of Vivaldo's typewriter, the sound of Ida's voice, the sound of the record player, attracted the attention of people coming up and down the stairs and the glimpse the open door afforded of Ida inflamed the transient imagination. People used the open door as an incitement—to stop, to listen, to stare, to knock, pretending that a friend of theirs had once lived in this very apartment, and did they know whatever had become of good old Tom or Nancy or Joanna? Or inviting them to a party upstairs or down the street, or inviting themselves to a party at Vivaldo's. Once, absolutely beside himself, Vivaldo had beaten from the landing to the streets a boy who stood in the hot shadow of the landing, his hands in his pockets and his eyes on Ida—or, rather, on the spot from which, with a furious cry and a curse, she had hastily removed herself. The boy had not taken his hands from his pockets, only kept up a small, ugly animal moaning; and fallen, when Vivaldo had pushed him through the street door, heavily, on one shoulder. The police came shortly afterward, their own combustible imaginations stiffening their ready civic pride. After that, they kept the doors not only closed but locked. Yet, the entire shapeless, unspeakable city seemed to be in the room with them, some summer nights.

He worked, she worked, he paced the room, she paced. She wanted him to become a "great" writer, but, unless *she* was working, she was incapable of being left alone. If she was working, the sound of her voice, the sound of her music, menaced, and, most often, drowned out that other orchestra in his head. If she was not working, she poured him another beer, ruffling his hair; she observed that his cigarette had burned itself out in the ashtray and lit him a new one; or she read over his shoulder, which he could not bear—but it was easier to bear this than to hear himself accused of having no respect for her intelligence. On the evenings they were together in the house, he really could not work, for he could not move far enough away from her, he could not enter himself. But he tried not to resent this, for the evenings she was away were worse.

Once or twice a week, sometimes, or once every two or three weeks, she went to Harlem, never inviting him to come along. Or she was sitting in with some musicians in Peekskill or Poughkeepsie or Washington or Philadelphia or Balti-

more or Queens. He drove down with her once, with the
other musicians, to a joint in Washington. But the atmosphere was deadly; the musicians had not wanted him along.
The people in the joint had liked him well enough but had
also seemed to wonder what he was doing there—or perhaps
it was only *he* who wondered it; and Ida had sung only two
songs, which did not seem much after such a long trip, and
she had not sung them well. He felt that this had something
to do with the attitude of the musicians, who seemed to want
to punish her, and with the uneasy defiance with which she
forced herself to face their judgment. It was only too clear
that if he had been a powerful white man, their attitudes
would have been modified by the assumption that she was
using *him;* but it was obvious that, as things were, he could
do her no good whatever and, therefore, he must be using
her. Neither did Ida have the professional standing which
would force them to accept him as the whim, the house pet,
or husband of a star. He had *no* function, they did: they
pulled rank on him, they closed ranks against him.

There was speedily accumulating, then, between Ida and
Vivaldo, great areas of the unspoken, vast minefields which
neither dared to cross. They never spoke of Washington,
nor did he ever again accompany her on such out-of-town
jaunts. They never spoke of her family, or of his. After his
long, tormenting Wednesday night, Vivaldo found that he
lacked the courage to mention the name of Steve Ellis. He
knew that Ellis was sending her to a more exclusive and
celebrated singing teacher, as well as to a coach, and intended to arrange a recording date for her. Ida and Vivaldo
buried their disputes in silence, in the mined field. It seemed
better than finding themselves hoarse, embittered, gasping,
and more than ever alone. He did not wish to hear himself
accused, again, of trying to stand between her and her career—did not wish to hear it because there was more than a
little truth to this accusation. Of course, he also felt that she,
although unconsciously, was attempting to stand between
himself and his fulfillment. But he did not want to say this.
It would have made too clear their mutual panic, their terror
of being left alone.

So, there they were, as the ghastly summer groaned and
bubbled on, he working in order not to be left behind by her,
and she working—in order to be free of him? or in order to
create a basis on which they could be, more than ever, together? "I've *got* to make it," she sometimes said, "I'm *going*

to make it. And you better make it, too, sweetie. I've just about had it, down here among the garbage cans."

As for Ellis:

"Vivaldo, if you want to believe I'm two-timing you with that man, that's your problem. If you want to believe it, you're *going* to believe it. I will not be put in the position of having to *prove* a damn thing. It's up to you. You don't trust me, well, so long, baby, I'll pack my bags and *go*."

Some nights, when Ida came in, from the restaurant, her singing teacher, her parents, wherever she had been, bringing him beer and cigarettes and sandwiches, her face weary and peaceful and her eyes soft with love, it seemed unthinkable that they could ever part. They ate and drank and talked and laughed together, and lay naked on their narrow bed in the darkness, near the open windows through which an occasional limp breeze came, and tasted each other's lips and caressed each other in spite of the heat, and made great plans for their indisputable tomorrow. And often fell asleep like that, at perfect ease with one another. But at other times they could not find each other at all. Sometimes, unable to reach her and unable to reach the people in his novel, he stalked out and walked the summer streets alone. Sometimes she declared she couldn't stand him another minute, his grumpy ways, and was going out to a movie. And sometimes they went out together, down to Benno's, or over to visit Eric —though these days, it was usually Eric and Cass.

Ida professed herself very struck by the change in Eric— she meant by this that she disapproved of surprises and that Eric had surprised her—and the implacable, unaccountable Puritan in her disapproved of his new and astonishing affair. She said that Cass was foolish and that Eric was dishonest.

Vivaldo's feelings were much milder—it was not Eric who had surprised him, but Cass. She had certainly jeopardized everything; and he remembered her declaration: *No, thank you, Vivaldo, I don't want to be protected any more.* And, insofar as his own confusion allowed him to consider hers at all, he was proud of her—not so much because she had placed herself in danger as because she knew she had.

A French movie in which Eric played a bit part came to New York that summer and the four of them made an appointment to go and see it. Ida and Vivaldo were to meet Eric and Cass at the box office.

"What does she think she's doing?" Ida asked. She and

Vivaldo were walking toward the theater through the July streets.

"She's trying to live," said Vivaldo, mildly.

"Oh, shit, baby, Cass is a grown woman with two kids. What about those kids? Eric's not the fatherly type, at least not with boys *that* age."

"What a filthy little moralist you are. What Cass does with Cass's life is her business. Not yours. Maybe she knows more about those kids than you do; maybe she's trying to live the way she thinks she ought to live so that they won't be afraid to do it when their time comes." He felt himself beginning to be angry. "And you don't know enough about Eric to talk about him that way."

"Those kids are going to hate her before it's over, believe me. And don't tell me I don't know about Eric; I knew all about him the minute I laid eyes on him."

"You knew what you'd *heard*. And you'd never heard that he was going to have an affair with Cass. So you're bugged."

"Eric may have *you* fooled, and he may have Cass fooled —of course, I think she's just fooling herself—but *I'm* not fooled. You'll see."

"You're not a singer at all, you're a fortuneteller. We should get you some big brass earrings and a vivid turban and set you up in business."

"Laugh, clown," she said.

"Well, what do you care? If he wants to make it with her and she wants to make it with him, what do *we* care?"

"Don't *you* care? Richard's *your* friend."

"Cass is more my friend than Richard," he said.

"She *can't* realize what she's doing. She's got a good man and he's really starting to get some place, and she can't find anything *better* to do than start screwing some poor-white faggot from Alabama. I swear, I don't understand white folks worth a damn."

"Eric's not poor-white; his family's very well off," he said, beginning to sweat with more than the heat, wishing her voice would cease.

"Well, I hope they haven't disowned him. Do you think Eric's ever going to make it as an actor?"

"I don't see what that has to do with anything. But, yes, I do, he's a very good actor."

"He's getting kind of old to be so unknown. What was he doing in Paris all that time?"

"I don't know, baby, but I hope he was having a ball. You

know? Like whatever he digs most, that's what I hope he was doing."

"Well," she said, "that isn't what he's doing now."

He sighed, telling himself to drop the subject or change it. But he said, "I just don't see why it should matter to you, that's all. So he likes a roll in the hay with a man. So what?"

"He wanted a roll in the hay with my brother, too," she said. "He wanted to make him as sick as he is."

"If anything happened between Eric and your brother, it didn't happen because Eric threw him down and raped him. Let me cool you, honey, you don't know as much about men as you think you know."

She turned on him a small, grim smile. "*If* anything happened. You're a damn liar, and a coward, too."

He looked at her; for that moment he hated her. "Why do you say that?"

"Because you know damn well what happened. It's only that you don't want to know—"

"Ida, it was none of my damn business, I never talked about it with Rufus *or* with Eric. Why *should* I have?"

"Vivaldo, you haven't got to *talk* about what's happening to *know* what's happening. Rufus never talked to me about what was happening to him—but I knew just the same."

He was silent for a moment. Then, "You're never going to forgive me, are you? for your brother's death."

Then she, too, was silent. He said, "I loved your brother, too, Ida. You don't believe that, I know, but I did. But he was just a man, baby. He wasn't a saint."

"I never said he was a saint. But I'm black, too, and I know how white people treat black boys and girls. They think you're something for them to wipe their pricks on."

He saw the lights of the movie theater three blocks down the Avenue. The summer streets were full. His throat closed and his eyes began to burn.

"After all this time we've been together," he said, at last, "you still think that?"

"Our being together doesn't change the world, Vivaldo."

"It does," he said, "for me."

"That," she said, "is because you're white."

He felt, suddenly, that he was going to scream, right there in the crowded streets, or close his heavy fingers around her neck. The lights of the movie theater wavered before him, and the sidewalk seemed to tilt. "You stop that," he said, in a voice which he did not recognize. "You stop that. You stop trying to kill me. It's not my fault I'm white. It's not my fault you're black. It's not my fault he's dead." He threw back his head, sharply, to scatter away his tears, to bring the lights into focus, to make the sidewalk even. And in another voice, he said, "He's dead, sweetheart, but we're alive. We're alive, and I love you, I love you. Please don't try to kill me." And then, "Don't you love me? Do you love me, Ida? Do you?" And he turned his head and looked at her.

She did not look at him; and she said nothing; said nothing for a block or more. The theater came closer and closer. Cass and Eric were standing under the marquee, and they waved. "What I don't understand," she said, slowly, "is how you can talk about love when you don't want to know what's happening. And *that's* not *my* fault. How can you say you loved Rufus when there was so much about him you didn't want to know? How can I believe you love me?" And, with a curious helplessness, she took his arm. "How can you love somebody you don't know anything about? You don't know where I've been. You don't know what life is like for me."

"But I'm willing," he said, "to spend the rest of my life finding out."

She threw back her head and laughed. "Oh, Vivaldo. You *may* spend the rest of your life finding out—but it won't be because you're willing." And then, with ferocity, "And it won't be *me* you'll be finding out about. Oh, Lord." She dropped his arm. She gave him a strange side glance; he could not read it, it seemed both pitying and cold. "I'm sorry to have hurt your feelings, I'm not trying to kill you. I know you're not responsible for—for the world. And, listen: I don't blame you for not being willing. I'm not willing, nobody's willing. Nobody's willing to pay their dues."

Then she moved forward, smiling, to greet Eric and Cass.

"Hello, kids," she said—and Vivaldo watched her, that urchin grin, those flashing eyes—"how you been making it?" She tapped Eric lightly on the cheek. "They tell me you're beginning to enjoy New York almost as much as you enjoyed Paris. How about that? We're not so bad over here, now, are we?"

Eric blushed, and humorously pursued his lips. "I'd enjoy it a whole lot more if you'd put your rivers and bridges in the middle of the city instead of having them all pushed off on the edges this way. You can't *breathe* in this city in the summertime; it's frightening." He looked at Vivaldo. "I don't know how you barbarians stand it."

"If it wasn't for us barbarians," said Vivaldo, "you mandarins would be in one hell of a fix." He kissed Cass on the

forehead, and struck Eric lightly on the back of the neck.
"It's good to see you, anyway."

"We've got good news," said Cass, "though I guess I really
ought to let Eric tell it."

"Well, we're not absolutely certain that it's good news,"
said Eric. He looked at Ida and Vivaldo. "Anyway, I think
we ought to keep them in suspense for a while. If they don't
think I'm the greatest thing they ever saw in this movie, why,
then, I think we just ought to let them find out what's happening when the general public finds out." And he threw his
chin in the air and swaggered toward the box office.

"Oh, Eric," cried Cass, *"can't* I tell them?" She said, to
Ida and Vivaldo, "It's got something to do with this movie
we're going to see."

"Well, you've got to tell us," Ida said, "or we simply won't
go in." She raised her voice in the direction of Eric's back:
"We *do* know other actors."

"Come on, Cass," said Vivaldo, "you've got to tell us
now."

But Cass looked again in Eric's direction, with a small,
frowning smile. *"Let* me tell them, sweetheart."

He turned, smiling, with the tickets in his hand. "I don't
know how to stop you," he said. He moved over to Cass, and
put one arm around her shoulder.

"Well," said Cass, smaller than ever, and more radiant
—and, as she spoke, Eric watched her with an amused and
loving smile—"Eric doesn't have much of a part in this
movie, he only appears in one or two scenes and he's only
got a couples of lines—"

"Three scenes," said Eric, *"one* line. If one of you sneezes,
you die."

"—but on the strength of *this*—" cried Cass.

"Well, not *only* on the strength of this," said Eric.

"Will you let the girl talk?" asked Vivaldo. "Go on, Cass."

"—on the strength of this particular performance"—

"—exposure," said Eric.

"Oh, shit," cried Vivaldo.

"He's a perfectionist," Cass said.

"He's going to be a dead one, too," said Ida, "if he doesn't
stop hogging this scene. Lord, would I hate to work with
you. Please go on, Cass."

"Well, telegrams and phone calls have been coming out of
Hollywood asking Eric if he will play—" and she looked up
at Eric.

"Well, don't stop now," cried Ida.

Eric, now, was very pale. "They've got some wild idea out there of making a movie version of *The Possessed*—"

"The Dostoievski novel," said Cass.

"Thanks," said Vivaldo, "and—?"

"They want me to play Stavrogin," said Eric.

A total silence fell, and they all stared at Eric, who looked uneasily back at them. There gleamed a small crown of sweat on his forehead, just below the hairline. Vivaldo felt a mighty tug of jealousy and fear. "Wow!" he said. Eric looked at him, seeming to see into his heart; and his brow puckered slightly, as though he were stiffening himself for a quarrel.

"It's probably going to be an awful movie," he said, "can you imagine them doing *The Possessed*? I didn't really take it seriously until my agent called me. And then Bronson called me, too, because, you see, there's going to be a kind of conflict with *Happy Hunting Ground*. We're set to go into rehearsal next month, and, who knows? maybe it'll be a hit. So we've got to iron that out."

"But they're willing to do almost anything to get Eric," Cass said.

"That's not entirely true," said Eric, "don't listen to her. They're just very interested, that's all. I don't believe anything until it happens." He took a blue handkerchief out of his back pocket and wiped his face. "Let's go in," he said.

"Baby," said Vivaldo, "you're going to be a star." He kissed Eric on the forehead. "You son of a bitch."

"Nothing is set," said Eric, and he looked at Cass. He grinned. "I'm really part of an economy drive. They can get me cheap, you know, and they've got almost everybody you ever heard of lined up for the other roles—so my agent explained to me that my name goes *below* the title—"

"*But* in equal size," said Cass.

"One of those *and introducing* deals," said Eric, and laughed. He looked pleased about his good news for the first time.

"Well, baby, it looks like you've made it now," said Ida. "Congratulations."

"Your clairvoyant Frenchman," Cass said, "was right."

"Only what are they going to do about that ante-bellum accent?" asked Vivaldo.

"Look," said Eric, "let's go see this movie. I speak French in it." He threw an arm around Vivaldo's shoulder. "Impeccably."

"Hell," Vivaldo said, "I don't really feel like seeing a

movie. I'd much rather take you out and get you stinking drunk."

"You're going to," said Eric, "as soon as the movie's over."

And they came, laughing, through the doors just as the French film began. The titles were superimposed over a montage of shots of Paris in the morning: laborers on their bicycles, on their way to work, coming down from the hills of Montmartre, crossing the Place de la Concorde, rolling through the great square before Notre Dame. In great close-ups, the traffic lights flashed on and off, the white batons of the traffic policemen rose and fell; it soon became apparent that one had already picked up the central character and would follow him to his destination; which, if one could judge from the music would be a place of execution. The film was one of those politics, sex, and vengeance dramas the French love to turn out, and it starred one of the great French actors, who had died when this film was completed. So the film, which was not remarkable in itself, held this undeniable necrophilic fascination. Working with this actor, being on the set while this man worked, had been one of the great adventures of Eric's life. And though Cass, Vivaldo, and Ida were interested in the film principally because Eric appeared in it, the attention which they brought to it was dictated by the silent intensity of Eric's adoration. They had all heard of the great actor, and they all admired him. But they could not see, of course, as Eric could, with what economy of means he managed great effects and turned an indifferent role into a striking creation.

On the other hand, just as the politics of the film were made helplessly frivolous by the French passion for argument and distrust of community, so was the male star's overwhelming performance rendered suspect by the question of just why so much energy and talent had been expended on so little.

Ida grabbed Vivaldo's hand in the darkness, and clung to it as though she were a child, mutely begging for reassurance and forgiveness. He pressed his shoulder very close to hers, and they leaned against one another. The film unrolled. Cass whispered to Eric, Eric whispered to Cass. Cass turned toward them, whispering, "Here he comes!" and the camera trucked into a crowded café, resting finally on a group of students. "That's our boy!" cried Ida, disturbing the people around them—who sounded, for a second, like the weirdest cloud of insects. Cass leaned over and kissed Eric on the

nose; and, "You look very good," Vivaldo whispered. Eric
was compelled to be still during this entire brief scene, while
the students around him wrangled; his head was thrown
back and up, against the wall, his eyes were closed; and he
seemed scarcely to move at all. Yet, the director had so
placed him that his drunken somnolence held the scene together, and emphasized the futility of the passionate talkers.
Someone jostled the table and Eric's position shifted slightly.
He seemed to be made of rubber, and seemed, indeed, to be
fleeing from the controversy which raged around him—in
which, nevertheless, he was fatally involved. Vivaldo had
been with Eric when he was drunk and knew that this was
not at all the way Eric behaved—on the contrary, it was the
Southern rebel and a certain steel-rod quality which came
out in Eric then; and Vivaldo, at the same time that he realized that Eric was doing a great deal by doing very little, also,
for the first time, caught a glimpse of who Eric really was. It
was very strange—to see more of Eric when he was acting
than when he was being, as the saying goes, himself. The
camera moved very little during this scene and Eric was always kept in range. The light in which he was trapped did
not alter, and his face, therefore, was exposed as it never was
in life. And the director had surely placed Eric where he had
because this face operated, in effect, as a footnote to the
twentieth-century torment. Under the merciless light, the
lined, tense, coarse-grained forehead also suggested the patient skull; an effect which was underlined by the promontory
of the eyebrows and the secret place of the eyes. The nose
was flaring and slightly pug, more bone, nevertheless, than
flesh. And the full, slightly parted lips were lonely and defenseless, barely protected by the stubborn chin. It was the
face of a man, of a tormented man. Yet, in precisely the way
that great music depends, ultimately, on great silence, this
masculinity was defined, and made powerful, by something
which was not masculine. But it was not feminine, either,
and something in Vivaldo resisted the word *androgynous*. It
was a quality to which great numbers of people would respond without knowing to what it was they were responding.
There was great force in the face, and great gentleness. But,
as most women are not gentle, nor most men strong, it was
a face which suggested, resonantly, in the depths, the truth
about our natures.

Eric, without moving his head, suddenly opened his eyes
and looked blankly around the table. Then he looked sick,
rose, and hurriedly vanished. All the students laughed. They

were caustic about their vanished comrade, feeling that the character represented by Eric lacked courage. The film ground on, and Eric appeared twice more, once, silent, deep in the background, during a youthful council of war, and, finally, at the very end of the film, on a rooftop, with a machine gun in his hand. As he delivered his one line—*"Nom de Dieu, que j'ai soif!"*—the camera shifted to show him framed in the sights of an enemy gun; blood suddenly bubbled from Eric's lips and he went sliding off the rooftop, out of sight. With Eric's death, the movie also died for them, and, luckily, very shortly, it was over. They walked out of the cool darkness into the oven of July.

"Who's going to buy me that drink?" Eric asked. He smiled a pale smile. It was something of a shock to see him, standing on the sidewalk, shorter than he had appeared in the film, in flesh and blood. "Anyway, let's get away from here before people start asking me for my autograph." And he laughed.

"It might happen, my dear," said Cass, "you've got great presence on the screen."

"The movie's not so much," said Vivaldo, "but you were terrific."

"I didn't really have anything to do," said Eric.

"No," said Ida, "you didn't. But you sure did the hell out of it."

They walked in silence for a few moments.

"I'm afraid I can only have one drink with you," Cass said, "and then I'll have to go home."

"That's right," Ida said, "let's don't be hanging out with these cats until all hours of the morning. I got too many people to face tomorrow. Besides"—she glanced at Vivaldo with a small smile—"I don't believe they've seen each other alone one *time* since Eric got off the boat."

"And you think we better give them an evening off," Cass said.

"If we don't give it to them, they going to take it. But, this way, we can make ourselves look good—and that always comes in handy." She laughed. "That's right, Cass, you got to be *clever* if you want to keep your man."

"I should have started taking lessons from you years ago," Cass said.

"Now, be careful," said Eric, mildly, "because I don't think that's very flattering."

"I was joking," Cass said.

"Well, I'm insecure," said Eric.

They walked into Benno's, which was half-empty tonight, and sat, in a rather abrupt and mysterious silence, at one of the tables in the back. This silence was produced by the fact that each of them had more on their minds than they could easily say. Their sexes, so to speak, obstructed them. Perhaps the women wished to talk to each other concerning their men, but they could not do this with the men present; and neither could Eric and Vivaldo begin to unburden themselves to each other in the presence of Ida and Cass. They made small-talk, therefore, about the movie they had seen and the movie Eric was to make. Even this chatter was constricted and cautious, there being an unavowed reluctance on Eric's part to go to Hollywood. The nature of this reluctance Vivaldo could not guess; but a certain thoughtfulness, a certain fear, played in Eric's face like a lighthouse light; and Vivaldo thought that perhaps Eric was afraid of being trapped on a height as he had previously been trapped in the depths. Perhaps he was afraid, as Vivaldo knew himself to be afraid, of any real change in his condition. And he thought, The women have more courage than we do. Then he thought, Maybe they don't have any choice.

After one drink, they put Ida and Cass in a cab, together. Ida said, "Now don't you wake me up when you come falling in," and Cass said, "I'll call you sometime tomorrow." They waved to their women and watched the red lights of the cab disappear. They looked at each other.

"Well!" Vivaldo grinned. "Let's make the most of it, baby. Let's go and get drunk."

"I don't want to go back into Benno's," Eric said. "Let's go on over to my place, I've got some liquor."

"Okay," said Vivaldo, "I'd just as soon see you pass out at your place as have to *drag* you to your place." He grinned at Eric. "I'm very glad to see you," he said.

They started toward Eric's house. "Yes, I've wanted to see you," said Eric, "but"—they looked at each other briefly, and both smiled—"we've been kept pretty busy."

Vivaldo laughed. "Good men, and true," he said. "I certainly hope that Cass isn't as—unpredictable—as Ida can be."

"Hell," said Eric, "I hope that you're not as unpredictable as *I* am."

Vivaldo smiled, but said nothing. The streets were very dark and still. On a side street, there stood a lone city tree on which the moonlight gleamed. "We're all unpredictable," he

finally said, "one way or another. I wouldn't like you to
think that you're special."

"It's very hard to live with that," said Eric. "I mean, with
the sense that one is never what one seems—never—and yet,
what one seems to be is probably, in some sense, almost exactly what one *is*." He turned his half-smiling face to Vivaldo.
"Do you know what I mean?"

"I wish I didn't," said Vivaldo, slowly, "but I'm afraid I
do."

Eric's building was on a street with trees, westbound, not
far from the river. It was very quiet except for the noise
coming from two taverns, one on either far corner. Eric had
visited each of them once. "One of them's gay," he said, "and
what a cemetery *that* is. The other one's for longshoremen,
and that's pretty deadly, too. The longshoremen never go to
the gay bar and the gay boys never go to the longshoremen's
bar—but they know where to find each other when the bars
close, all up and down this street. It all seems very sad to me,
but maybe I've been away too long. *I* don't go for back-alley
cock-sucking. *I* think sin should be fun."

Vivaldo laughed, but thought, with wonder and a little
fear, My God, he *has* changed. He never talked like this before. And he looked at the quiet street, at the shadows
thrown by houses and trees, with a new sense of its menace,
and its terrifying loneliness. And he looked at Eric again, in
very much the same way he had looked at him in the film,
wondering again who Eric was, and how he bore it.

They entered Eric's small, lighted vestibule and climbed
the stairs to his apartment. One light, the night light over
the bed, was burning, "To keep away robbers," Eric said;
and the apartment was in its familiar state of disorder, with
the bed unmade and Eric's clothes draped over chairs and
hanging from knobs.

"Poor Cass," Eric laughed, "she keeps trying to establish
some order here, but it's uphill work. Anyway, the way
things are between us, I don't give her much time to do much
in the way of straightening up." He walked about, picking up
odds and ends of clothing, which he then piled all together
on top of the kitchen table. He turned on the kitchen light
and opened his icebox. Vivaldo flopped down on the unmade
bed. Eric poured two drinks and sat down opposite him on a
straight-backed easy chair. Then there was silence for a moment.

"Turn out that kitchen light," Vivaldo said, "it's in my
eyes."

Eric rose and switched off the kitchen light and came back with the bottle of whiskey and put it on the floor. Vivaldo flipped off his shoes and drew his legs up, playing with the toes of one foot.

"Are you in love with Cass?" he asked, abruptly.

Eric's red hair flashed in the dim light, as he looked down into his drink, then looked up at Vivaldo. "No. I don't think I'm in love with her. I think I wish I were. I care a lot about her—but, no, I'm not in love."

And he sipped his drink.

"But she's in love with you," said Vivaldo. "Isn't she?"

Eric raised his eyebrows. "I guess she is. She thinks she is. I don't know. What does it mean, to be in love? Are you in love with Ida?"

"Yes," said Vivaldo.

Eric rose and walked to the window. "You didn't even have to think about it. I guess that tells me where *I* am." He laughed. With his back to Vivaldo, he said, "I used to envy you, you know that?"

"You must have been out of your mind," said Vivaldo. "Why?"

"Because you were normal," Eric said. He turned and faced Vivaldo.

Vivaldo threw back his head and laughed. "Flattery will get you nowhere, son. Or is that a subtle put-down?"

"It's not a put-down at all," said Eric. "But I'm glad I don't envy you any more."

"Hell," said Vivaldo, "I might just as easily envy *you*. You can make it with both men and women and sometimes I've wished I could do that, I really have." Eric was silent. Vivaldo grinned. "We've all got our troubles, Buster."

Eric looked very grave. He grunted, noncommittally, and sat down again. "You've wished you could—you *say*. And I wish I couldn't."

"*You* say."

They looked at each other and smiled. Then, "I hope you get along with Ida better than I did with Rufus," Eric said.

Vivaldo felt chilled. He looked away from Eric, toward the window; the dark, lonely streets seemed to come flooding in on them. "*How*," he asked, "did you get along with Rufus?"

"It was terrible, it drove me crazy."

"I figured that." He watched Eric. "Is that all over now? I mean—is Cass kind of the wave of your future?"

"I don't know. I thought I could make myself fall in love with Cass, but—but, no. I love her very much, we get on beautifully together. But she's not all tangled up in my guts the way—the way I guess Ida is all tangled up in yours."

"Maybe you're just not in love with *her*. You haven't got to be in love every time you go to bed. You haven't *got* to be in love to have a good affair."

Eric was silent. Then, "No. But once you *have* been—!"

And he stared into his drink. "Yes," Vivaldo said at last, "yes, I know."

"I think," said Eric, "that I've really got to accept—or decide—some very strange things. Right away."

He walked into the dark kitchen, returned with ice, and spiked his drink, and Vivaldo's. He sat down again in his straight chair. "I've spent years now, it seems to me, thinking that one fine day I'd wake up and all my torment would be over, and all my indecision would end—and that no man, no boy, no *male*—would ever have power over me again."

Vivaldo blushed and lit a cigarette. "*I* can't be sure," he said, "that one fine day, I won't get all hung up on some boy —like that cat in *Death in Venice*. So *you* can't be sure that there isn't a woman waiting for you, just for you, somewhere up the road."

"Indeed," said Eric, "I can't be sure. And yet I must decide."

"*What* must you decide?"

Eric lit a cigarette, drew one foot up, and hugged one knee. "I mean, I think you've got to be truthful about the life you *have*. Otherwise, there's no possibility of achieving the life you *want*." He paused. "Or *think* you want."

"Or," said Vivaldo, after a moment, "the life you think you *should* want."

"The life you think you *should* want," said Eric, "is always the life that looks safest." He looked toward the window. The one light in the room, coming from behind Vivaldo, played on his face like firelight. "When I'm with Cass, it's fun, you know, and sometimes it's, well, really quite fantastic. And it makes me feel kind of restful and protected—and strong—there *are* some things which only a woman can give you." He walked to the window, peering down through the slats in the Venetian blinds as though he were awaiting the moment when the men in their opposing camps would leave their tents and meet in the shadow of the trees. "And yet, in a way, it's all a kind of superior calisthenics. It's a great chal-

lenge, a great test, a great game. But I don't really feel that
—terror—and that anguish and that joy I've sometimes felt
with—a few men. Not enough of myself is invested; it's
almost as though I'm doing something—for Cass." He
turned and looked at Vivaldo. "Does that make sense to
you?"

"I think it does," said Vivaldo. "I think it does."

But he was thinking of some nights in bed with Jane,
when she had become drunk enough to be insatiable; he was
thinking of her breath and her slippery body, and the eerie
impersonality of her cries. Once, he had had a terrible
stomach-ache, but Jane had given him no rest, and finally, in
order to avoid shoving his fist down her throat, he had
thrown himself on her, hoping, desperately, to exhaust her
so that he could get some sleep. And he knew that this was
not what Eric was talking about.

"Perhaps," said Vivaldo, haltingly, thinking of the night
on the roof with Harold, and Harold's hands, "it's something
like the way I might feel if I went to bed with a man only because I—liked him—and he wanted me to."

Eric smiled, grimly. "I'm not sure that there is a comparison, Vivaldo. Sex is too private. But if you went to bed
with a guy just because he wanted you to, you wouldn't have
to take any responsibility for it; you wouldn't be doing any
of the work. He'd do all the work. And the idea of being passive is very attractive to many men, maybe to most men."

"It is?" He put his feet on the floor and took a long swallow of his drink. He looked over at Eric and sighed and
smiled. "You make the whole deal sound pretty rough, old
buddy."

"Well, that's the way it looks from where I'm sitting."
Eric grimaced, threw back his head, and sipped his whiskey.
"Maybe I'm crying because I wanted to believe that, somewhere, for some people, life and love are easier—than they
are for me, than they are. Maybe it was easier to call myself
a faggot and blame my sorrow on that."

Then silence filled the room, like a chill. Eric and Vivaldo
stared at each other with an oddly belligerent intensity.
There was a great question in Eric's eyes and Vivaldo turned
away as though he were turning from a mirror and walked
to the kitchen door. "You really think it makes no difference?"

"I don't know. Does the difference make any difference?"

"Well," said Vivaldo, tapping with his thumbnail against
the hinges of the door, "I certainly think that the real ball

game is between men and women. And it's physically easier."
He looked quickly at Eric. "Isn't it? And then," he added,
"there are children." And he looked quickly at Eric again.

Eric laughed. "I never heard of two cats who wanted to
make it failing because they were the wrong size. Love always find a way, dad. I don't know anything about baseball,
so I don't know if life's a baseball game or not. Maybe it is
for you. It isn't for me. And if it's children you're after, well,
you can do that in five minutes and you haven't got to love
anybody to do it. If all the children who get here every year
were brought here by love, wow! baby, what a bright world
this would *be!*"

And now Vivaldo felt, at the very bottom of his heart, a
certain reluctant hatred rising, against which he struggled
as he would have struggled against vomiting. "I can't decide," he said, "whether you want to make everybody as
miserable as you are, or whether everybody *is* as miserable as
you are."

"Well, don't put it that way, baby. How happy are *you?*
That's got nothing to do with me, nothing to do with how I
live, or what I think, or how miserable I am—how are *you*
making it?"

The question hung in the room, like the smoke which
wavered between Eric and Vivaldo. The question was as
thick as the silence in which Vivaldo looked down, away
from Eric, searching his heart for an answer. He was frightened; he looked up at Eric; Eric was frightened, too. They
watched each other. "I'm in love with Ida," Vivaldo said.
Then, "And sometimes we make it, beautifully, beautifully.
And sometimes we don't. And it's hideous."

And he remained where he was, in the doorway, still.

"I, too, am in love," said Eric, "his name is Yves; he's
coming to New York very soon. I got a letter from him
today."

He stood up and walked to his desk, picked up the play
and opened it and took out an airmail envelope. Vivaldo
watched his face, which had become, in an instant, weary
and transfigured. Eric opened the letter and read it again. He
looked at Vivaldo. "Sometimes we make it, too, and it's
beautiful. And when we don't, it's hideous." He sat down
again. "When I was talking before about accepting or deciding, I was thinking about him." He paused, and threw his
letter on the bed. There was a very long silence, which
Vivaldo did not dare to break.

"I," said Eric, "must understand that if I dreamed of

escape, and I *did*—when this thing with Cass began, I thought that perhaps here was my opportunity to change, and I was *glad*—well, Yves, who is much younger than I, will also dream of escape. I must be prepared to let him go. He *will* go. And I think"—he looked up at Vivaldo—"that he *must* go, probably, in order to become a man."

"You mean," said Vivaldo, "in order to become himself."

"Yes," said Eric. And silence came again.

"All I can do," said Eric, at last, "is love him. But this means—doesn't it?—that I can't delude myself about loving someone else. I can't make any promise greater than this promise I've made already—not now, not now, and maybe I'll never make any greater promise. I can't be safe and sorry, too. I can't act as though I'm free when I know I'm not. I've got to live with that, I've got to learn to live with that. Does that make sense? or am I mad?" There were tears in his eyes. He walked to the kitchen door and stared at Vivaldo. Then he turned away. "You're right. You're right. There's nothing here to decide. There's everything to accept."

Vivaldo moved from the door, and threw himself face down on the bed, his long arms dangling to the floor. "Does Cass know about Yves?"

"Yes. I told her before anything happened." He smiled. "But you know how that is—we were trying to be honorable. Nothing could really have stopped us by that time; we needed each other too much."

"What are you going to do now? When does"—he gestured toward the letter, which was somewhere beneath his belly button—"Yves get here?"

"In about two weeks. According to that letter. It may be a little longer. It may be sooner."

"Have you told Cass that?"

"No. I'll tell her tomorrow."

"How do you think she'll take it?"

"Well, she's always known he was on his way. I don't know how she'll take—his actual *arrival*."

In the streets, they heard footsteps, walking fast, and someone whistling.

Eric stared at the wall again, frowning heavily. Other voices were heard in the street. "I guess the bars are beginning to close," said Eric.

"Yes." Vivaldo leaned up, looking toward the blinds which held back the jungle. "Eric. How's one going to get through it all? How can you live if you can't love? And how can you live if you *do?*"

And he stared at Eric, who said nothing, whose face gleamed in the yellow light, as mysteriously impersonal and as fearfully moving as might have been a death mask of Eric as a boy. He realized that they were both beginning to be drunk.

"I don't see how I can live with Ida, and I don't see how I can live without her. I get through every day on a prayer. Every morning, when I wake up, I'm surprised to find that she's still beside me." Eric was watching him, perfectly rigid and still, seeming scarcely to breathe, only his unmoving eyes were alive. "And yet"—he caught his breath—"sometimes I wish she weren't there, sometimes I wish I'd never met her, sometimes I think I'd go anywhere to get this burden off me. She never lets me forget I'm white, she never lets me forget she's colored. And I don't care, I don't care—did Rufus do that to you? Did he try to make you pay?"

Eric dropped his eyes, and his lips tightened. "Ah. He didn't *try*. I paid." He raised his eyes to Vivaldo's. "But I'm not sad about it any more. If it hadn't been for Rufus, I would never have had to go away, I would never have been able to deal with Yves." And then, rising and walking to the window, from which more and more voices rose, "Maybe that's what love is for."

"Are you sleeping with anyone besides Cass?"

Eric turned. "No."

"I'm sorry. I just thought you might be. I'm not sleeping with anyone except Ida."

"We can't be everywhere at once," said Eric.

They listened to the footfalls and voices in the street: someone was singing, someone called, someone was cursing. Someone ran. Then silence, again.

"You know," said Eric, "it's true that you can make kids without love. But if you *do* love the person you make the kids with, it must be something fantastic."

"Ida and I could have great kids," said Vivaldo.

"Do you think you will?"

"I don't know. I'd love to—but"—he fell back on the bed, staring at the ceiling—"I don't know."

He allowed himself, for a moment, the luxury of dreaming of Ida's children, though he knew that these children would never be born and that this moment was all he would ever have of them. Nevertheless, he dreamed of a baby boy who had Ida's mouth and eyes and forehead, his hair, only curlier, his build, *their* color. What would that color be? From the streets, again, came a cry and a crash and a roar. Eric

switched off the night light and opened the blinds and
Vivaldo joined him at the window. But now there was nothing to see, the street was empty, dark, and still, though an
echo of voices, diminishing, floated back.

"One of the last times I saw Rufus," Vivaldo said, abruptly
—and stopped. He had not thought about it since that moment; in a way, he had never thought about it at all.

"Yes?" He could barely make out Eric's face in the darkness. He turned away from Eric and sat down on the bed
again, and lit a cigarette. And in the tiny flare, Eric's face
leaped at him, then dropped back into darkness. He watched
the red-black silhouette of Eric's head against the dim glow
of the Venetian blinds.

He remembered that terrible apartment again, and Leona's
tears, and Rufus with the knife, and the bed with the twisted
gray sheet and the thin blanket: and it all seemed to have
happened many, many years ago.

But, in fact, it had only been a matter of months.

"I never told this to anybody before," he said, "and I really
don't know why I'm telling you. It's just that the last time I
saw Rufus, before he disappeared, when he was still with
Leona"—he caught his breath, he dragged on his cigarette
and the glow brought the room back into the world, then
dropped it again into chaos—"we had a fight, he said he was
going to kill me. And, at the very end, when he was finally in
bed, after he'd cried, and after he'd told me—so many terrible things—I looked at him, he was lying on his side, his eyes
were half open, he was looking at me. I was taking off my
pants, Leona was staying at my place and I was going to stay
there, I was afraid to leave him alone. Well, when he looked
at me, just before he closed his eyes and turned on his side
away from me, all curled up, I had the weirdest feeling that
he wanted me to take him in my arms. And not for sex,
though maybe sex would have happened. I had the feeling
that he wanted someone to hold him, to hold him, and that,
that night, it had to be a man. I got in the bed and I thought
about it and I watched his back, it was as dark in that room,
then, as it is in this room, now, and I lay on my back and I
didn't touch him and I didn't sleep. I remember that night as
a kind of vigil. I don't know whether he slept or not, I kept
trying to tell from his breathing—but I couldn't tell, it was
too choppy, maybe he was having nightmares. I loved Rufus,
I loved him, I didn't want him to die. But when he was
dead, I thought about it, thought about it—isn't it funny?
I didn't know I'd thought about it as much as I have—and I

wondered, I guess I still wonder, what would have happened if I'd taken him in my arms, if I'd held him, if I hadn't been —afraid. I was afraid that he wouldn't understand that it was—only love. Only love. But, oh, Lord, when he died, I thought that maybe I could have saved him if I'd just reached out that quarter of an inch between us on that bed, and held him." He felt the cold tears on his face, and he tried to wipe them away. "Do you know what I mean? I haven't told Ida this, I haven't told anyone, I haven't thought about it, since he died. But I guess I've been living with it. And I'll never know. I'll never know."

"No," said Eric, "you'll never know. If I had been there, I'd have held him—but it wouldn't have helped. His little girl tried to hold him, and that didn't help."

He sat down on the bed beside Vivaldo. "Would you like a cup of coffee?"

"Hell, no." Vivaldo dried his eyes with the back of his hand. "Let's have another drink. Let's watch the dawn come up."

"Okay," Eric started to move away. Vivaldo grabbed his hand.

"Eric—" He watched Eric's dark, questioning eyes and the slightly parted, slightly smiling lips. "I'm glad I told you about that. I guess I couldn't have told anybody else."

Eric seemed to smile. He took Vivaldo's face between his hands and kissed him, a light, swift kiss, on the forehead. Then his shadow vanished, and Vivaldo heard him in the kitchen.

"I'm out of ice."

"The hell with the ice."

"Water?"

"No. Well, maybe a little."

Eric returned with two glasses and put one in Vivaldo's hand. They touched glasses.

"To the dawn," said Eric.

"To the dawn," Vivaldo said.

Then they sat together, side by side, watching the light come up behind the window and insinuate itself into the room. Vivaldo sighed, and Eric turned to look at his lean, gray face, the long cheeks hollowed now, and the stubble coming up, the marvelous mouth resigned, and the black eyes staring straight out—staring out because they were beginning to look inward. And Eric felt, for perhaps the first time in his life, the key to the comradeship of men. Here was Vivaldo, long, lean, and weary, dressed, as he almost always was, in black and white; his white shirt was open, almost to the navel, and the shirt was dirty now, and the hair on his chest curled out; the hair on his head, which was always too long, was tousled, and fell over his forehead; and he smelled Vivaldo's sweat, his armpits and his groin, and was terribly aware of his long legs. Here Vivaldo sat, on Eric's bed. Not a quarter of an inch divided them. His elbow nearly touched Vivaldo's elbow, as he listened to the rise and fall of Vivaldo's breath. They were like two soldiers, resting from battle, about to go into battle again.

Vivaldo fell back on the bed, one hand covering his forehead, one hand between his legs. Presently, he was snoring, then he shuddered, and turned into Eric's pillow, toward Eric's wall. Eric sat on the bed, alone, and watched him. He took off Vivaldo's shoes, he loosened Vivaldo's belt, turning Vivaldo to face him. The morning light bathed the sleeper. Eric made himself another drink, with ice this time, for the ice was ready. He thought of reading Yves's letter again, but he knew it by heart; and he was terrified of Yves's arrival. He sat on the bed again, looking at the morning. . . . *Mon plus cher. Je te previendra la jour de mon arrivée. Je prendrai l'avion. J'ai dit au revoir à ma mère. Elle a beaucoup pleurée. J'avoue que ça me faisait quelque chose. Bon. Paris est mortelle sans toi. Je t'adore mon petit et je t'aime. Comme j'ai envie de te serre très fort entre mes bras. Je t'embrasse. Toujours à toi. Ton* YVES.

Oh, yes. Somewhere, someone turned on a radio. The day was here. He finished his drink, took off his shoes, loosened his belt, and stretched out beside Vivaldo. He put his head on Vivaldo's chest, and, in the shadow of that rock, he slept.

Ida told the taxi driver, "Uptown, please, to Small's Paradise," then turned, with a rueful smile, to Cass.

"*Their* night," she said, indicating the vanished Eric and Vivaldo, "is just beginning. So is mine, only mine won't be as much fun."

"I thought you were going home," Cass said.

"Well, I'm not. I've got some people to meet." She looked thoughtfully at her fingernails, then looked over to Cass. "I couldn't tell Vivaldo, so don't you tell him, please. He just gets upset when he's around—some of those musicians. I can't blame him. I really can't blame them, either; I know how they feel. But I don't like for them to take it out on Vivaldo, he's having a rough enough time as it is."

And, after a moment, she added, under her breath, "So am I."

Cass said nothing, for she was too astonished. So far from imagining herself and Ida to be friends, she had long ago decided that Ida disliked and distrusted her. But she did not sound that way now. She sounded lonely and troubled.

"I wish you'd come up and have one drink with me up there," Ida said. She kept twisting the ring on her little finger.

Cass thought, at once, I'll feel terribly out of place up there, and if you're meeting someone, what's the good of my coming along? But she sensed, somehow, that she could not say this, that Ida needed a woman to talk to, if only for a few minutes, even if the woman were white.

"Okay," she said, "but just one drink. I've got to hurry home to Richard." As she said this, both she and Ida laughed. It was almost the first time they had ever laughed together; and this laughter revealed to Cass that Ida's attitude toward her had been modified by Ida's knowledge of her adultery. Perhaps Ida felt that Cass was more to be trusted and more of a woman, now that her virtue, and her safety, were gone. And there was also, in that sudden and spontaneous laughter, the very faintest hint of blackmail. Ida could be freer with Cass now, since the world's judgment, should it ever be necessary to face it, would condemn Cass yet more cruelly than Ida. For Ida was not white, not married, nor a mother. The world assumed Ida's sins to be natural, whereas those of Cass were perverse.

Ida said, "Men are a bitch, aren't they, baby?" She sounded sad and weary. "I don't understand them, I swear I don't."

"I always thought you did," said Cass, "much better than I ever have."

Ida smiled. "Well, that's all a kind of act. Besides it's not hard to deal with a man if you don't *give* a damn about him. Most of the jokers I've had to deal with weren't worth shit. And I've always expected all of them to be like that." Then she was silent. She looked over at Cass, who sat very still, looking down. The cab was approaching Times Square. "Do you know what I mean?"

"I don't know if I do, or not," Cass said. "I guess I don't. I've only dealt with—two men—in my whole life."

Ida looked at her, speculatively, a small, sardonic smile touching her lips. "That's very hard to believe. It's hard to imagine."

"Well! I was never very pretty. I guess I led a kind of sheltered life. And—I got married very young." She lit a cigarette, she crossed her legs.

Ida looked out at the lights, and the crowds. "I'm wondering if I'm ever going to marry. I guess I'm not. I'll never marry Vivaldo, and"—she tapped her ring again—"it's hard to see what's coming, up the road. But I don't seem to see a bridegroom."

Cass was silent. Then, *"Why* will you never marry Vivaldo? Don't you love him?"

Ida said, "Love doesn't have as much to do with it as everybody seems to think. I mean, you know, it doesn't change everything, like people say. It can be a goddamn pain in the ass." She shifted, restlessly, in their narrow, dark space, and looked out of the window again. "Sure, I love Vivaldo; he's the sweetest man I've ever known. And I know I've given him a rough time sometimes. I can't help it. But I can't marry him, it would be the end of him, and the end of me."

"Well, why?" She paused; then, carefully, "You don't mean just because he's white—?"

"Well, yes," said Ida, forcefully, "in a way, I *do* mean that. That probably sounds terrible to you. I don't care about the color of his skin. I don't mean that." She stopped, clearly trying to discover what she *did* mean. "I've only known one man better than Vivaldo, and that man was my brother. Well, you know, Vivaldo was his best friend—and Rufus was *dying,* but Vivaldo didn't know it. And I was miles away, and I *did!"*

"How do you know that Vivaldo didn't know it? You're being very unjust. And *your* knowing it didn't stop anything, didn't change anything—"

"Maybe nothing can be stopped, or changed," Ida said, "but you've got to *know,* you've got to know what's happening."

"But, Ida, nobody really does know what's happening—not really. Like, perhaps you know things that I don't know. But isn't it possible that I also know things that you don't know? I know what it's like to have a child, for example. You don't."

"Oh, hell, Cass, I can *have* a damn baby, and then I'll know. Babies aren't my kick, but, you know, I can find out if I want to. The way Vivaldo carries on, I'm likely to find out, whether I want to or not," and, incongruously, she giggled. "But"—she sighed—"it doesn't work the other way

around. *You* don't know, and there's no way in the world
for you to find out, what it's like to be a black girl in this
world, and the way white men, and black men, too, baby,
treat you. You've never decided that the whole world was
just one big whorehouse and so the only way for you to make
it was to decide to be the biggest, coolest, hardest whore
around, and make the world pay you back that way." They
were in the park. Ida leaned forward and lit a cigarette with
trembling hands, then gestured out the window. "I bet you
think we're in a goddamn park. You don't know we're in one
of the world's great jungles. You don't know that behind
all them damn dainty trees and shit, people are screwing and
sucking and fixing and dying. Dying, baby, right now while
we move through this darkness in this man's taxicab. And
you don't know it, even when you're told; you don't know
it, even when you see it."

She felt very far from Ida, and very small and cold. "How
can we know it, Ida? How can you blame us if we don't
know? We never had a chance to find out. I hardly knew
that Central Park existed until I was a married woman."
And she, too, looked out at the park, trying to see what Ida
saw; but, of course, she saw only the trees and the lights and
the grass and the twisting road and the shape of the buildings
beyond the park. "There were hardly any colored people in
the town I grew up in—how am I to know?" And she hated
herself for her next question, but she could not hold it back:
"Don't you think I deserve some credit, for trying to be
human, for not being a part of all that for—walking out?"

"What the hell," asked Ida, "have you walked out on,
Cass?"

"That world," said Cass, "that empty life, that meaningless life!"

Ida laughed. It was a cruel sound and yet Cass sensed, very
powerfully, that Ida was not trying to be cruel. She seemed
to be laboring, within herself, up some steep, unprecedented
slope. "Couldn't we put it another way, honey—just for
kicks? Couldn't we, sort of, blame it on nature? and say that
you saw Richard and he got you hot, and so you didn't really
walk out—you just got married?"

Cass began to be angry; and she asked herself, Why? She
said, "No. Long before I met Richard, I knew that that
wasn't the life for me." And this was true, and yet her voice
lacked conviction. And Ida, relentlessly, put Cass's unspoken question into words.

"And what would have happened if Richard hadn't come?"

"I don't know. But this is silly. He *did* come. I *did* leave."

Now the air thickened between them, as though they were on opposite sides of a chasm in the mountains, trying to discern each other through the cloud and the fog, but terribly frightened of the precipice at their feet. For she had left Richard, or had, anyway, betrayed him—and what did that failure mean? And what was she doing, now, with Eric, and where was the meaning there? She began, dimly and unwillingly, to sense the vast dimensions of Ida's accusation at the same time that her ancient, incipient guilt concerning her life with Richard nosed its way, once more, into the front hall of her mind. She had always seen much farther than Richard, and known much more; she was more skillful, more patient, more cunning, and more single-minded; and he would have had to be a very different, stronger, and more ruthless man, *not* to have married her. But this was the way it always had been, always would be, between men and women, everywhere. Was it? She threw her cigarette out of the window. *He* did *come. I* did *walk out.* Had she, indeed? The cab was approaching Harlem. She realized, with a small shock, that she had not been here since the morning of Rufus's funeral.

"But, imagine," Ida was saying, "that he came, *that* man who's *your* man—because you always know, and he damn sure don't come every day—and there wasn't any place for you to walk out of or into, because he came too late. And no matter when he arrived would have been too late—because too much had happened by the time you were born, let alone by the time you met each other."

I don't believe that, Cass thought. That's too easy. I don't believe it. She said, "If you're talking of yourself and Vivaldo—there are other countries—have you ever thought of that?"

Ida threw back her head and laughed. "Oh, yes! And in another five or ten years, when we get the loot together, we can pack up and go to one of those countries." Then, savagely, "And what do you think will have happened to us in those five years? How much will be left?" She leaned toward Cass. "How much do you think will be left between you and Eric in five years—because I *know* you know you're not going to marry him, you're not *that* crazy."

"We'll be friends, we'll be friends," said Cass. "I hope we'll be friends forever." She felt cold; she thought of Eric's hands and lips; and she looked at Ida again.

Ida had turned again to the window.

"What you people don't know," she said, "is that life is a *bitch,* baby. It's the biggest hype going. You don't have any experience in paying your dues and it's going to be rough on you, baby, when the deal goes down. There's lots of back dues to be collected, and I know damn well you haven't got a penny saved."

Cass looked at the dark, proud head, which was half-turned away from her. "Do you hate white people, Ida?"

Ida sucked her teeth in anger. "What the hell has that got to do with anything? Hell, yes, sometimes I hate them, I could see them all dead. And sometimes I don't. I *do* have a couple of other things to occupy my mind." Her face changed. She looked down at her fingers, she twisted her ring. "If any *one* white person gets through to you, it kind of destroys your—single-mindedness. They say that love and hate are very close together. Well, that's a fact." She turned to the window again. "But, Cass, ask yourself, look out and ask yourself—wouldn't you hate all white people if they kept you in prison here?" They were rolling up startling Seventh Avenue. The entire population seemed to be in the streets, draped, almost, from lamp posts, stoops, and hydrants, and walking through the traffic as though it were not there. "Kept you here, and stunted you and starved you, and made you watch your mother and father and sister and lover and brother and son and daughter die or go mad or go under, before your very eyes? And not in a hurry, like from one day to the next, but, every day, every day, for years, for generations? Shit. They keep you here because you're black, the filthy, white cock suckers, while they go around jerking themselves off with all that jazz about the land of the free and the home of the brave. And they want you to jerk yourself off with that same music, too, only, keep your distance. Some days, honey, I wish I could turn myself into one big fist and grind this miserable country to powder. Some days, I don't believe it has a right to exist. Now, you've never felt like that, and Vivaldo's never felt like that. Vivaldo didn't want to know my brother was dying because he doesn't want to know that my brother would still be alive if he hadn't been born black."

"I don't know if that's true or not," Cass said, slowly, "but I guess I don't have any right to say it *isn't* true."

"No, baby, you sure don't," Ida said, "not unless you're really willing to ask yourself how *you'd* have made it, if they'd dumped on you what they dumped on Rufus. And you can't ask yourself that question because there's no way in the world for you to know what Rufus went through, not in this world, not as long as you're white." She smiled. It was the saddest smile Cass had ever seen. "That's right, baby. That's where it's at."

The cab stopped in front of Small's.

"Here we go," said Ida, jauntily, seeming, in an instant, to drag all of herself up from the depths, as though she were about to walk that mile from the wings to the stage. She glanced quickly at the meter, then opened her handbag.

"Let me," said Cass. "It's just about the only thing that a poor white woman can still do."

Ida looked at her, and smiled. "Now, don't you be like that," she said, "because you *can* suffer, and you've got some suffering to do, believe me." Cass handed the driver a bill. "You stand to lose everything—your home, your husband, even your children."

Cass sat very still, waiting for her change. She looked like a defiant little girl.

"I'll never give up my children," she said.

"They *could* be taken from you."

"Yes. It *could* happen. But it won't."

She tipped the driver, and they got out of the cab.

"It happened," said Ida, mildly, "to my ancestors every day."

"Maybe," said Cass, with a sudden flash of anger, and very close to tears, "it happened to all of us! Why was my husband ashamed to speak Polish all the years that he was growing up?—and look at him now, he doesn't *know* who he is. Maybe we're worse off than you."

"Oh," said Ida, "you are. There's no maybe about that."

"Then have a little mercy."

"You're asking a lot."

The men on the sidewalk looked at them with a kind of merciless calculation, deciding that they were certainly unattainable, that their studs or their johns were waiting inside; and, anyway, three white policemen, walking abreast, came up the Avenue. Cass felt, suddenly, exposed, and in danger and wished she had not come. She thought of herself, later, alone, looking for a taxi; but she did not dare say anything to Ida. Ida opened the doors, and they walked in.

"We're really not dressed for this place," Cass whispered.

"It doesn't matter," Ida said. She stared imperiously over the heads of the people at the bar, into the farther room, where the bandstand seemed to be, and the raised dance floor. And her arrogance produced, out of the smoke and confusion, a heavy, dark man who approached them with raised eyebrows.

"We're with Mr. Ellis's party," said Ida. "Will you lead us to him, please?"

He seemed checked; seemed, indeed almost to bow. "Oh, yes," he said. "Please follow me." Ida moved back slightly, to allow Cass to go before her, giving her the briefest of winks as she did so. Cass felt overcome with admiration and with rage, and at the same time she wanted to laugh. They walked, or, rather, marched through the bar, two lone and superbly improbable women, whose respectability had been, if not precisely defined, placed beyond the gates of common speculation. The place was crowded, but at a large table which gave the impression, somehow, of taking up more than its share of space, sat Steve Ellis, with two couples, one black and one white.

He rose, and the waiter vanished.

"I'm delighted to see you again, Mrs. Silenski," he said, smiling, holding out that regal hand. "Each time I see Richard, I beg to be remembered to you—but has he ever given you any of my messages? Of course not."

"Of course not," Cass said, laughing. She felt, suddenly, unaccountably, extremely lighthearted. "Richard simply has no memory at all. But I kept imagining that you would come back to see us, and you never have."

"Oh, but I will. You'll be seeing much more of me, dear lady, than you have the courage to imagine." He turned to the table. "Let me introduce you all." He gestured toward the dark couple. "Here are Mr. and Mrs. Barry—Mrs. Silenski." He bowed ironically in Ida's direction. "Miss Scott." Ida responded to this bow with an ironical half-curtsey.

Mr. Barry rose and shook their hands. He wore a small mustache over narrow lips; and he smiled a tentative smile which did not quite mask his patient wonder as to who *they* were. His wife looked like a retired showgirl. She glittered and gleamed, and she was one of those women who always seem to be dying to get home and take off their cruel and intricate and invisible lacings. Her red lower lip swooped or buckled down over her chin when she smiled, which was always. The other couple were named Nash. The male was red-faced, gray-haired, heavy, with a large cigar and a self-satisfied laugh; he was much older than his wife, who was pale, blond and thin, and wore bangs. Ida and Cass were dis-

tributed around the table, Ida next to Ellis, Cass next to
Mrs. Barry. They ordered drinks.

"Miss Scott," said Ellis, "spends a vast amount of her
time pretending to be a waitress. Don't ever go anywhere
near the joint she works in—I won't even tell you where it is
—she's the *worst*. As a waitress. But she's a great singer.
You're going to be hearing a lot from Miss Ida Scott." And
he grabbed her hand and patted it hard for a moment, held
it for a moment. "We might be able to persuade those boys
on the stand to let her sing a couple of numbers for us."

"Oh, please. I didn't come dressed for anything. Cass
picked me up at work, and we just came on as we were."

Ellis looked around the table. "Does anyone object to the
way Miss Scott is dressed?"

"My God, no," said Mrs. Barry, swooping and buckling
and perspiring and breathing hard, "she's perfectly charm-
ing."

"If a man's word means anything," said Mr. Nash, "I
couldn't care less *what* Miss Scott took it into her beautiful
head to wear. There are women who look well in—well, I
guess I better not say that in front of my wife," and his
heavy, merry laugh rang out, almost drowning the music for
a few seconds.

His wife did not, however, seem to be easily amused.

"Anyway," said Ida, "they've got a vocalist, and she won't
like it. If *I* was the vocalist, *I* wouldn't like it."

"Well. We'll see." And he took her hand again.

"I'd much rather not."

"We'll *see*. Okay?"

"All right," said Ida, and took her hand away, "we'll see."

The waiter came and set their drinks before them. Cass
looked about her. The band was out, the stage was empty;
but on the dance floor a few couples were dancing to the
juke box. She watched one large, ginger-colored boy dancing
with a tall, much darker girl. They danced with a concentration at once effortless and tremendous, sometimes very close
to one another, sometimes swinging far apart, but always
joined, each body making way for, responding to, and com-
menting on the other. Their faces were impassive. Only the
eyes, from time to time, flashed a signal or acknowledged an
unexpected nuance. It all seemed so effortless, so simple;
they followed the music, which also seemed to follow them;
and yet Cass knew that she would never be able to dance that
way; never. Never? She watched the girl; then she watched
the boy. Part of their ease came from the fact that it was the

boy who led—indisputably—and the girl who followed; but it also came, more profoundly, from the fact that the girl was, in no sense, appalled by the boy and did not for an instant hesitate to answer his rudest erotic quiver with her own. It all seemed so effortless, so simple, and yet, when one considered whence it came, it began to be clear that it was not at all simple: on the contrary, it was difficult and delicate, dangerous and deep. And she, Cass, who watched them with such envy (for first she watched the girl, then she watched the boy) began to feel uneasy; but they, oddly, on the gleaming floor, under the light, were at ease. In what sense, and for what reason, and why would it be forever impossible for her to dance as they did?

Mr. Barry was saying, "We have been hearing the most wonderful things about your husband, Mrs. Silenski. I've read his book, and I must say"—he smiled his cordial smile, everything about him was held within decent bounds—"it's a very remarkable achievement."

For an instant, Cass said nothing. She sipped her drink and watched his face, which was as smooth as a black jelly-bean. At first, she was tempted to dismiss the face as empty. But it was not empty; it was only that it was desperately trying to empty itself, decently, inward; an impossibility leading to God alone could guess what backing up of bile. Deep, deep behind the carefully hooded and noncommittal eyes, the jungle howled and lunged and bright dead birds lay scattered. He was like his wife, only he would never be able to step out of his iron corsets.

She felt very sorry for him, then she trembled; he hated her; and somehow his hatred was connected with her barely conscious wish to have the ginger-colored boy on the floor make love to her. He hated her—therefore?—far more than Ida could, and was far more at the mercy of his hatred; which, from ceaseless trampling down, yearned to go upward, blowing up the world.

But he could not afford to know this.

She said, smiling, with stiff lips, "Thank you very much."

Mrs. Barry said, "You must be very proud of your husband."

Cass and Ida glanced briefly at each other, and Cass smiled and said, "Well, I've always been proud of him, really; none of this comes as any surprise to me."

Ida laughed. "That's the truth. Cass thinks Richard can do *no* wrong."

"Not even when she catches him at it." Ellis grinned.

Then, "We've been together quite a lot lately, and he often speaks of what a happy man he is."

For some reason, this frightened her. She wondered when, and how often, Richard and Ellis met and what Richard really had to say. She swallowed her fear. "Blind faith," she said, inanely, "I've got it," and thought, *God*. She looked toward the dance floor. But that particular couple had vanished.

"Your husband's a lucky man," said Mr. Barry. He looked at his wife, and reached for her hand. "So am I."

"Mr. Barry's just become a part of our publicity department," Ellis said. "We're awfully proud to have him on board. And I'm sorry if I sound like I'm bragging—hell, I'm not sorry, I *am* bragging—but I think it represents a tremendous breakthrough in our pussyfooting, hidebound industry." He grinned, and Mr. Barry smiled. "And hidebound so soon!"

"It was hidebound the instant it was born," said Mr. Nash, "just as your cinema industry was hidebound, and for the same reason. It immediately became the property of the banks—part of what you people quaintly call free enterprise, though God knows there's nothing free about it, and nothing even remotely enterprising about the lot of you."

Cass and Ida stared at him. "Where are you from?" Cass demanded.

He smiled at her from a great, tolerant distance. "Belfast," he said.

"Oh," cried Ida, "I have a friend whose father was born in Dublin! Do you know Dublin? Is it very far from Belfast?"

"Geographically? Yes, some distance. Otherwise, the distance is negligible—though the population of either city would hang me if they heard me say so." And he laughed his cheerful, lubricated laugh.

"What have you got against us?" Cass asked.

"I? Why, nothing," said Mr. Nash, laughing, "I make a great deal of money out of you."

"Mr. Nash," said Ellis, "is an impresario who no longer lives in Belfast."

"Free enterprise, you see," said Mr. Nash, and winked at Mr. Barry.

Mr. Barry laughed. He leaned toward Mr. Nash. "Well, I'm on the side of Mrs. Silenski. What *have* you got against our system? I think we've all made great strides under it." He raised one bony hand, one manicured finger. "What would you replace it with?"

"What," asked Cass, unexpectedly, *"does* one replace a dream with? I wish I knew."

Mr. Nash laughed, then stopped, as if embarrassed. Ida was watching her—watching her without seeming to watch. Then Cass sensed, for the first time in her life, the knowledge that black people had of white people—though what, really, did Ida know about her, except that she was lying, was unfaithful, and was acting? and was in trouble—and, for a second, she hated Ida with all her heart. Then she felt very cold again, the second passed.

"I suppose," said Ida, in an extraordinary voice, "that one replaces a dream with reality."

Everybody laughed, nervously. The music began again. She looked again toward the dance floor, but those dancers were gone. She grabbed her drink as though it were a spar, and held it in her mouth as though it were ice.

"Only," said Ida, "that's not so easy to do." She held her drink between her two thin hands and looked across at Cass. Cass swallowed the warm fluid she had been holding in her mouth, and it hurt her throat. Ida put down her drink and grabbed Ellis by the hand. "Come on, honey," she said, "let's dance."

Ellis rose. "You will excuse us," he said, "but I am summoned."

"Indeed you are," said Ida, and smiled at them all, and swept onto the dance floor. Ellis followed, rather like something entangled in her train.

"She reminds me of the young Billie Holiday," said Mr. Barry, wistfully.

"Yes, I'd love to hear her sing," said Mrs. Nash—rather venomously, and most unexpectedly. They all turned expectantly toward her, as though this were a seance and she were the medium. But she sipped her drink and said nothing more.

Cass turned again toward the dance floor, watching Ida and Ellis. The light was still as bright, the floor somewhat more crowded; the juke box blared. There was a vast amount of cunning, conscious or not, in Ida's choice of a costume for the place. She wore a very simple pale orange dress, and flat shoes, and very little make-up; and her hair, which was usually piled high, was pulled back tonight and held tightly in a severe, old-maidish bun. Therefore, she looked even younger than she was, almost like a very young girl; and the effect of this was to make Ellis, who was so much shorter than she, look older than he was, and more corrupt. They became an odd and unprecedented beauty and the beast up there; and, for the first time consciously, Cass wondered about their real relationship to one another. Ida had said that she did not want Vivaldo "bugged" by any of the musicians; but she had not come to meet any musicians. She had come to meet Ellis. And she had brought Cass along as a kind of smoke screen—and she and Ellis could not have met often in public before. In private then? And she wondered about this as she watched them. Their dance, which was slow and should have been fluid, was awkward and dry and full of hesitations. She was holding him at bay, he could not lead her; yet, she was holding him fast.

"I wonder if his wife knows where he is." Mrs. Nash again, *sotto voce*, to her husband, with a small, smug smile.

Cass thought of Vivaldo, then thought of Richard, and immediately hated Mrs. Nash. *You evil-minded whore*, she thought, and broke the table's uneasy silence by saying:

"Mrs. Ellis and Miss Scott have known each other for quite a long time, long before Mrs. Ellis's marriage."

Why did I say that? she wondered. *She can easily find out if I'm lying.* She looked steadily at Mrs. Nash, making no attempt to hide her dislike. *She won't, though. She hasn't got the wit or the guts.*

Mrs. Nash looked at Cass with that absolutely infuriating superciliousness achieved only by chambermaids who have lately become great ladies. "How strange that is," she murmured.

"Not at all," Cass said, recklessly, "they both worked in the same factory."

Mrs. Nash watched her, the faintest tremor occurring somewhere around her upper lip. Cass smiled and looked briefly at Mr. Nash. "Did you and your wife meet in Belfast?"

"No," said Mr. Nash, smiling—and Cass felt, with a surge of amusement and horror, how much his wife despised him at that moment—"we met in Dublin, while I was there on a business trip." He took his wife's limp hand. Her pale eyes did not move, her pale face did not change. "The most important trip I ever made."

Ah, yes, thought Cass, *I don't doubt it, for both of you.* But suddenly she felt weary and inexplicably sad. What in the world was she doing here, and why was she needling this absurd little woman? The music changed, becoming louder and swifter and more raucous; and all their attention returned, with relief, to the dance floor. Ida and Ellis had begun a new dance; or, rather, Ida had begun a new cruelty. Ida was suddenly dancing as she had probably not danced since her adolescence, and Ellis was attempting to match her—he could certainly not be said to be leading her now, either. He tried, of course, his square figure swooping and breaking, and his little boy's face trying hard to seem abandoned. And the harder he tried—*the fool!* Cass thought —the more she eluded him, the more savagely she shamed him. He was not on those terms with his body, or with hers, or anyone's body. He moved his buttocks by will, with no faintest memory of love, no hint of grace; his thighs were merely those of a climber, his feet might have been treading grapes. He did not know what to do with his arms, which stuck out at angles to his body as though they were sectioned and controlled by strings, and also as though they had no communion with his hands—hands which had grasped and taken but never caressed. Was Ida being revenged? or was she giving him warning? Ellis's forehead turned slick with sweat, his short, curly hair seemed to darken, Cass almost heard his breathing. Ida circled around him, in her orange dress, her legs flashing like knives, and her hips cruelly grinding. From time to time she extended to him, his fingers touched, her lean, brown, fiery hand. Others on the floor made way for them—for her: it must have seemed to Ellis that the music would never end.

But the juke box fell silent, at last, and the colored lights stopped whirling, for the band was coming on again. Ida and Ellis returned to the table.

The lights began to dim. Cass stood up.

"Ida," she said, "I promised to have one drink, and I have, and now I must go. I really must. Richard will kill me if I stay out any longer."

Her voice unaccountably shook, and she felt herself blushing as she said this. At the same time, she realized that Ida was in an even more dangerous mood now than she had been before her dance.

"Oh, call him up," Ida said. "Even the most faithful of wives deserves a night out."

Cass, very nearly, in her fear and despair, sank slowly into her seat again; but Ellis, mopping his brow, and gleaming, was more cheerful than ever. "I don't think that's necessarily so," he said—and wrung from the table the obligatory laugh—"and, anyway, Mrs. Silenski is responsible for a very heavy investment. Her husband is very valuable, we must take good care of his morale." Ida and Cass watched each other. Ida smiled.

"Will Richard's morale suffer if you do not get home?"

"Unquestionably," said Cass. "I must go."

Ida's face changed, and she looked down. She seemed, abruptly, weary and sad. "I guess you're right," she said, "and there's no point in putting it off." She looked at Ellis. "Walk her to a cab, sweetie."

"My pleasure," said Ellis.

"Good night, all," said Cass. "I'm sorry I have to run, but I must." She said, to Ida, "I'll see you soon—?"

"Shall I expect to see you at the usual place?"

"If it's still standing," Cass said, after a moment, "yes." She turned and made her way through the darkening room, with Ellis padding behind her. They gained the street, she feeling limp and frightened. Ellis put her into a cab. The cab was driven by a young Puerto Rican.

"Good night, Mrs. Silenski," Ellis said, and gave her his wet, hard hand. "Please give Richard my best, and tell him I'll be calling him in a couple of days."

"Yes, I'll tell him. Thank you. Good night."

He was gone, and she was alone in the cab, behind the unspeaking shoulders of the Puerto Rican. Idly, she sought out his face in the glass, then looked down, lighting a cigarette. The cab began to move. She did not look out. She sat huddled in the darkness, burning with a curious kind of shame. She was not ashamed—was she?—of anything she had done; but she was ashamed, as it were in anticipation, of what she might, now, helplessly, find herself doing. She had been using Ida and Vivaldo as smoke screens to cover her affair with Eric: why should not Ida use *her,* then, to cover from Vivaldo her assignation with Ellis? She had silenced *them,* in relation to Richard—now she was silenced, in relation to Vivaldo. She smiled, but the smoke she inhaled was bitter. When she had been safe and respectable, so had the world been safe and respectable; now the entire world was bitter with deceit and danger and loss; and which was the greater illusion? She was uncomfortably aware of the driver, his shoulders, his untried face, his color, and his soft, dark eyes. He glanced at her from time to time in the mirror —after all, she had glanced at him first; and her mood, perhaps, had set up a tension between them, a sexual tension. She thought, again, unwillingly, of the ginger-colored boy on the dance floor. And she knew (as though her mind, for a moment, were a clear pool, and she saw straight down into its depths) that, yes, yes, had he touched her, had he insisted, he could have had his way, she would have been glad. She would have been glad to know his body, even though the body might be all that she could know. Eric's entrance into her, her fall from—grace?—had left her prey to ambiguities whose power she had never glimpsed before. Richard had been her protection, not only against the evil in the world, but also against the wilderness of herself. And now she would never be protected again. She tried to feel jubilant about this. But she did not feel jubilant. She felt frightened and bewildered.

The driver coughed. The cab stopped for a red light, just before entering the park, and the driver lit a cigarette. She, too, lit a fresh cigarette: and the two tiny flames almost seemed to be signaling one another. Just so, she now remembered, as the cab lurched forward, had she wandered, aimlessly and bitterly, through the city, when Richard first began to go away from her. She had wanted to be noticed, she had wanted a man to notice her. And they had: they had noticed that she was a sexual beggar, no longer young. Terrifying, that the loss of intimacy with one person results in the freezing over of the world, and the loss of oneself! And terrifying that the terms of love are so rigorous, its checks and liberties so tightly bound together.

There were many things she could not demand of Eric. Their relationship depended on her restraint. She could not go to him now, for example, at two in the morning: this liberty was not in their contract. The premise of their affair, or the basis of their comedy, was that they were two independent people, who needed each other for a time, who would always be friends, but who, probably, would not always be lovers. Such a premise forbids the intrusion of the future, or too vivid an exhibition of need. Eric, in effect, was marking time, waiting—waiting for something to be resolved. And when it was resolved—by the arrival of Yves, the signing of a contract, or the acceptance, in Eric, of a sorrow neither of them could name—she would be locked out of his bed. He would use everything life had given him, or taken from him, in his work—*that* would be his life. He was too proud to use her, or anyone, as a haven, too proud to accept any resolution of his sorrow not forged by his own hands. And she could not be bitter about this, or even sorrowful, for this was precisely why she loved him. Or, if not why, the *why* of such matters being securely locked away from human perception, it was this quality in him which she most admired, and which she knew he could not live without. Most men could—did: this was why she was so menaced.

Therefore, she too, was marking time, waiting—for the blow to fall, for the bill to come in. Only after she had paid this bill would she really know what her resources were. And she dreaded this moment, dreaded it—her terror of this moment sometimes made her catch her breath. The terror was not merely that she did not know how she would rebuild her life, or that she feared, as she grew older, coming to despise herself: the terror was that her children would despise her. The rebuilding of her own life might have reduced itself, simply, to moving out of Richard's house—*Richard's* house! how long had she thought of it as Richard's house?—and getting a job. But holding the love of her children, and helping them to grow from boys into men—this was a different matter.

The cab driver was singing to himself, in Spanish.

"You have a nice voice," she heard herself say.

He turned his head, briefly, smiling, and she watched his young profile, the faint gleam of his teeth, and his sparkling eyes. "Thank you," he said. "We are all singers where I come from." His accent was heavy, and he lisped slightly.

"In Puerto Rico? there can't be very much to sing about."

He laughed. "Oh, but we sing, anyway." He turned to her again. "There is nothing to sing about here, either, you know—nobody sings here."

She smiled. "That's true. I think singing—for pleasure, anyway—may have become one of the great American crimes."

He did not follow this, except in spirit. "You are all too serious here. Cold and ugly."

"How long have you been here?"

"Two years." He smiled at her again. "I was lucky, I work hard, I get along." He paused. "Only, sometimes, it's lonely. So I sing." They both laughed. "It makes the time go," he said.

"Don't you have any friends?" she asked.

He shrugged. "Friends cost money. And I have no money and no time. I must send money home to my family."

"Oh, are you married?"

He shrugged again, turning his profile to her again, not

smiling. "No, I am not married." Then he grinned. "That also costs money."

There was a silence. They turned into her block.

"Yes," she said, idly, "you're right about that." She pointed to the house. "Here we are." The cab stopped. She fumbled in her handbag. He watched her.

"*You* are married?" he asked at last.

"Yes." She smiled. "With two children."

"Boy or girl?"

"Two boys."

"That is very good," he said.

She paid him. "Good-bye. I wish you well."

He smiled. It was a really friendly smile. "I also wish you well. You are very nice. Good night."

"Good night."

She opened the door and the light shone full on their faces for a moment. His face was very young and direct and hopeful, and caused her to blush a little. She slammed the cab door behind her, and walked into her house without looking back. She heard the cab drive away.

The light was on in the living room, and Richard, fully dressed except for his shoes, lay on the sofa, asleep. He was usually in bed, or at work, when she came home. She stared at him for a moment. There was a half-glass of vodka on the table next to him, and a dead cigarette in the ashtray. He slept very silently and his face looked tormented and very young.

She started to wake him, but left him there, and tiptoed into the room where Paul and Michael slept. Paul lay on his belly, the sheet tangled at his feet, and his arms thrown up. With a shock, she saw how heavy he was, and how tall: he was already at the outer edge of his boyhood. It had happened so fast, it seemed almost to have happened in a dream. She looked at the sleeping head and wondered what thoughts it contained, what judgments, watched one twitching leg and wondered what his dreams were now. Gently, she pulled the sheet up to his shoulders. She looked at the secretive Michael, curled on his side like a worm or an embryo, hands hidden between his legs, and the hair damp on his forehead. But she did not dare to touch his brow: he woke too easily. As quietly as possible, she retrieved his sheet from the floor and laid it over him. She left their room and walked into the bathroom. Then she heard, in the living room, Richard's feet hit the floor.

She washed her face, combed her hair, staring at her weary face in the mirror. Then she walked into the living room. Richard sat on the sofa, the glass of vodka in his hands, staring at the floor.

"Hello," she said. "What made you fall asleep in here?" She had left her handbag in the bathroom. She walked to the bar and picked up a package of cigarettes and lit one. She asked, mockingly, "You weren't, were you, waiting up for me?"

He looked at her, drained his glass, and held it out. "Pour me a drink. Pour yourself a drink, too."

She took his glass. Now, his face which in sleep had looked so young, looked old. A certain pain and terror passed through her. She thought, insanely, as she turned her back on him, of Cleopatra's lament for Antony: *His face was as the heavens.* Was that right? She could not remember the rest of it. She poured two drinks, vodka for him, whiskey for her. The ice bucket was empty. "Do you want ice?"

"No."

She handed him his drink. She poured a little water into her whiskey. She looked, covertly, at him again—her guilt began. *His face was as the heavens, Wherein were set the stars and moon.*

"Sit down, Cass."

She left the bar and sat down in the easy chair facing him. She had left the cigarettes on the bar. *Which kept their course and lighted, This little O, the earth.*

He asked, in a friendly tone, "Where are you just coming from, Cass?" He looked at his watch. "It's past two o'clock."

"I often get in past two o'clock," she said. "Is this the first time you've noticed it?" She was astounded at the hostility in her voice. She sipped her drink. Her mind began to play strange tricks on her: her mind was filled, abruptly, with the memory of a field, long ago, in New England, a field with blue flowers in patches here and there. The field was absolutely silent and empty, it sloped gently toward a forest; they were hidden by tall grass. The sun was hot. Richard's face was above her, his arms and his hands held and inflamed her, his weight pressed her down into the flowers. A little way from them lay his army cap and jacket; his shirt was open to the navel, and the rough, glinting hairs of his chest tortured her breasts. But she was resisting, she was frightened, and his face was full of pain and anger. Helplessly, she reached up and stroked his hair. *Oh, I can't.*

*We're getting married, remember? And I'm going over-
seas next week.*

Anybody can find us here!

*Nobody ever comes this way. Everybody's gone away.
Not here.*

Where?

"No," he said, with a dangerous quietness, "it's not the
first time I've noticed it."

"Well. It doesn't matter. I've just left Ida."

"With Vivaldo?"

She hesitated, and he smiled. "We were all together earlier.
Then she and I went up to Harlem and had a drink."

"Alone?"

She shrugged. "With lots of other people. Why?" But before he could answer, she added, "Ellis was there. He said
he's going to call you in a couple of days."

"Ah," he said, "Ellis was there." He sipped his drink.
"And you left Ida with Ellis?"

"I left Ida with Ellis's party." She stared at him. "What's
going on in your mind?"

"And what did you do when you left Ida?"

"I came home."

"You came straight home?"

"I got into a taxi and I came straight home." She began to
be angry. "What are you cross-examining me for? I will
not *be* cross-examined, you know, not by you, not by anyone."

He was silent—finished his vodka, and walked to the bar.
"I think you're drunk enough already," she said, coldly. "If
you have a question you want to ask me, ask it. Otherwise,
I'm going to bed."

He turned and looked at her. This look frightened her, but
she willed herself to be calm. "You are *not* going to bed for a
while yet. And I have a great many questions I want to ask
you."

"You may ask," she said. "I may not answer. You've
waited a very long time, it seems to me, to ask me questions.
Maybe you've waited too long." They stared at each other.
And she saw, with a sense of triumph that made her ill, that,
yes, she was stronger than he. She could break him: for, to
match her will, he would be compelled to descend to strata-
gems far beneath him.

And her mind was filled again with that bright, blue field.
She shook with the memory of his weight, her desire, her
terror, and her cunning. *Not here. Where? Oh, Richard.*

The cruel sun, and the indifferent air, and the two of them burning on a burning field. She knew that, yes, she must now surrender, now that she had him; she knew that she could not let him go; and, oh, his hands, his hands. But she was frightened, she realized that she knew nothing: *Can't we wait? Wait. No. No.* And his lips burned her neck and her breasts. *Then let's go to the woods. Let's go to the woods.* And he grinned. The memory of that grin rushed up from its hiding place and splintered her heart now. *You'd have to carry me, or I'd have to crawl, can't you feel it?* Then, *Let me in, Cass, take me, take me, I swear I won't betray you, you know I won't!*

"I love you, Cass," he said, his lips twitching and his eyes stunned with grief. "Tell me where you've been, tell me why you've gone so far away from me."

"Why *I*," she said, helplessly, "have gone away from *you?*" The smell of crushed flowers rose to her nostrils. She began to cry.

She did not look down. She looked straight up at the sun; then she closed her eyes, and the sun roared inside her head. One hand had left her—where his hand had been, she was cold.

I won't hurt you.
Please.
Maybe just a little. Just at first.
Oh, Richard. Please.
Tell me you love me. Say it. Say it now.
Oh, yes. I love you. I love you.
Tell me you'll love me forever.
Yes. Forever. Forever.

He was looking at her, leaning on the bar, looking at her from far away. She dried her eyes with the handkerchief he had thrown in her lap. "Give me a cigarette, please."

He threw her the pack, threw her some matches. She lit a cigarette.

"When was the last time you saw Ida and Vivaldo? Tell me the truth."

"Tonight."

"And you've been spending all this time—every time you come in here in the early morning—with Ida and Vivaldo?"

She was frightened again, and she knew that her tone betrayed her. "Yes."

"You're lying. Ida hasn't been with Vivaldo. She's been with Ellis. And it's been going on a long time." He paused. "The question is—where have *you* been? Who's been with

Vivaldo while Ida's been away—till two o'clock in the morning?"

She looked at him, too stunned for an instant, to calculate. "You mean, Ida's been having an affair with Steve Ellis? For how long? And how do *you* know that?"

"How do *you*—*not* know it?"

"Why—every time I saw them, they seemed perfectly natural and happy together—"

"But many of the times you say you've been with them, you couldn't have been with them, because Ida's been with *Steve!*"

She still could not quite get it through her head, even though she knew that it was true and although she knew that precious seconds were passing, and that she must soon begin to fight for herself. "How do you *know?*"

"Because Steve told me! He's got a real thing about her, he's going out of his mind."

Now, she did begin to calculate—desperately, cursing Ida for not having given her warning. But how could she have? She said, coldly, "Ellis at the mercy of a great passion—? Don't make me laugh."

"Oh, I know you think we're made of the coarsest of coarse clay, and are insensitive to all the higher vibrations. I don't care. You *can't* have been seeing much of Ida—that I know. Have you been seeing much of Vivaldo? Answer me, Cass."

She said, wonderingly—for it was *this* she could not get through her head: "And Vivaldo doesn't *know*—"

"And you don't, either? You're the only two in town who don't. What mighty distractions have you two found?"

She winced and looked up at him. She saw that he was controlling himself with a great and terrible effort; that he both wanted to know the truth, and feared to know it. She could not bear the anguish in his eyes, and she looked away.

How could she ever have doubted that he loved her!

"Have you been seeing a lot of Vivaldo? Tell me."

She rose and walked to the window. She felt sick—her stomach seemed to have shrunk to the size of a small, hard, rubber ball. "Leave me alone. You've always been jealous of Vivaldo, and we both know why, though you won't admit it. Sometimes I saw Vivaldo, sometimes I saw Vivaldo with Ida, sometimes I just walked around, sometimes I went to the movies."

"Till two o'clock in the morning?"

"Sometimes I've come in at midnight, sometimes I've

come in at four! Leave me alone! Why is it so important to you now? I've lived in this house like a ghost for months, half the time you haven't *known* I was here—what does it matter now?"

His face was wet and white and ugly. "*I* have lived here like a ghost, not you. I've known you were here, how could I not know it?" He took one step toward her. He dropped his voice. "Do you know how you made your presence known? By the way you look at me, by the contempt in your eyes when you look at me. What have I done to deserve your contempt? What have I done, Cass? You loved me once, you loved me, and everything I've done I've done for you."

She heard her voice saying coldly, "Are you sure? For me?"

"Who else? who *else*? You *are* my life. Why have you gone away from me?"

She sat down. "Let's talk about this in the morning."

"No. We'll talk about it now."

He walked about the room—in order, she sensed, not to come too close to her, not to touch her; he did not know what would happen if he did. She covered her face with one hand. She thought of the ginger-colored boy and the Puerto Rican, Eric blazed up in her mind for a moment, like salvation. She thought of the field of flowers. Then she thought of the children, and her stomach contracted again. And the pain in her stomach somehow defeated lucidity. She said, and knew, obscurely, as she said it, that she was making a mistake, was delivering herself up, "Stop torturing yourself about Vivaldo —we have not been sleeping together."

He came close to the chair she sat in. She did not look up.

"I know that you've always admired Vivaldo. More than you admire me."

There was a terrible mixture of humility and anger in his tone, and her heart shook; she saw what he was trying to accept. She almost looked up to reach out to him, to help him and comfort him, but something made her keep still.

She said, "Admiration and love are very different."

"Are they? I'm not so sure. How can you touch a woman if you know she despises you? And if a woman admires a man, what is it, really, that she admires? A woman who admires you will open her legs for you at once, she'll give you anything she's got." She felt his heat and his presence above her like a cloud; she bit one knuckle. "You did—you did, for me, don't you remember? Won't you come back?"

Then she did look up at him, tears falling down her face. "Oh, Richard. I don't know if I can."

"Why? Do you despise me so much?" She looked down, twisting the handkerchief. He squatted beside the chair. "I'm sorry we've got so far apart—I really don't even know how it happened, but I guess I got mad at you because—because you seemed to have so little respect for"—he tried to laugh—"my success. Maybe you're right, I don't know. I know you're smarter than I am, but how are we going to eat, baby, what else can I do? Maybe I shouldn't have let myself get so jealous of Vivaldo, but it seemed so logical, once I thought about it. Once I thought about it, I thought about it all the time. I know he must be alone a lot, and—and you've been alone." She looked at him, looked away. He put one hand on her arm; she bit her lip to control her trembling. "Come back to me, please. Don't you love me any more? You can't have stopped loving me. I can't live without you. You've always been the only woman in the world for me."

She could keep silence and go into his arms, and the last few months would be wiped away—he would never know where she had been. The world would return to its former shape. Would it? The silence between them stretched. She could not look at him. He had existed for too long in her mind—now, she was being humbled by the baffling reality of his presence. Her imagination had not taken enough into account—she had not foreseen, for example, the measure or the quality or the power of his pain. He was a lonely and limited man, who loved her. Did she love him?

"I don't despise you," she said. "I'm sorry if I've made you think that." Then she said nothing more. Why tell him? What good would it do? He would never understand it, she would merely have given him an anguish which he would never be able to handle. And he would never trust her again.

Did she love him? And if she did, what should she do? Very slowly and gently, she took her arm from beneath his hand; and she walked to the window. The blinds were drawn against the night, but she opened them a little and looked out: on the lights and the deep black water. Silence rang its mighty gongs in the room behind her. She dropped the blinds, and turned and looked at him. He sat, now, on the floor, beside the chair that she had left, his glass between his feet, his great hands loosely clasped below his knees, his head tilted up toward her. It was a look she knew, a listening, trusting look. She forced herself to look at him; she might never see that look again; and it had been her sustenance so long! His face was the face of a man entering middle age, and it was also—and always would be, for her—the face of a boy. His sandy hair was longer than usual, it was beginning to turn gray, his forehead was wet, and his hair was wet. Cass discovered that she loved him during the fearful, immeasurable second that she stood there watching him. Had she loved him less, she might have wearily consented to continue acting as the bulwark which protected his simplicity. But she could not do that to Richard, nor to his children. He had the right to know his wife: she prayed that he would take it.

She said, "I have to tell you something, Richard. I don't know how you'll take it, or where we can go from here." She paused, and his face changed. *Be quick!* she told herself. "I have to tell you because we can never come back together, we can never have any future if I don't." Her stomach contracted again, dryly. She wanted to run to the bathroom, but she knew that that would do no good. The spasm passed. "Vivaldo and I have never touched each other. I've"—*be quick!*—"been having an affair with Eric."

His voice, when he spoke, seemed to have no consciousness behind it, to belong to no one; it was a mere meaningless tinkle on the air: "Eric?"

She walked to the bar and leaned on it. "Yes."

How the silence rang and gathered! "Eric?" He laughed. *"Eric?"*

It's his turn now, she thought. She did not look at him; he was rising to his feet; he stumbled, suddenly drunken, to the bar. She felt him staring at her—for some reason, she thought of an airplane trying to land. Then his hand was on her shoulder. He turned her to face him. She forced herself to look into his eyes.

"Is that the truth?"

She felt absolutely cold and dry and wanted to go to sleep. "Yes, Richard. That's the truth."

She moved away and sat down in the chair again. She had, indeed, delivered herself up: she thought of the children and fear broke over her like a wave, chilling her. She stared straight before her, sitting perfectly still, listening: for no matter what else was lost, she would not give up her children, she would not let them go.

"It's *not* true. I don't believe you. Why Eric? Why did you go to him?"

"He has something—something I needed very badly."

"What is that, Cass?"

"A sense of himself."

"A sense of himself," he repeated, slowly. "A sense of himself." She felt his eyes on her, and also felt, with dread, how slowly the storm in him gathered, how long it would take to break. "Forgive your coarse-grained husband, but I've always felt that he had no sense of himself at all. He's not even sure he knows what's between his legs, or what to do with it—but I guess I have to take that back now."

Here we go, she thought.

She said, wearily, helplessly, "I know it sounds strange, Richard." Tears came to her eyes. "But he's a very wonderful person. I know. I know him better than you do."

He said, making a sound somewhere between a grunt and a sob, "I guess you *do*—though *he* may have preferred it the other way around. Did you ever think of that? You must be one of the very few women in the world—"

"Don't, Richard. Don't. It won't change anything, it won't help."

He came and stood over her. "Let's get this straight. We've been married almost thirteen years, and I've been in love with you all that time, and I've trusted you, and, except for a couple of times in the army, I haven't had anything to do with any other woman. Even though I've thought about it. But it never seemed worth it. And I've worked, I've worked very hard, Cass, for you and our children, so we could be happy and so our marriage would work. Maybe you think that's old-fashioned, maybe you think I'm dumb, I don't know, you're so much more—*sensitive* than I am. And now—and then—" He walked over to the bar and set his glass down. "Suddenly, for no reason, just when it begins to seem that things are really going to work out for us, all of a sudden—you begin to make me feel that I'm something that stinks, that I ought to be out of doors. I didn't know what had happened, I didn't know where you'd gone—all of a sudden. I've listened to you come into this house and go and look at the boys, and then crawl into bed—I swear, I could hear every move you made—and I'd stay on in the office like a little boy, because I didn't know how, *how,* to come close to you again. I kept thinking, She'll get over it, it's just some strange kind of feminine shift that I can't understand. I even thought, my God, that maybe you were going to have another baby and didn't want to tell me yet." He bowed his head on the bar. "And, Jesus, Jesus—Eric! You walk in and tell me you've been sleeping with Eric." He turned and looked at her. "How long?"

"A few weeks."

"Why?" She did not answer. He came toward her again. "Answer me, baby. Why?" He leaned over her, imprisoning her in the chair. "Is it that you wanted to hurt me?"

"No. I never wanted to hurt you."

"Why, then?" He leaned closer. "Did you get bored with me? Does he make love to you better than I; does he know tricks I don't know? Is that it?" He wrapped the fingers of one hand in her hair. "Is that it? Answer me!"

"Richard, you're going to wake the children—"

"Now she worries about the children!" He pulled her head forward, then slammed it back against the chair, and slapped her across the face, twice, as hard as he could. The room dropped into darkness for a second, then came reeling back, in light; tears came to her eyes, and her nose began to bleed. "Is that it? Did he fuck you in the ass, did he make you suck his cock? Answer me, you bitch, you slut, you *cunt!"*

She tried to throw back her head, choking and gasping, she felt her thick blood on her lips, and it fell onto her breasts. "No, Richard, no, no. Please, Richard."

"Oh, God. Oh, God." He fell away from her, and, as though in a dream, she saw his great body stagger to the sofa; and he fell beside the sofa, on his knees, weeping. She listened, listened to hear a sound from the children, and looked toward the door, where they would be standing if they were up; but they were not there, there was no sound. She looked at Richard, and covered her face for a moment. She could not bear the sound of his weeping, or the sight of those breaking shoulders. Her face felt twice its size; when she took her hands away, they were covered with blood. She rose, and staggered into the bathroom.

She ran the water, the bleeding slowly began to stop. Then she sat down on the bathroom floor. Her mind swung madly back and forth, like the needle of some broken instrument. She wondered if her face would be swollen in the morning, and how she would explain this to Paul and Michael. She thought of Ida and Vivaldo and Ellis, and wondered what Vivaldo would do when he discovered the truth; and felt very sorry for him, sad enough for her tears to begin again, dripping down on her clenched hands. She thought of Eric, and wondered if she had also betrayed *him* by telling Richard the truth. And what would she say to Eric now, or he to her? She did not want, ever, to leave the white, lighted haven of the bathroom. The center of her mind was filled with the sight and sound of Richard's anguish. She wondered if there was any hope for them, if there was anything left between them which they could use. This last question made her rise at last, her dry belly still contracting, and take off her bloody dress. She wanted to burn it, but she put it in the dirty-clothes hamper. She walked into the kitchen and put coffee on the stove. Then she walked back into the bathroom, put on a bathrobe, and took the cigarettes out of her handbag. She lit a cigarette and sat down at the kitchen table. It was three o'clock in the morning. She sat and waited for Richard to rise and come to her.

BOOK THREE

TOWARD
BETHLEHEM

How with this rage shall beauty hold a plea,
Whose action is no stronger than a flower?
—SHAKESPEARE, *Sonnet* LXV

CHAPTER 1

Vivaldo dreamed that he was running, running, running, through a country he had always known, but could not now remember, a rocky country. He was blinded by the rain beating down, the tough, wet vines dragged at his legs and feet, and thorns and nettles tormented his hands and arms and face. He was both fleeing and seeking, and, in his dream, the time was running out. There was a high wall ahead of him, a high, stone wall. Broken glass glittered on top of the wall, sharp points standing straight up, like spears. He was reminded of music, though he heard none: the music was created by the sight of the rain which fell in long, cruel, gleaming shafts, and by the bright glass which reared itself bitterly against it. And he felt an answering rearing in his own body, a pull fugitive and powerful and dimly troubling, such as he might have felt for a moment had there been the movement and power of a horse beneath him. And, at the same time, in his dream, as he ran or as he was propelled, he was weighed down and made sick by the certainty that he had forgotten—forgotten—what? some secret, some duty, that would save him. His breath was a terrible captive weight in his chest. He reached the wall. He grasped the stone with his bleeding hands, but the stone was slippery, he could not hold it, could not lift himself up. He tried with his feet; his feet slipped; the rain poured down.

And now he knew that his enemy was upon him. Salt burned his eyes. He dared not turn; in terror he pressed himself against the rough, wet wall, as though a wall could melt or could be entered. He had forgotten—what? how to escape or how to defeat his enemy. Then he heard the wail of trombones and clarinets and a steady, enraged beating on the drums. They were playing a blues he had never heard before, they were filling the earth with a sound so dreadful that he knew he could not bear it. Where was Ida? she could help

him. But he felt rough hands on him and he looked down
into Rufus's distorted and vindictive face. *Go on up*, said
Rufus, *I'm helping you up. Go up!* Rufus's hands pushed and
pushed and soon Vivaldo stood, higher than Rufus had ever
stood, on the wintry bridge, looking down on death. He knew
that his death was what Rufus most desired. He tried to look
down, to beg Rufus for mercy, but he could not move without falling off the wall, or falling on the glass. From far
away, far beyond this flood, he saw Ida, on a sloping green
meadow, walking alone. The sun was beautiful on her blue-
black hair and on her Aztec brow, and gathered in a dark,
glinting pool at the hollow of her throat. She did not look
toward him, walked in a measured way, looking down at the
ground; yet, he felt that she saw him, was aware of him
standing on the cruel wall, and waited, in collusion with her
brother, for his death. Then Rufus came hurtling from the
air, impaling himself on the far, spiked fence which bounded
the meadow. Ida did not look; she waited. Vivaldo watched
Rufus's blood run down, bright red over the black spikes,
into the green meadow. He tried to shout, but no words
came; tried to reach out to Ida and fell heavily on his hands
and knees on the rearing, uplifted glass. He could not bear
the pain; yet, he felt again the random, voluptuous tug. He
felt entirely helpless and more terrified than ever. But there
was pleasure in it. He writhed against the glass. *Don't kill
me, Rufus. Please. Please. I love you.* Then, to his delight
and confusion, Rufus lay down beside him and opened his
arms. And the moment he surrendered to this sweet and overwhelming embrace, his dream, like glass, shattered, he heard
the rain at the windows, returned, violently, into his body, became aware of his odor and the odor of Eric, and found that
it was Eric to whom he clung, who clung to him. Eric's lips
were against Vivaldo's neck and chest.

Vivaldo hoped that he was dreaming still. A terrible sorrow entered him, because he was dreaming and because he
was awake. Immediately, he felt that he had created his
dream in order to create this opportunity; he had brought
about something that he had long desired. He was frightened
and then he was angry—at Eric or at himself? he did not
know—and started to pull away. But he could not pull away,
he did not want to, it was too late. He thought to keep his
eyes closed in order to take no responsibility for what was
happening. This thought made him ashamed. He tried to re-
construct the way in which this monstrous endeavor must
have begun. They must have gone to sleep, spoon-fashion.

Eric curled against him—oh, what did this cause him, nearly, to remember? He had curled his legs, himself, around Eric, since Eric's body was there; and desire had entered this monastic, this boyish bed. Now it was too late, thank God it was too late; it was necessary for them to disentangle themselves from the drag and torment of their undershorts, their trousers, and the sheets. He opened his eyes. Eric was watching him with a small half-smile, a troubled smile, and this smile caused Vivaldo to realize that Eric loved him. Eric really loved him and would be proud to give Vivaldo anything Vivaldo needed. With a groan and a sigh, with an indescribable relief, Vivaldo came full awake and pulled Eric closer. It had been a dream and not a dream, how long could such dreams last? this one could not last long. Instantaneously, then, they each seemed to become intent on carrying this moment, which belonged to them, as far as it would go. They kicked their trousers to the floor, saying nothing—what was there to say?—and not daring to let go of one another. Then, as in a waking dream, helpless and trustful, he felt Eric remove his shirt and caress him with his parted lips. Eric bowed and kissed Vivaldo on the belly button, half-hidden in the violent, gypsy hair. This was in honor of Vivaldo, of Vivaldo's body and Vivaldo's need, and Vivaldo trembled as he had never trembled before. And this caress was not entirely pleasant. Vivaldo felt terribly ill at ease, not knowing what was expected of him, or what he could expect from Eric. He pulled Eric up and kissed him on the mouth, kneading Eric's buttocks and stroking his sex. How strange it felt, this violent muscle, stretching and throbbing, so like his own, but belonging to another! And this chest, this belly, these legs, were like his, and the tremor of Eric's breath echoed his own earthquake. Oh, what was it that he could not remember? It was his first sexual encounter with a male in many years, and his very first sexual encounter with a friend. He associated the act with the humiliation and the debasement of one male by another, the inferior male of less importance than the crumpled, cast-off handkerchief; but he did not feel this way toward Eric; and therefore he did not know what he felt. This tormented self-consciousness caused Vivaldo to fear that their moment might, after all, come to nothing. He did not want this to happen, he knew his need to be too great, and they had come too far, and Eric had risked too much. He was afraid of what might happen if they failed. Yet, his lust remained, and rose, and chafing within and battering against the labyrinth of his bewilderment; his

lust was unaccustomedly arrogant and cruel and irresponsi-
ble, and yet there was mingled in it a deep and incomprehen-
sible tenderness: he did not want to cause Eric pain. The
physical pain he had sometimes brought to vanished, phan-
tom girls had been necessary for them, he had been unlock-
ing, for them, the door to life; but he was now involved in
another mystery, at once blacker and more pure. He tried
to will himself back into his adolescence, grasping Eric's
strange body and stroking that strange sex. At the same time,
he tried to think of a woman. (But he did not want to think
of Ida.) And they lay together in this antique attitude, the
hand of each on the sex of the other, and with their limbs entangled, and Eric's breath trembling against Vivaldo's chest.
This childish and trustful tremor returned to Vivaldo a sense
of his own power. He held Eric very tightly and covered
Eric's body with his own, as though he were shielding him
from the falling heavens. But it was also as though he were, at
the same instant, being shielded—by Eric's love. It was
strangely and insistently double-edged, it was like making
love in the midst of mirrors, or it was like death by drowning.
But it was also like music, the highest, sweetest, loneliest
reeds, and it was like the rain. He kissed Eric again and again,
wondering how they would finally come together. The male
body was not mysterious, he had never thought about it at all,
but it was the most impenetrable of mysteries now; and this
wonder made him think of his own body, of its possibilities
and its imminent and absolute decay, in a way that he had
never thought of it before. Eric moved against him, and beneath him, as thirsty as the sand. He wondered what moved in
Eric's body which drove him, like a bird or a leaf in a storm,
against the wall of Vivaldo's flesh; and he wondered what
moved in his own body: what virtue were they seeking, now,
to share? what was he doing here? This was as far removed
as anything could be from the necessary war one underwent
with women. He would have entered her by now, this woman
who was not here, her sighs would be different and her surrender would never be total. Her sex, which afforded him his
entry, would nevertheless remain strange to him, an incitement and an anguish, and an everlasting mystery. And even
now, in this bright, laboring and doubting moment, with only
the rain as his witness, he knew that he was condemned to
women. What was it like to be a man, condemned to men?
He could not imagine it and he felt a quick revulsion, quickly
banished, for it threatened his ease. But at the very same
moment his excitement increased: he felt that he could do

with Eric whatever he liked. Now, Vivaldo, who was accustomed himself to labor, to be the giver of the gift, and
enter into his satisfaction by means of the satisfaction of a
woman, surrendered to the luxury, the flaming torpor of
passivity, and whispered in Eric's ear a muffled, urgent plea.

The dream teetered on the edge of nightmare: how old
was this rite, this act of love, how deep? in impersonal time,
in the actors? He felt that he had stepped off a precipice into
an air which held him inexorably up, as the salt sea holds the
swimmer: and seemed to see, vastly and horribly down, into
the bottom of his heart, that heart which contained all the
possibilities that he could name and yet others that he could
not name. Their moment was coming to its end. He moaned
and his thighs, like the thighs of a woman, loosened, he
thrust upward as Eric thrust down. How strange, how
strange! Was Eric, now, silently sobbing and praying, as he,
over Ida, silently sobbed and prayed? But Rufus had certainly thrashed and throbbed, feeling himself mount higher,
as Vivaldo thrashed and throbbed and mounted now. *Rufus.
Rufus.* Had it been like this for him? And he wanted to ask
Eric, What was it like for Rufus? What was it like for him?
Then he felt himself falling, as though the weary sea had
failed, had wrapped him about, and he were plunging down
—plunging down as he desperately thrust and struggled upward. He heard his own harsh breath, coming from far away;
he heard the drumming rain; he was being overtaken. He remembered how Ida, at the unbearable moment, threw back
her head and thrashed and bared her teeth. And she called
his name. And Rufus? Had he murmured at last, in a strange
voice, as he now heard himself murmur. *Oh, Eric. Eric.* What
was that fury like? *Eric.* He pulled Eric to him through the
ruined sheets and held him tight. And, *Thank you,* Vivaldo
whispered, *thank you, Eric, thank you.* Eric curled against
him like a child and salt from his forehead dripped onto
Vivaldo's chest.

Then they lay together, close, hidden and protected by
the sound of the rain. The rain came down outside like a
blessing, like a wall between them and the world. Vivaldo
seemed to have fallen through a great hole in time, back to
his innocence; he felt clear, washed, and empty, waiting to be
filled. He stroked the rough hair at the base of Eric's skull,
delighted and amazed by the love he felt. Eric's breath
trembled against the hairs of his chest; from time to time he
touched Vivaldo with his lips. This luxury and this warmth
made Vivaldo heavy and drowsy. He slowly began drifting

off to sleep again, beams of light playing in his skull, behind his eyes, like the sun. But beneath this peace and this gratitude, he wondered what Eric was thinking. He wanted to open his eyes, to look into Eric's eyes, but this was too great an effort and risked, furthermore, shattering his peace. He stroked Eric's neck and back slowly, hoping this his joy was conveyed by his fingertips. At the same time he wondered, and it almost made him laugh, *after all that shit I was talking last night,* what he was doing, in this bed, in the arms of this man? who was the dearest man on earth, for him. He felt fantastically protected, liberated, by the knowledge that, no matter where, once the clawing day descended, he felt compelled to go, no matter what happened to him from now until he died, and even, or perhaps especially, if they should never lie in each other's arms again, there was a man in the world who loved him. All of his hope, which had grown so pale, flushed into life again. He loved Eric: it was a great revelation. But it was yet more strange and made for an unprecedented steadiness and freedom, that Eric loved him. "Eric—?"

They opened their eyes and looked at each other. Eric's dark blue eyes were very clear and candid, but there was a terrible fear in their depth, too, waiting. Vivaldo said, "It was wonderful for me, Eric." He watched Eric's face. "Was it for you?"

"Yes," Eric said, and he blushed. They spoke in whispers. "I suppose that I needed it, more than I knew."

"It may never happen again."

"I know." There was a silence. Then, "Would you *like* it to happen again?"

Then Vivaldo was silent, feeling frightened for the first time. "I don't know how to answer that," he said. "Yes— yes and no. But, just the same, I love you, Eric, I always will, I hope you know that." He was astonished to hear how his voice shook. "Do you love me? Tell me that you do."

"You know I do," said Eric. He stared into Vivaldo's worn, white face and raised one hand to stroke the stubble which began just below the cheekbone. "I love you very much, I'd do anything for you. You must have known it, no? somewhere, for a very long time. Because I must have loved you for a very long time."

"Is that true? I didn't *know* I knew it."

"I didn't know it, either," Eric said. He smiled. "What a funny day this is. It begins with revelations."

"They're opening up," said Vivaldo, "all those books in

heaven." He closed his eyes. The telephone rang. "Oh, shit."

"More revelations." Eric grinned. He reached over Vivaldo for a cigarette, and lit it.

"It's too *early*, baby. Can't we go back to sleep?"

The phone rang and rang.

"It's one o'clock," said Eric. He looked doubtfully from
Vivaldo to the ringing telephone. "It's probably Cass.
She'll call back."

"Or it may be Ida. She probably *won't* call back."

Eric picked up the receiver. "Hello?"

Vivaldo heard, dimly, from far away, Cass's voice rushing
through the wires. "Good morning, baby, how are you?"
cried Eric. Then he fell into silence. Something in the quality
of that silence caused Vivaldo to come full awake and sit
straight up. He watched Eric's face. Then he lit himself a
cigarette, and waited.

"Oh," said Eric, after a moment. Then, "Jesus. Oh, my
poor Cass." The voice went on and on, Eric's face becoming
more troubled and more weary. "Yes. But now it *has* happened. It's here. It's upon us." He looked briefly at Vivaldo,
then looked over at his watch. "Yes, certainly, where?" He
looked toward the window. "Cass, it doesn't *look* as though
it's likely to let up." Then, "Please, Cass. Please don't." His
face changed again, registering shock; he glanced at Vivaldo,
and said quickly, "Vivaldo's here. *We* didn't go anywhere,
we just stayed here." A dry, bitter smile touched his lips.
"That's what they say and it sure as hell is pouring to beat
the band now." He laughed. "No, nobody lives without
clichés—what?" He listened. He said, gently, "But I'm going
to be in rehearsal very soon, Cass, and I *may* be going to the
Coast, and besides—" He looked over at Vivaldo with a
heavy, helpless frown. "Yes, I understand that, Cass. Yes. At
four. Okay. You hold on, baby, you just hold on."

He hung up. He sat for a moment, turned, staring toward
the rain, then lowered his gaze to Vivaldo with a small smile,
both sad and proud. He looked at his watch again, put out
his cigarette, and lay back, staring at the ceiling, his head
resting on his arms. "Well. Guess what. The shit has hit the
fan. Cass got in late last night and she and Richard had a
fight—about us. Richard knows about us."

Vivaldo whistled, his eyes very big. "I knew you shouldn't
have answered that phone. What a mess. Is Richard on his
way down here with a shotgun? and *how* did he find out?"

Eric looked strangely guilty, then he said, "Oh, Cass
wasn't at her most coherent, I don't really know. Anyway,

how he found out hardly matters now, since he *has*." He sat up. "Apparently, he *has* been suspicious—but he was suspicious of *you*—"

"Of *me?* He must be crazy!"

"Well, Cass kept coming to see you all the time, that's what she told him, anyway—"

"And what did he think Ida was doing while Cass and I were screwing? Reading us bedtime stories?"

Again, Eric looked uncomfortable, but he laughed. "I don't know what he thought. Anyway, Cass says that he's very bitter against you because"—he faltered for a moment and looked down—"because you knew about the affair and you're supposed to be his friend and you didn't tell him." He watched Vivaldo. "Do you think you should have told him?"

Vivaldo put out his cigarette. "What a wild idea. I'm nobody's goddamn Boy Scout. Besides, you and Cass are my friends, not Richard."

"Well, he didn't know that; you've known him much longer than you've known me, and—Richard doesn't really like me very much—so he'd naturally expect you to be loyal to him."

Vivaldo sighed. "There's a hell of a lot that Richard doesn't know and that's too bad but it's not my fault. And he's being dishonest. He *knows* that we haven't really been friends for a long time. And I *won't* be made to feel guilty." Then he grinned. "I've got enough to feel guilty about."

"*Do* you feel guilty?"

They stared at each other for a moment. Vivaldo laughed. "That wasn't what I had in mind. But, no, I don't feel guilty and I hope to God that I never feel guilty again. It's a monstrous waste of time."

Eric looked down. "Yes, Cass says that Richard may try to see *you* today."

"Sounds just like him. Well, I'm not at home." Suddenly, he laughed. "Wouldn't it be funny if Richard came *here?*"

"And found you here, you mean?" They laughed, rolling in the bed like children. "I wonder what he'd think."

"Poor man. He wouldn't know *what* to think."

They looked at each other and began to laugh again. "We certainly aren't giving him an awful lot of sympathy," Eric said.

"That's true." Vivaldo sat up and lit two cigarettes, giving one to Eric. "The poor bastard must really be suffering; after all, he doesn't know what hit him." They were silent. "And I'm sure Cass isn't laughing."

"No. Not at Richard, not at anything. She sounded half out of her mind."

"Where was she calling from?"

"Home. Richard had just gone out."

"I wonder if he really did go to my house. Maybe I should call and see if Ida's there." But he did not move toward the phone.

"It's all just about as messy as it can possibly be," Eric said, after a moment, "Richard's talking about suing for divorce and getting custody of the children."

"Yes, and he's probably gone out shopping for a brand with the letter *A* on it and if he could, he'd arrange for Cass to peddle her ass in the streets and drop dead of syphilis. Slowly. Because the cat's been wounded, man, in his self-esteem."

"Well," said Eric, slowly, "he *has* been wounded. You haven't got to be—admirable—in order to feel pain."

"No. But I think that perhaps you can begin to *become* admirable if, when you're hurt, you don't try to pay back." He looked at Eric and put one hand on the back of Eric's neck. "Do you know what I mean? Perhaps if you can accept the pain that almost kills you, you can use it, you can become better."

Eric watched him, smiling a strange half-smile, with his face full of love and pain. "That's very hard to do."

"One's got to *try*."

"I know." He said, very carefully, watching Vivaldo, "Otherwise, you just get stopped with whatever it was that ruined you and you make it happen over and over again and your life has—ceased, really—because you can't move or change or love any more."

Vivaldo let his hand fall. He leaned back. "You're trying to tell me something. What is it that you're trying to tell me?"

"I was talking about myself."

"Maybe. But I don't believe you."

"I just hope," said Eric, suddenly, "that Cass will never hate me."

"Why should she hate you?"

"I can't do her much good. I *haven't* done her much good."

"You don't know that. Cass knew what she was doing. I think she had a much clearer idea than you—because you, you know," and he grinned, "you aren't very clear-headed."

"I think I was hoping—perhaps *we* were hoping—that Richard would never find out and that Yves would get here—before—"

"Yes. Well, life isn't ever that tidy."

"*You're* very clear-headed," Eric said.

"Naturally." He grinned and reached out and pulled Eric to him. "And you must do the same for me, baby, when I'm in trouble. Be *clear*-headed."

"I'll do my best," said Eric, gravely.

Vivaldo laughed. "No one could ever hate you. You're much too funny." He pulled away. "What time are you meeting Cass?"

"At four. At the Museum of Modern Art."

"God. How's she going to get away? Or is Richard coming along?"

Eric hesitated. "She isn't sure that Richard's coming back today."

"I see. I think, maybe, we'd better have a cup of coffee—? I'm going to the john." And he leaped out of bed and slammed the bathroom door behind him.

Eric walked into the kitchen, which was only slightly less disordered than he now felt himself to be, and put coffee on the stove. He stood there a moment, watching the blue flame in the gloom of the small room. He took down two coffee cups and found the milk and sugar. He returned to the big room and cleared the night table of books and of urgently scrawled notes—nearly all of which, beneath his eyes, as he wrote them on small scraps of paper, had hardened into irrelevance—and emptied the ashtray. He picked up his clothes, and Vivaldo's, from the floor, piling them on a chair, and straightened the sheets on the bed. He put the cups and the milk and sugar on the night table, discovered that there were only five cigarettes left, and searched in his pockets for more, but there were none. He was hungry, but the refrigerator was empty. He thought that, perhaps, he could find the energy to dress and run down to the corner delicatessen for something—Vivaldo was probably hungry, too. He walked to the window and peeked out through the blinds. The rain poured down like a wall. It struck the pavements with a vicious sound, and spattered in the swollen gutters with the force of bullets. The asphalt was wide and white and blank with rain. The gray pavements danced and gleamed and sloped. Nothing moved—not a car, not a person, not a cat; and the rain was the only sound. He forgot about going to the store, and merely watched the rain, comforted by the anonymity and the violence—this violence was also peace. And just as the speeding rain distorted, blurred, blunted, all the familiar outlines of walls, windows, doors, parked cars, lamp posts, hydrants, trees, so Eric, now, in his silent watching, sought to blur and blunt and flee from all the conundrums which crowded in on him. *How will I ever get to the museum in all this rain?* he wondered: but did not dare to wonder what he would say to Cass, what she would say to him. He thought of Yves, thought of him with a sorrow that was close to panic, feeling doubly faithless, feeling that the principal support of his life had shifted—had shifted and would shift again, might fail beneath the dreadful, the accumulating and secret weight. Faintly, from the closed door behind him, he heard Vivaldo whistling. How could he not have known what he was capable of feeling for Vivaldo? And the answer drummed at him as relentlessly as the falling rain fell: he had not known because he had not dared to know. There were so many things one did not dare to know. And were they all patiently waiting, like demons in the dark, to spring from hiding, to reveal themselves, on some rainy Sunday morning?

He dropped the blind and turned back into the room. The telephone rang. He stared at it sourly, thinking *More revelations,* and picked up the receiver.

His agent, Harman, shouted in his ear. "Hello there— Eric? I'm sorry to bother you on a Sunday morning, but you're a pretty hard man to reach. I was thinking of sending you a telegram."

"Am I hard to find? I've just been staying home, it seems to me, curled up with that lovely script."

"Don't shit *me,* sweetheart. I know you've got a hard on for that play, but it's not *that* big. You just haven't been answering your phone. Listen—"

"Yes?"

"About your screen test—you got a pencil?"

"Wait a minute."

He found a pencil on his desk, and a scrap of paper, and returned to the phone.

"Go ahead, Harman."

"You're not going to the Coast. It's fixed up for you to do it here. You know where the Allied Studios are?"

"Yes, naturally."

"Well, it's set for Wednesday morning. Allied, at ten. Listen. Can you have lunch with me tomorrow?"

"Yes. I'd love to."

"Good. I'll fill you in on all the details. Downey's okay?"

"Right. What time?"

"One o'clock. Now—you still with me?"

"All ears, baby."

"Well, we finally got that *meshugena* of a broken-down movie star in town and the rehearsal date is definitely set for a week from tomorrow."

"Next week?"

"*Right.*"

"Wonderful. God, I'll be so glad to be working again."

Vivaldo came out of the bathroom, seeming unutterably huge in his blank, white nakedness, and walked into the kitchen. He looked critically at the coffee pot, came back into the room, and threw himself into the bed.

"You're going to be working from now on, Eric. You're on your way, sweetheart; you're going to go right over the top, and, baby, I couldn't be more delighted."

"Thanks, Harman. I certainly hope you're right."

"I've been in the business longer than you've been in the world, Eric. I know a winner when I see one and I've never made a mistake, not about that. You be good now, I'll see you tomorrow. Good-bye."

"Good-bye."

He put down the receiver, filled with a fugitive excitement.

"Good news?"

"That was my agent. We're going into rehearsal next week and we're doing my screen test Wednesday." Then his triumph blazed up in him and he turned to Vivaldo. "Isn't that fantastic?"

Vivaldo watched him, smiling. "I think we ought to drink to *that*, baby." He watched as Eric picked up the empty bottle from the floor. "Ah. Too sad."

"But I've got a little bourbon," Eric said.

"Crazy."

Eric poured two bourbons and lowered the flame under the coffee. "Bourbon's really much more fitting," he said, happily, "since that's what they drink in the South, where I come from."

He sat on the bed again, and they touched glasses.

"To your first Oscar," said Vivaldo.

Eric laughed. "That's touching. To your Nobel prize."

"That's *very* touching." Eric pulled the sheet up to his navel. Vivaldo watched him. "You're going to be very lonely," he said, suddenly.

Eric looked over at Vivaldo, and shrugged. "So are you, if it comes to that. If it comes to *that*," he added, after a moment, "I'm lonely now."

Vivaldo was silent for a moment. When he spoke, he

sounded very sad and gentle. "Are you? *Will* you be—when your boy gets here?"

Then Eric was silent. "No," he said, finally. He hesitated. "Well—yes and no." Then he looked at Vivaldo. "Are you lonely with Ida?"

Vivaldo looked down. "I've been thinking about that—or I've been trying not to think about that—all morning." He raised his eyes to Eric's eyes. "I hope you don't mind my saying—well, hell, anyway, you know it—that I'm sort of hiding in your bed now, hiding even in your arms maybe—from Ida, in a way. I'm trying to get something straight in my mind about my life with Ida." He looked down again. "I keep feeling that it's up to me to resolve it, one way or another. But I don't seem to have the guts. I don't know how. I'm afraid to force anything because I'm afraid to lose her." He seemed to flounder in the depths of Eric's silence. "Do you know what I mean? Does it make any sense to you?"

"Oh, yes," said Eric, bleakly, "it makes sense, all right." He looked over at Vivaldo with a smile, and dared to say, "Maybe, at this very moment, while both of us are huddled here, hiding from things which frighten us—maybe you love me and I love you as well as we'll ever love, or be loved, in this world."

Vivaldo said, "I don't know if I can accept that, not yet. Not yet. As *well*—maybe. Well, surely." He looked up at Eric. "But it's not, really, is it? very complete. Look. This day is almost over. How long will it be before such a day comes for us again? Because we're not kids, we know what life is like, and how time just vanishes, runs away—I can't, really, like from moment to moment, day to day, month to month, make you less lonely. Or you, me. We aren't driven in the same directions and I can't help that, any more than you can." He paused, watching Eric with enormous, tormented eyes. He smiled. "It would be wonderful if it could be like that; you're very beautiful, Eric. But I don't, really, dig you the way I guess you must dig me. You know? And if we tried to arrange it, prolong it, control it, if we tried to take more than what we've—by some miracle, some miracle, I swear—stumbled into, then I'd just become a parasite and we'd both shrivel. So what can we really do for each other except—just love each other and be each other's witness? And haven't we got the right to hope—for more? So that we can really stretch into whoever we really are? Don't you think so?" And, before Eric could answer, he took a large swallow of his whiskey and said in a different tone, a lower voice, "Because, you know, when I was in the bathroom, I was thinking that, yes, I loved being in your arms, holding you"—he flushed and looked up into Eric's face again—"why not, it's warm, I'm sensual, I like—you—the way you love me, but" —he looked down again—"it's not my battle, not my *thing*, and I know it, and I can't give up my battle. If I do, I'll die and if I die"—and now he looked up at Eric with a rueful, juvenile grin—"you won't love me any more. And I want you to love me all my life."

Eric reached out and touched Vivaldo's face. After a moment, Vivaldo grabbed his hand. "For you, the moon, baby," Eric said. His voice, to his surprise, was a grave, hoarse whisper. He cleared his throat. "Do you want some coffee now?"

Vivaldo shook his head. He emptied his glass and put it on the table.

"Drink up," he said to Eric.

Eric finished his drink. Vivaldo took the glass from him and set it down.

"I don't want any coffee now," he said. He opened his arms. "Let's make the most of our little day."

By ten minutes to four, Eric was, somehow, showered, shaved, and dressed, with his raincoat and his rain cap on. The coffee was too hot, he only managed to drink half a cup. Vivaldo was still undressed.

"You go on," he said. "I'll clean up a little and I'll lock the door."

"All right." But Eric dreaded leaving in the same way that Vivaldo dreaded getting dressed. "I'll leave you the cigarettes, I'll buy some."

"That's big of you. Go on, now. Give my love to Cass."

"Give *my* love," he said, "to Ida."

They both grinned. "I'm going to call her," Vivaldo said, "just as soon as you get your ass out of here."

"*Okay*, I'm gone." Yet, at the door, he stopped, looking at Vivaldo, who stood in the center of the room, holding a cup of coffee. He stared at the floor with a harsh bewilderment in his face. Then he felt Eric's eyes and looked up. He put down his coffee cup and walked to the door. He kissed Eric on the mouth and looked into his eyes.

"See you soon, baby."

"Yes," said Eric, "see you soon." He opened the door and left.

Vivaldo listened to him go down the stairs. Then he walked to the window and opened the blinds and watched

him. Eric appeared in the street as though he had been running, or as though he had been propelled. He looked first in
one direction and then in the other; then, his hands in his
pockets, head lowered and shoulders raised, he walked the
long block, hugging the sides of buildings. Vivaldo watched
him till he turned the corner.

Then he turned back into the room, pale with assessments,
with guilt deliciously beginning to gnaw at the rope with
which he had tied it, sharpening its teeth for him. And yet,
at the same time, he felt radiantly, wonderfully spent. He
poured himself another small drink and sat on the edge of
the bed. Slowly, he dialed his number.

The receiver was lifted almost at once, and Ida's voice
came at him: with the force of an electric shock. "Hello?"

In the background, he heard Billie Holiday singing *Billie's
Blues.*

"Hello, sugar. This is your man, checking on his woman."

"Do you know what time it is? Where the hell are you?"

"I'm at Eric's. We passed out here. I'm just pulling myself
together."

There was a peculiar relief in her voice. He was aware of
it because she tried to hide it. "You've been there all *night?*
ever since I left you?"

"Yes. We came on over here and started talking and
finished up Eric's whiskey. And he had quite a lot of whiskey
—so, you see."

"Yes, I know you think it's against the law to stop drinking
as long as there's anything left to drink. Listen. Has Cass
called?"

"Yes."

"Did you talk to her?"

"No. Eric did."

"Oh? What did Eric tell you?"

"What do you mean, what did Eric tell me?"

"I mean, what did Cass *say?*"

"She said she was in trouble. Richard's found out about
them."

"Isn't that awful? What else did she say?"

"Well—I think that that sort of cluttered up her mind.
She doesn't seem to have said anything else. Did you know
anything about all this?"

"*Yes.* Richard was here. Has he been there?"

"No."

"Oh, Vivaldo, it was awful. I felt so sorry for him. I
thought that you *might* be at Eric's, but I said you'd gone off

to see your family in Brooklyn and I didn't have the phone number or the address. It's very sad, Vivaldo, he's very bitter, he wants to hurt you. He feels that you betrayed him—"

"Yes, well, I think it may be easier for him to feel that way. How long was he there?"

"Not long. Only about ten minutes. But it seemed longer. He said some terrible things—"

"I'm sure. Does he still want to see me?"

"I don't know." There was a pause. "Are you coming home now?"

"Yes, right away. Are you going to be there?"

"I'll be here. Come on. Oh. Where's Eric?"

"He's gone—uptown—"

"To meet Cass?"

"Yes."

She sighed. "Lord, what a mess. Come on home, sweetie, if Richard's going to shoot you you don't want him to do it while you're wandering around Eric's house. That would really be too much."

He laughed. "You're right. You seem to be in a good mood today."

"I'm really in a terrible mood. But I'm being brave about it, I'm pretending to be Greer Garson."

He laughed again. "Does it help?"

"Well, no, baby, but it makes everything pretty funny."

"All right. I'll be along in a minute."

"Okay, sweetie. 'Bye."

"Good-bye."

He hung up with an exultant relief that no trouble seemed to be awaiting him at home with Ida. He felt that he had got away with something. He stepped into Eric's shower, scrubbed and sang; but when he stepped out he realized that he was terribly hungry and weak. While he was dressing, Eric's doorbell rang.

He was sure that it was Richard, at last, and he hurriedly buckled his belt and pulled on his shoes before pressing the buzzer. He started, idiotically, to make up the bed, but realized that there would not be time, and, anyway, it could not possibly make any difference to Richard whether the bed was made or not. He waited, hearing the downstairs door open and close. He opened Eric's door. But he heard no footsteps. A voice called, "Eric Jones!"

"Here!" cried Vivaldo. He let out his breath. He walked to the landing. A Western Union boy came up the steps.

"You Eric Jones?"

"He's gone out. But I can take it."

The boy handed him a telegram and a book for him to sign. He gave the boy twenty cents and walked back into the apartment. He thought that the telegram came, probably, from Eric's agent or producer; but he looked at it more carefully and realized that it was a cable and that it came from Europe. He propped it against Eric's telephone. He scribbled a note: *I've borrowed your other raincoat. NOTE CABLEGRAM.* He paused. Then he scribbled, *It was a great day.* And added, *love, Vivaldo.* He placed the note in the center of Eric's desk, weighting it down with an ink bottle.

Then he was ready; he looked about the room. The bed was still unmade; he left it that way; the bottle was still on the floor, the glasses on the night table. Everything was absolutely still, silent, except for the rain. He looked again at the cablegram, which leaned lightly, charged, waiting, against the telephone. Telegrams always frightened him a little. He closed the door behind him, tested it to make certain that it was locked, and walked out, at last, into the unfriendly rain.

Eric saw her at once, standing near the steps, just beyond the ticket-taker. She was pacing in a small circle and her back, as he entered, was to him. She wore her loose brown raincoat and her head was covered with a matching hood; and she played with the tip, white bone in the shape of a claw, of her thin umbrella. The museum was crowded, full of the stale, Sunday museum stink, aggravated, now, by the damp. He came through the doors behind a great cloud of windy, rainy, broad-beamed ladies; and they formed, before him, a large, loud, rocking wall, as they shook their umbrellas and themselves and repeated to each other, in their triumphant voices, how awful the weather was. Three young men and two young girls, scrubbed and milky, gleaming with their passion for improvement and the ease with which they moved among abstractions, were surrendering their tickets and passing through the barrier. Others were on the steps, going down, coming up, stationary, peering at each other like half-blinded birds and setting up a hideous whirr, as of flying feathers and boastful wings. Cass, small, pale, and old-fashioned in her hood, restlessly pacing, disenchantedly watched all this; she glanced indifferently toward the resounding ladies, but did not see him; he was still trying to get through, or around, the wall. He looked toward the people on the steps again, wondering why Cass had wished to meet here; it was only too probable that these sacred and sterile

halls contained, blocking a corridor or half-hidden by a
spinning mass of statuary, someone that they knew. Cass
resignedly lit a cigarette, half-turning in her small, imaginary
cage. People now came crushing in through the doors behind
him, and their greater pressure spat him past the ladies. He
touched Cass on the shoulder.

At his touch, she seemed to spring. Her eyes came alive
at once, and her pale lips tensed. And her smile was pale. She
said, "Oh. I thought you'd never get here."

He had surmounted a desperate temptation not to come at
all, and had half-hoped that he would not find her there.
She was so pale and seemed, in this cold, dazzling place, so
helpless, that his heart turned over. He was half an hour late.
He said, "Dear Cass, please forgive me, it's hard to get anywhere in weather like this. How are you?"

"Dead." She did not move, merely stared at the tip of her
cigarette as though she were hypnotized by it. "I've had no
sleep." Her voice was very light and calm.

"You picked a strange place for us to meet."

"Did I?" She looked unseeingly around; then looked at
him. The blank despair in her face seemed to take notice, in
the far distance, of him, and her face softened into sorrow.
"I guess I did. I just thought—well, nobody's likely to over-
hear us, and I—I just couldn't think of any other place."

He had been about to suggest that they leave, but her white
face and the fact of the rain checked him. "It's all right,"
he said. He took her arm, they started aimlessly up the steps.
He realized that he was terribly hungry.

"I can't stay with you very long, because I left the kids
alone. But I told Richard that I was coming out—that I was
going to try to see you today."

They reached the first of a labyrinthine series of rooms,
shifting and crackling with groups of people, with bright
paintings above and around them, and stretching into the
far distance, like tombstones with unreadable inscriptions.
The people moved in waves, like tourists in a foreign graveyard. Occasionally, a single mourner, dreaming of some vanished relationship, stood alone in adoration or revery before
a massive memorial—but they mainly evinced, moving restlessly here and there, the democratic gaiety. Cass and Eric
moved in some panic through this crowd, trying to find a
quieter place; through fields of French impressionists and
cubists and cacophonous modern masters, into a smaller
room dominated by an enormous painting, executed, princi-

pally, in red, before which two students, a girl and a boy, stood holding hands.

"Was it very bad, Cass? last night?"

He asked this in a low voice as they stood before a painting in cool yellow, of a girl with a long neck, in a yellow dress, with yellow hair.

"Yes." Her hood obscured her face; it was hot in the museum; she threw the hood back. Her hair was disheveled on the brow and trailing at the neck: she looked weary and old. "At first, it was awful because I hadn't realized how much I'd hurt him. He *can* suffer, after all," and she looked at Eric quickly, and looked away. They moved away from the yellow painting and faced another one, of a street with canals, somewhere in Europe. "And—no matter what has happened since, I *did* love him very much, he was my whole life, and he'll always be very important to me." She paused. "I suppose he made me feel terribly guilty. I didn't know that would happen. I didn't think it could—but—it did." She paused again, her shoulders sagging with a weary and proud defeat. Then she touched his hand. "I hate to tell you that— but I must try to tell you all of it. He frightened me, too, he frightened me because I was suddenly terribly afraid of losing the children and I cannot live without them." She moved one hand over her brow, uselessly pushing up her hair. "I didn't *have* to tell him; he didn't really know, he didn't suspect you at all, of course; he thought it was Vivaldo. I told him because I thought he had a right to know, that if we were going to—continue—together, we could begin again on a new basis, with everything clear between us. But I was wrong. Some things cannot *be* clear."

The boy and girl were coming to their side of the room. Cass and Eric crossed over, to stand beneath the red painting. "Or perhaps some things *are* clear, only one won't face those things. I don't know. . . . Anyway—I didn't think he'd threaten me, I didn't think he'd try to frighten me. If *he* were leaving *me*, if he were being unfaithful to *me*— unfaithful, what a word!—I don't think I'd try to hold him that way. I don't think I'd try to punish him. After all—he doesn't belong to me, nobody *belongs* to anybody."

They began walking again, down a long corridor, toward the ladies. "He said these terrible things to me, he said that he would sue me for divorce and take Paul and Michael away from me. And I listened to him, it didn't seem real. I didn't see how he could say those things, if he'd ever loved

me. And I watched him. I could see that he was just saying
these things to hurt me, to hurt me because he'd been hurt—
like a child. And I saw that I'd loved him like that, like a
child, and now the bill for all that dreaming had come in.
How can one have dreamed so long? And I thought it was
real. Now I don't know what's real. And I felt betrayed, I
felt that I'd betrayed myself, and you, and everything—of
value, everything, anyway, that one aspires to become, one
doesn't want to be simply another gray, shapeless monster."
They passed the cheerful ladies and Cass looked at them with
wonder and with hatred. "Oh, God. It's a miserable world."

He said nothing, for he did not know what to say, and
they continued their frightening promenade through the icy
and angular jungle. The colors on the walls blared at them—
like frozen music; he had the feeling that these rooms would
never cease folding in on each other, that this labyrinth was
eternal. And a sorrow entered him for Cass stronger than any
love he had ever felt for her. She stood as erect as a soldier,
moving straight ahead, and no bigger, as they said in the
South, than a minute. He wished that he could rescue her,
that it was within his power to rescue her and make her life
less hard. But it was only love which could accomplish the
miracle of making a life bearable—only love, and love itself
mostly failed; and he had never loved her. He had used her
to find out something about himself. And even this was not
true. He had used her in the hope of avoiding a confrontation with himself which he had, nevertheless, and with a
vengeance, been forced to endure. He felt as far removed
from Cass now, in her terrible hour, as he was physically
removed from Yves. Space howled between them like a
flood. And whereas, with every moment now, Yves was coming closer, defeating all that water, and, as he approached,
becoming more unreal, Cass was being driven farther away,
was already in the unconquerable distance where she would
be wrapped about by reality, unalterable forever, as a corpse
is wrapped in a shroud. Therefore, his sorrow, now that he
was helpless, luxuriously stretched and reached. "You'll
never be a monster," he said, "never. What's happening is
unspeakable, I know, but it can't defeat you. You can't go
under, you've come too far."

"I think I know what I *won't* be. But what I'm going to become—that I don't see at all. And I'm afraid."

They passed not far from a weary guard, who looked
blinded and dazzled, as though he had never been able to
escape the light. Before them was a large and violent canvas

in greens and reds and blacks, in blocks and circles, in dag-
gerlike exclamations; it took a flying leap, as it were, from
the wall, poised for the spectator's eyeballs; and at the same
time it seemed to stretch endlessly and adoringly in on itself,
reaching back into an unspeakable chaos. It was aggressively
and superbly uncharming and unreadable, and might have
been painted by a lonely and bloodthirsty tyrant, who had
been cheated of his victims. "How horrible," Cass murmured, but she did not move; for they had this corner, except
for the guard, to themselves.

"You said once," he said, "that you wanted to grow. Isn't
that always frightening? Doesn't it always hurt?"

It was a question he was asking himself—of course; she
turned toward him with a small, grateful smile, then turned
to the painting again.

"I'm beginning to think," she said, "that growing just
means learning more and more about anguish. That poison
becomes your diet—you drink a little of it every day. Once
you've seen it, you can't stop seeing it—that's the trouble.
And it can, it can"—she passed her hand wearily over her
brow again—"drive you mad." She walked away briefly,
then returned to their corner. "You begin to see that you
yourself, innocent, upright you, have contributed and do
contribute to the misery of the world. Which will never end
because we're what we are." He watched her face from
which the youth was now, before his eyes, departing; her girl-
hood, at last, was falling away from her. Yet, her face did
not seem precisely faded, or, for that matter, old. It looked
scoured, there was something invincibly impersonal in it.
"I watched Richard this morning and I thought to myself, as
I've thought before, how much responsibility I must take for
who he is, for what he's become." She put the tip of her
finger against her lips for a moment, and closed her eyes. "I
score him, after all, for being second-rate, for not having any
real passion, any real daring, any real thoughts of his own.
But he never did, he hasn't changed. I was delighted to give
him *my* opinions; when I was with him, *I* had the daring and
the passion. And he took them all, of course, how could he
tell they weren't his? And I was happy because I'd succeeded
so brilliantly, I thought, in making him what I wanted him
to be. And of course he can't understand that it's just that
triumph which is intolerable now. I've made myself—less
than I might have been—by leading him to water which he
doesn't know how to drink. It's not *for* him. But it's too late
now." She smiled. "He doesn't have any real work to do,

that's his trouble, that's the trouble with this whole unspeakable time and place. And I'm trapped. It doesn't do any good to blame the people or the time—one is oneself all those people. We *are* the time."

"You think that there isn't any hope for us?"

"Hope?" The word seemed to bang from wall to wall. "Hope? No, I don't think there's any hope. We're too empty here"—her eyes took in the Sunday crowd—"too empty—here." She touched her heart. "This isn't a country at all, it's a collection of football players and Eagle Scouts. Cowards. We think we're happy. We're not. We're doomed." She looked at her watch. "I must get back." She looked at him. "I only wanted to see you for a moment."

"What are you going to do?"

"I don't know yet. I'll let you know when I do. Richard's gone off, he may not be back for a couple of days. He wants to think, he says." She sighed. "I don't know." She said, carefully, looking at the painting, "I imagine, for the sake of the children, he'll decide that we should weather this, and stick together. I don't know if I want that or not, I don't know if I can bear it. But he won't sue me for divorce, he hasn't got the courage to name you as corespondent." Each to the other's astonishment, laughed. She looked at him again. "I can't come to you," she said.

There was a silence.

"No," he said, "you can't come to me."

"So it's really—though I'll see you again—good-bye."

"Yes," he said. Then, "It had to come."

"I know. I wish it hadn't come as it *has* come, but"—she smiled—"you did something very valuable for me, Eric, just the same. I hope you'll believe me. I hope you'll never forget it—what I've said. I'll never forget you."

"No," he said, and suddenly touched her arm. He felt that he was falling, falling out of the world. Cass was releasing him into chaos. He held on to her for the last time.

She looked into his face, and she said, "Don't be frightened, Eric. It will help me not to be frightened, if you're not. Do that for me." She touched his face, his lips. "Be a man. It can be borne, everything can be borne."

"Yes." But he stared at her still. "Oh, Cass. If only I could do more."

"You can't," she said, "do more than you've done. You've been my lover and now you're my friend." She took his hand in hers and stared down at it. "That was you you gave me for a little while. It was really you."

They turned away from the ringing canvas, into the crowds again, and walked slowly down the stairs. Cass put up her hood; he had never taken off his cap.

"When will I see you?" he asked. "Will you call me, or what?"

"I'll call you," she said, "tomorrow, or the day after." They walked to the doors and stopped. It was still raining.

They stood watching the rain. No one entered, no one left. Then a cab rolled up to the curb and stopped. Two women, wearing plastic hoods, fumbled with their umbrellas and handbags and change purses, preparing to step out of the cab.

Without a word, Eric and Cass rushed out into the rain, to the curb. The women ran heavily into the museum. Eric opened the cab door.

"Good-bye, Eric." She leaned forward and kissed him. He held her. Her face was wet but he did not know whether it was rainwater or tears. She pulled away and got into the cab.

"I'll be expecting your call," he said.

"Yes. I'll call you. Be good."

"God bless you, Cass. So long."

"So long."

He closed the door on her and the cab moved away, down the long, blank, shining street.

Darkness was beginning to fall. The lights of the city would soon begin to blaze: it would not be long, now, before these lights would carry his name. An errant wind, a cold wind, ruffled the water in the gutter at Eric's feet. Then everything was still, with a bleakness that was almost comforting.

Ida heard Vivaldo's step and rushed to open the door for him, just as he began fumbling for his key. She threw back her head and laughed.

"You look like you narrowly escaped a lynching, dad. And where did you get that coat?" She looked him up and down, and laughed again. "Come on in, you poor, drowned rat, before the posse gets here."

She closed the door behind him and he took off Eric's coat and hung it in the bathroom and dried his dripping hair. "Do we have anything to eat in this house?"

"Yes. Are you hungry?"

"Starving." He came out of the bathroom. "What did Richard have to say?"

She was in the kitchen with her back to him, digging in the cupboard beneath the sink where the pots and pans were kept. She came up with a frying pan; looked at him briefly; and this look made him feel that Richard had managed, somehow, to frighten her.

"Nothing very pleasant. But it's not important now." She put the pan on the stove and opened the icebox door. "I think you and Cass were his whole world. And now both of you have treated him so badly that he doesn't know where he is." She took tomatoes and lettuce and a package of pork chops out of the icebox and put them on the table. "He tried to make me angry—but I just felt terribly sad. He'd been so hurt." She paused. "Men are so helpless when they're hurt."

He came up behind her and kissed her. "Are they?"

She returned his kiss, and said gravely, "Yes. You don't believe it's happening. You think that there must have been some mistake."

"How wise you are!" he said.

"I'm not wise. I'm just a poor, ignorant, black girl, trying to get along."

He laughed. "If you're just a poor, ignorant, black girl, trying to get along, I'd sure hate like hell to tangle with one who'd made it."

"But you wouldn't know. You think women tell the truth. They don't. They can't." She stepped away from him, busy with another saucepan and water and flame. And she gave him a mocking look. "Men wouldn't *love* them if they did."

"You just don't like *men*."

She said, "I can't say that I've met very many. Not what *I* call men."

"I hope I'm one of them."

"Oh, there's hope for you," she said, humorously, "you might make it yet."

"That's probably," he said, "the nicest thing you've ever said to me."

She laughed, but there was something sad and lonely in the sound. There was something sad and lonely in her whole aspect, which obscurely troubled him. And he began to watch her closely, without quite knowing that he was doing so.

She said, "Poor Vivaldo. I've given you a hard time, haven't I, baby?"

"I'm not complaining," he said, carefully.

"No," she said, half to herself, running her fingers

thoughtfully through a bowl of dry rice, "I'll say that much for you. I dish it out, but you sure as hell can take it."

"You think maybe," he said, "that I take too much?"

She frowned. She dumped the rice into the boiling water. "Maybe. Hell, I don't think women know what they want, not a damn one of them. Look at Cass—do you want a drink," she asked, suddenly, "before dinner?"

"Sure." He took down the bottle and the glasses and took out the ice. "What do you mean—women don't know what they want? Don't *you* know what you want?"

She had taken down the great salad bowl and was slicing tomatoes into it; it seemed that she did not dare be still. "Sure. I thought I did. I was sure once. Now I'm not so sure." She paused. "And I only found that out—last night." She looked up at him humorously, gave a little shrug, and sliced savagely into another tomato.

He set her drink beside her. "What's happened to confuse you?"

She laughed—again he heard that striking melancholy. "Living with you! Would you believe it? I fell for that jive."

He dragged his work stool in from the other room and teetered on it, watching her, a little above her.

"*What* jive, sweetheart, are you talking about?"

She sipped her drink. "That love jive, sweetheart. Love, love, love!"

His heart jumped up; they watched each other; she smiled a rueful smile. "Are you trying to tell me—without my having to ask you or anything—that you love me?"

"Am I? I guess I am." Then she dropped the knife and sat perfectly still, looking down, the fingers of one hand drumming on the table. Then she clasped her hands, the fingers of one hand playing with the ruby-eyed snake ring, slipping it half-off, slipping it on.

"But—that's wonderful." He took her hand. It lay cold and damp and lifeless in his. A kind of wind of terror shook him for an instant. "Isn't it? It makes me very happy—*you* make me very happy."

She took his hand and rested her cheek against it. "Do I, Vivaldo?" Then she rose and walked to the sink to wash the lettuce.

He followed her, standing beside her, and looking into her closed, averted face. "What's the matter, Ida?" He put one hand on her waist; she shivered, as if in revulsion, and he let his hand fall. "Tell me, please."

"It's nothing," she said, trying to sound light about it, "I told you, I'm in a bad mood. It's probably the time of the month."

"Now, come on, baby, don't try to cop out that way."

She was tearing the lettuce and washing it, and placing it in a towel. She continued with this in silence until she had torn off the last leaf. She was trying to avoid his eyes; he had never seen her at such a loss before. Again, he was frightened. "What *is* it?"

"Leave me alone, Vivaldo. We'll talk about it later."

"We will *not* talk about it later. We'll talk about it now."

The rice came to a boil and she moved hastily away from him to turn down the flame.

"My Mama always told me, honey, you can't cook and talk."

"Well, stop *cooking!*"

She gave him that look, coquettish, wide-eyed, and amused, which he had known so long. But now there was something desperate in it; had there always been something desperate in this look? "But you *said* you were hungry!"

"Stop that. It's not funny, okay?" He led her to the table. "I want to know what's happening. Is it something Richard said?"

"I am not trying to be funny. I *would* like to feed you." Then, with a sudden burst of anger, "It's got nothing to do with Richard. What, after all, can Richard *say?*"

He had had some wild idea that Richard had made up a story about himself and Eric, and he had been on the point of denying it. He recovered, hoping that she had not been aware of his panic; but his panic increased.

He said, very gently, "Well, then, what *is* it, Ida?"

She said, wearily, "Oh, it's too many things, it goes too far back, I can never make you understand it, never."

"Try me. You say you love me. Why can't you trust me?"

She laughed. "Oh. You think life is so simple." She looked up at him and laughed again. And this laughter was unbearable. He wanted to strike her, not in anger, only to make the laughter stop; but he forced himself to stand still, and did nothing. "Because—I know you're older than I am—I always think of you as being much younger. I always think of you as being a very nice boy who doesn't know what the score is, who'll maybe never find out. And I don't want to be the one to teach you."

She said the last in a venomous undertone, looking down again at her hands.

"Okay. Go on."

"Go *on?*" She looked up at him in a strange, wild way. "You want me to go *on?*"

He said, "Please stop tormenting me, Ida. Please go on."

"*Am* I tormenting you?"

"You want it in writing?"

Her face changed, she rose from the table and walked back to the stove. "I'm sure it must seem like that to you," she said—very humbly. She moved to the sink and leaned against it, watching him. "But I wasn't trying to torment you—whenever I did. I don't think that I thought about that at all. In fact, I know I didn't, I've never had the time." She watched his face. "I've just realized lately that I've bitten off more than I can chew, certainly more than I can swallow." He winced. She broke off suddenly: "Are you sure you're a man, Vivaldo?"

He said, "I've got to be sure."

"Fair enough," she said. She walked to the stove and put a light under the frying pan, walked to the table and opened the meat. She began to dust it with salt and pepper and paprika, and chopped garlic into it, near the bone. He took a swallow of his drink, which had no taste whatever; he splashed more whiskey into his glass. "When Rufus died, something happened to me," she said. She sounded now very quiet and weary, as though she were telling someone else's story; also, as though she herself, with a faint astonishment, were hearing it for the first time. But it was yet more astonishing that he now began to listen to a story he had always known, but never dared believe. "I can't explain it. Rufus had always been the world to me. I loved him."

"So did I," he said—too quickly, irrelevantly; and for the first time it occurred to him that, possibly, he was a liar; had never loved Rufus at all, but had only feared and envied him.

"I don't need your credentials, Vivaldo," she said.

She watched the frying pan critically, waiting for it to become hot enough, then dropped in a little oil. "The point, anyway, at the moment, is that *I* loved him. He was my big brother, but as soon as I knew anything, I knew that I was stronger than he was. He was nice, he was really very nice, no matter what any of you might have thought of him later. None of you, anyway, knew anything about him, you didn't know how."

"You often say that," he said, wearily. "Why?"

"How could you—how *can* you?—dreaming the way you dream? You people think you're free. That means you think you've got something other people want—or need. Shit." She grinned wryly and looked at him. "And you *do*, in a way. But it isn't what you think it is. And you're going to find out, too, just as soon as some of those other people start getting what you've got now." She shook her head. "I feel sorry for them. I feel sorry for you. I even feel kind of sorry for myself, because God knows I've often wished you'd left me where I was—"

"Down there in the jungle?" he taunted.

"Yes. Down there in the jungle, black and funky—and myself."

His small anger died down as quickly as it had flared up. "Well," he said, quietly, "sometimes I'm nostalgic, too, Ida." He watched her dark, lonely face. For the first time, he had an intimation of how she would look when she grew old. "What I've never understood," he said, finally, "is that you always accuse me of making a thing about your color, of penalizing you. But you do the same thing. You always make me feel white. Don't you think that hurts me? You lock me out. And all I want is for you to be a part of me, for me to be a part of you. I wouldn't give a damn if you were striped like a zebra."

She laughed. "Yes, you would, really. But you say the cutest things." Then, "If I lock you out, as you put it, it's mainly to protect you—"

"Protect me from what? and I don't *want* to be protected. Besides—"

"Besides?"

"I don't believe you. I don't believe that's why. You want to protect yourself. You want to hate me because I'm white, because it's easier for you that way."

"I don't hate you."

"Then why do you always bring it up? What *is* it?"

She stirred the rice, which was almost ready, found a colander, and placed it in the sink. Then she turned to face him.

"This all began because I said that you people—"

"Listen to yourself. *You people!*"

"—didn't know anything about Rufus—"

"Because we're white."

"No. Because he was black."

"Oh. I give *up*. And, anyway, why must we always end up talking about Rufus?"

"I had started to tell you something," she said, quietly; and watched him.

He swallowed some more of his whiskey, and lit a cigarette. "True. Please go on."

"Because I'm black," she said, after a moment, and sat at the table near him, "I know more about what happened to my brother than you can ever know. I watched it happen—from the beginning. I was there. He shouldn't have ended up the way he did. That's what's been so hard for me to accept. He was a very beautiful boy. Most people aren't beautiful, I knew that right away. I watched them, and I knew. But he didn't because he was so much nicer than I." She paused, and the silence grumbled with the sound of the frying pan and the steady sound of the rain. "He loved our father, for example. He really loved him. I didn't. He was just a loud-mouthed, broken-down man, who liked to get drunk and hang out in barber shops—well, maybe he didn't like it but that was all he could find to do, except work like a dog, for nothing—and play the guitar on the week ends for his only son." She paused again, smiling. "There was something very nice about those week ends, just the same. I can still see Daddy, his belly hanging out, strumming on that guitar and trying to teach Rufus some down-home song and Rufus grinning at him and making fun of him a little, really, but very nicely, and singing with him. I bet my father was never happier, all the days of his life, than when he was singing for Rufus. He's got no one to sing to now. He was so proud of him. He bought Rufus his first set of drums."

She was not locking him out now; he felt, rather, that he was being locked in. He listened, seeing, or trying to see, what she saw, and feeling something of what she felt. But he wondered, just the same, how much her memory had filtered out. And he wondered what Rufus must have looked like in those days, with all his bright, untried brashness, and all his hopes intact.

She was silent for a moment, leaning forward, looking down, her elbows on her knees and the fingers of one hand restlessly playing with her ring.

"When Rufus died, all the light went out of that house, all of it. That was why I couldn't stay there, I knew I couldn't stay there, I'd grow old like they were, suddenly, and I'd end up like all the other abandoned girls who can't find anyone to protect them. I'd always known I couldn't end up like that, I'd always known it. I'd counted on Rufus to get me out of there—I knew he'd do anything in the world for me, just like I would for him. It hadn't occurred to me that it wouldn't happen. I *knew* it would happen."

She rose and returned to the stove and took the rice off the fire and poured it into the colander and ran water over it; put water in the saucepan and put it back on the fire, placing the colander on top of it and covering the rice with a towel. She turned the chops over. Then she sat down.

"When we saw Rufus's body, I can't tell you. My father stared at it, he stared at it, and stared at it. It didn't look like Rufus, it was—terrible—from the water, and he must have *struck* something going down, or in the water, because he was so broken and lumpy—and ugly. *My* brother. And my father stared at it—at it—and he said, They don't leave a man much, do they? His own father was beaten to death with a hammer by a railroad guard. And they brought his father home like that. My mother got frightened, she wanted my father to pray. And he said, he shouted it at the top of his lungs, Pray? *Who*, pray? I bet you, if I ever get anywhere near that white devil you call God, I'll tear my son and my father out of his white hide! Don't you never say the word Pray to me again, woman, not if you want to *live*. Then he started to cry. I'll never forget it. Maybe I hadn't loved him before, but I loved him then. That was the last time he ever shouted, he hasn't raised his voice since. He just sits there, he doesn't even drink any more. Sometimes he goes out and listens to those fellows who make speeches on 125th Street and Seventh Avenue. He says he just wants to live long enough—long enough—"

Vivaldo said, to break the silence which abruptly roared around them, "To be paid back."

"Yes," she said. "And I felt that way, too."

She walked over to the stove again.

"I felt that I'd been robbed. And I *had* been robbed—of the only hope I had. By a group of people too cowardly even to know what they had done. And it didn't seem to me that they deserved any better than what they'd given me. I didn't care what happened to them, just so they suffered. I didn't really much care what happened to me. But I wasn't going to let what happened to Rufus, and what was happening all around me, happen to me. I was going to get through the world, and get what I needed out of it, no matter how."

He thought, *Oh, it's coming now,* and felt a strange, bitter relief. He finished his drink and lit another cigarette, and watched her.

She looked over at him, as though to make certain that he was still listening.

"Nothing you've said so far," he said, carefully, "seems to

have much to do with being black. Except for what you make out of it. But nobody can help you there."

She sighed sharply, in a kind of rage. "That could be true. But it's too easy for you to say that."

"Ida, a lot of what you've had to say, ever since we met, has been—too easy." He watched her. "Hasn't it?" And then, "Sweetheart, suffering doesn't *have* a color. Does it? Can't we step out of this nightmare? I'd give anything, I'd give anything if we could." He crossed to her and took her in his arms. "Please, Ida, whatever has to be done, to set us free—let's do that."

Her eyes were full of tears. She looked down. "Let me finish my story."

"Nothing you say will make any difference."

"You don't know that. Are you afraid?"

He stepped back. "No." Then, "Yes. Yes. I can't take any more of your revenge."

"Well, I can't either. Let me finish."

"Come away from the stove. I can't eat now."

"Everything will be ruined."

"Let it be ruined. Come and sit down."

He wished that he were better prepared for this moment, that he had not been with Eric, that his hunger would vanish, that his fear would drop, and love lend him a transcendent perception and concentration. But he knew himself to be physically weak and tired, not drunk, but far from sober; part of his troubled mind was far away, gorging on the conundrum of himself.

She put out the fire under the frying pan and came and sat at the table. He pushed her drink toward her, but she did not touch it.

"I knew there wasn't any hope uptown. A lot of those men, they got their little deals going and all that, but they don't really have anything, Mr. Charlie's not going to let them get but so far. Those that really do have something would never have any use for me; I'm too dark for them, they see girls like me on Seventh Avenue every day. I knew what they would do to me."

And now he knew that he did not want to hear the rest of her story. He thought of himself on Seventh Avenue; perhaps he had never left. He thought of the day behind him, of Eric and Cass and Richard, and felt himself now being sucked into the rapids of a mysterious defeat.

"There was only one thing for me to do, as Rufus used to say, and that was to hit the A train. So I hit it. Nothing was clear in my mind at first. I used to see the way white men watched me, like dogs. And I thought about what I could do to them. How I hated them, the way they looked, and the things they'd say, all dressed up in their damn white skin, and their clothes just so, and their little weak, white pricks jumping in their drawers. You could do any damn thing with them if you just led them along, because they wanted to do something dirty and they knew that you knew how. All black people knew that. Only, the polite ones didn't say dirty. They said real. I used to wonder what in the world they did in bed, white people I mean, between themselves, to get them so sick. Because they *are* sick, and I'm telling you something that I know. I had a couple of girl friends and we used to go out every once in a while with some of these shitheads. But they were smart, too, they knew that they were white, and they could always go back home, and there wasn't a damn thing you could do about it. I thought to myself, Shit, this scene is not for me. Because I didn't want their little change, I didn't want to be at their mercy. I wanted them to be at mine."

She sipped her drink.

"Well, you were calling me all the time about that time, but I didn't really think about you very much, not seriously anyway. I liked you, but I certainly hadn't planned to get hung up on a white boy who didn't have any money—in fact, I hadn't planned to get hung up on anybody. But I liked you, and the few times I saw you it was a kind of—*relief*—from all those other, horrible people. You were really nice to me. You didn't have that look in your eyes. You just acted like a real sweet boy and maybe, without knowing it, I got to depend on it. Sometimes I'd just see you for a minute or so, we'd just have a cup of coffee or something like that, and I'd run off—but I felt better, I was kind of protected from their eyes and their hands. I was feeling so sick most of the time through there. I didn't want my father to know what I was doing and I tried not to think about Rufus. That was when I decided that I ought to try to sing, I'd do it for Rufus, and then all the rest wouldn't matter. I would have settled the score. But I thought I needed somebody to help me, and it was then, just at that time that I—" She stopped and looked down at her hands. "I think I wanted to go to bed with you, not to have an affair with you, but just to go to bed with somebody that I *liked*. Somebody who wasn't old, because all those men are old, no matter how young they are. I'd only been to bed with one boy I liked, a boy on our block, but he got religion, and so it all stopped and he got married. And there weren't any other colored men, I was afraid, because look what happened to them, they got cut down like grass! And I didn't see any way out, except—finally—you. And Ellis."

Then she stopped. They listened to the rain. He had finished his drink and he picked up hers. She looked down, he had the feeling that she could not look up, and he was afraid to touch her. And the silence stretched; he longed for it to end, and dreaded it; there was nothing he could say.

She straightened her shoulders and reached out for a cigarette. He lit it for her.

"Richard knows about me and Ellis," she said in a matter-of-fact tone, "but that's not why I'm telling you. I'm telling you because I'm trying to bring this whole awful thing to a halt. If that's possible."

She paused. She said, "Let me have a sip of your drink, please."

"It's yours," he said. He gave it to her and poured himself another one.

She blew a cloud of smoke toward the ceiling. "It's funny the way things work. If it hadn't been for you, I don't think Ellis would ever have got so hung up on me. *He* saw, better than I did, that I really liked you and that meant that I could really like somebody and so why not him, since he could give me so much more? And I thought so, too, that it was a kind of dirty trick for life to play on me, for me to like you better than I liked him. And, after all, the chances of its lasting were just about equal, only with him, if I played it right, I might have something to show for it when it was all over. And he was smart, he didn't bug me about it, he said, Sure, he wanted me but he was going to help me, regardless, and the one thing had nothing to do with the other. And he did— he was very nice to me, in his way, he was as good as his word, he was nicer to me than anyone had ever been before. He used to take me out to dinner, to places where nobody would know him or where it wouldn't matter if they did. A lot of the time we went up to Harlem, or if he knew I was sitting in somewhere, he'd drop in. He didn't seem to be trying to hype me, not even when he talked about his wife and his kids—you know? He sounded as though he really *was* lonely. And, after all, I owed him a lot—and—it was nice to be treated that way and to know the cat had enough money to take you anywhere, and—ah! well, it started, I guess I'd always known it was going to start, and then, once it started,

I didn't think I could stand it but I didn't know how to stop it. Because it's one thing for a man to be doing all these things for you while you're not having an affair with him and it's another thing for him to be doing them after you've *stopped* having an affair with him. And I had to go on, I had to get up there on top, where maybe I could begin to breathe. But I saw why he'd never been upset about you. He really is smart. He was *glad* I was with you, he told me so; he was glad I had another boy friend because it made it easier for him. It meant I wouldn't make any scenes, I wouldn't think I'd fallen in love with him. It gave him another kind of power over me in a way because he knew that I was afraid of your finding out and the more afraid I got, the harder it was to refuse him. Do you understand that?"

"Yes," he said, slowly, "I think I understand that."

They stared at each other. She dropped her eyes.

"But, you know," she said, slowly, "I think you knew all the time."

He said nothing. She persisted, in a low voice, "Didn't you?"

"You told me that you weren't," he said.

"But did you believe me?"

He stammered: "I—I *had* to believe you."

"Why?"

Again, he said nothing.

"Because you were afraid?"

"Yes," he said at last. "I was afraid."

"It was easier to let it happen than to try to stop it?"

"Yes."

"Why?"

Her eyes searched his face. It was his turn to look away.

"I used to hate you for that sometimes," she said, "for pretending to believe me because you didn't want to know what was happening to me."

"I was trying to do what I thought you wanted! I was afraid that you would *leave* me—you *told* me that you would!" He rose and stalked the kitchen, his hands in his pockets, water standing in his eyes. "I worried about it, I thought about it—but I put it out of my mind. You had made it a matter of my trusting you—don't you remember?"

He looked at her with hatred, standing above her; but she seemed to be beyond his anger.

"Yes, I remember. But you didn't start trusting me. You just gave in to me and pretended to trust me."

"What would you have done if I had called you on it?"

"I don't know. But if you had faced it, I would have had to face it—as long as you were pretending, I had to pretend. I'm not blaming you. I'm just telling it to you like it is." She looked up at him. "I saw that it could go on a long time like that," and her lips twisted wearily. "I sort of had you where I wanted you. I'd got my revenge. Only, it wasn't *you* I was after. It wasn't *you* I was trying to beat."

"It was Ellis?"

She sighed and put one hand to her face. "Oh. I don't know, I really don't know what I was thinking. Sometimes I'd leave Ellis and I'd come and find you here—like my dog or my cat, I used to think sometimes, just waiting. And I'd be afraid you'd be here and I'd be afraid you'd gone out, afraid you'd ask me, *really* ask me where I'd been, and afraid you wouldn't. Sometimes you'd try, but I could always stop you, I could see in your eyes when you were frightened. I hated that look and I hated me and I hated you. I could see how white men got that look they so often had when they looked at me; somebody had beat the shit out of them, had scared the shit out of them. long ago. And now I was doing it to you. And it made it hard for me when you touched me, especially—" She stopped. picked up her drink, tasted it, set it down. "I couldn't stand Ellis. You don't know what it's like, to have a man's body over you if you can't stand that body. And it was worse now, since I'd been with you, that it had ever been before. Before, I used to watch them wriggle and listen to them grunt, and, God, they were so solemn about it, sweating yellow pigs. and so *vain*, like that sad little piece of meat was making miracles happen, and I guess it was, for them—and I wasn't touched at all, I just wished I could make them come down lower. Oh, yes, I found out all about white people, *that's* what they were like, alone, where only a black girl could see them, and the black girl might as well have been blind as far as they were concerned. Because they knew they were white. baby, and they ruled the world. But now it was different, sometimes when Ellis put his hands on me, it was all I could do not to scream, not to vomit. It had *got* to me, it had got *to* me, and I felt that I was being pumped full of—I don't know what, not poison exactly, but dirt, *waste*, filth, and I'd never be able to get it out of me, never be able to get that stink out of me. And sometimes, sometimes, sometimes—" She covered her mouth, her tears spilled down over her hand, over the red ring. He could not move. "Oh, Lord Jesus. I've done terrible things. Oh, Lord. Sometimes. And then I'd come home to you. He always had that funny little smile when I finally left him, that smile he has, I've seen it many times now, when he's outsmarted somebody who doesn't know it yet. He can't help it, that's him, it was as though he were saying, 'Now that I'm through with you, have a nice time with Vivaldo. And give him my regards.' And, funny, funny—I couldn't hate him. I saw what he was doing, but I couldn't hate him. I wondered what it felt like, to be like that, not to have any real feelings at all, except to say, Well, now, let's do this and now let's do that and now let's eat and now let's fuck and now let's go. And do that all your life. And then I'd come home and look at you. But I'd bring him with me. It was as though I was dirty, and you had to wash me, each time. And I knew you never could, no matter how hard we tried, and I didn't hate him but I hated you. And I hated me."

"Why didn't you stop it, Ida? You could have stopped it, you didn't have to go on with it."

"Stop it and go where? Stop it and do what? No, I thought to myself, Well, you're in it now, girl, close your eyes and grit your teeth and get through it. It'll be worth it when it's over. And that's why I've been working so hard. To get away."

"And what about me? What about us?"

She looked up at him with a bitter smile. "What about us? I hoped I'd get through this and then we'd see. But last night something happened, I couldn't take it any more. We were up at Small's Paradise—"

"Last night? You and Ellis?"

"Yes. *And* Cass."

"Cass?"

"I asked her to come and have a drink with me."

"Did you leave together?"

"No."

"So that's why she got in late last night." He looked at her. "It's a good thing I didn't come home then, isn't it?"

"What would you have done," she cried, "if you had? You'd have sat at that typewriter for a while and then you'd have played some music and then you'd have gone out and got drunk. And when I came home, no matter *when* I came home, you'd have believed any lie I told you because you were afraid not to."

"What a bitch you are," he said.

"Yes," she said, with a terrible sobriety, "I know." She lit a cigarette. The hand that held the match trembled. "But I'm trying not to be. I don't know if there's any hope for me or not." She dropped the match on the table. "He made me sing with the band. They didn't really want me to, and I didn't want to, but they didn't want to say No, to him. So I sang. And of course I knew some of the musicians and some of them had known Rufus. Baby, if musicians don't want to work with you, they sure can make you know it. I sang *Sweet Georgia Brown,* and something else. I wanted to get off that stand in the worst way. When it was over, and the people were clapping, the bass player whispered to me, he said, 'You black white man's whore, don't you never let me catch you on Seventh Avenue, you hear? I'll tear your little black pussy *up.'* And the other musicians could hear him, and they were grinning. 'I'm going to do it twice, once for every black man you castrate every time you walk, and once for your poor brother, because I loved that stud. And he going to thank me for it, too, you can bet on that, black girl.' And he slapped me on the ass, hard, everybody could see it and, you know, those people up there aren't fools, and before I could get away, he grabbed my hand and raised it, and he said, 'She's the *champion,* ain't she, folks? Talk about walking, this girl ain't *started* walking!' And he dropped my hand, hard, like it was too hot or too dirty, and I almost fell off the stand. And everybody laughed and cheered, they knew what he meant, and I did, too. And I got back to the table. Ellis was grinning like it was all a big joke. And it was. On me."

She rose, and poured herself a fresh drink.

"Then he took me to that place he has, way over on the East River. I kept wondering what I was going to do. I didn't know what to do. I watched his face in the taxicab. He put his hand on my leg. And he tried to take my hand. But I couldn't move. I kept thinking of what that black man had said to me, and his face when he said it, and I kept thinking of Rufus, and I kept thinking of you. It was like a merry-go-round, all these faces just kept going around in my mind. And a song kept going around in my head, *Oh, Lord, is it I?* And there he sat, next to me, puffing on his cigar. The funny thing was that I knew if I really started crying or pleading, he'd take me home. He can't stand scenes. But I couldn't even do that. And God knows I wanted to get home, I hoped you wouldn't be here, so I could just crawl under the sheets and die. And, that way, when you came home, I could tell you everything before you came to bed, and—maybe—but, no, we were going to his place and I felt that I deserved it. I felt that I couldn't fall much lower, I might as well go all the way and get it over with. And then we'd see, if there was any-

thing left of me after that, we'd see." She threw down about
two fingers of whiskey and immediately poured herself another drink. "There's always farther to fall, always, always."
She moved from the table, holding her glass, and leaned
against the icebox door. "And I did everything he wanted, I
let him have his way. It wasn't me. It wasn't me." She gestured aimlessly with her glass, tried to drink from it, dropped
it, and suddenly fell on her knees beside the table, her hands
against her belly, weeping.

Stupidly, he picked up the glass, afraid that she would cut
herself. She was kneeling in the spilled whiskey, which had
stained the edges of her skirt. He dropped the broken glass in
the brown paper bag they used for garbage. He was afraid to
go near her, he was afraid to touch her, it was almost as
though she had told him that she had been infected with the
plague. His arms trembled with his revulsion, and every act
of the body seemed unimaginably vile. And yet, at the same
time, as he stood helpless and stupid in the kitchen which had
abruptly become immortal, or which, in any case, would
surely live as long as he lived, and follow him everywhere, his
heart began to beat with a newer, stonier anguish, which destroyed the distance called pity and placed him, very nearly,
in her body, beside the table, on the dirty floor. The single
yellow light beat terribly down on them both. He went to her,
resigned and tender and helpless, her sobs seeming to make
his belly sore. And, nevertheless, for a moment, he could not
touch her, he did not know how. He thought, unwillingly, of
all the whores, black whores, with whom he had coupled,
and what he had hoped for from them, and he was gripped in
a kind of retrospective nausea. What would they see when
they looked into each other's faces again? "Come on, Ida,"
he whispered, "come on, Ida. Get up," and at last he touched
her shoulders, trying to force her to rise. She tried to check
her sobs, she put both hands on the table.

"I'm all right," she murmured, "give me a handkerchief."

He knelt beside her and thrust his handkerchief, warm
and wadded, but fairly clean, into her hand. She blew her
nose. He kept his arm around her shoulder. "Stand up," he
said. "Go wash your face. Would you like some coffee?"

She nodded her head, Yes, and slowly rose. He rose with
her. She kept her head down and moved swiftly, drunkenly,
past him, into the bathroom. She locked the door. He had
the spinning sensation of having been through all this before.
He lit a flame under the coffee pot, making a mental note to

break down the bathroom door if she was silent too long, if she was gone too long. But he heard the water running, and, beneath it, the sound of the rain. He ate a pork chop, greedily, with a piece of bread, and drank a glass of milk; for he was trembling, it had to be because of hunger. Otherwise, for the moment, he felt nothing. The coffee pot, now beginning to growl, was real, and the blue fire beneath it and the pork chops in the pan, and the milk which seemed to be turning sour in his belly. The coffee cups, as he thoughtfully washed them, were real, and the water which ran into them, over his heavy, long hands. Sugar and milk were real, and he set them on the table, another reality, and cigarettes were real, and he lit one. Smoke poured from his nostrils and a detail that he needed for his novel, which he had been searching for for months, fell, neatly and vividly, like the tumblers of a lock, into place in his mind. It seemed impossible that he should not have thought of it before: it illuminated, justified, clarified everything. He would work on it later tonight; he thought that perhaps he should make a note of it now; he started toward his worktable. The telephone rang. He picked up the receiver at once, stealthily, as though someone were ill or sleeping in the house, and whispered into it, "Hello?"

"Hello, Vivaldo. It's Eric."

"Eric!" He was overjoyed. He looked quickly toward the bathroom door. "How did things go?"

"Well. Cass is beautiful, as you know. But life is grim."

"As I know. Has anything been decided?"

"Not really, no. She just called me a few minutes ago—I haven't been home long. Oh, thanks for your note. She thinks that she might go up to New England for a little while, with the kids. Richard hasn't come home yet."

"Where is he?"

"He's probably out getting drunk."

"Who with?"

"Well, Ellis, maybe—"

They both halted at the name. The wires hummed. Vivaldo looked at the bathroom door again.

"You knew about that, Eric, didn't you, this morning?"

"Knew about what?"

He dropped his voice lower, and struggled to say it: "Ida. You knew about Ida and Ellis. Cass told you."

There was silence for a moment. "Yes." Then, "Who told *you?*"

"Ida."

"Oh. Poor Vivaldo." After a moment: "But it's better that way, isn't it? I didn't think that *I* was the one to tell you—especially—well, especially not this morning."

Vivaldo was silent.

"Vivaldo—?"

"Yes?"

"Don't you think I was right? Are you sore at me?"

"Don't be silly. Never in this world. It's—much better this way." He cleared his throat, slowly, deliberately, for he suddenly wanted to weep.

"Vivaldo, it's a terrible time to ask you, I know—but do you think it's at all likely that you—and Ida—will feel up to coming over to my joint tomorrow night, or the night after?"

"What's up?"

"Yves will be here in the morning. I know he'd like to meet my friends."

"That was the cablegram, huh?"

"Yes."

"Are you glad, Eric?"

"I guess so. Right now, I'm just scared. I don't know whether to try to sleep—it's so *early*, but it feels like midnight—or go to a movie, or what."

"I'd love to go to a movie with you. But—I guess I can't."

"No. When will you let me know about tomorrow?"

"I'll call you later tonight. Or I'll call you in the morning."

"Okay. If you call in the morning and miss, call back. I've got to go to Idlewild."

"What time is he getting in?"

"Oh, at dawn, practically. Naturally. Seven A.M., something convenient like that."

Vivaldo laughed. "Poor Eric."

"Yes. Life's catching up with us. Good night, Vivaldo."

"Good night, Eric."

He hung up, smiling thoughtfully, switched on his work-table lamp, and scribbled his note. Then he walked into the kitchen, turned off the gas, and poured the coffee. He knocked on the bathroom door.

"Ida? Your coffee's getting cold."

"Thank you. I'll be right out."

He sat down on his work stool, and, presently, here she came, scrubbed and quiet, looking like a child. He forced himself to look into her eyes; he did not know what she would see in them; he did not know what he felt.

"Vivaldo," she said, standing, speaking quickly, "I just want you to know that I wouldn't have been with you so

long, and wouldn't have given you such a hard time, if"—
she faltered, and held on with both hands to the back of a
chair—"I didn't love you. That's why I had to tell you everything I've told you. I mean—I know I'm giving you a tough
row to hoe." She sat down, and picked up her coffee. "I had
to say that while I could."

She had the advantage of him, for he did not know what
to say. He realized this with shame and fear. He wanted to
say, *I love you,* but the words would not come. He wondered what her lips would taste like now, what her body
would be like for him now: he watched her quiet face. She
seemed utterly passive; yet, she was waiting, in a despair
which steadily chilled and hardened, for some word, some
touch, of his. And he could not find himself, could not summon or concentrate enough of himself to make any sign at
all. He stared into his cup, noting that black coffee was not
black, but deep brown. Not many things in the world were
really black, not even the night, not even the mines. And
the light was not white, either, even the palest light held within itself some hint of its origins, in fire. He thought to himself
that he had at last got what he wanted, the truth out of Ida,
or the true Ida; and he did not know how he was going to
live with it.

He said, "Thank you for telling me—everything you've
told me. I know it wasn't easy." She said nothing. She made
a faint, steamy sound as she sipped her coffee, and this sound
was unaccountably, inexpressibly annoying. "And forgive
me, now, if I don't seem to know just what to say, I'm maybe
a little—stunned." He looked over at her, and a wilderness
of anger, pity, love, and contempt and lust all raged together
in him. She, too, was a whore; how bitterly he had been betrayed! "I'm not trying to deny anything you've said, but just
the same, there are a lot of things I didn't—don't—understand, not really. Bear with me, please give me a little
time—"

"Vivaldo," she said, wearily, "just one thing. I don't want
you to be *understanding.* I don't want you to be kind, okay?"
She looked directly at him, and an unnamable heat and tension flashed violently alive between them, as close to hatred
as it was to love. She softened and reached out, and touched
his hand. "Promise me that."

"I promise you that," he said. And then, furiously, "You
seem to forget that I love you."

They stared at each other. Suddenly, he reached out and
pulled her to him, trembling, with tears starting up behind

his eyes, burning and blinding, and covered her face with
kisses, which seemed to freeze as they fell. She clung to him;
with a sigh she buried her face in his chest. There was nothing erotic in it; they were like two weary children. And it
was she who was comforting him. Her long fingers stroked
his back, and he began, slowly, with a horrible, strangling
sound, to weep, for she was stroking his innocence out of
him.

By and by, he was still. He rose, and went to the bathroom
and washed his face, and then sat down at his worktable. She
put on a record by Mahalia Jackson, *In the Upper Room,*
and sat at the window, her hands in her lap, looking out over
the sparkling streets. Much, much later, while he was still
working and she slept, she turned in her sleep, and she called
his name. He paused, waiting, staring at her, but she did not
move again, or speak again. He rose, and walked to the window. The rain had ceased, in the black-blue sky a few stars
were scattered, and the wind roughly jostled the clouds along.

CHAPTER 2

The sun struck, on steel, on bronze, on stone, on glass, on the gray water far beneath them, on the turret tops and the flashing windshields of crawling cars, on the incredible highways, stretching and snarling and turning for mile upon mile upon mile, on the houses, square and high, low and gabled, and on their howling antennae, on the sparse, weak trees, and on those towers, in the distance, of the city of New York. The plane tilted, dropped and rose, and the whole earth slanted, now leaning against the windows of the plane, now dropping out of sight. The sky was hot, blank blue, and the static light invested everything with its own lack of motion. Only things could be seen from here, the work of people's hands: but the people did not exist. The plane rose up, up, as though loath to descend from this high tranquillity; tilted, and Yves looked down, hoping to see the Statue of Liberty, though he had been warned that it could not be seen from here; then the plane began, like a stone, to drop, the water rushed up at them, the motors groaned, the wings trembled, resisting the awful, downward pull. Then, when the water was at their feet, the white strip of the landing flashed into place beneath them. The wheels struck the ground with a brief and heavy thud, and wires and lights and towers went screaming by. The hostess' voice came over the speaker, congratulating them on their journey, and hoping to see them soon again. The hostess was very pretty, he had intermittently flirted with her all night, delighted to discover how easy this was. He was drunk and terribly weary, and filled with an excitement which was close to panic; in fact, he had burned his way to the outer edge of drunkenness and weariness, into a diamond-hard sobriety. With the voice of the hostess, the people of this planet sprang out of the ground, pushing trucks and waving arms and crossing roads and vanishing into, or erupting out of buildings. The voice of the hostess asked the passengers please to remain seated until the aircraft had come to a complete halt. Yves touched the package which contained the brandy and cigarettes he had bought in Shannon, and he folded his copies of *France-Soir* and *Le Monde* and *Paris-Match*, for he knew that Eric would like to see them. On the top of a brightly colored building, people were driven against the sky; he looked for Eric's flaming hair, feeling another excitement, an excitement close to pain, well up in him. But the people were too far away, they were faceless still. He watched them move, but there was no movement which reminded him of Eric. Still, he knew that Eric was there, somewhere in that faceless crowd, waiting for him, and he was filled, all at once, with an extraordinary peace and happiness.

Then the plane came slowly to a halt. As the plane halted, the people in the cabin seemed, collectively, to sigh, and discovered that the power of movement had been returned to them. Off came safety belts, down came packages, papers, and coats. The faces they had worn when hanging, at the mercy of mysteries they could not begin to fathom, in the middle of the air, were now discarded for the faces which they wore on earth. The housewife, traveling alone, who had been, during their passage, a rather flirtatious girl, became a housewife once again: her face responded to her proddings as abjectly as her hat. The businessman who had spoken to Yves about the waters of Lake Michigan, and the days when he had hiked and fished there, relentlessly put all of this behind him, and solemnly and cruelly tightened the knot in his tie. Yves was not wearing a tie, he was wearing a light blue shirt, with short sleeves, and he carried a light sport jacket; and he thought now, with some terror, that this had probably been a mistake; he was not really in America yet, after all, and might not be allowed to enter. But there was nothing he could do about it now. He straightened his collar and put on his jacket and ran his fingers through his hair—which was probably too long. He cursed himself and wished that he could ask one of his fellow passengers for reassurance. But his seatmate, a young man who played the organ in Montana, was now frowning and breathing hard and straightening as much of himself as could decently be reached. He had been very friendly during the journey and had even asked Yves to come and see him, if he ever came to Montana; but now Yves realized that he had not been given any address, and that he knew only the man's first name, which was Peter. And it was only too clear that he could not ask for any information now. Nearly everyone on the plane knew—for he had been very high-spirited and talkative—that he was French, and coming to the States for the first time; and some of them knew that he had a friend in New York, who was an actor. This had all seemed perfectly all right while they were in the middle of the air. But now, on the ground, and in the light, hard and American, of sober second thought, it all seemed rather suspect. He felt helplessly French: and he had never felt French before. And he felt their movement away from him, decently but definitely, with nervous, and, as it were, backward smiles; they were making it clear that he could make no appeal to them, for they did not know who he was. It flashed through him that of course he had a test to pass; he had not yet entered the country; perhaps he would not pass the test. He watched them fill the aisles, and he moved backward from them, into his familiar loneliness and contempt. "Good luck," said his seatmate quickly, and took his place in the line; he would probably have said the same words, as quickly, and in the same tone of voice, to a friend about to be carried off to prison. Yves sighed, and remained in his seat, waiting for the load in the aisle to lighten. He thought, bleakly, *Le plus dur reste à faire.*

Then he joined the line, and moved slowly toward the door. The hostesses stood there, smiling and saying good-bye. The sun was bright on their faces, and on the faces of the disembarking passengers; they seemed, as they turned and disappeared, to be stepping into a new and healing light. He held his newspapers under one arm, shifted his package from hand to hand, straightened his belt, trembling. The hostess with whom he had flirted was nearest the door. *"Au revoir,"* she said, with the bright and generous and mocking smile possessed by so many of his countrywomen. He suddenly realized that he would never see her again. It had not occurred to him, until this moment, that he could possibly have left behind him anything which he might, one day, long for and need, with all his heart. *"Bon courage,"* she said. He smiled and said, *"Merci, mademoiselle. Au revoir!"* And he wanted to say, *Vous êtes très jolie,* but it was too late, he had hit the light, the sun glared at him, and everything wavered in the heat. He started down the extraordinary steps. When he hit the ground, a voice above him said, *"Bonjour, mon gar. Soyez le bienvenu."* He looked up. Eric leaned on the rail of the observation deck, grinning, wearing an open white shirt and khaki trousers. He looked very much at ease, at home, thinner than he had been, with his short hair spinning and flaming about his head. Yves looked up joyously, and waved, unable to say anything. *Eric*. And all his fear left him, he was certain, now, that everything would be all right. He whistled to himself as he followed the line which separated him from the Americans, into the examination hall. But he passed his examination with no trouble, and in a very short time; his passport was eventually stamped and handed back to him, with a grin and a small joke, the meaning but not the good nature of which escaped him. Then he was in a vaster hall, waiting for his luggage, with Eric above him, smiling down on him through glass. Then even his luggage belonged to him again, and he strode through the barriers, more high-hearted than he had ever been as a child, into that city which the people from heaven had made their home.

Istanbul, Dec. 10, 1961